PENGUIN BOOKS
My Boyfriend is a Vampire

Eva Knight, the paranormal alter ego of Helena Hunting, loves all things romance and spice. When she isn't busy writing spicy college vampire romance, she's devouring her favorite romance novels, or binge-watching dark comedies on Netflix with her void kitty, Pumpkin. Her favorite non-reading pastimes include running (on purpose), Scrabble (when she can find someone to play with her), cribbage (with her dad) and cross-stitching gnomes (the actual act of cross-stitching, not collecting gnomes who cross-stitch).

T0333036

My Boyfriend is a Vampire

EVA KNIGHT

PENGUIN BOOKS

PENGUIN BOOKS

UK | USA | Canada | Ireland | Australia
India | New Zealand | South Africa

Penguin Books is part of the Penguin Random House group of companies
whose addresses can be found at global.penguinrandomhouse.com

First published by Penguin Books 2023
001

Copyright © Helena Hunting, 2022

The moral right of the author has been asserted

Set in 12.5/14.75pt Garamond MT
Typeset by Falcon Oast Graphic Art Ltd
Printed and bound in Great Britain by Clays Ltd, Elcograf S.p.A.

The authorized representative in the EEA is Penguin Random House Ireland,
Morrison Chambers, 32 Nassau Street, Dublin D02 YH68

A CIP catalogue record for this book is available from the British Library

ISBN: 978-1-405-95779-3

www.greenpenguin.co.uk

Kidlet, you're such a gift. If you read past this page it's probably going to get awkward. I love you.

I

Hazy

'These textbooks must weigh a hundred pounds.' I adjust my backpack, but there's no relief from the one digging into the base of my spine.

'You could get the ebook version and save your back,' Satya says.

'I know, but the reading experience is different. I feel like I retain the information better when I read from a hard copy.'

'I get what you mean, but even paperbacks are infinitely lighter than those bricks you're carting around.' Satya pats her own backpack.

'Think of it this way, you've gotten your cardio and your weight training in one shot,' Alyssa says brightly.

The three of us are seniors, all in our final year of our undergraduate degrees. Although I'm in it for the long haul since I'm pre-med. Satya plans to start her master's next year and Alyssa is still deciding what's next. We met in the dorms as freshmen, rented an off-campus house during sophomore year and have been inseparable since.

We make a left down Frat Row and I fight with myself not to reach into my pocket and retrieve my phone, but lose the battle after we pass the first house with a shirtless, half-lit guy lounging on the front porch. I pretend to check my messages when really I'm looking at my reflection in the black screen.

'So transparent, Hazy,' Satya says with a roll of her eyes.

'More transparent than a mesh football jersey,' Alyssa agrees.

'I'm not giving in to bad decisions this year. I'm just making sure I look good while making excellent, non-toxic ones,' I reply defensively.

'I'll believe it when I see it,' Satya grumbles.

'I bet a fully loaded meat-za from Bobby's Bestest Pizza that you fold tonight. There will be alcohol and Blaine will invariably be shirtless, and you've proven to be a sucker for lanky guys with sort-of-abs,' Alyssa says.

Satya's eyes light up. 'Ohhh, I raise that bet and add two dozen wings that Hazy doesn't make it down the street without ending up in his bedroom.'

'You two are the literal worst. I'm not sleeping with Blaine this year. Not even once. I've learned my lesson.' Although they are correct about the alcohol-shirtless-lanky-guy attraction, and Blaine happens to fit that bill perfectly. He's also good at providing orgasms, but *only* when he's on top and he does this angle thing with my left leg. Still, a college guy who takes the time to provide an O before he gets his own is sort of like a four-leaf clover, hence the reason I keep falling back into bed with him once a year. And then I remember all the reasons we don't work. Usually once he opens his mouth post-sex and reminds me why we broke up in the first place by being his tactless self.

'You said that last year,' Alyssa reminds me.

'And the year before that,' Satya adds.

'And –'

'I know, I know.' I raise a hand to stop Alyssa. 'And the year before that, but seriously, I mean it this time.'

Last year we hooked up during the first week. Then I had to deal with the awkward aftermath of having slept with my ex, who is also the co-editor in chief at the school paper, for which I work.

'Has he texted yet?' Satya asks.

'Yes, but I haven't responded.'

The texts started two days ago, neatly corresponding with his return to college. He spent the summer abroad, doing what, I have no idea. I haven't spoken to him since the spring semester ended. I apply fresh lip gloss, though, in case I run into him. I do want to look my best when I invariably turn him down for a frolic between the sheets.

'Holy crap!' Alyssa stops walking and because I'm preoccupied with my lips, I run right into her backpack.

'Am I high?' Satya asks and rubs her eyes.

'Not unless the campus cafe is serving special cookies this year.' I stop checking myself out and follow their gaze. 'What the fuckballs?' I glance at our surroundings to make sure we're on the right street.

'The haunted house,' Alyssa mutters. 'It doesn't look haunted anymore.'

'It wasn't like this yesterday.' I blink hard a couple of times, but the mirage before me doesn't shift or change. 'I swear I couldn't see it through the freaking forest in the front yard.' I stare up at the majestic three-story brick home.

The bushes that line the perimeter have been trimmed to waist level, revealing a beautiful umbrella tree. There's a lattice archway covered in lush green vines dotted with purple and white flowers. The path leading to the front door is made of natural stone and is punctuated with lovely pink rose bushes. It looks like something out of a fairy tale instead of a horror movie. The only things that need some TLC are the front porch and the faded shutters.

'Are you sure?' Satya asks.

'Positive. I was talking to Alyssa when I passed it.'

I went to the store to grab chips and salsa for our Mexican night, which consisted of nachos and margaritas. On the way back I came up Frat Row because I have a fascination with the derelict house. I always call Alyssa or Satya when I pass the house, in case a ghost tries to kidnap me. Not that I believe in ghosts, but the house is extra creepy.

The front door opens and a guy wearing a plain white T-shirt, khaki shorts and a pair of running shoes steps onto the porch.

I swear all the air is sucked out of my lungs as I take in the rest of him. He's tall and lean with sun-kissed skin, chestnut hair that's styled in such a way that he looks like he could fit into the hipster crowd, but he's clean-shaven with high cheekbones, a rugged jawline and full lips that have a natural pout. In short, he's gorgeous.

'Hey there!' A head pops out from behind a huge bush in the middle of the yard that's being shaped into . . . something I can't yet identify.

Satya screams and Alyssa startles. I'm still busy staring at the hot guy so my gasp comes three seconds later.

'So sorry. Didn't mean to scare you.' A guy steps out from behind the bush, and sets the electric hedge trimmer on the ground, then wipes his hands on his shorts.

'I'm Hunter. We just moved into the neighborhood.' He extends a hand and Satya, who is closest to him, takes it.

He looks like every jock I've ever met. Huge shoulders, massive biceps, legs as thick as tree trunks. He's also sporting a full beard and his hair is a month past needing a trim. It curls around his ears and at the nape of his neck.

'Hey. Hi. Hello. I'm Satya, this is Alyssa and Hazy, short for Hazel.' She thumbs over her shoulder at us, then motions to the front yard. 'You've really transformed the place.'

'Yeah, things were out of control. We took care of the inside first, now it's just getting the exterior to look as pretty as my bush clover.' He pats the bush he's standing beside. 'You all live on the street?'

'One block over,' Alyssa says.

'Nice. Do you go to Burnham College, too, then?'

'Yeah, we're all seniors, I'm an English major, Alyssa is taking Classics and Hazel is our resident brainiac and pre-med.'

'Oh yeah?' He peeks around Satya to get a look at me. 'My brother is pre-med, too.' He brings his fingers to his lips and whistles shrilly. 'Hey, God, come meet our neighbors.'

He's hidden behind one of the ornate, peeling columns. His head appears and then the rest of him as he sets his paint can near the stairs and ambles down the stone pathway.

'This is Godric. Godric, this is Satya, Alyssa and Hazy, short for Hazel, who is also pre-med.'

Godric's gaze moves to me, and I forget how to speak. His eyes are a rich deep brown that reminds me of delicious,

5

dark maple syrup and I can't stop looking at him. He's ridiculously beautiful in a way that's difficult to process.

He holds out his hand and I stare at it for half a second too long before I reach for it. He has long slender fingers. The kind that would be perfect for delicate surgery. They wrap around mine and for reasons I don't understand, my lady parts start tingling. Similar to the kind of tingles I get when I'm reading one of my steamy romance novels, or when I'm taking care of my personal needs before bed, or in the shower, or whenever I need some stress relief.

I need to stop thinking about self-gratification.

'Hi, I'm Hazy.' I don't know if it's in my head or not, but I worry that sounded more like a moan than actual words.

'Yeah, I caught that.' One corner of his mouth tips up in a wry grin.

I'm being all awkward.

Hunter coughs into his fist.

Godric drops my hand and runs his through his hair, then tucks his thumbs into his pockets.

'What fraternity are you guys part of?' Alyssa asks, thankfully breaking the awkward silence I've created.

'Beta Epsilon Delta,' Hunter says.

'Huh, I've never heard of it.' Satya plays with the end of her ponytail.

Alyssa arches an eyebrow. 'BED for short?'

'Better than Theta Iota Theta.' I point across the street. The symbols are painted on the front of the house. At least it's not the initials.

'TIT for short,' Hunter snorts, then schools his expression. 'Not that it's funny or anything.'

'It's totally funny. My personal favorite is Delta Iota

6

Kappa. They're down the other end of the street.' Satya motions in the direction we came from.

'So are you three part of a sorority?' Hunter seems to be the chatty one.

I keep trying to steal glances at Godric, but every time I do his gaze shifts back to me. There's something about him, beyond the fact that he looks like he stepped out of the pages of a magazine. I have the desire to drag him into a dark room and have my wicked way with him, but at the same time my gut churns with anxious energy.

I catch movement in my peripheral vision, followed by tapping. I drag my gaze to the stunning house behind Godric and Hunter in time to see a figure standing at a second-floor window before the curtain falls shut.

'Uh.' I point to the house. 'Is it the two of you living here? There are rumors that this place is haunted.'

Hunter chuckles. 'Nah, that's our younger brother, Laz. He's got bad social anxiety, so he keeps to himself a lot, but you'll meet him eventually. Maybe.'

'Right. Well, it's good that you don't have ghosts living in the house with you.' *Why aren't me and words friends today?*

A door slams from somewhere close by and everyone but me turns to look in the direction of the noise. I'm too busy trying to check out Godric again. And the tingles are back, not just in my nether regions, but also in my nipples. *What the hell is going on with my body?*

Godric's brow furrows, his gaze homed in on whoever is across the street, and his upper lip curls slightly.

I finally drag my eyes away from his lovely face in time to see Blaine sprinting toward me, one side of his cocky mouth quirked up in a salacious grin.

'Hey, new dudes! Welcome to the neighborhood. Party tonight at my place.' Blaine drops to one knee, grabs me around the waist and tosses me over his shoulder. My backpack slides off my arms and lands on the ground. 'Hazy, baby, why are you ignoring all my messages?'

Obviously, he's been working out a lot this summer.

'Blaine! Put me down! I was in the middle of a conversation.' I reach out a hand, which Alyssa tries to grab, but Blaine is quick, rushing across the street with me slung over his shoulder like a giant sack of potatoes.

Satya looks unsurprised and Alyssa looks resigned.

Godric's lips pull down at the corners and he takes a single step forward as I hear him ask, 'Does your friend need help?'

Alyssa or Satya's responses are cut off as Blaine carries me up the steps to his front porch and into the house. I'm immediately hit with the stench of dude-bro; a combination of takeout food, dirty sneakers and a general lack of cleaning.

Blaine's roommate and friend, Justin, is sitting on the couch, a bag of Doritos propped against his leg. He's wearing lemon-yellow Speedos, and that is all. His legs are spread wide, giving me an eyeful of the outline of his twig and berries. Justin plays on the football team. He's not unattractive, but his incessant need to wear banana hammocks in public and scratch his balls and then rummage around in a bowl of chips for the folded ones speaks to his entire personality.

'Hey, Hazy, have a good summer?' Justin asks before he shoves a chip into his mouth.

'Yup. Got to work at a lab for most of it, so that was fun.

You?' I grab onto the doorframe as Blaine tries to carry me through to the kitchen.

'I washed cars. It was boring as fuck.'

'I'm sorry to hear that.' I lose my grip on the doorframe and we're on the move again.

'Put me down, Blaine! You are not carrying me up the stairs like this! If you drop me, something will break and that's not how I want to start my year!' I punch him in the side of the thigh without thinking.

'Ah! Shit!' His leg buckles and his hold on me relaxes.

I put my hands out to stop my face from hitting the floor as I slide down his back, landing on the filthy linoleum. I suppress a gag as I get a load of dust bunnies living under their stove.

I do a graceless tuck and roll and scramble to my feet, then try to make a run for it, but Blaine has been on the track team for years, so he's fast and agile. He spreads both his arms and then backs me into the corner of the L-shaped counter.

'Why are you so intent on avoiding me?' He settles a palm on either side of me to box me in.

This is Blaine's go-to move when he wants to entice me into bed. I am loath to admit it's worked more than once.

I cross my arms to prevent him from getting closer. 'I've been busy.'

'Not too busy to flirt with the new guys across the street.' His expression darkens. 'There's something going on over there. Yesterday it was a forest and today that house looks like it belongs on an HGTV show.'

I roll my eyes. 'Everything is suspect to you. And I wasn't flirting with the new guys. We were saying hi and

9

welcoming them to the neighborhood. It's called being polite, you should give it a try sometime.'

'I'm always polite.'

'Is that what you call throwing me over your shoulder like some kind of caveman while I was in the middle of a conversation?'

'You've been ghosting my messages.' He slides a finger between my crossed arms and tugs. 'I missed you this summer.'

'You could have texted any time prior to the last two days.' Not that I wanted him to.

'I was giving you space.'

When it becomes apparent that I won't uncross my arms, he switches tactics and pushes my hair over my shoulders; his hands get tangled in the overly long, dark waves. I needed to cut it about a year ago and now it nearly reaches my waist. It's a lot, but I'm kind of attached to it.

Once his fingers are free, he strokes along the edge of my jaw with his thumb. 'Come upstairs so we can talk in private.'

He leans in, as though he's planning to kiss me, and I tip my head back to escape the nearness of his mouth.

My hormones are already firing, nipples peaked under my shirt, but not because of Blaine's lame attempt to get me into his bed. Again. It's bizarre that less than ten minutes ago I was worried about the possibility of repeating history, and now all I want to do is get another eyeful of his new neighbor so I can figure out why my body is going all haywire.

I bat his hand away. 'I'm not getting naked with you, Blaine.'

He smirks. 'Come on, Hazy. You know I always make you feel good.'

Ugh, he's so cocky. The inevitable orgasm no longer seems worth the ego inflation.

Thankfully, the front door opens and closes with a slam, providing the distraction I need to shove on his chest and slip around him.

'Lys! Babe, you finally come to your senses? You gonna let me take you on that date this year?' Justin asks, his mouth clearly full of Doritos based on the garbled quality of the question.

'Not even if you were the last man on the face of this planet,' she replies, her eyes firmly locked on me as I move toward her and Satya.

'Come on.' Alyssa extends a hand and I take it as Blaine grabs my other arm.

'Don't go, Hazy,' he whines.

They pull on me from both directions, like I'm a tug-of-war rope.

'Hey, Blaine, back this year for a victory lap?' Satya inspects her nails.

Blaine was supposed to graduate last year.

'I'm trying to improve my grades so I can apply for programs overseas. Leave Hazy here, she wants to hang out with me.'

He's still holding my hand, but no longer yanking on it.

Alyssa gives me her disapproving mom face. 'We're trying to save both of you from making the same mistake for the fourth year in a row.'

'The only mistake Hazy keeps making is breaking it off again before we even have a chance to find out if we'd work.'

This line, coming from a different guy, might melt my heart, but Blaine always wants what he can't have, and currently that's me.

'You're like gasoline and a lit match in the middle of a dry forest. Never a good combo.' Alyssa tugs on my hand. 'Didn't you say something about needing to wax before the party tonight?'

'Yes!' I pull my hand free from his and slide between Alyssa and Satya. 'Gotta roll.'

'Alyssa, I liked you. Why you doing me dirty like this?' Blaine's frown reminds me of an unimpressed Kermit the Frog.

'I'm trying to save you from drama. And myself. And Satya.'

'Preach.' Satya brings up the rear, mostly to prevent Blaine from getting close to me.

'Party starts at eight. It's only a matter of time, Hazy.' His certainty irks me more than a toilet paper roll with one sheet left.

'I'm turning over a new leaf this year, Blaine, and it includes not ending up under you,' I call over my shoulder as Alyssa and Satya hustle me to the door.

'Later, Hazy, Satya,' Justin says while cupping his balls through his Speedos.

Satya and I say bye in unison.

'Lys, I love you.'

'You love your ball sack.' Alyssa fires the bird over her shoulder.

I drag in a couple of deep breaths once we're outside. That entire house smells like the inside of a gym bag.

Godric and Hunter are both on ladders, holding paint

brushes and cans of paint, freshening up the shutters. I check out Godric's butt. I wonder what the jiggle factor would be if I gave it a hearty smack.

Maybe I'm getting my period. That could explain all this hormonal nonsense. 'Thanks for saving me from that mistake. Again.'

'No problem,' Alyssa and Satya say in unison.

'That Godric guy couldn't take his eyes off of you.' Alyssa glances over her shoulder before we round the corner. 'And I'm pretty sure he's staring at you right now.'

'Seriously?' I'm halfway to looking over my shoulder but Alyssa pokes me in the ribs. 'Ow.'

'Don't look.' She threads her arm through mine. 'He'll probably be at the party tonight. You'll get to see him again soon enough.'

2

After much time spent picking exactly the right bathing suit, cover up and flip-flops combo, and then changing three more times before returning to the original outfit, Satya, Alyssa and I are party ready.

Alyssa takes me by the shoulders, her expression serious. 'What is the one thing you will not do tonight?'

'Allow Blaine's pecs to entice me back into his bed.'

'And why won't you allow this?'

'Because it will invariably lead to me requiring an ice cream intervention, and the first four to eight weeks of the semester will be spent in a pit of overwhelming self-loathing for making the same mistake, again,' I recite.

'You know, we could skip the party tonight,' Satya suggests.

Alyssa and I give her a disbelieving look.

Satya shrugs. 'It's a legitimate option.'

'We cannot waste all this effort.' I motion to our reflection in the mirror across the room. 'I will not let my hormones dictate my actions tonight. At least not where Blaine is concerned.'

'I believe in you.' Satya's tone is unconvinced.

'I'm not drinking tonight,' I declare.

'We're going to a keg party, how are you going to avoid booze?' Satya asks.

'I'm bringing a travel mug of iced tea, and if I cave,

I'll halve it with soda so I can remain on the right side of tipsy.'

'Sounds reasonable. And like a smart plan.'

We gather our phones and our travel mugs and head over to Frat Row.

The party is in full swing when we arrive. Justin has changed into Speedos with an American flag print and is lounging in one of the many chairs around the pool.

He lifts his megaphone as we push through the gate. 'Alyssa, you look like a wet dream!'

Alyssa rolls her eyes, cups her hands around her mouth and shouts, 'I know, and your dreams are as close as you'll ever get to this.' She punctuates her statement with a spin.

'One day you'll go out with me.'

'When hell freezes over!' she shouts back.

'Hazy! I'm glad you're finally here. We should go to my room and have that chat.' Blaine appears out of nowhere and slings his arm over my shoulder, pulling me into his side. He's wet from the pool and smells like a brewery.

'I'm good, but thanks for the offer.' I push his hand off my shoulder.

'What're you drinking? Can I get you a cooler?'

I tap the side of my travel mug. 'Got it covered, but thanks.'

Someone calls his name, and he frowns down at me. 'I'll be back for you later.'

'I'm not going to change my mind, but good for you for persevering.'

'I guess we'll see who's right in the end, won't we?' He walks backward across the lawn, smirking.

I wrinkle my nose as he spins around, heading for the

group of people who just arrived. 'His overconfidence is unappealing.' Although in the past he's been right about me folding.

'Yeah,' Alyssa and Satya say in unison.

It's a balmy night and the pool is full of people with travel mugs like ours, or if they're unprepared, red plastic cups. I'm sure at this point the pool is five percent alcohol and juice.

I scan the partygoers, looking for the new neighbors across the street, but they don't seem to be here. The night is young, though.

Satya spots a guy from one of her English classes last semester, so she goes over to say hi, and Alyssa makes eye contact with a guy she's had a crush on since sophomore year, but hasn't had the guts to approach him until now.

'Go, now, before you overthink it.' I nudge her in his direction.

'Wish me luck.'

'You don't need luck.' I tap her on the butt and send her on her way.

I take a sip of my iced tea, but it makes a terrible slurping sound, signaling my need for a refill. And a trip to the ladies room.

I scan the yard and spot Blaine with a group of people, engaged in conversation. Alyssa is talking to the hottie crush and Satya is chatting up the dude from her English class. With everyone occupied, I slip into the house, use the bathroom, apply a fresh coat of lip gloss, and refill my travel mug with ice-cold water this time.

I step back outside and scan the yard. A behemoth of a dude is standing on the end of the diving board. Everyone has moved to the edge of the pool. I cross my fingers that whoever they are and whatever they're planning, it doesn't end with a trip to the ER and some stitches. It's happened before.

He bounces a couple of times and rolls his neck on his shoulders before he raises his arms, as if he's preparing to dive. He pushes off the board and gets an incredible amount of height and then he tucks himself into a ball and spins in the air, landing in the pool with a splash that soaks nearly everyone.

Shrieks and claps follow as he pops out of the water, hands raised in victory as he does a slow spin. Which is when I realize it's Hunter, one of the new guys who lives across the street.

My heart stutters because Hunter's presence means that his brother Godric might be here. I scan the yard but come up empty at first. Until I move toward the edge of the deck. And then I spot him in the shadows, leaning against the side of the house, looking delicious and painfully bored.

He's also dressed . . . not like everyone else. He's wearing a blazer with the sleeves rolled up that reminds me of eighties movies. He's also alone. But I can see a group of girls about twenty feet away from him doing the whole glance and giggle thing.

I don't give myself time to second-guess. I hop down the steps and head in his direction, flip-flops aggressively slapping the concrete patio. The closer I get, the faster my heart beats. He's wearing a pair of sky-blue board shorts with a pink palm tree pattern. His blazer is unbuttoned and he's shirtless underneath. Which means I have an incredible view of the line down the center of his body that bisects his defined abs. The only thing that isn't visible is the delectable V leading to the divining rod of lust.

Heat flashes over my skin the closer I get. I'm half a second from chickening out when his gaze swings my way. Recognition flares and he tips his head, so I continue my approach.

'Hey. Hi. Hello.' Awesome. My awkward is in full effect. 'I'm Hazy, we met earlier today.' I wrap both hands around my travel mug, to keep from doing something clichéd like play with my hair or drag a finger along my collarbone to draw attention to my cleavage.

My right hand lifts, as though it's interpreting the thought as a command, but I grasp my metal straw with the silicone bendy tip instead. I bring it to my lips and take a quick sip.

'I recall.' His gaze lands on my mouth before moving over me. 'Your friends seemed rather concerned about your welfare earlier.'

'Yeah. Blaine and I have . . . history.'

The right side of his mouth curls up, as though I've made a joke.

'But he's mostly harmless.'

Godric makes a sound. 'He seems a bit . . . handsy.'

I nod. 'Yeah, he is that.'

He blinks twice. 'Is that something you find appealing?'

'Not particularly, no.'

'And yet, here you are.' He sips his drink, which I realize is in an actual glass, rather than a plastic cup or a travel mug. And it's not just any old glass, it's crystal, with a pretty pattern etched into it. Like something I might find in my Great-Grandma Gertie's china hutch.

'That's not the safest choice of glassware for a party like this,' I blurt.

His eyebrows draw together. 'I'm sorry?'

I tap the glass in his hand. 'Is this crystal?'

'It is. As befits a fine Scotch.'

'I'd stay away from the pool with that if I were you. In my freshman year some idiot smashed a beer bottle beside the pool, and they missed some of the bigger pieces. A sophomore girl got a shard lodged in her heel. It looked like a damn shark attack happened in the pool. There was a cloud of blood and everything. And when they pulled the shard out the wound started gushing all over the place.'

Godric's placid expression shifts slightly, his brow lifting. But my mouth keeps running.

'I don't know if they hit a vein or what, but blood started pouring out of the bottom of her foot. She needed something like twenty stitches. And she was on the girls' volleyball team, but she couldn't play for weeks and she had to walk on crutches for, like, the first month of school. I couldn't believe how much blood there was. Like so much blood.' *Why can't I stop talking about blood?*

Godric swallows thickly, and when he speaks his voice is low and gravely and sounds almost like a growl. 'Is that right?'

'Once I cut my foot on a zebra mussel when we went on vacation and I almost passed out from the sight of blood, but that had nothing on the sophomore who cut her foot on the beer bottle. That was next level. Almost like horror movie bloody, you know?' *I need to stop talking.* 'I didn't pass out, but this girl, she totally passed out and hit her head on

19

the concrete and then she needed even more stitches, and she ended up with a mild concussion.'

As I continue to word-vomit this horrible story I begin to sweat, which I attribute to the mortification over not being able to cease the nonsense I'm spewing. But that's not the only issue. I have the irrational desire to wrap myself around Godric like cellophane and shove my tongue in his mouth. Or maybe it's not all that irrational because it would stop me from talking.

Suddenly a guy appears beside Godric, and I suck in a gasping breath and take a step back. He's a few inches shorter than Godric, with hair the color of night, pale skin that looks like it doesn't see the sun much, and he's dressed in a long-sleeved black shirt, black dress pants and black boots.

His eyes dart to me for a split second and then land on Godric, who drags his intense gaze away from me.

The emo guy blinks twice. 'You forgot to take your medication. You need to do that. Immediately. Or the consequences will be catastrophic.'

Godric and the emo guy stare each other down for several long seconds.

Godric casually sips his Scotch. 'You're being rather dramatic, don't you think, Laz?'

Emo guy, now identified as Laz, cocks one dark, villainous eyebrow. 'Am I?'

Godric slowly turns his attention back to me. 'I'm sorry, my brother likes to make a big deal out of every little thing, but I'd like to avoid catastrophic consequences, so I should probably go.'

'Oh, I get it. I take my birth control pill at the same time every night like clockwork.' Ugh, way to go, talking about birth control with someone I hardly know. 'You can never be too careful when it comes to medication.' *What the hell am I even saying?*

Godric's mouth curls up in a lopsided grin that makes my vagina feel like it's going to explode.

My reaction to this guy is disarming.

'It was nice to see you again, Hazy.'

'It was nice to see you too, God . . . ric.'

And with that, the two of them turn in a synchronized spin and disappear around the side of the house, leaving me alone with my mortification.

3

It's Monday morning and the first day of classes. It doesn't matter how many days pass, every time I think about my conversation with Godric at Blaine's party I have the same reaction, and that's to hide inside my shirt until the rush of embarrassment passes.

Each time the flush of mortification spreads across my chest and up to my cheeks. It's horrible. I plan to avoid walking down Frat Row for the rest of the year.

Alyssa and Satya are still asleep because they both worked their schedules to avoid classes before ten in the morning. I, on the other hand, have an 8:30 class every Monday, Wednesday and Friday, but Tuesdays and Thursdays are free, apart from my Tuesday night class. Does it suck to have an early class three days a week? Sort of. But it's biochem and one of my favorite courses, so I'll take the early mornings if it means I get two days out of the week to focus on reading and completing assignments.

To prevent further embarrassing interactions, I avoid walking past Godric's place on the way to campus. It also means I'm unlikely to see Blaine outside of the school paper office. There's no chance he'll be able to throw me over his shoulder and get me into his bedroom when we're on campus. I also heard that he hooked up with some sophomore girl at one of the other parties last week, so maybe he will back off and stop trying to get me to sleep with him. A girl can dream.

I don't account for the extra minutes I add to my walk by going the long way around, so I'm cutting it close when I get to campus. I rush up the steps to the science building with only minutes to spare and push through the doors to the lecture theater.

There are about two hundred students in this class and almost every seat is filled. I scan the room, my stomach sinking when I spot Blaine near the front. He's usually in at least one of my classes every semester, so this isn't a surprise, but it is unwelcome. I spot a vacant seat four rows from the back, far away from Blaine. As I approach, the guy in the seat in front of the empty one turns his head slightly, and I catch a glimpse of his profile. *Godric.*

There's a girl beside him with curly dark hair who keeps fiddling with her glasses and tugging at the collar of her shirt every time he opens his mouth and speaks to her. *I feel you, girl. He's so hot he incinerates panties.* I scan the room for another empty seat, but all that remains is a left-handed desk at the front of the room close to Blaine. And the professor is standing at the podium, ready to begin, so I excuse my way down the aisle and cross my fingers that Godric doesn't turn around for the next fifty minutes.

Of course, because I'm in a rush and apparently clumsy as an ox this morning, I kick the back of his chair when I sit down. 'I'm so sorry,' I mumble.

He stiffens momentarily, then glances over his shoulder. That infernal lopsided grin of his makes an appearance. Heat works its way up my chest and floods my cheeks. I have the urge to apologize for the party last week and my word-vomiting, but I bite my lips together.

'Good morning, Hazy.'

'Morning, God . . . ric.'

The professor clears his throat and Godric returns his attention to the front of the class.

I can't concentrate on anything apart from the smell of Godric's cologne and the way he keeps masterfully flipping a pen between his fingers, back and forth, almost like a metronome, the timing seemingly perfect. It's mesmerizing.

For the next twenty minutes I watch that pen. I have a small, portable tablet with a keyboard for taking notes, as do most of the students around me. But all Godric has is his pen, textbook and a notebook. Old-school. Except all he's done so far is flip that pen and take no notes. Maybe he's recording the lecture?

Professor Barton asks a question that I don't catch because I'm too engrossed in Godric. When I glance at my tablet screen, I realize I've started several sentences with *Godric is hot.* I've also written *Don't talk about blood or stitches if he asks you a question.*

After several seconds in which many people flip furiously through their textbooks, Godric lazily raises his hand.

Professor Barton pushes his glasses up his nose. 'Young man, fifth row from the back. Your name, please?'

'Godric Hawthorn, professor.'

'Mr Hawthorn, please go ahead.'

That pen of his continues to flip between his fingers, back and forth, as relentless as it is consistent.

'Enzymes can be classified into seven categories according to the type of reaction they catalyze.'

If I'd been paying closer attention, I could have answered this one. I recite the categories under my breath along with him.

'These categories are oxidoreductases, transferases, hydrolases, lyases, isomerases, ligases and translocases.'

He sounds like he's reciting it from his textbook, but in a sexy voice. Memorizing facts would be a lot more fun if Godric was reading them to me. Preferably shirtless. Naked would make it impossible to focus. He glances over his shoulder once finished, another half-smile tipping the corner of his mouth. Maybe I wasn't being as quiet as I thought.

Professor Barton nods. 'That is exactly right, and I expect that within the next week the rest of you will be able to provide that information with the same level of ease and confidence as Mr Hawthorn.'

Twice more Professor Barton pauses his lecture to ask a question, and while other students can partially answer, it's Godric who fills in whatever blanks are left. Maybe he's a savant. Or he's read ahead and has a photographic memory.

When class ends, I hustle out, not wanting to risk speaking to Godric again, concerned I'll say something mortifying. I'd prefer to avoid a scenario like that in front of my entire biochemistry class. I spend the next hour in the library, then head to my advanced microbiology course. Monday I have three classes, and Tuesday and Wednesday I have three-hour night classes, but it's all worth it to end my Friday at two-thirty in the afternoon with a lab.

After my third and final class of the day – I don't run into Godric again, and I'm on the fence as to whether that's a good thing or not – I head to the student commons so I can pop into the student paper office. It's a shared space with several other student-run initiatives. We have a meeting tomorrow to discuss next week's edition, our assignments, and to welcome the freshmen recruits.

Blaine is already there, leafing through articles for this week's edition.

'Hey. What happened to you last week at the party? I saw you chatting with the neighbor guy. What's his name? Garrett?' Blaine flips his pen between his fingers but fumbles it and it rolls off his desk and onto the floor. I don't bend to pick it up for him.

'I heard you boned a sophomore from the Beta Pi sorority.' That's not what I heard at all, but it's fun to watch him get flustered.

'Who told you that?'

I shrug. 'Why does it matter?'

'Tina isn't a sophomore, she's a junior from Theta Nu. I'd been drinking, and you turned me down more than once.'

I cross my arms. 'Seems like I made the right choice.'

He continues to offer an explanation I don't need. 'Tina wanted no strings. She's working on her master's thesis and doesn't have time for feelings, which suited us both since my feelings are still attached to you, and you hurt my feelings by brushing me off more than once. Besides, you were all over the guy who lives across the street from me, while you were at a party at *my* house. Did you leave with him?' He frowns at the possibility.

I used to find this kind of blunt honesty from Blaine endearing, now it's just frustrating. I ignore the part about his feelings. 'Why do you care?'

'What do you know about him and the guys he lives with?' He picks up another pen and starts with the flipping thing but fumbles it on the trip back to his pointer finger.

'Their names are Godric, Hunter and Laz and they're brothers. Why do you care so much about these dudes, apart from the fact that you think I passed up jumping back into your bed so I could jump into one of theirs?'

'Is that what you did, Hazy? Did you jump into bed with one of them?' His frown deepens. 'Or more than one?'

I make a face. 'First of all, that's a super inappropriate question. Secondly, it's none of your business.' I run my middle finger across my eyebrow. 'Have you had a chance to read my article yet?'

I wrote a short piece on the importance of safeguarding peer connections during the first month of college. Mostly I focus on the science department and any science-y news: research projects, awards, and academic findings of note.

'I'll get to it tonight. You could come over later, we could review it together.' He has the audacity to look hopeful.

'I have to wash my hair.'

He scans my head with a critical eye. 'Your hair looks fine. You can wash it after.'

'I'm not coming over. Just email me the article with the proposed changes.' I don't wait for him to answer before I turn on my heel and leave.

On the way home – I take the long way – Satya requests that I pick up Bibb lettuce and water chestnuts so we can make chicken lettuce wraps for dinner. We have a corner store on the other side of Frat Row and an actual grocery store one block in the opposite direction. My avoidance route home takes me closer to the grocery store, so I continue in that direction. I message back to ask if we're low on anything else that's light enough for me to carry home.

It's hot this afternoon and sweat trickles down my spine and the back of my neck. While having physical textbooks makes it easier to mark and tab sections for tests, Satya might have a point about the lightness of ebooks. It would save me from carting half my bodyweight in science textbooks around every day.

By the time I arrive at the grocery store my back is damp with perspiration, as are my temples. The doors open and a blast of cool air hits me, causing my skin to pebble with goosebumps. I grab a cart and consider tossing my backpack in, but there's probably a wet spot down the center of my back from all the sweating and this store is frequented by the college students who live in the area, so I suffer through the pressure at the base of my spine.

I grab the things we need for dinner, then make my way to the other side of the store to pick up essentials like chocolate and chips.

Just as I reach the bakery section to grab a German chocolate cake – despite it being from a grocery store, it's still the best one I've ever had – a shiver rips through me and the hairs on the back of my neck rise. I look up, expecting to see a vent above me, but nothing. I give my head a shake, and turn my cart around, ready to head for the checkout.

Which is when I spot Godric loping down the baked goods aisle toward me. As usual, he looks good enough to eat. Unlike me, he's not a sweaty, gross mess. His hair is styled neatly and he's wearing a pair of gray shorts and a black band T-shirt. It stretches across his chest and shoulders, the sleeves conforming to his biceps.

He stops in front of the chocolate desserts and adds a few things to his cart. Which contains the makings for a steak dinner.

He stills for a moment, then tips his chin up, inhaling deeply. His jaw tics and his fists clench as his head turns fractionally in my direction. I'm sweaty, I probably smell bad and there's a good chance the liner I put on this morning is smudged under my eyes. I will him not to turn around, but my silent directive is unheeded. His cart angles toward my end of the aisle, followed by his body.

And like every single other time I've found myself near him, my body reacts. Muscles below the waist clench. Heat works its way up my neck into my cheeks, and despite the cold air pumping through the vents, I'm suddenly overheated. In my mind I abandon my cart and launch myself at him. He catches me, hands cupping my ass, as I wrap myself around him . . .

His gaze locks with mine and for a split second I almost believe he can see right inside my head, and that the same fantasy that's playing out for me is also playing out for him.

I raise a hand, waving as I call out, 'Hey, Godric!' My voice is ridiculously pitchy.

Instead of responding, he breaks our prolonged eye contact and spins his cart around, heading in the opposite direction. Without so much as a wave of acknowledgement.

Well, that was humiliating. He couldn't even give me a head nod. I might not look my hottest, but totally ignoring me is a real jerk move.

Having a class with him three times a week is going to suck.

Fingers crossed we don't have the same lab.

4

After being ignored in the supermarket, I make a point of arriving to class early on Wednesday and Friday so I can grab a seat closer to the front of the room and hopefully avoid any accidental eye contact/proximity with Godric. Being snubbed sucks and I would prefer not to endure that again. I'm also trying to avoid being seen by Blaine. He hasn't realized we're in the same class yet, too busy flirting with whoever he's sitting next to. I snag a seat at the end of an aisle, close to an exit so I'm able to duck out as soon as class is over.

Despite my careful planning, I find I'm unable to stop myself from checking the class for the supermarket ignorer before I bolt. And both times I spot Godric talking to that girl with the curly hair and the glasses. Maybe they're friends, or they know each other from somewhere, or they're dating. If it's the latter, then he probably shouldn't have been checking me out the other day. I also spot him on campus a few times over the course of the week. Out of those sightings, only once does he offer me a half-smile of acknowledgement; the rest of the time he either doesn't notice me, or he's ignoring me.

After biochem I hit the library between classes, meet up with Satya and Alyssa for a late lunch, then head to my lab. It's my final class of the week and one I've been looking forward to. I arrive as the class before mine is filing out, and duck behind a column when I spot Blaine in the hall, chatting up another classmate. I also recognize the curly-haired girl I've seen Godric talking to leaving the class as well, but there's no Godric with her this time.

I pick a seat with a decent view of the door and set up my tablet and notebook in preparation for today's lab. Students file in, some in pairs, and take the seats around me. As the class fills, so does my relief, because it looks like Godric isn't in my lab.

But then, because the universe clearly has something against me, Blaine walks through the door and scans the room. I wish for the power of invisibility, but like a beacon in the night, his gaze homes in on me. Ending up with Blaine as my lab partner for an entire semester is the worst possible option. Blaine is the guy who ekes out passing grades and leaves it to his lab partners to do all the work. I would know, since I've been his partner before.

Blaine's eyes flare, as if I'm a surprise. Which I am, since I've avoided his notice all week. As he moves toward me, a highly recognizable figure steps through the door. And suddenly, the slim chance that Godric has the same lab as me becomes a one hundred percent chance.

His brow furrows as he takes in Blaine heading for my table, then his expression lifts when he sees me. Between one blink and the next, Godric has managed to skirt around Blaine and make it all the way across the room to the empty seat beside me.

His lopsided smile is annoyingly adorable. 'Hi, Hazy.'

Today he's wearing a pair of light-wash denim, and a yellow shirt that reads *Department of Redundancy Department*.

'Hi.' I didn't expect him to acknowledge me, so I don't know what else to say.

'Do you have a partner yet?' Godric's gaze shifts to the empty stool two feet from mine.

'Yeah. Ron Weasley is wearing Harry's invisibility cloak.' Ugh. That was embarrassingly weak. 'I mean, no?' It's more question than statement. I'm so confused.

Blaine gets stopped by a girl with a bob who I've seen in other classes over the years.

'You sound unsure.' Godric runs a hand through his perfect hair, but instead of making a mess of it, the strands fall right back into place, swooping elegantly across his forehead. 'Are you waiting for someone else?' He tips his head in Blaine's direction.

For half a second I consider saying yes, since I would prefer not to suffer from the emotional whiplash he's giving me, but I don't want to get stuck with Blaine. It's quite the conundrum. 'You can be my partner. If you want. I mean no, I'm not waiting for anyone.' I motion to the empty seat.

Blaine gives me an unimpressed look, but takes a seat beside his newest, unwitting victim.

'Great.' Godric's grin widens and he drops onto the stool beside me.

And like the last time I was this close to him, awkward things start happening to my body that I can't quite get a handle on. The hairs on my arms rise, and I have the sudden urge to run, which is not normally something I would do on purpose, unless I urgently need to use the bathroom, or there's a sale on German chocolate cakes. But at the same time my nipples harden, my vagina tingles, my imagination heads for the closest gutter and dives straight down into the dirty, smutty abyss. In my head, Godric apologizes for ignoring me, I tell him it's fine, and suddenly we're naked, me spread out on the lab station with Godric's face between my thighs. It's very conflicting.

My body doesn't seem to care about my actual feelings as heat pools low in my belly, and everything below the waist clenches. That warmth travels through my veins and climbs up my chest, causing my neck to feel itchy and my cheeks to explode with color.

Godric pauses with his fingers on the zipper of his backpack and his gaze shifts my way. His maple-syrup eyes caress my face, and still, those lurid images keep flipping through my mind in an excessively graphic slideshow of sexy times.

The next two hours are going to be hellishly long if I can't get a handle on myself around this man.

'How's your week been? I haven't seen you around, apart from when you're rushing out of biochem.' He sets a spiral-bound notebook and a pen on the desk in front of him and relocates his backpack to the floor next to mine. A metallic buzz comes from inside, but he ignores it.

'Oh, it's uh . . . it's been busy. You know how first weeks are.' I fidget with my pen and my tablet, rearranging them on the desk. It gives me something to do with my hands and somewhere to look that isn't his face. I realize the polite thing to do is to ask a question in return, so eventually I drag my gaze back to him. 'How's your first week been? It must be tough to start your senior year at a new college.'

Godric shrugs, and the hint of a smile turns up one corner of his delicious mouth. 'I'm used to moving around a lot. A change of scenery is always welcome, especially when it includes someone like you.'

I can't even imagine what my expression must be, but I can feel my mouth trying to pucker and pull down at the same time, and my eyebrows are trying to touch each other. 'Are you fucking with me?'

It's Godric's turn to look confused. 'I'm sorry, what?'

I lean in and lower my voice. 'Do you honestly think you can come in here looking all –' I flail a hand in his direction – '*GQ Magazine* pretty, dropping compliments, and I'm supposed to do what? Get all swoony about it? Next thing you know, you'll be pushing the whole write-up for the lab on me, which, let me be clear, isn't going to happen. I don't care how nice you are to look at, you want to be my lab partner, you better pull your weight on the write-ups.'

He grins. 'You think I'm nice to look at?'

I roll my eyes. 'Of course that was your takeaway. Freaking frat boys are all the same.'

I glance around the room, there are still a couple of people without a partner. One is a guy who almost blew up a lab I was in last year. The other is a girl who I know for a fact is a perfectionist. I collect my things anyway. Like hell I'm spending the next sixteen weeks dealing with a pretty frat boy who's nice to me one second and ignoring me the next, and likely going to pawn off all the lab write-ups on me. Which is exactly what Blaine would do if he was my partner. I might be projecting a wee bit.

'I'm not a frat boy.'

'You live in a frat house.' I mean, I'm pointing out the obvious, but still.

He lowers his voice. 'I'm not like the Blaines of this world.'

I glance in Blaine's direction. He's busy turning on the charm with his new lab partner; all smiles and attentiveness.

I drop my voice. 'You don't routinely throw women you've previously bedded over your shoulder like a caveman and try to entice them back into your bed by reminding them of the fact that you can bring the O?' I wish I'd switched tables four sentences ago.

'I find it incredibly unbelievable that he thinks about anyone but himself in bed.'

I take a hard right, because this conversation isn't one I want to have with Godric, especially not with Blaine sitting less than fifteen feet away. 'I saw you on Monday in the grocery store,' I blurt. 'I thought maybe you ignored me because of all the nonsense I spewed at you at the party. And then I started thinking that maybe that brother of yours said the things that he said because he was saving you from me. But then you sat beside me today, and now I don't know what to think.'

More buzzing comes from Godric's bag, but he continues to ignore it. 'He wasn't trying to save me from you, he was trying to save you from me. Fortunately, he's not here so no one can do any saving.'

'Why would he want to save me from you in the first place?'

He rubs his bottom lip with this thumb. 'My social skills aren't always up to par.'

'I totally relate to the social skills issue. Sometimes when I get nervous my mouth keeps moving and words keep coming out that shouldn't and I'm incapable of stopping them. Kind of like now.' I clasp my hands and set them on the desk in front of me, hoping it will help reduce the fidgetiness that seems to come from having Godric's undivided attention.

There is a slight pause and I'm about to fill the awkward silence with something embarrassing but he saves me from myself.

'I'm sorry about the grocery store. I didn't expect to see you and I wasn't . . . in the best headspace for conversation. I didn't mean to be a jerk.'

'It's fine. I was sweaty and not looking my best self.' I decide it would be a good idea to change the subject. 'What other classes do you have this semester? I think this is the only one we have together.'

'Unfortunately, I think you're right, but at least we get to be lab partners.' He picks up his pen and starts flipping it between his fingers, like he did in class on Monday.

Godric rattles off a number of courses, some of which I have next semester, but two I have this semester. We must be in different sections.

I'm about to ask more about his classes, but his brother Hunter appears beside him.

'Stop ignoring your text messages and look at your phone.' His gaze swings from Godric to me. 'Hi, Hazy, it's nice to see you again.'

I lift a hand in a wave. 'You too, Hunter.'

He turns his attention back to Godric. 'Seriously, dude, we talked about this. You can't skip breakfast every day or there are going to be problems.' He stresses the word breakfast.

'I'll deal with it later,' he mutters.

'You're pushing it, God.'

I glance around the room. Several people are watching the exchange. The girl in front of Godric is rubbing her arm, which has broken out in goosebumps. I lift my gaze to the ceiling, but she's not sitting under one of the vents. Weird.

'I've got it under control.'

'Laz does not agree.' Hunter spins around and walks out of the class.

Godric reaches into his backpack and retrieves his phone. He angles it towards him as he keys in his passcode and pulls up his messages. His eyebrows pull together while his lips turn down in a frown. He shakes his head on a sigh and shoves his phone back in his bag.

'Everything okay?' I ask.

Godric nods, but before he can say anything, the professor walks into the room and takes his place at the front of the class. It's almost a relief because it means I can't keep saying awkward things.

The first lab isn't very exciting. It's the usual swabbing of bacteria and putting it in Petri dishes to see what grows over the next week. But we do get to add two strains of the flu virus to the samples, so we have something interesting to compare it against when we review our findings next week and complete our lab.

As we're cleaning up during the last five minutes of class I suggest we divide up the lab components for our report. That way, when we meet next week all we have to do is plug in our findings.

Godric slides his notebook into his bag. 'Or we could go for coffee and work on them together.'

'You want to go for coffee?'

'Unless you have another class.' He zips up his backpack. 'Or maybe you're busy?'

'No, I don't have another class. I'm done for the day.'

I stuff my tablet, notebook and pencil case into my own backpack and zip it up.

Godric gives me another disarming smile that sends butterflies flitting around in my stomach. 'I'm done, too.' He shoulders his bag. 'Are you up for that coffee?'

'Sure. That way, we go into the weekend with one less assignment hanging over our heads.' Because there's no way Godric is asking me on an actual coffee date. It's for studying purposes only. At least this is what I'm telling myself. I like to expect the worst so I'm not setting myself up for disappointment.

'And I can prove that I plan to pull my weight on the lab reports,' he says dryly.

Ah, there it is, the real reason for suggesting coffee. Good job setting my personal expectations low. 'You can't blame me for being wary. Statistically, you only acknowledge my existence in a positive way twenty-five percent of the time.'

He frowns. 'That seems abysmally low.'

'The numbers don't lie.'

'I'll need to work on improving that then, huh?'

'Smiles are free.' I thread my arms through my own backpack straps and follow him into the hall.

He moves in close to me, his arm grazing mine as we navigate our way through the throng of students leaving one class or rushing to another. We end up stuffed in the back corner of an elevator. I find it curious that the guys seem to give him extra space. He's tall and broad, but not exceptionally imposing.

When we reach the ground floor he steps to the side and puts his hand over the censor to prevent the door from closing on me. He also waits until I'm in the foyer before he crosses the threshold. He holds the door for me as we leave the building, and then we fall into step beside each other on our way to the student cafe, and I manage not to ask any weird, awkward questions. But when we reach the cafe, there's a line and not an empty table in sight. While the weather isn't terrible, clouds have rolled in and the sky is threatening rain.

Godric rubs the back of his neck. 'How would you feel about getting coffees to go and going back to one of our places to work on this, instead of trying to play musical chairs?'

'We could do that. Lys and Satya both have class until four. What about your brothers?' My body is already going haywire at the thought of having Godric inside my house. I can't figure out if it excites or unnerves me. Maybe both? It's hard to get a read on him.

'Hunter has class until five, but he's probably skipping so he can start the weekend early. And Laz rarely leaves the house. He has mostly night and online courses.'

'His social anxiety is that bad?'

'People stress him out, so he avoids them for the most part,' Godric replies.

I tap my lip. 'Hmm, well, I don't want to stress anyone out. Maybe my place is the better option.'

Lys and Satya usually stop at the bar for a beer before they come home. Any other day and I might stick around campus and grab one with them, but getting a lab report out of the way seems like a smart plan.

'Your place it is.'

I order an iced coffee with oat milk and Godric orders

a mocha frappé topped with whipped cream, chocolate syrup and an entire double-chocolate cookie on top.

'I sort of figured you for a black coffee kind of guy.'

Godric graces me with a lopsided grin. 'That's more Laz's style, not mine. I have a thing for all things chocolatey.'

'And steak, apparently.'

He quirks an eyebrow. 'How do you know that?'

I shrug and fight the blush threatening to stain my cheeks. 'Your grocery cart was full of meat and cupcakes.'

His smile turns into a smirk. 'Are you judging me on my eating habits?'

'Not judging, just observing.' I let my gaze move over his long, lean frame. 'And you seem like the kind of guy who can get away with eating pounds of red meat and a six-pack of cupcakes, and then washing it all down with one of those sugar-and-calorie-filled, I'm-pretending-to-be-coffee beverages, and still never gain an ounce.'

'Yeah, I can basically eat anything I want, whenever I want, without worrying.' His smile turns wry, almost like he's making a joke.

The barista calls our names, and we pick up our coffees and leave the crowded cafe.

Unfortunately, we pass by the student commons on the way through campus, and run into Blaine. He's sitting on a bench with two of the freshman recruits who have joined the student paper this year. They're hanging off his every word, like he holds the answers to all of life's mysteries.

I felt that way when he was a sophomore, and I was a freshman. He's frustratingly charismatic, and annoyingly pretty. We dated second semester of my freshman year, but it was on-again-off-again the entire time. He wasn't intentionally being a douche, but his tendency toward blunt honesty once we passed the getting-to-know-you stage often made him sound like one. I would have to explain why what he'd said was offensive, and he would apologize for the a-hole things that came out of his mouth, and that apology would always include orgasms. For a while, the orgasms were enough of an incentive to keep coming back.

But then summer happened, and he traveled to wherever his parents decided to send him for four months, and I stuck around and got a job. Relationships are hard enough when you're living in the same town, going to the same college. Long distance, with a guy who routinely stuck his foot in his mouth, seemed like torture I didn't need. So we broke up.

But come the end of summer, he started texting, asking to see me, telling me he missed me and, of course, like the nineteen-year-old, horny idiot I was, I couldn't pass up the O-pportunity. It took some time, but I think I've finally figured out why he keeps perpetuating the cycle. He always wants what he can't have, and for some reason I'm at the top of that list every fall. He lays on the charm until he gets into my pants, and then goes back to being his bluntly honest self.

Blaine abandons his new groupies, and shouts my name at an obnoxious volume as he crosses the quad.

'I'm sorry in advance for whatever nonsense Blaine spits out at us. I'd ignore him, but if I do, he'll probably up his persistence, and I'd like to avoid that,' I say.

'I expected him to make a bigger fuss about my being your partner in the lab.'

'I'm sure he'll find creative ways to show me how he feels about that.'

'And you dated him.' Godric seems appropriately mystified by this. His expression is a mix of displeasure, disbelief and – judging by the sudden dark slant of his gaze and the tic in his jaw – a hint of murderous rage.

I should find that look disconcerting. However, for reasons I don't get, my heart does this fluttery thing and my stomach flip-flops.

'Yeah. My hormones were an issue back in the day, and he really struggles with not getting what he wants, which apparently is me, until he finds someone new to fixate on.'

Godric doesn't have a chance to respond because Blaine is right in front of us.

'That was quite the move you pulled in the lab. I'm sure Hazy was just being nice by letting you be her lab partner, but you should know she and I have history. Isn't that right, Hazy?' He picks me up and swings me around in a circle, but my feet drag on the ground, and I hang there limply, not making the whole swinging me around like a doll thing easy for him.

'I wasn't just being nice. And in our case it's better not to repeat history.'

'My feelings for you are as constant as the north star,' Blaine declares.

'They're only constant when there isn't someone else to charm the pants off of.' This is so awkward.

'I didn't even know we had the same class until I saw you in the lab, otherwise I would have focused all my attention on you.' He sets me on my feet. 'We still need to have that talk.' He tries to touch my hair, but I step out of reach

42

and position myself slightly behind Godric. I'm absolutely using him as a shield and I don't feel bad about it at all.

'We already had that talk, more than once.'

'We should have it again.'

'It seems kind of pointless.' I don't give him a chance to argue, tacking on, 'You still haven't given me my article back with edits, FYI.'

'You can come over tomorrow and we can work through them together.'

'I can't. I have plans all weekend. You can email them to me like you do with everyone else. Anyway, we gotta get going. We have a lab assignment to work on.' I take a step back and Blaine's gaze shifts to Godric.

'How are you settling into the neighborhood? You see any ghosts in your place yet? I've heard it's haunted.'

Godric gives him a tight smile. 'No ghosts so far. Just a fair amount of dust and spiders. The caretaker passed away and we failed to find a replacement.'

'Oh yeah?' Blaine's eyes light up. 'How'd he die?'

'Seriously, Blaine?' I squeeze Godric's biceps. 'You do not need to answer that.'

'Sorry, my bad. It's the reporter in me. That house has been empty for as long as I've been at Burnham. I didn't even know it was still habitable. How'd you manage to get the place? Was it for sale or something?'

'It belonged to my great-uncle,' Godric replies.

'Great-uncle, huh? And you live there with your brothers, is that right?' Blaine keeps throwing out the questions.

'Yeah, that's right.'

'And you're in fourth year, yeah? What about your brothers? I met the one last week – Hudson I think? Big dude. My roommate plays football, if you think he might want to try out. They're always looking to recruit new players.'

Godric rubs his lips to hide a smile. 'Football isn't Hunter's sport of choice. He's more into rock climbing and trail running. Dabbles in archery. Really lives up to his name.'

'Huh. Well. If he changes his mind, you know where I live.' Blaine pulls out the gun fingers. He alternates those with the thumbs up.

'That I do.'

'What about the other brother? I haven't met him yet, have I? There's a party this weekend down the street at Delta Iota Kappa, they're not as fun as the ones my house throws, but still not bad. You should bring him out.'

'I'll see what I can do, he's pretty reclusive, though.'

'Okay, well!' I clap my hands and startle myself. 'We should get going if we want to make it home before it starts raining.' I point to the sky, which has lightened up considerably in the last twenty minutes. 'Don't forget to email me my article so I'm not editing it five minutes before it's due for formatting,' I remind Blaine.

'See you around.' Godric nods to him.

I don't know if I imagine it, but his tone makes it sound more like a threat than a goodbye.

'I have a question.' Godric says as we walk away. He glances over his shoulder, his jaw clenching. 'Actually, I have more than one question.'

'Okay. Ask away.'

He adjusts the strap of his backpack, that furrow in his brow deepening in the most enticing way. Serious Godric is as attractive as smiling Godric and annoyed Godric. 'Is he always that obnoxious? Or does he save that for his interactions with you?'

I snort-chuckle. 'He has a hard time letting go. He perseverates on things, and one of those happens to be me.'

'Because you dated four years ago?' Godric looks at me like I'm a puzzle he's trying to solve.

'Yeah, but don't hold it against me, please.'

Godric's smile turns wry. 'I would never judge a person based solely on one questionable boyfriend choice. How long did you go out for?'

'Why?'

Godric side-eyes me. 'Just curious.'

'About?'

'You.'

'But why are you curious about me?'

He rubs at his bottom lip, as if he's trying to hide a grin. 'Why shouldn't I be curious about you?'

I do not want to find him charming. 'You're infuriating, you know that, right?'

'I'm aware. Do you find that appealing?'

'No. Not even a little,' I lie.

'Hmm. Would it help if I told you you're unlike anyone I've ever met?'

'That's a nice way of saying I'm a weirdo.'

'You have an interesting way of turning compliments into insults.'

'And you have an interesting way of answering questions that leads to more questions.' And I think I like it.

Since I'm with Godric, and Blaine is still on campus, we take the shorter route back to my place. When we get there, I usher Godric inside and give him a tour of the main floor, starting with the small galley kitchen that was probably renovated sometime in the early eighties and hasn't been touched since.

'This is where we make food.'

The floor is yellowed linoleum that may have once been lighter, but years of foot traffic has worn the center strip. The sink is full of dirty dishes; most of them belong to Satya since she seems to have an allergy to putting them in the dishwasher.

'It's quaint,' Godric says.

'It's old and run-down, but it's functional.'

I step through the doorway into our equally small living room. In one corner is an ancient lounger that used to belong to my dad, and beside that is an equally ancient couch that sags horribly in the middle. The coffee table boasts several coasters with inappropriate sayings on them, and across from the couch is a flat-screen TV, which the three of us bought by pooling our resources when we first moved in.

'And this is where we watch romantic comedies and develop unrealistic expectations of relationships.'

One side of Godric's mouth tips up. 'Laz loves romantic comedies.'

That gives me pause. 'Your emo brother?'

'Emo?'

'Or maybe he identifies as goth? He's the one who extracted you from the party, right? He looks more like he'd enjoy horror films, or psychological thrillers.'

'Mm. You can't always judge a book by its cover. He can't stand horror films. They irk him.'

'Interesting. What kind of movies do you like?' I ask.

'Depends on the day, what kind of movies do you think I'd like?'

I tap my lip and give him a slow once-over, not because I need to, but because checking him out is becoming my favorite pastime apart from binge-watching college romance dramas. 'I feel like you're a fan of post-apocalyptic sci-fi.'

He smiles. 'That's very specific.'

'Am I right, though?'

'Pretty spot on, actually.'

'What else do you enjoy?'

His gaze moves over my face, and I almost feel it like a caress. 'You.'

'If you tell me you could watch me all day, I'm sending you home.'

He laughs and rubs the back of his neck. 'Sorry. I'm out of practice with the whole flirting thing.'

'It's cute.' I squeeze his biceps in reassurance, and because it's an excuse to touch him.

Godric's lips turn down. 'Cute is how people refer to kittens and puppies and babies.'

'Your attempts at flirting can be added to that list.' This is good, I can do the banter thing with him.

47

'I don't know that I want to be on the cute list,' he gripes.

I bite back a grin and point past the staircase leading to the bedrooms on the second floor. Across from it are two doors. One is a random closet that seems slightly pointless, but we use it as a pantry and a place to store the vacuum cleaner. The other leads to the small powder room with wallpaper that's been around so long it's back in style. 'If you need to use the bathroom, it's just there.'

'I'm good, but thanks.'

I don't offer to show him the second floor. Having him in my house is enough of a challenge, and taking him upstairs, where there's a bed, is a bad idea.

'Do you want to work in the living room, or would you rather sit at the kitchen table?' I'm back to trying to strangle my fingers.

'Either works.' He leaves it open for me to make the final decision.

'We'll have enough room to spread out in the kitchen.' I shut down an image of me lying naked on the table. I glance at Godric, hoping that only sounded suggestive to me. Based on his impassive expression, I'm the solo ball of hormones.

We return to the kitchen, and I grab the cloth from the sink, giving it a sniff test before I use it to wipe down the table. It smells like it needs to be washed. I toss it aside and grab a fresh one from the drawer. Once I've wiped the table free of dried syrup droplets and coffee rings, Godric and I unpack our backpacks.

'Are you hungry? I can put out some snacks if you'd like.' He's a guy, and they have notoriously bottomless stomachs.

'I'm fine either way.' Godric sets his notebook and his pen on the table.

'We have chocolate.'

Godric grins. 'I do love chocolate.'

'I'll throw some stuff on a plate.' I pull out the plastic tray we use for charcuterie boards, which is something that happens often, especially on a Friday night when none of us is particularly motivated to cook. I push up on my tiptoes, straining to reach the box of crackers on the top shelf. I'm not particularly short, but the top shelf is always a stretch.

I suck in a breath when Godric comes up behind me and his chest brushes my shoulder as he plucks the box from the shelf and sets the crackers on the counter. 'Is this what you needed?'

'Yeah, thanks.' I wish I could get a handle on myself around this guy. Being stuck at self-gratification station for a lot of months is making it tough to keep my hormones in check.

Godric leans against the edge of the counter. 'Can I help?'

I point to the cupboard behind him. 'You'll find our extensive chocolate stash on the top shelf. There should be cookies up there, too – double-chocolate fudge, if I remember correctly.'

'Now you're speaking my language.'

While Godric retrieves the excessively large chocolate bars we store on the top shelf and three boxes of cookies, I get to work on assembling the rest of our snack board, half of which ends up filled with sweet treats.

It suddenly occurs to me to ask, 'Do you have any allergies?'

'I can eat pretty much anything.'

'Good to know.'

I add a handful of cashews, and cube some cheese, although all we have is old cheddar, and some Swiss. I add a few crackers and round out the board with bunches of red grapes.

Once the board is ready, we move it to the kitchen table and set it between us, with the chocolate treats angled toward Godric.

He grabs a cookie from the plate and devours it in two bites. 'God, I love chocolate,' he half groans.

'It's second only to orgasms.' I slap a hand over my mouth. 'I didn't just say that.'

Godric chokes on his cookie.

I get up and give him a couple of hearty pats on the back. 'I'm so sorry, please don't die.'

He huffs another laugh. 'A cookie can't take me down. And please don't apologize, your unfiltered comments are highly entertaining.'

'More like highly embarrassing.' I'm flustered all over again. 'We should probably tackle the lab write-up.' I drop back into my chair and flip open my tablet.

Thankfully, my brain remains on task while we work on the lab report and I don't say anything else embarrassing.

'Do you have any brothers or sisters?' Godric asks as he notes the methods and materials used in the lab.

'I have four older brothers. Which was awesome and awful at the same time.' This is better. Normal conversation is good.

'Why? Were they overprotective?'

'They could be, especially with me being the youngest.'

He flips his pen between his fingers. 'How much older are they?'

'My oldest brother, Curtis, is in his early thirties, Dawson and Devon are twenty-eight and twins, and Francis is twenty-five. They were mostly in college or out of the house by the time I hit high school, except for Francis, but he was a senior when I was a freshman, so there wasn't a lot of overlap there, thankfully. They didn't have too many opportunities to ruin my social life, not that I had much of one in high school.'

Godric rests his elbow on the table and props his chin on his fist. 'Why the lack of social life?'

'I was too busy with school and studying to be bothered with much else.'

'Was that by choice?'

'I come from a long line of overachievers. My dad is a biochemical engineer, and my mom is a neurosurgeon. I grew up in a house full of science-y people. We watched a lot of Discovery channel and built Lego models on the weekends.'

'Sounds like my kind of weekend.' He regards me intently. 'What field of medicine are you most interested in?'

'Molecular genetics has always fascinated me.'

Godric's eyes light up. 'There's such artistry in human DNA, isn't there?'

'Right? The double helix structure is a thing of beauty.'

'A true masterpiece, unique to each individual,' he agrees.

'Exactly. There's so much to study and learn. Like how the body adapts and changes with every new generation.'

'Humans are quite a revolutionary species, always evolving. Always changing.'

'Yes!' I agree with him, then prop my chin on my fist,

mirroring him. 'What about you? Are there any doctors in your family? What field are you interested in pursuing?'

'My mother is in medicine and her focus has always been on blood disorders.'

'That's such an important field.'

'It truly is. It's our life force. We can't survive without it.' His voice grows gruff and he clears his throat.

'What about your brothers? What are they studying? How old are they? Is it just the three of you?' I pick up a cube of cheese and pop it in my mouth.

His gaze darts away and his smile seems secretive again, which I don't understand. 'I'm twenty-four, I took a year off before I started my undergraduate degree. Hunter is two years older, and this is his second degree, his first is in ancient history, and now he's studying social deviance.'

'Wow. Degree number two, that's impressive.'

'Hunter has a range of interests, so narrowing it down isn't always easy for him. Laz is two years younger and working on a degree in computer science.'

'Ah, that makes you the middle child.'

'Mm. Yes, I should be notoriously misunderstood, but that's Laz.' He reaches for another cookie.

'The three of you must be close if you're all going to Burnham together. How'd you manage that anyway?'

'Laz and Hunter applied, and were offered admission, and I put in for a transfer. It's sort of a family tradition to go here.'

'Where did you transfer from?'

'We were up in Alaska, and I was tired of the cold, and it was time for a change. My great-uncle's house made it easy to move. Besides, if I hadn't switched schools, I wouldn't be sitting here with you, proving that I'll pull my weight when it comes to lab reports.'

I roll my eyes. 'I maintain that my concerns were valid and directly impacted by your grocery store snubbing.'

'I'm sorry about that.' His tongue darts out to skim his bottom lip, and I track the movement. 'I was saving you from my bad mood.'

'So you keep saying.' And then I do something ridiculously girlie by ducking my head and tucking my hair behind my ear.

He tips his head, a wry grin tugging at his luscious mouth. 'I'm still not sure you believe me.'

I don't have time to come up with a snippy reply, because the front door opens, and Satya yells, 'It's Friyay! Let's get our comfy clothes on and eat ourselves into a coma!'

She bounces around the corner, swinging her bra around in the air above her head. 'Oh shit.' Her bra goes flying and lands on the counter.

Godric sits back, which is when it registers that we were both leaning in. I want to throw tacks at Satya for interrupting what may or may not have been a moment.

'Oh, hey now! I didn't realize you had a friend over.' Satya's eyes widen in mild accusation as she plasters an awkward smile on her face and crosses her arms over her chest to hide her nipples, which are currently visible through her white shirt.

Godric's lips turn up in a slightly uncomfortable smile. 'Hi, you're Satya, right?'

'That's me!' She starts to wave, then quickly recrosses her arms. 'You're Godric. You live in the haunted house across from Blaine the Pain.'

'That's a fitting name.'

'It really is.' She nods a few times and side-steps over to the counter to retrieve her bra. 'I'm just going to change into something that doesn't have a real waistband. And I'm not gonna come back downstairs for a while, so you kids have fun doing whatever you're doing.' She does some sort of weird moonwalk dance out of the kitchen.

A few seconds later she yelps as she runs up the stairs, I'm guessing because free-boobing it, while lovely, isn't the best when rushing to her room.

'I'm sorry that happened.' I motion to where Satya was moments ago. 'It's kind of her thing, you know? Every time she walks through the door, she takes off her bra and frees the girls. And it's Friday, or Fri*yay*, and the end of the first week of classes, so there's even more of a reason to celebrate and free the twins, you know?' I wish I stopped myself at sorry.

Godric's gaze drops from my face to my chest, but springs right back up. His tongue pokes at his top lip. 'Do you usually join in?'

'Depends on what bra I'm wearing. Some are more comfortable than others.' I motion to the space where my roommate was standing moments ago. 'Satya's got a lot going on in the girls department, so releasing them from their underwire prison at the end of the day would probably be similar to, oh, removing a jockstrap?' I motion unnecessarily to my lady business, which is now flushed with embarrassment, along with my cheeks. 'I imagine that freeing the boys after they've been cooped up in a cup for several hours must feel pretty good.' I glance down, but his legs are crossed so I'm looking at his knee.

54

Godric taps his lips, thoughtfully. 'Cups aren't known for being comfortable, but it's a lot better than getting a puck in the balls.'

'You play hockey?' I run my gaze over his long, lean frame. I would have thought more along the lines of volleyball, or possibly baseball.

'Hunter plays, and sometimes he forces me to practice with him. I do see your point, though. In the future, if we end up here working on an assignment, don't let me hold you back. I would hate for you to be uncomfortable.'

'How very considerate of you.' I gather up the papers strewn all over the table and tap them into a neat pile.

'Considerate is my middle name.' He passes me one of the sheets that slipped out of the pile.

I slide it back in with the rest of them. 'Ow.' Blood wells in the small slice across my index finger. 'Paper cuts are the worst.' I bring my finger to my lips, licking over the wound. The metallic tang of blood hits my tongue and I shift my gaze to Godric.

His nostrils flare and his eyes go wide. He turns away and grabs something from his bag, but drops it on the floor. The small pill bottle makes a sound like maracas. He snatches it from the floor, unscrews the cap and pops a pill into his mouth, swallowing it dry. His chair scrapes across the floor as he pushes it back and gets to his feet.

'I should go, I need to go.' He grabs his backpack from the floor and jams his notebook in along with the rest of his things.

'Is everything okay?' I have no idea what happened to set him off.

'Yeah, everything is fine. I just . . . I told Laz I'd be home by five. Thanks for having me over.' He zips his backpack and slings it over his shoulder and heads for the door.

I follow him to the foyer where he's already jamming his feet into his shoes. He wrenches the door open before stepping onto the front porch. It isn't until he's halfway down the front walk that he turns to face me. He runs a hand roughly through his hair and grips the back of his neck, his smile stiff and his jaw tight.

'Thanks again, Hazy. If I don't run into you before, I'll see you in class on Monday.' And with that, he spins on his heel and rushes down the street, leaving me with whiplash once again.

6

I don't see Godric over the weekend. If I'd been on the ball, I would've traded numbers with him before he left on Friday, but at the same time he was in one hell of a rush.

Although it's the second time he's had to leave because of the whole medication thing. Maybe he has a serious condition. Maybe he's part of the reason his mom studied blood disorders. Or maybe I'm turning it into a bigger deal than it needs to be. It's possible I misinterpreted the whole leaning into each other thing. As a result, I've spent much of the weekend over-analyzing our entire interaction on Friday, from beginning to end.

On Monday morning, I get up nice and early, shower, and take care of my personal needs while fantasizing about Godric. The orgasm is so intense it takes me to my knees in the shower and I'm all wobbly-legged for a good five minutes afterward. When I'm able to make my limbs work, I moisturize my entire body and try on five outfits before I settle on what to wear.

I scan the fridge for something appealing for breakfast, but my stomach is doing flip-flops and I'm nervous about seeing Godric.

I take the route to campus that passes his house on the off chance that I might run into him. But I don't have the guts to knock on his door. Instead, I slow walk past his house and nearly trip over the sidewalk because I'm not paying attention to where I'm going.

I arrive fifteen minutes early for class. Which means I get the pick of the best seats. I grab one in the middle of the room, but at the end of the row, close to one of the exits, so it's easy to get from this class to my next one. I slouch down when I spot Blaine heading for the front of the class.

I nervously check my make-up to ensure that my face doesn't look like a hot mess, and that my hair isn't doing anything weird. I'm in the middle of reapplying my candy apple-flavored lip gloss when I sense rather than see Godric. It's in the way the hairs on the back of my neck suddenly stand on end and heat blossoms low in my belly, spreading through me like wildfire.

A moment later a figure appears beside me. Godric is dressed in a pair of dark-washed jeans, and a black band shirt.

He offers me a lopsided grin. 'Hey.'

'Hey.' I stuff my lip gloss back in my bag.

He shifts from foot to foot and adjusts the strap of his messenger bag, nodding to the seat beside me, which is currently occupied by my backpack. He looks the tiniest bit unsure of himself. 'Are you saving that for someone special?'

I cock an eyebrow. 'You gonna run away again on me if I let you sit there?'

He bites his lips together. 'I had to get home.'

'Uh-huh.'

'My brother needed my help.'

'If you say so.' I move my backpack to the floor and stand to give him room to get by me.

He faces me as he shuffles past, his diaphragm lightly grazing my chest. If my nipples could scream with excitement, they would.

'I was serious about my social skills not being the best.' He drops into the seat next to me, his gaze moving over my face on a slow sweep like he's trying to see inside my head.

'I guess you weren't lying.'

He makes a face. 'I did kind of rush out, didn't I?'

'Uh-huh.' I wait for more of an explanation, but apparently that's all I'm getting.

'How was your weekend? I didn't see you at the DIK party.' He pulls his notebook out of his messenger bag and flips it open to a fresh page.

'Satya hooked up with a guy in one of her English classes last weekend and he lives on Frat Row. The experience was less than memorable, so we decided the better option was to stay home and watch movies with gratuitous violence. Did Laz come out?'

'Nah, he's not big on the party scene on a good day, and neither am I, to be honest. I only went because I'd hoped you would be there.'

This opens up the perfect segue. 'We could swap numbers, that way you can message me, and ask if I'm going.'

'That'd be great.' He holds up his phone, snapping a quick pic. He smiles and pokes at the screen before he hands me the device. My first and last name are already programmed in. 'You just have to add your number.'

I click on the contact image and, as expected, it's highly unflattering. 'You can't use this picture, it's awful.'

'You look cute.'

I narrow my eyes.

He bites his bottom lip and leans in, dropping his voice to a whisper, his breath warm against my cheek. 'Just let me keep it until I take one I like more.'

I guess we're back to being on the hot side instead of the cold.

My whole body reacts to his statement, and heat rushes through my veins. Lurid images of me straddling him in the middle of the lecture theater clog my brain.

He leans back and the image in my head vaporizes. 'How do you do that?'

'Do what?'

I shake my head. 'Nothing. Never mind.' I add my number and send myself a text, then pass his phone back and check mine so I can add his name to his contact. I also snap a quick photo, but unlike mine, his is infuriatingly perfect. He's all angles and raw masculinity.

The professor arrives and class begins. I take notes on my tablet with my stylus while Godric takes handwritten ones. He has beautiful cursive. It's a lost art, and now I know why he always uses a pen and paper to take notes. His penmanship is as attractive as the rest of him.

I spend a good part of the class admiring Godric's notes. Unfortunately, that means my own are lacking. I did read ahead, and I have a decent memory for facts, but I've heard from other students that Professor Barton tends to elaborate and explore concepts in greater detail during his lectures. On the upside, there's a somewhat decent chance Godric will let me borrow his if I need to. Hopefully.

At the end of class, we pack up our things and head outside. It's another warm, beautiful, sunny day, and I'm disappointed that I can't spend the next hour outside, enjoying the weather, since fall is around the corner. Soon it will be jacket weather, and while I love the fall colors, I always mourn the loss of shorts and T-shirt weather.

As if Godric can read my mind, he turns to me when we reach the bottom of the stairs. 'Do you want to grab a coffee?'

The answer is a resounding yes. I would much prefer to spend the next hour sitting in the sunshine, drinking an iced coffee while staring at his lovely face, but Blaine has already managed to ruin my plans before I can even make them.

'Honestly, I would love that, but unfortunately, Blaine didn't send my article back until late last night.' Despite me emailing him three times. 'I have to run over to the student commons and give it a final edit before it goes to print this afternoon.'

Godric's expression darkens, and his lips pull down in a frown, as if he feels the same way about my unexpected plans. 'Didn't you ask for that on Friday?'

'Yup.'

His frown deepens. 'Why was he so late, then?'

'Because he's being difficult.' If I texted him, it might help expedite things, but then he's likely to start in on the whole me coming over to talk, which he doesn't do in emails. I adjust my backpack, my textbook is digging into my spine again. It's an annoyance, much like Blaine. 'If it makes you feel any better, coffee with you sounds way better than editing my piece, with Blaine hanging over my shoulder, giving me his version of constructive criticism.'

Godric taps agitatedly on the strap of his messenger bag. 'Can I ask you a question?'

'Sure. As long as you can talk and walk; I want to get in and get out of that office as quickly as possible. And I told Blaine I'd meet him there by ten.' If I'm late, my piece might not run, since everything is due by ten-thirty.

Godric lopes along beside me, his strides measured to match mine. 'Why do you let that putz get away with this shit?'

I sigh. 'He's not always like this. Mostly he's upset about not getting his way, but he'll get over it.' Eventually. Hopefully sooner rather than later. 'I love working on the paper, it's sort of my passion project. Almost everything I do is science and data-based, which I also love, but the school paper gives me an opportunity to do something semi-creative. The trade-off is dealing with Blaine's sometimes fragile ego.'

'I could come up and wait for you,' he offers when we reach the student center.

I consider that for a moment, but I have a feeling showing up with Godric in tow will only exacerbate the problem rather than solve it. 'There's no reason to subject yourself to more of Blaine than necessary.'

'Mm.' He tips his head fractionally. 'And yet you continue to do it.'

'Because I love writing for the paper. And I'll be damned if I'm going to let Blaine take that away from me.' A dandelion fluff lands on his shirt, so I pick it off and watch it float away on a wish.

But before I can drop my hand, he covers it with his, pressing it flat against his pec. 'Can I text you later?'

I'm disarmed by the sudden physical contact and his exceptionally earnest expression. My whole body seems to warm with his touch, and I can feel his heart beating under my palm. A rapid *thump-thump*. Like maybe he's nervous I'll say no. 'Um, yeah, sure. If you want.'

His mouth quirks up in a shy smile. 'Groovy. I look forward to sending you a message.' He drops his hand and mine falls to my side.

'Cool.' Since when did asking permission to text me become sexy? And when did the term 'groovy' come back in style?

'Good luck with Blaine the Pain.' He winks and brushes past me, disappearing into the throng of bodies, leaving me totally discombobulated.

I'm in a heightened state as I enter the student center. Part of me would like to take a minute to collect myself before I deal with Blaine. It's 9:57 and if I'm any later, the probability that my article won't run becomes infinitely higher. If that happens, the chance I'll lose my shit on Blaine increases at an exponential rate. Freaking out on him in public will only make me look bad, so my options are limited. Which means I must face my ex while my whole body is pinging with sexual tension. So fun.

When I get to the office, I've calmed down slightly.

Blaine is sitting behind his desk, with a red pen in one hand, and a mug of coffee in the other, with the phrase *I'm awesome, which makes you awesome by proxy* stamped on it. His ego is ridiculous.

His gaze lifts from his computer screen to me as I push through the door. He glances at the clock on the wall. 'You're cutting it close.' As if it's my fault, not his.

I cross my arms and glare. I wish I could laser-beam the smug look off his face. I'm already tired of his nonsense, and that's saying something, since I've only had to deal with him for a week.

Godric has a point, though. If I allow Blaine to keep acting like this, then I'm reinforcing his behavior. 'I wouldn't be cutting it close if you'd sent my article back before eleven last night. I was already in bed.'

'If you'd come over this weekend it wouldn't have been a problem.' He flips his red pen between his fingers and, as expected, drops it on the swivel back to his pointer. I don't know why he's so bad at the pen flip thing, but I find it slightly fascinating and gratifying that Godric is one million times better at it than he is.

I glance around the office to make sure we're alone before I plant my fists on the edge of his desk and lean in. 'Look, I know what you're doing, and it won't work.'

Blaine folds his hands together and leans in, mouth pulling down in a frown. 'And what is it that I'm trying to do, Hazy?'

'The same thing that you did last year. And it's not going to fly.' I lower my voice and give him a smirky smile. 'You need to come to terms with the fact that I am not sleeping with you this year. In fact, I will never, ever sleep with you again. The sooner you accept that, the sooner we can move past this ridiculous phase where you spend the next two months giving me shitty stories to cover and send me back a goddamn PDF with handwritten comments in the margins because your ego is bruised. It's juvenile and it will *not* continue.'

His right eye twitches. It's what happens when he's faced with unexpected confrontation. 'Word kept crashing on me, it was the only way I could get the article back to you.

I tried texting to let you know this, but you don't respond – and that's on you, Hazy.'

When I open my mouth to speak, he holds up a finger. 'And I'd like to remind you that you are the one who chose to write a piece on making friends. It's fluff and not front-page news. Which puts it at the bottom of my editing pile along with the piece on peaceful cohabitation with neighborhood raccoons. Maybe you should adjust your attitude and be grateful that your article is running at all.'

I'm beginning to regret not accepting Godric's offer to hang out with me. It looks like Blaine has moved past the 'try to charm my pants off' phase directly to the 'unfortunate douche' phase. I remind myself that blunt honesty which straddles the asshole line is one of Blaine's personality flaws. 'It's not a fluff piece, it's based on student mental health, which is paramount, especially during the first semester. I included statistics pulled from graduate studies to support my findings, and interviewed students and staff. Your first-page news this week is focused on frosh week and frat parties. How is that life-changing for anyone, apart from potentially experiencing the worst hangover of their entire existence? It's a shameless plug for your freaking fraternity.' I rub my temples, a headache knocking. 'I don't even know why I'm bothering with this. Arguing it with you is like trying to reason with an under-slept toddler.'

I spin around and head for the desk I usually sit at when I'm working on an article or proofing pieces. Except someone else's things are all over it, which means there's a very good chance Blaine is redirecting all his charm at one of the new freshman girls.

'Hold on.'

I'm not stupid enough to believe he'll apologize. The word 'sorry' is not in Blaine's vocabulary. I grit my teeth and take a breath so I don't launch myself at him or stab him with his pen. That would definitely impact my ability to write for the paper.

I don't turn around. 'What?'

'I've been doing some research.'

Now I spin to face him. 'On how to be the biggest asshole in the universe?'

Blaine blinks several times. 'Being honest doesn't make me an asshole.'

'Doesn't it?' We have a fifteen-second stare down, neither of us speaking or looking away.

Finally, he opens his mouth, ignoring my question. 'I've been looking into that house with those three guys across the street. Apparently, it's owned by a Godric Hawthorn, which is kind of ironic since that's your new boyfriend's name.'

'First of all, he's not my new boyfriend. He's a friend, who also happens to be a boy, and we have a class together.' I don't know why I feel the need to justify this to Blaine of all people. 'Secondly, what if his uncle died and left the house to him? Did you think of that?'

Blaine makes his constipated face. 'Don't you think it's weird that house has been empty for years. In fact, I did some digging, and it's been over two decades since anyone has lived there. Why wouldn't his uncle rent it out? Why has it been empty all this time? Don't you find it strange that these dudes show up out of nowhere, and none of them are freshmen?' He raises a finger and slaps it with his other hand. It's a weird thing he does when he's trying to make a point. 'They're all in the middle of degrees.' He raises a second finger and slaps it. 'And they're brothers who go to exactly the same school.'

'It's a family tradition to go to Burnham,' I snap. Godric and his brothers better not become Blaine's newest fixation. I'd almost rather him keep trying to get me to sleep with him again than have him obsess over Godric.

'Or maybe they're running from something.' He spins a pen between his fingers, and it goes flying across the room.

'You mean bears, since they moved here from Alaska? Why do you have to turn this into some twisted mystery in which they're the bad guys?' Last year, when I started dating a guy in second semester, Blaine did some digging on him and found out he had a juvenile record for graffiti. He was in the art program and pretty anti-establishment, so it wasn't a huge surprise.

'Excuse me for being concerned about your well-being since you're spending time with one of these guys. What do you honestly know about them? And have you met the third brother? I've never even seen him, and he lives across the street from me. How do we even know he exists?'

'I've met him once.' For like five seconds, but that's irrelevant. 'He's real, so you can put that conspiracy theory to bed. Honestly, Blaine, you're creating drama where there isn't any.'

'Don't you think it's weird that a guy like him would be interested in someone like you?'

I prop my hands on my hips, already regretting the question before I ask it. 'What does that mean? Someone like *me*?'

'He's like a ten, and you're . . .' He gives me a look like I'm supposed to fill in the blank for him.

'And I'm . . .' I make a *go on* motion. 'Go ahead and rate me.'

He purses his lips, like maybe he's trying to curb his horrible honesty, but it only lasts a few seconds before he blurts, 'You're a solid seven on a good day.'

While I expected his charming side to take a gutter dive, I didn't anticipate it would happen so quickly, or be quite so brutal. Blaine has two types. Tall, leggy women who look like they probably haven't eaten a plate of fries since they were eleven . . . and me. I'm aware that as a curvy, shorter woman I don't fit some random, archaic, media-driven ideal of what women should look like, but I'm smart, sassy, cute, and I've got a great ass and a nice rack. 'So you're trying to say I'm reaching above my hotness scale with Godric.'

'You don't really match,' Blaine says.

'Based on that logic you're also a seven,' I point out.

Blaine makes his constipated Kermit face. 'No. I'm an eight, maybe an eight and a half, but you gave great blow jobs and you were kind of a freak in the sheets, so that helped balance things out for us.'

'Wow. Your misogyny is mind-blowing.' And his fragile ego can't handle my rejection, apparently.

'You're the one who encouraged me to rate you. I'm just being honest out of concern for your well-being.' He points to the clock. 'You should get on it if you want your piece to make it in this week's run.'

I walk away because I'm not sure how easy it will be to make a relationship with Godric work if I'm behind bars for murder.

7

Godric texts me later that evening asking if I was able to get my piece edited in time. He uses full sentences and punctuation in text messages. It's kind of cute. We sit beside each other on Wednesday, but on Friday I'm running behind. When I get to class the seats on either side of him are already taken, the curly-haired girl on his left, and some other girl on his right. Dejected, I take a seat in the back corner. Both girls are pretty and Blaine's comment about me being a seven is like a sliver I can't quite extract. As a result it makes me feel vulnerable. I slip out of class as soon as it ends so I can avoid Godric until our lab.

I'm mostly over not sitting beside Godric by the time we get to the lab, especially since he apologizes for not being able to save me a seat in class. Having him as a lab partner is amazing. He's enthusiastic and makes even the most rudimentary lab assignment riveting. It doesn't hurt that he smells good, or that our shoulders are constantly touching.

We inspect our flu-infected samples and talk through the differences. I love that we're both so passionate about our findings that we completely tune out everyone around us.

Unfortunately, at the end of class, Godric gets a message from his brother and has to rush off. I think this time he's telling the truth.

I don't know much about Laz apart from the fact that he has social anxiety and prefers solitude over spending time with others. My brother Francis is like that. Being an introvert in a family of extroverts can be a challenge, especially when our other brothers tend to be the life of the party. Francis is usually the last one to show up for holiday events, and he spends most of the evening drinking spiked egg-nog and observing or giving one-word answers while the rest of our brothers get loud and rowdy.

Godric texts me around dinner to ask if I'm going to the party on his street. Satya is back in the saddle, and she's ready to ride the next horse, which means we are one thousand percent going to the party.

'Is that your hottie boyfriend texting to find out what your Friday night plans are?' Alyssa holds one shirt under her chin and then another, trying to decide which one will make her eyes pop. The one on the right is a sequined tank in baby blue. While it's been warm during the day, once the sun goes down, the temperature does, too. Alyssa hangs both shirts over my computer chair, tugs her shirt over her head, drops it on the floor and picks up the sequined top. It might not be practical, but it will make a statement, which Alyssa is fond of.

'He's not my boyfriend.' I lay several shirts on my bed, so I can pick the one that will accentuate my curves best.

'You're spending an awful lot of time together.' Satya picks up a pencil and gets to work on her eyebrows.

'We have a class together,' I point out.

'Yeah, but you're not texting all your other classmates, are you?' Alyssa says.

'We're lab partners, we have to work on reports together,' I say.

'But he's not texting about lab reports, he's texting about

the party tonight because he wants to see you. And you're pulling out all your best boob tops. It's only a matter of time before your lab partner status becomes couple status.' Alyssa props her hands on her hips. 'Is this too much? It's probably too much, isn't it?'

Satya gives her the thumbs up. 'It's the perfect amount of too much.'

'I concur. That shirt commands attention. Also, you'll be frozen about an hour into the party if you're outside, which means you can probably get some guy to take a shirt off for you. It's a win-win situation.' I tap my lip as I pull two shirts from the line-up and toss them aside. 'Maybe I need to wear something more understated tonight.'

Alyssa and Satya both give me a look. 'Why would you do that?'

I chew on the inside of my lip. I haven't said anything about Blaine's shitty comments earlier this week, but they're eating at me and if ever there was a time I needed the encouragement of my friends, it's now. 'Blaine told me Godric and I aren't evenly matched.'

'What the hell does that mean, and who the fuck is Blaine to give his unsolicited matchmaking advice?' Alyssa practically snarls.

I explain what happened.

'Oh hell, no. You are no seven. You're a ten all the way, baby.' Satya smacks my butt. 'Women pay damn good money to have an ass like yours. Fuck him and his patriarchal, bullshitting, gaslighting ass. The only reason he said that is because he can't handle that you're moving on. What a dickbag.'

'Save your blow job skills for someone who deserves

them. If he's there tonight I'm shoving him in the pool,' Alyssa says. 'Ugh. Why is he such a giant asshole?'

'I seriously considered stabbing him with his pen, but orange isn't my color.'

'Mm. It really doesn't work with your lovely olive skin tone, does it?' Alyssa crosses over to my bed and picks out the boobiest shirt of them all. 'I think this is what you need to wear tonight. And I highly recommend fawning all over Godric. Like be extra touchy-feely. Maybe even make out with him in front of Blaine. I bet that will make him lose his mind.'

'Uh, well . . . we haven't even kissed, so I'm not sure the whole making out in front of everyone who lives in our neighborhood is on the menu, but I'm happy to pat his pecs and liberally squeeze his biceps.'

'Wait. Hold the phone. You haven't kissed yet?' Alyssa and Satya exchange dumbfounded looks. 'But he's always looking at you like he wants to devour you, and you're always looking at him like you're thinking about humping him regardless of the audience.'

They're not wrong. At least on my end. It's nice to hear that he looks at me like I'm edible and not a seven.

I shake my head and tug my current shirt over my head so I can put on the boobalicious one. 'Not yet. There was one time when it sort of seemed like it might be headed in that direction, but nothing happened, so . . .'

Satya grimaces. 'That was last Friday, wasn't it? When he was over working on some science-y thing with you in the kitchen. I totally clam dammed that kiss. I'm sorry.'

I wave her off and shimmy into my shirt. 'The timing was wrong anyway.' And he basically bolted three minutes later. 'I can't imagine that it would've been less awkward for you to walk in with us making out as opposed to before we started making out. Maybe tonight will be the night.' I hold up my crossed fingers. I'd love to get out of this limbo zone. Half the time I don't know if I'm coming or going with Godric.

'I think you probably need to take the reins on this one. Maybe he's super progressive and waiting for you to make the first move,' Alyssa says.

'Maybe.' I hadn't considered that. And he has mentioned on more than one occasion that his social skills need some work. It's possible he's afraid to make the first move.

We finish getting ready for the party and I send Godric a message to let him know that we're heading over. He responds a few seconds later that he and Hunter are already there.

I do a final breath freshness check, make sure my deodorant is doing its job, reapply my cotton candy-flavored lip gloss, grab my travel mug, and the three of us head down the street and around the corner to the party.

It takes me five seconds to find Godric. Mainly because he's leaning against the side of the house near the gate leading to the backyard, and everyone who enters must pass him to get to the action.

His eyes flare and his gaze drops to my cleavage and springs back up to my face. 'Oh, wow. You look. Wow. Red looks great on you.'

'Thanks. You look pretty delicious yourself.' I give him a full-body once-over. He's wearing a pair of jeans and another band shirt. That seems to be his go-to outfit. Or shirts with funny sayings.

Satya nudges me and Alyssa gives me her 'told you' eyebrows. They say hi, but don't stick around, heading across the lawn to where the guys throwing the party are currently doing keg stands.

'This will probably get messy fast if that's anything to go by.' I cringe when the current beer-funneler can't chug fast enough and ends up getting sprayed in the face and then dropped on the lawn. Hooting and hollering follows.

'I've already seen a bunch of pukers.' Godric takes a sip from his flask, and then another before tapping it against my travel mug. 'What's your poison tonight?'

'Tequila sunrise. Heavy on the tequila, low on the sunrise. Are you drinking straight Scotch again tonight?'

'I am.' Godric smiles and tips his flask back, taking a long sip. 'But I'm taking the welfare of people's feet into consideration this evening and not drinking out of something breakable.'

'So thoughtful.'

'I'm mostly seeking your approval.' He takes another long swig.

'Well you definitely have it.' I take a small sip of my own drink. 'Everything work out with your brother? Is he okay?'

'Hmm?'

'Laz. You had to rush out after the lab.'

'Ah, yes.' He nods once and focuses his attention on the swimming pool where girls in bikinis lounge, and guys flexing their abs do cannonballs into the water. 'He needed my help, but he's fine now.'

'That's good.'

He doesn't elaborate and I don't push for more information.

Someone turns on the outside speakers and blasts hard rock. Along with the increase in music volume comes an increase in human volume. And the more people who show up the louder it gets. Godric doesn't seem to have a problem hearing anything I say, but every time he replies, I ask him to repeat himself. I honestly don't mind that he has to lean in so close that his lips graze my cheek more than once. But I'm a lot shorter than he is and the constant hunching can't be easy.

'It's hard to hear over the music, want to ditch the party and go back to your place?' I ask. When all he does is stare down at me for several long seconds, I add, 'Unless you want to stay?' Maybe I've been reading things all wrong. Maybe I'm in the friend zone. The thought makes my stomach sink.

Godric shakes his head slowly, his gaze dropping to my chest and quickly moving back to my lips before his eyes meet mine. It's the reassurance I need. He wouldn't be checking me out if I was friend material.

'I don't want to stay.' His tongue pokes at his bottom lip and he rubs the back of his neck. 'But Laz is home. When I left, he was in the living room, watching a romantic comedy. He wasn't in the best mood, and he isn't the friendliest person in the world even on a good day, so I can't guarantee you'll enjoy meeting him.'

'Oh, well, we could go back to my place if you prefer. I don't mind either way.' But my room looks like a fashion bomb hit it. There are still clothes lying all over the place and probably a couple of bras hanging from my bed post. 'I can handle an emo brother, but it's totally up to you.' I drag my fingers along the collar of my shirt, shamelessly drawing more attention to my cleavage.

He follows the path of my finger, his lips parting and

his tongue running across his top teeth. 'We can go back to my place, it's closer anyway.'

'You're sure?' I bite my lip and bat my lashes.

'Positive. Want to go?' His voice is low and gravely.

'I'll let Alyssa and Satya know that I'm taking off with you. I'll be right back.' I give his biceps a quick squeeze and rush off to find my friends. We have a strict rule; never leave without telling each other.

I find Alyssa with some of the guys from the street. Since we've been living here for three years, we know them all pretty well. They're sort of like unruly brothers, entertaining in small doses. Two of them are so hammered they can barely stand, but the third guy is new this year, and he's hanging off Alyssa's every word.

She smiles when she sees me heading her way, but then her brow furrows. 'Where's your hottie?'

'Waiting in the wings.' I thumb over my shoulder. 'We're going back to his place.'

'Hell yeah you are!' she yells and raises her hand. 'Don't leave me hanging.'

'Could you be any more obvious?' I grab her arm, pulling it back down.

'Go get it, girl.' She swats me on the ass.

'Have you seen Satya?'

'Yeah, she's with that guy she dated in second semester last year.'

'The one with the pierced peen or the one with the gold tooth?'

'The one with the gold tooth.'

'Right, okay. Well, let's hope she doesn't regret that choice again.'

76

'Oh, I won't let her go home with him, don't worry.' Alyssa hugs me. 'Now go. Tomorrow morning we're going for pancakes and you're going to tell us all the delicious details.'

'Wish me luck.'

'You don't need it, but I'm sending all the good make-out vibes your way.'

I'm halfway across the lawn when Blaine jumps in front of me. Based on his weaving and the bleariness in his eyes, he's wasted already.

'Hazy, baby, look at you,' he slurs. He makes an A-okay sign with his hand and then brings the O to his eye and moves it like it's a camera lens toward my cleavage. 'I miss you.'

Before Blaine has a chance to say something worse, Godric appears out of nowhere and takes my hand in his, angling his body so he's mostly blocking Blaine from view.

'Are you ready for me . . .' He lifts my hand, but instead of kissing my knuckle he turns it over, palm facing up, and presses his lips to the inside of my wrist. 'To take you home,' he finishes.

Yeah, I'm not in the friend zone. I feel that contact through my entire body. I seriously need to get him alone so I can find out what his lips feel like when they're on mine. 'I absolutely am.'

'If you'll excuse us.' His hot gaze turns ice cold as it moves to Blaine, whose eyes go wide as he takes a quick step back. He stumbles over his own feet and lands on his ass.

Godric guides me away from Blaine, toward the gate, his fingers pressed gently into the base of my spine. His nostrils flare and his jaw tics. He drops his head, and his lips brush my ear. 'What did he say to you?'

'Nothing that bears repeating.' I lace my fingers with his and am about to turn sideways so I can make it through the gap between two groups of people, but when they see us coming, they shift out of the way.

'I don't like the way Blaine looks at you,' Godric says once we're through the gate and heading down the driveway, away from the loud music and the raucous party.

I squeeze his hand. 'That makes two of us. But let's not let Blaine be a dark cloud on our evening just because he's perfected the art of being a skeeze.'

Godric makes a low sound in the back of his throat. 'Mm. He really is adept at being awful, isn't he?'

He releases my hand as we cross the street. I fall into step beside him as we make our way toward his house. Beyond the party it's quiet on the street, likely because everyone who lives around here is currently in the backyard we just left. Godric's front porch is lit up, but the rest of the windows are dark, apart from one on the second floor. It's the same window through which I saw Laz tapping on the glass, so I assume it's his bedroom.

The house no longer has a creepy, ominous vibe. The bush in the front yard has been shaped into a head, the top of which is in full bloom, making it look like a flowering head of hair. The flowers that line the stone path leading to the front porch are also in full bloom: dark purple violets interspersed with white lilies and pale pink roses. That they're still in bloom is impressive considering our zinnias are struggling through their final bloom of the season. The porch, which was in rough shape that first day I met Godric and Hunter, now looks fresh and welcoming. Three chairs line the wooden deck, a small table set between them, each holding a small potted plant.

'You guys did an incredible job giving this place a face-lift.' My gaze skims the ivy spilling over the side of the hanging baskets that frame the porch as I pass.

'That was mostly Laz, although Hunter is also a fan of gardening.' Godric slides a key into the lock and opens the front door, ushering me inside.

I toe off my flats and leave them on the mat at the front door, where several pairs of shoes are lined up in a neat row. Even the front hall boasts elegant finishes. There's a closet to the right, its door dark wood, with ornate designs carved into it and an old brass handle.

'Laz must be in his bedroom.' Godric peeks around the corner. 'Want a tour?'

'I would love one.' It's hard to believe that only two weeks ago I thought this place was a haunted wreck.

I follow him into the living room that looks like it's been transplanted from a movie set in the fifties. Everything is dark wood, with the same ornate designs carved into them as the door to the front hall closet. Even the furniture looks like it's from another century; the fabrics are deep, rich tones with subtle patterns. It's almost like being in a time warp. The drapery seems like it's from a bygone era and the wallpaper has a velvet textured finish to it. Along one wall is a sideboard boasting several different bottles of whiskey and Scotch; the same crystal glasses Godric was drinking from at Blaine's party are lined up in a perfect row. The only thing that seems out of place is the massive flat-screen

TV recessed into the wall, but it's one that's meant to look like a picture frame. The art is a Van Gogh, which seems on brand with the house itself.

'Can I get you a drink?' Godric motions to the bar. 'As you can see, I'm a fan of Scotch and whiskey.' He crosses over and opens one of the doors, retrieving a bottle of red wine. 'I have a Merlot, or a Cabernet Sauvignon if you prefer your wine full-bodied, and Hunter has beer in the fridge, but he's a fan of small breweries and likes his ale on the hoppy side.'

'Merlot would be perfect, thank you.'

Godric makes quick work of uncorking the bottle. He pours the deep red liquid into one of the crystal goblets. He also sets his flask on the sideboard and pours himself a glass of Scotch before continuing with the tour.

We pass through the living room to a formal dining room that would comfortably seat twelve. Everything is rich and lush and looks very much like the past has made its way into the present. The kitchen is straight out of the 1950s, with a white-on-white color scheme and what looks like original appliances, but they must be new. I run my hand over the butcher block island.

'This kitchen is a chef's dream. Who's the cook in the house? And please don't tell me the pizza place down the street.'

Godric smiles that secretive smile of his. 'Laz spends the most time in the kitchen – apart from watching romantic comedies, experimenting with food is one of his favorite pastimes. However, Hunter is the barbecuer of the family, and I'm the baker.'

'Of all things chocolatey and delicious?'

'Mm. Mostly. I'm on a mission to find the perfect brownie recipe.'

'We might need to have a bake-off, because I happen to have a brownie recipe that is utterly delectable.'

'I would love to do that with you.' Godric tips his head fractionally. 'Although, I don't think there's much I wouldn't enjoy doing with you.'

My heart does a little leap and my stomach twists and flips. 'We'll have to make it a date, then.'

We smile at each other, but the sound of someone moving around above us has Godric's gaze lifting to the ceiling. His right eye twitches and he motions for me to follow him again.

We pass through the kitchen and step into the hallway. To the right is the front door, and on the left are two doors. One has a set of stairs that disappear into darkness. Some of the basements in this area are finished, but not all. The house we live in has a crawlspace where we keep our holiday decorations and not much else.

Godric pushes another door open to reveal a small, two-piece bathroom with a pedestal sink and wallpaper with an ocean theme. 'The powder room, if you need it.'

We continue down the hall to another set of stairs, this one leading to the second floor. The newel post is ornately carved, and the banister is smooth dark wood with a glossy finish. The stairs are the same dark wood but covered in a runner with a Gothic-era pattern.

Now I understand why his uncle never rented this place out. College kids would ruin this beautiful house within a matter of months. Only people who can appreciate the artistry of it should live inside these walls. We stroll down the hall to the flight of stairs that leads to the second floor. I take them slowly, pausing to admire the framed photos on the wall.

'These are family photos?' My gaze skips over them, taking in the grainy black and white that's yellowed with age. Each generation defined by the outfits they wear.

'Yes. My father and my uncles lived here when they went to college, and theirs before that, and so on. Family tradition and all that.'

His fingers caress the dip in my spine and I continue up the stairs, leaving the wall of pictures behind.

The runner that lines the stairs continues down the hallway on the second floor. Gorgeous wall sconces light the way, casting shadows that look like flowers on the pretty, pale wallpaper. We pass a door on the right, the low tones of melancholic music filtering into the hall.

'That's Laz's room.' We move past it, to another closed door. 'And this is Hunter's room.'

At the end of the hall is another staircase, this one narrower, leading to the third floor. Godric turns to me at the base of the staircase. 'My bedroom is just up here, if you'd like to see it.'

'I absolutely would.'

He smiles. 'I was hoping you'd say that.'

8

My heart skips a beat as he flicks on the light, illuminating the narrow staircase. The first stair creaks under my foot, but the rest of the ascent is silent, apart from my shaky inhalation. I swear I can hear my heart thundering in my chest. Warmth travels through my veins at the top of the stairs as Godric reaches around me to turn on the light, bathing his room in a soft, golden glow.

It's everything I expect from Godric. The space is huge, with vaulted ceilings. The room is decorated in black and gray scale, with a dramatic pop of color at the window seat that faces the front of the house. The burgundy velvet curtains are the perfect complement to the dark tones and black-finished walnut bed that is the central focus of the room. The four-poster king frame boasts heavy midnight-black drapery. They swag elegantly, tied back to the posts with the promise of privacy with one quick tug. It's decadent and sensual, and I feel like I'm about to spontaneously combust.

I have no idea how long I stand there, but it's enough time for my imagination to concoct a million dirty sexual acts on those luxurious black sheets. I bet they're silk. The most amazing feature, though, is the crystal chandelier that hangs above his bed, the teardrops refracting rainbows on the dark comforter.

'Your room is amazing. I feel like it probably would have

been better to go to my place first, because now that I've seen your bedroom, I'm not sure I want you to see mine.' I cross over to the bed and run my hand along the comforter. I was right about it being silk.

'I'm sure your room is just as fabulous as you are.' Godric stands in the doorway and leans against the jamb, sipping his Scotch.

'I have the periodic elements poster on my wall. And the quilt on my bed was made by my grandma. I've had it forever and I don't have the heart to part with it. But it's shades of orange, brown and green, so matching my room to that color scheme isn't the best.' It's taking everything in me not to dive-bomb onto his bed in hopes that the smell of him will stick to me and I'll get to rub it all over my own sheets and marinate in the scent of his cologne all night.

It's a combination of bergamot, sandalwood and sage and it's divine.

I set my wine glass on his nightstand, which is black like everything else in the room, and turn to face Godric. He's still leaning against the door jamb. Maybe Alyssa and Satya are right, maybe I need to be the one to make the first move. I can be bold. Not get naked bold but entice him to come over here and make out with me bold. I hoist myself up onto the edge of his bed. It's raised, so my feet dangle a good foot off the ground.

'Your bed is amazing.' I run my hand over the comforter, watching rainbows jump along my hand.

'And made all the more attractive with you sitting on it.' He swirls his Scotch and takes another sip.

One side of his mouth turns up in a half-smile that

unleashes a kaleidoscope of butterflies in my stomach and a flood of heat between my thighs.

'The only thing that would make it better is if you were over here with me.' I pat the empty space beside me. I'm nervous but hopeful.

He pushes off the jamb, pulling the door closed behind him. He doesn't come over to me right away, though. Instead, he crosses to the other side of the room, pausing at his dresser. He sets his Scotch down, opens the top drawer and retrieves something. A moment later he pops a pill in his mouth and washes it down with Scotch.

He closes the drawer and moves a few feet in my direction to where a vintage record player from a different era sits on an equally vintage table. They're both in perfect condition. The only turntables I've seen are the ones old-school DJs use. Half of me wants to leave my spot on his very comfortable bed to get a closer look, but the other half wants him to come to me so we can finally relieve some of the sexual tension that's been growing between us like ivy.

'How do you feel about old-school Radiohead?' Godric pulls a record free from the protective sleeve.

'How old-school are we talking? *OK Computer* Radiohead or *The Bends*? Or maybe *Pablo Honey*?'

He drops the needle, and the strains of 'Creep' filter through the room, which is ironic since last week I went on a Radiohead kick after listening to the nineties noon hour on my favorite streaming platform. I ended up down a Radiohead rabbit hole that started with *Pablo Honey*.

I wrinkle my nose. 'Is this your version of mood music?'

He sips his Scotch, hiding a chagrined smile behind the

crystal. 'You were wearing a Radiohead T-shirt last week, so I thought maybe you had a fondness for nineties indie music. Should I change it to something else? A different band? A different album?'

I shake my head and run my hand over the comforter. 'Just trying to figure out if the song choice is meant to be a warning, or if you have the same eclectic taste in music I do.'

'I can appreciate most music. Except screamo and death metal, those are hard nopes. Otherwise, I can pretty much find something in every genre to enjoy.' Finally, he abandons the record player and makes his way across the room.

Thom Yorke croons about being a weirdo and we both smile. My heart slams around in my chest, my palms start to sweat, and all my sensitive parts perk up as they usually do when Godric is this close. I don't know that I've gotten used to the feelings he evokes, but I have learned to expect my body's response to him.

He takes a step closer, bringing him within arm's reach. I pluck his crystal glass from his hand and set it on the nightstand beside mine. When I part my legs he steps forward. My knees are conveniently at waist height thanks to how high off the ground the bed is. The inside of my knees skim across his hips as he fills the space between mine. There isn't even skin-to-skin contact and my body is already humming with anticipation.

All I want to do is wrap myself around him so I can feel every inch of his body pressed against mine. Preferably naked, but I'll settle for fully clothed if I can finally, *finally* find out what his lips feel like against mine.

'Hey.' I hook my finger into one of his belt loops.

He grins, that secretive, sly grin that makes my body sing. 'Hey.'

'I like your bedroom.' I run a hand over his comforter. 'I'm a particularly huge fan of your bed.' The tension is killing me slowly.

'Are you now?' His voice is a soft caress I feel everywhere.

I nod and bite my lip. I will him to do something, anything, but he just continues to stand in front of me, the inside of my knees resting against his hips, the space between us infinitesimal and infinite at the same time. I wish he'd make the first move, but I don't think that's going to happen.

It has to be me.

'I think we're finally alone now.' I skim the back of his hand with my fingertips. Brief contact that begs for touch without asking.

'I think you're right.' He strokes a single finger from my temple to my chin.

Like every other time, I feel that touch through my entire body. It's a fire rushing through my veins.

His hot gaze dips to my mouth. 'And what would you like to do, Hazy, now that we're alone?'

'Hmm.' I poke at my top lip, digging deep and shoring up all my courage. 'Well, there is one thing that I've been thinking about for a while now.' I slide a hand up his chest and around the back of his neck. My fingers slip into the silken strands of his hair at the nape and curl around them.

'And what is that?' He tucks an errant curl behind my ear.

'Maybe I should show you rather than tell you.' I tilt my chin up.

Godric's eyes are hooded, his gaze dark as he runs his tongue along his bottom lip. His jaw tics and he exhales through his nose. For a moment he looks uncertain, and he mutters something that sounds like, 'I can do this. It'll be fine.'

It seems a lot like we're both over-thinking this whole thing. I tug on the back of his neck and pull his lips to mine. It's a soft brush at first, tentative, that same uncertainty seeping through. But it doesn't last. Godric's palm comes to rest against the side of my neck, and his thumb sweeps along the edge of my jaw.

'You are dangerously difficult to resist.' His lips meet mine again, lingering this time. A low, deep sound rumbles through him, not quite a groan, not quite a growl.

Heat rushes through me, setting every nerve ending on fire, and all I want is to get closer, to taste more of him. I stroke along the seam of his lips, seeking entrance. And another deep sound follows, and then his tongue pushes past my lips. I expect to taste the woodsy flavor of Scotch, but instead I'm hit with sweetness, as though he's been eating candy. Maybe it wasn't a pill he popped, maybe it was a fruity breath mint.

I make a low, needy sound and stroke my tongue against his, soaking up that sweetness. I want more of it, more of him. I slide my fingers deeper into his hair, gripping the strands as I angle my head and open wider, trying to push my way into his mouth to get another taste of him. I'm hit with an incredible wave of calm, followed by a spike of desire.

I try to pull him closer, but he's not budging, no matter how hard I tug, so I scramble to my knees and press the front of my body against his. He makes a surprised sound and the hand cupping my face slides into my hair, his fingers curling around the strands, tugging hard enough to cause a delicious sting. His other arm wraps around my waist, holding me against him.

'God, your mouth tastes amazing.' I suck his bottom lip between mine.

I'm ravenous for more. Needy and frantic. A starved animal desperate to devour.

The sound he makes causes the hairs on my arm to stand on end, but I'm mindless with want. I can't decide what I want to do next. Strip my clothes off or try to get him onto this giant, incredible bed with me. I pull on the front of his shirt, but he's immovable as a mountain.

I groan in frustration, and bite his bottom lip, dragging the flesh through my teeth. I'm not gentle about it either. And that incredible sweetness hits my tongue again, sending another wash of calm over me, warming me from the inside. The idea of ceasing this kiss seems preposterous. Godric groans a curse, his tongue pushing back inside my mouth, tangling again. I catch it between my teeth and suck.

Suddenly, I have the oddest, uncomfortable feeling that we're no longer alone. I crack a lid. Godric's long lashes caress his cheek, but his brows are slanted, a sharp line between them. I catch movement in my peripheral vision as an object comes flying across the room and beans him in the head. We both startle and suddenly the metallic tang of blood hits my tongue. He pulls away, his dark eyes flaring, along with his nostrils. One side of his mouth curls up and he makes a noise that's almost a snarl.

I touch my lip and glance down to find a smear of red across the pad of my index finger. 'I cut my lip.'

I look up in time to see a dark-haired figure disappear through the bedroom door, and at the same time the bathroom door slams so hard it rattles the glasses on the nightstand and causes the record to skip. And I'm suddenly alone.

'What the hell?' I clamber off the bed and my knees buckle. I grab for the comforter to stop myself from becoming a heap on the floor.

My entire body is trembling, all my senses having gone haywire. I feel like I'm in the middle of a fight-or-flight response and can't explain why, apart from the fact that I'm pretty sure Godric's younger brother was spying on us while we were making out. Which is creepy and weird on its own, but now Godric is locked in the bathroom and I'm shaking like I have low blood sugar while Radiohead blares through the speakers.

It takes several deep breaths before I feel steady enough to stand without holding onto something. I cross over to the bedroom door and grab the knob, but it's been a good thirty seconds or more. If Godric's brother was spying on us, he's probably back in his room. But if he isn't, and he's on the other side of the door, do I want to deal with him? I don't know the answer to that.

There's a key in the ancient door. The next question is, will I feel safer locking out his brother, or locking me in here with Godric? I swallow thickly but turn the key until it clicks.

Then I face the closed bathroom door. I pass his dresser on the way, and pause when I catch my reflection in the mirror. There's a streak of blood on my chin. I lean to inspect it, running my tongue over my lip. I taste the sweetness of Godric's mouth, which causes another wave of goosebumps to flash across my skin, combined with the metallic tang of blood, but I don't see a cut anywhere on my lip. Strange.

Why the hell would his brother come into his room and throw something at him while we were kissing? Unless he was being a dick?

I glance at the bed, but I don't see anything on top of the comforter. Whatever his brother threw at him must have landed on the floor. What if he'd missed and hit me instead?

My head is all over the place and my heart is slamming around in my chest. I'm shaking and breathing like I just finished running a marathon. My hormones are still firing on all cylinders and my stomach churns with anxiety.

I tiptoe over to the bathroom. I don't know why I'm trying to be stealthy, other than I feel like I'm waiting for the jump scare in a horror movie.

The water is running in the bathroom. Maybe I was being too forward? Maybe he is old-fashioned and wants to take things slow, which could explain why it's taken two weeks for us to kiss. Maybe that should've been a conversation we had before I attacked his lips with my lips.

I rap twice on the bathroom door. 'Godric? Are you okay?'

He's silent for so long I wonder if he hasn't heard me, but the water shuts off and he calls out, 'I'm sorry. I need a minute.'

I want to ask why the heck his brother was in the room

with us, but I feel like that conversation needs to happen when I can see his face. I cross over to his bed and chug half my glass of wine. It gets rid of the sweet taste of Godric's mouth, and the shakes slowly subside. I don't sit down on the bed. Instead, I head over to the window seat. Maybe I should have sat over here in the first place. Maybe it would have been less intimidating than his bed.

Several minutes pass, and the longer I'm out here while he remains in the bathroom, the more awkward it feels to stay. And the more weirded out I get about his brother being in here with us. After what must be a good five minutes, I decide I've waited long enough.

I cross over to the bathroom and knock once. 'I'm going to go home.'

I wait a few seconds for him to open the door, but all I get back is a quiet, 'I'm sorry.'

I leave his room feeling like a complete idiot. I don't think it could get any more awkward than it already is, except if I run into Laz in the hall. I unlock the door, and open it a crack, poking my head out. But I'm at the top of the stairs so all I can see is the dimly lit hall at the bottom of the equally dimly lit staircase. I leave the door ajar, and hustle down the stairs as quietly as possible. When I reach the bottom, I take a deep breath, my hand shaking and my nerves shot for reasons I don't understand. I peek around the corner, relieved to find the hall empty.

I steel myself with another deep breath, and speed walk down the hall, not stopping until I've passed Laz's room and I reach the next flight of stairs. I don't breathe either. I pause for the briefest of moments on the way down the stairs, checking out the family photos that span the wall.

As fascinated as I am, I'm more interested in avoiding Laz should he be lurking around on the main floor somewhere.

I take the rest of the stairs at a jog and cringe when the floor creaks under my feet as I reach the foyer. I slide my feet into my shoes – thank heaven for slip-ons – and open the front door, stepping out into the warm dark night. I close the door behind me and rush down the flower-lined path. Music comes from across the street. It sounds like someone is playing an acoustic guitar in one of the backyards. There are lights on at Blaine's place. And someone is moving around in the living room. Or maybe it's just the breeze.

I don't look back at Godric's house until I'm on the sidewalk. Lights dot the windows on both the second and the third floor. I swear I see the curtains move on the second floor, in the room that I know to be Laz's. I fight the urge to fire the middle finger his way. I have no idea why he was in Godric's room, or what just happened, but all I want to do is escape this embarrassment. Monday is going to be so awkward.

9

The house is quiet when I push through the front door, which is good because explaining why I'm home to my roommates is not high on my to-do list.

I trudge upstairs and flop down on my grandma-made comforter. That kiss started out great. At least for me it did. And then he got beaned in the head. I don't understand why his brother would do that, or why Godric felt the need to lock himself in the bathroom.

The longer I lie on my bed, staring at the cobwebs decorating the light overhead – it's not nearly as nice as the one hanging over Godric's bed – replaying the kiss in my head, I wonder if there's more to Godric locking himself in the bathroom. Maybe I'm a terrible kisser. Maybe he didn't want to tell me that to my face.

That idea is all it takes for the stupid, emotional, embarrassment tears to start falling. I'm not a huge crier and the fact that now is the time my eyes start leaking annoys me in an irrational way. This is what I get for going after what I want, I guess. Why are boys so confusing?

Half an hour of stupid tears later, or more, or less, I'm not sure – all I know is that I've done an exceptional amount of sniffle-crying – my phone buzzes with a message.

Godric: *I'm sorry. It's not you, it's me.*

It's literally the worst text message a person could receive. The *it's me, not you* absolutely means that it is me. I haven't even mustered the emotional courage to respond when another message appears below the first one.

Godric: *Shit.*

Followed by another.

Godric: *I'm so sorry. I'm terrible at texting. I realize now that me saying it's me and not you is the last thing anyone ever wants to hear, let alone in a text message. If you've taken it to mean that it is you, let me be clear that YOU are not the problem. I messed up. That was not the best way to handle the situation. I really do like you. A lot. I also like kissing you. A lot. If you would come to the door maybe we could have a do-over. If you're interested in a do-over. If you're not, I'll also understand. I'll be disappointed, obviously. But I don't want to pressure you either way.*

I read the very long message over three times. It must take me so long to respond that he sends another message.

Godric: *If you'd rather postpone the do-over I'd understand that, too. Maybe I should leave.*

And a few seconds later.

Godric: *I should probably leave.*

I type out a quick reply.

Hazy: *I'll be down in a minute, don't go anywhere.*

I roll off my bed and get a load of my reflection in the mirror. My eyes are puffy, and my face is blotchy, not a winning combo. I stop in the bathroom – Godric can wait for me to get my face under control – splash cold water on my cheeks to calm the redness, and use eyedrops to make it look less like I've been crying over him locking himself in the bathroom after we kissed. The doorbell rings. I take a few, deep calming breaths and head downstairs.

I open the door to find Godric pacing.

Between one blink and the next he's across the porch,

standing in front of me. 'I am so, so sorry, Hazy.' His brow is furrowed; the creases somehow make his face even prettier than usual.

I cross my arms to prevent him from getting closer and also to form a barricade between him and my heart. 'What happened up there?' I make a general motion in the direction of his house.

He runs a hand through his lovely hair, which I realize now is quite the mess. Clearly, his hands have been in it since I left his place.

'I just . . . I haven't kissed a hu——' He stops and his jaw works as he drops his head for a moment. 'It's been a long time since I've been attracted to anyone like I am to you. And longer since I've kissed a . . . woman. I was . . . overwhelmed, is the best way I can describe it. It was sensory overload, and I couldn't get a handle on myself. I was embarrassed and unable to deal with all the sensations and I didn't want you to see me lose control like that.' He blows out a breath. 'I'm sorry, Hazy. Really and truly.'

As I absorb his words, things click into place. The way Godric routinely hangs back at parties, staying on the fringe. How he prefers to avoid the campus cafe when it's crowded and overly noisy. How he always looks like he's concentrating hard when he touches me. Godric may very well have a sensory processing disorder. My brother Francis has one. He's constantly blocking out noise with headphones, and overly busy restaurants can be a lot for him. The excessive stimulus makes him anxious. It could explain why Godric didn't try to kiss me until I basically pushed him into it tonight.

'I'm sorry if I came on too strong,' I reply.

His eyes flare. 'Don't be sorry. I love your take-charge attitude. Never change that.' He steps closer and tucks both of his hands in his pockets, then removes them and clasps them behind his back. 'I've been thinking about kissing you since the first time we met. To be quite honest, it's hard to focus on anything but your lips when I'm around you. And now I've gone and ruined our first kiss.'

My heart skips a couple of beats at his admission. At least now I know I'm not alone in feeling like I'm going to combust whenever I'm around him. 'You didn't ruin it.'

'I locked myself in a bathroom because I couldn't get a handle on my emotions, I absolutely ruined it.' His expression shifts to one of hopefulness. 'But if you're interested, we could give it another try. Maybe erase that bad memory with a better one?'

'I'd be willing to give it a shot.' I roll back on my heels and my tongue darts out to wet my bottom lip in preparation.

He tracks the movement as he draws closer, his toes nearly touching mine. 'Permission to try that kiss again requested.'

I tip my chin up. 'Permission granted.'

Godric's gaze moves over my face in a slow caress that I feel everywhere. My heart flutters and my palms grow damp as his hand appears in my peripheral vision. When his fingertips skim my cheek, goosebumps break out across my arms and the familiar tightness in my stomach becomes a delicious ache. And still, I wait for him to drop his head, for his lips to touch mine.

I already know it's going to be a great kiss. As long as he doesn't bolt again.

He exhales a warm, sweet breath against my lips as he

cups my cheek gently in his palm. And then finally, *finally* his lips brush over mine. Once. Twice. Three times, before it becomes an insistent press.

He groans and I moan.

His free arm wraps around my waist and he pulls me flush against him. I loop both arms over his shoulders and link my fingers behind his neck. The urge to slide them into his hair is strong, but then I'll try to angle his head and take the lead, and it's better if he's in control, especially if sensory processing is an issue.

After a few seconds I part my lips in invitation. And he takes it, thank God. His tongue slides against mine and once again I'm hit with another shot of sweetness, as though he finished sucking a candy before he arrived.

If I had better vertical, I would attempt to wrap my entire body around his and never let him go. But again, that would be me taking control, and for now I need to let him have it.

I have no idea how long we kiss for, but eventually I find myself pressed up against the side of the house, with Godric's thigh between my legs. And I am shamelessly, and I mean *shamelessly*, dry humping him for all I'm worth.

Eventually, he breaks the kiss and brushes his nose against mine. It's so sweet, just like his decadent mouth. If this is how he kisses, I can't wait to find out what other skills he has in the bedroom.

'Will you go out with me? On a date?' Godric asks.

I was half a second away from asking him if he wanted to come inside and see my bedroom – screw the fact that there is a pile of used tissues on my bed from all my ridiculous crying, post-failed first kiss. So it takes me a few seconds to switch mental gears and process his question. 'A date?'

'Dinner and a movie, maybe?' Godric adds. He's adorably hot right now.

Mostly I want to tear his clothes off, but maybe after dinner and a movie we'll get past first base. 'Yes. I'd absolutely love to go on a date.'

His smile makes my insides all melty. 'Are you busy tomorrow night?'

'I am now.'

His grin widens. 'I can pick you up at seven?'

'That would be great.'

'Groovy.' He leans in and presses his lips to mine.

But I wrap my hand around the nape of his neck and press up on my toes to prolong the contact. We end up making out again for another half a millennium. I'm panting and my entire body is humming with need by the time it ends.

He brings my hand to his mouth, but at the very last second he flips it over and presses his lips to the inside of my wrist. 'Until tomorrow.'

10

Hazy: *what is dress code for this restaurant?*

Godric: *Dress code is typically business casual.*

Hazy: *so a dress?*

Godric: *If you like wearing dresses then yes, if not pants are also fine.*

Godric: *Or if you prefer, capris are an option.*

Godric: *Culottes are also a possible choice.*

Hazy: *culottes? I think those went out of style in 1982*

Godric: *This is accurate, although still an option, maybe just not a stylish one.*

Hazy: *I don't think you've seen me in a dress yet*

Godric: *I believe I have not.*

Hazy: *would you like to see me in a dress?*

Godric: *You could wear a burlap sack, all that matters to me is being able to spend time with you and seeing your beautiful face. However, burlap isn't the most comfortable fabric, or so I hear.*

Hazy: *I have no burlap sack available, but I do have dresses.*

Godric: *I look forward to seeing you in a dress then. Seven never seemed so far away.*

I pull several dresses from my closet and call in reinforcements in the form of my roommates. 'I need help.'

Satya sashays into my room and plunks herself down

in my computer chair. 'Look no further, your prep team is here and ready to turn you into an irresistible smoke show.'

Alyssa flops into the beanbag chair opposite her.

Half an hour later, my curvy body is poured into a cute LBD, my hair is curled and my make-up is done. I opt for gloss instead of lipstick so I can kiss Godric without worrying about it being smeared over both of our faces. I predict that I'll have very little in the way of restraint when it comes to making out with him.

At 6:58 the doorbell rings.

Alyssa and Satya clap their hands and squeal like grade schoolers.

'*Ahhhh!* He's early!'

Alyssa pushes me out of my bedroom and into the hall.

'Wait! My heels!'

Satya grabs them from the floor and Alyssa gets down on one knee, as if she's planning to help me with them.

'I'm good, I can put my own shoes on.'

'Right. Yes. Sorry.' Alyssa backs off.

I slip my feet into the open-toed burgundy heels. It's a pop of color and it matches my clutch, which is this cool beaded number that looks like a math textbook, but cuter.

I carefully rush down the stairs, Satya and Alyssa following like nervous mother birds. They quickly throw themselves down on the couch and turn on the TV, to make it look like they've been sitting there the entire time, while I smooth my hands over my hips, take a deep breath, plaster a smile on my face and throw open the door.

The air leaves my lungs on a whoosh.

Even on a bad day, Godric looks good. He's always fashionably, if not sometimes eclectically, dressed. But tonight he's taken his hotness to a whole new level. He's wearing a pair of black dress pants with a sharp crease down the center of each leg, teamed with a long-sleeve, black button-down that's rolled up to expose his gloriously defined forearms – I had no idea how appealing forearms could be until he walked into my life. The black on black has been complemented with a black satin tie. But what launches this outfit into a whole different stratosphere of yum is the fact that he's paired it with old-school, black and white brogues. He's like Johnny Cash's hot grandson.

'Wow. Hey. Yum.' Is my stellar greeting.

One side of his mouth quirks up in a wry grin, and his hot gaze moves over me. Just because I've finally had his lips on mine, it doesn't mean I've become immune to my body's reaction to his eyes on me. Or his general presence. On the contrary, my lady parts are applauding his arrival.

Godric steps forward, takes my hand and lifts it to his lips. 'You look absolutely stunning, Hazy.' As I've come to expect, he flips my hand palm up, and presses his lips to the inside of my wrist. 'And you smell entirely edible.'

It dawns on me, as he inhales while kissing the inside of my wrist, that if I wore perfume, this would be one of my preferred pulse points. But Alyssa is allergic to most fragrances so none of us wear strong scents. Body lotion and deodorant is where it ends. But I'm not about to tell Godric that, because I'm more than happy to have those lips of his anywhere he wants to put them.

For a moment it looks like he's about to pull me into him and lay one on me, but then his gaze shifts to where Alyssa and Satya are sitting on the couch. *The Vampire*

Diaries is playing in the background, the volume too low for me to hear.

He doesn't let go of my hand, but he does raise the other one in a wave. 'Alyssa, Satya, always lovely to see you.'

They're both grinning like Cheshire cats. 'The pleasure is ours,' they say in unison and then start giggling.

I shoot them both a warning look.

'Have fun,' Alyssa says.

'But not too much,' Satya snickers.

Godric looks like he's fighting a laugh. 'I promise to be on my best behavior.'

'That's no fun,' Satya says, still grinning.

'Okay, well, we should probably be going. We don't want to be late.' I step out onto the front porch in hopes that we can escape before my roommates embarrass the hell out of me. I'm plenty capable of doing that all on my own.

But as I'm pulling the door closed, Satya yells, 'Try not to get an indecent exposure charge!'

'And if you're planning another make-out session you can always relocate it from the front porch to your bedroom so the whole neighborhood doesn't witness it!' Alyssa calls.

'Unless you're both into exhibitionism!' Satya adds.

I flip them the bird and pull the door closed. 'Sorry about that.'

'No apology necessary. If I'd had better control of myself last night we would've been making out in the privacy of my bedroom, instead of in full view on your front porch.' Godric keeps hold of my hand as we make our way down the porch steps.

It isn't until we're standing on the driveway that I realize there's a car parked in it. And it's not Alyssa's old Ford Focus that was passed down to her from her brother when he traded up for a family sedan, or my ancient Jetta that once belonged to my oldest brother when he was in high school.

It's as if Godric dressed to match his car. It's sleek and black and looks like something straight out of the 1950s. I let out a low whistle. 'Holy shit balls. Whose car is this?'

'It belonged to our great-uncle.'

'It's awesome.'

He follows me to the passenger side and opens the door, maintaining his hold on my hand. But before I can slide into my seat his free hand comes up to cup my cheek. I tip my chin up and he tips his down.

His eyes spark, and the hairs on the back of my neck rise. My stomach clenches and my breath catches.

'Hi,' he murmurs.

'Hi,' I whisper.

His lips meet mine. I'm sure he means to keep it chaste, but I suck his bottom lip between mine and give it a nibble.

He groans and wraps his arm around my waist. I moan and thread my fingers through his hair. We tip our heads further and part our lips.

The front door opens, and Satya shouts, 'Either go out for dinner or hit the bedroom!'

I fire the bird over my shoulder, but we break apart. 'To be continued.'

Godric exhales a long, slow breath, his nostrils flaring. 'Dinner will be the most incredible torment.' He steps back and helps me into the car before closing the door and rounding the hood.

I run my hand along the leather seat and take in the modern interior and the obvious upgrades. The stereo looks like it's the original, with the radio dial and everything, but a USB port has been added. Everything is black and white and chrome.

I lean across and pull the handle, opening the door for Godric. He smiles as he takes his place behind the wheel.

'This is a cool car.'

'Laz has a thing for bringing old cars into the twenty-first century.' He slides the key into the ignition and turns the engine over.

'Does he also have a thing for creeping on you when you have girls in your room?' I slap a hand over my mouth. 'I'm sorry, that was not a nice thing to say.'

Godric pauses, his hand on the gearshift. 'He didn't realize I had company and he feels bad for interrupting.'

'He threw something at you.'

'I left my extra pills in the kitchen. It's a bad habit.' He clears his throat and rubs his bottom lip with his thumb. 'He was reminding me to take my medication by lobbing it at me, but he didn't realize you were with me until it was too late. He's pretty embarrassed about the whole thing.'

'Oh. Well, tell him it's okay. We all make mistakes.'

'I'll pass on the message.' He puts the car in gear and pulls out of the driveway, making a right toward downtown.

Godric didn't tell me where we're going for dinner, just to dress for a night out.

'Can I ask you a question?' I fiddle with the handle on my purse.

'Of course.'

'It's personal,' I warn. I'm trying to piece together

the appealing puzzle that is Godric Hawthorn. Half the time he seems wise beyond his years, and yet there are moments – like locking himself in the bathroom – when he also seems as though he's struggling to figure out college life, like the rest of us.

He glances at me for a moment before focusing on the road again. 'Okay.'

'Do you have some kind of . . . illness? I don't mean to be nosy, but maybe it's something I need to be aware of? In case something happens when I'm with you? I understand if you're not comfortable talking about it, though. You don't have to answer if you don't want to, I just thought . . . we're spending a lot of time together.' I'm nervous now, and my stupid palms are starting to sweat. 'My uncle was a diabetic, and for a long time he took pills to manage it. Type two, but as he got older the pills stopped being effective and he started taking insulin every day. And then it increased to several times a day. And once he had a reaction because he thought he was eating the diabetic chocolates, but he was eating the regular ones, and we ended up having to take him to the hospital. It was during Christmas, on a full moon, which is the worst combination in the history of the universe when it comes to hospital visits, apparently. But he was okay in the end. Mostly it scared the crap out of everyone. And since Laz seems to be particularly concerned about your well-being a lot of the time, I wondered if maybe that was the reason?' My voice is all pitchy and reedy.

Godric clears his throat and waits a moment, possibly since it's hard to tell if I'm done yammering at him. 'I have a blood disorder, and it's sort of like diabetes in that I take medication to keep it under control.'

'Is it serious?' All sorts of horrible things go through my mind. Leukemia is a blood disorder and while sometimes it's manageable, sometimes it's not. I realize I really, *really* like Godric. And I don't think it would take very much for that like to turn into something bigger. The thought of there being a time limit on us, while frightening, doesn't change the fact that my feelings for him are deepening.

'No, it's not the kind of serious you're probably thinking about. Sorry if it came out sounding like I had some life-altering illness.' He reaches across the center console and takes my hand. He lifts it to his lips and presses them against my knuckles. 'It's completely manageable, but it's not something that will ever go away. Does that help at all?'

'Yeah. That helps. That must be a hard thing to talk about because my mind went to the worst-case scenario immediately,' I admit.

'I could see that on your face. I probably should've said something about it before now, but it can be an awkward subject. Laz is hypervigilant. It's just the way he is, but it doesn't impact my life or my ability to live it.'

'That's good to hear.'

We arrive at the restaurant and Godric finds a parking spot. But before we exit the car, he slides his hand under my curtain of hair and sweeps his thumb along the column of my throat. 'I was hoping I could steal a kiss before we have to manage ourselves in public for several hours.'

'I was hoping you would say something like that.'

We both lean in and tip our heads, lips connecting. Our tongues meet, and once again, that sweetness coats my throat and along with it comes that strange, familiar sensation; almost as though I've taken a sedative and consumed an energy drink at the same time. I can't say I dislike it, but having my body revving into fifth gear before we sit in a restaurant for the next two hours is a special brand of torment.

Eventually, Godric breaks the kiss. 'To be continued, again.'

He's out of the car and around to the passenger side before I even have a chance to catch my breath.

The restaurant isn't typical by anyone's standards. It's a century-old estate house on the edge of town with a sprawling property and lush gardens in various stages of bloom. It's set high up on a hill, one side overlooking the city, the other the dense woods that lead to the rural communities on the outskirts of town. It's a beautiful marrying of city and country in a grand, Gothic home. And it's exactly the kind of place I'd expect Godric to like.

We take an elevator to the third-floor terrace and we're seated by an outdoor fire with a stunning view of the rolling hills and the forest. There's only one other table out here and we're separated by a lattice barrier thick with ivy and clematis.

'This is a huge step up from TGI Friday's,' I say, once the host has left us to browse the drink menu.

Godric gives me a wry grin. 'Is this too much for you? I can take you somewhere more low-key if you want.'

'No, no, you don't need to do that. This is gorgeous.' But I'm probably going to blow my entertainment budget for the next month if we're splitting the bill.

The server comes to take our drink order. The wine

menu is seven pages long and I can't find a single familiar name.

'Did you like the wine you had at my place last night?'

'Yes!' I practically shout. 'That was incredible.'

'We'll take a bottle of that, then.'

The server leaves and I lean in and whisper, 'If I drink a bottle of wine I'll be too wasted to walk.'

Godric winks. 'Don't worry, I won't make you drink it on your own.'

I remind myself that Godric is well over six feet, and that guys have a much higher tolerance. When the server returns, Godric orders the shrimp and lobster dainties with garlic butter as an appetizer. It's as delicious and decadent as it sounds, although I'm grateful I have breath mints handy for after dinner.

There are no prices on the menu, just descriptions. I throw caution and my bank card to the wind and order the steak, like Godric, except I ask for medium while he gets his rare.

Once the server has left to put in our order, I turn my attention back to Godric. 'Are you the only one in your family with a blood disorder? What is it? Is it okay for me to ask questions about this? I don't want to push, but obviously I'm curious.'

Godric reaches across the table and lines our fingers up. 'I don't mind. And no, I'm not the only one with a blood disorder. It's genetic, and both of my parents are carriers. You probably haven't heard of it. It's very rare and there aren't a lot of studies about it, which is why my mother became a hematologist.'

'Is that why you chose to study molecular genetics?'

Godric nods. 'Medicine evolves like humans do. We make new discoveries every day, and studying my own condition helps me understand what makes me different from everyone else.'

'That's such a great outlook.'

'It doesn't do us any good to wish away our differences. Studying them and learning how to manipulate them to our advantage is the best way to make new connections and new strides in medicine. Good can always come from the things originally perceived as bad.'

'Sort of like how botulism has been isolated and extracted for medicinal purposes beyond getting rid of wrinkles,' I say.

Godric chuckles. 'Yes, exactly. Here's this horrible, silent, scentless bacteria that can shut down a person's entire respiratory system when ingested, but when isolated and manipulated, it can provide relief for migraine and chronic pain sufferers.'

'It's about pushing past the limitations,' I say.

'And finding alternatives,' Godric agrees. 'And not being defined by one aspect of what makes us who we are.'

'And I love that you're devoting your future to understanding what you're facing. It's bold and brave.'

The server arrives with our entrees, and we continue to talk, the discussion moving on to less intense topics. I carefully cut my steak into small pieces, chewing slowly so I can savor every bite, as we share stories about our families and what it was like growing up with four brothers versus Godric's two. I wonder if this is what it's like to really find someone who complements me. Someone with similar interests and hobbies, who gets excited about the same things I do. It goes far beyond physical attraction. I'm just as attracted to Godric's mind as I am to the rest of him.

'I enjoy everything about you,' Godric says as I dab at my mouth with my serviette after I've finished the last bite of my steak.

'I enjoy everything about you, too. Especially your lips on mine. That's a particular favorite.'

He grins. 'Have I mentioned how much I love this dress on you?'

'You have.' I skim along the edge of the collar, which dips low and does a great job of accentuating my best assets, which have garnered a lot of Godric's attention.

'It bears repeating that you look good enough to eat this evening.' He reaches across the table and takes my hand in his, turning it to press a kiss to the inside of my wrist. His lips curve in a salacious smile. 'Although, you always look edible.'

The server appears, breaking the delicious tension, and forcing Godric's lips to leave my skin. I sort of want to kick the server for interrupting, but at the same time, launching myself over the table at Godric and tackling him to the ground so we can make out in yet another public place seems like a great way to get that indecent exposure charge my roommates warned me about.

Godric doesn't even look at the server when he orders the chocolate lava cake for dessert and requests only one spoon.

Dessert is the most extensive foreplay in the history of the universe. Godric feeds me bite after bite. And when I get some on my lip, he wipes it off with his finger. Before he can wipe the gooey chocolate on his serviette I latch onto his hand and wrap my lips around his finger. It's a million percent highly suggestive. Godric makes a low sound in the back of his throat and my entire body zings with carnal anticipation.

'How committed are you to the movie part of this date?' I ask, my voice a husky whisper.

His brow furrows. 'Do you want the date to end?'

My eyes flare. 'Hell no. But if I have to wait another two hours before I get to make out with you again, I might spontaneously combust.'

'That sounds dangerous.'

'Mm.' I nod, my expression serious. 'I hear it's hard to come back from spontaneous combustion.'

'What should we do instead?'

'Alyssa and Satya were planning to go to a friend's place to play Jackbox.'

'What's Jackbox?'

'An interactive game where you draw or write silly things and then try to beat the other players.'

'You want to play Jackbox instead of go to a movie?' Godric seems rightfully confused.

'No. If Alyssa and Satya are out it means my place should be empty. But let me check to make sure.'

My house is preferable, and avoids any potentially awkward interactions with his brother. I fire off a quick message to our group chat, to see if my roommates still plan to attend trivia night.

A few seconds later, I get a thumbs up from Alyssa and a short video clip of her and Satya sitting on a very old couch before she pans out to show the rest of the room, which is full of people with phones in their hands. It seems antisocial, but it's really not.

Satya: *guess we should message before we come home*

Several GIFs follow, including one that says *you go, girl* and another where endless hotdogs keep falling on a girl's upturned face.

'My house is empty.' I drop my phone back into my purse. 'Are you interested in continuing this date in my bedroom?'

I I

Godric doesn't answer with words. Instead, he pushes back his chair and holds out his hand as he stands. I slip mine into his palm and allow him to pull me to my feet.

'What about the bill?' I ask, as we leave behind the view of the gardens and the forest in the distance.

'It's already taken care of.' He slips his arm through mine so my hand rests on top of his forearm, like we're in an old movie.

'But you didn't give him your credit card. And what if I wanted to split the tab?'

He pauses to glance down at me. 'I asked you on a date, it's only proper that I pay. And they have my card on file.'

I arch a delicate eyebrow.

He frowns. 'I don't understand your expression.'

The whole 'proper' comment I'll deal with later. 'How often do you come here?'

'Once a week.'

'Once a week?' I'm an echo now. But this place is seriously swanky. And it must be ridiculously expensive. I took a picture of the bottle of wine so I could look up the price later. But beyond this place being super high-end, I have other more burning questions, such as, 'Who do you come here with?'

We reach the elevator, which has its own attendant standing outside. He doesn't get in with us, but he seems to know Godric. He tips his hat and says, 'Goodnight, Mr Hawthorn. Goodnight, ma'am.'

We step into the elevator and the doors close. Godric turns to me, and I see his smile reflected from several different angles since this elevator is all mirrors. It's almost a smirk. 'I come here with my brothers. It's our favorite place. Who else would I be with, Hazy?'

That curly-haired girl comes to mind. I lift a shoulder and let it fall. 'Dunno. Maybe this is where you take all your first dates.' Oh my God, I sound like a jealous girlfriend.

Godric bites his bottom lip and bends until his lips graze my ear. 'I like you in green.'

When he leans back, I narrow my eyes. 'You weren't supposed to call me out like that, Godric.'

'You're the only woman I'm interested in dating.' His smile falls, his expression darkening like a storm cloud. 'Are you interested in anyone else?'

'No.'

'Good.' He runs his hand down his tie and clears his throat before he continues. 'I'm glad we're on the same page, then.'

The elevator door slides open and Godric steps back, giving me space since he was all up in mine. He links our arms again as we cross the restaurant.

A manager comes striding over before we can reach the door. 'Mr Hawthorn, I hope dinner was to your liking tonight.'

'It was excellent, thank you, Bernard. My compliments to the chef.'

Bernard turns to me. 'Ma'am, I hope you enjoyed the terrace view.'

'It was spectacular.'

'Wonderful, wonderful.' He claps his hands. 'I hope we'll see you both again soon.'

Godric thanks him again and I have a feeling if I'd had to pay half the tab, it would have thrown off my entire monthly budget.

When we step outside, I'm hit with the lush, fragrant scent of blooming flowers. Part of me would like to walk through the gardens because they're stunning – and who knows when or if I'll be back here? But a bigger part of me realizes that there's a very good chance we'll get carried away.

Heading straight home is the right choice because the moment we're in the car, I'm across the driver's side, suctioning my lips to Godric's. It slips my mind that I've been eating garlic, and that my mouth probably tastes like a combination of that and a hint of chocolate lava cake. Unsurprisingly, Godric manages to taste like candy. I didn't see him pop any before we got in the car, although it's very possible he nabbed one on the way out and I didn't notice because I was too busy worrying about the cost of dinner. Godric, being the courteous man he is, indulges me in a short make-out session. And like every other time I've kissed him, I'm flooded with a familiar wave of serenity, followed by the intense need to take my clothes off.

Eventually, he takes my face in his hands and disengages our lips. 'To be continued, yet again.'

The entire ride home Godric peppers the hand he's holding with kisses, and I twist in my seat so I can stare at his pretty face. Yeah. I think I'm already falling for this guy. Which shouldn't be possible, but here I am, all mooneyes over him. As soon as he pulls into the driveway I'm out of the car, rushing up the front steps. I'm clumsy and over-excited so I drop the keys on the mat and bend to pick them up again. Godric strolls up the steps, all calm and composed, wearing a salacious smile.

'You need to stop that,' I grumble as I try to get the key in the lock again.

He leans against the side of the house, while I continue to struggle. 'I need to stop what, Hazy?'

My name sounds sinful in his mouth.

I make a circle motion around my face. 'This. The cock-iness. The smirk. I want to lick it right off your face.' I grimace because that sounded way better in my head than it did coming out of my mouth.

'There are other, far more interesting places on my body that would appreciate the attention of your tongue,' he says.

I drop the keys again, but somehow, he catches them before they hit the ground.

Before I have a chance to question his incredible reflexes, he winds his arm around my waist, and his mouth covers mine. All it takes is the sweetness of his mouth and the decadent stroke of his tongue against mine and any thoughts, words or questions I had melt into desire. I'm not sure how long we make out on the front porch, but the only thing that stops us is the sound of the neighbor's dog barking.

I reluctantly allow him to remove his lips from mine so he can slide the key into the lock, which he does with no trouble. I pull him in by his tie and slam the door behind him, flipping the lock. I kick off my shoes, lace my fingers with his and drag him towards the staircase. 'Let me show you my bedroom.' There's a sweatshirt thrown over the newel post and one of Satya's many bras. I knock it to the floor and continue upstairs.

'That's Alyssa's room.' I point to the closed door on the right. 'And that's Satya's.' I thumb to the one across the hall. 'And this is mine.' I shoulder open the door at the end of the hall and flick on the light.

My room looks a lot like it was hit by a hurricane of clothes. 'Shit.' My bed is covered in a pile of dresses that did not make the cut for tonight. 'Let me put a few things away.'

I reluctantly release Godric's hand and scoop up my discarded dresses, several pairs of sexy panties, a few equally sexy bras and hustle them over to my closet. I toss them inside and slam the door shut before everything can tumble back out. One of the bras manages to escape. I kick it under my computer desk.

By the time I'm done, Godric has closed the door and is stalking toward me, slowly, like a predator sizing up his prey. Which is a weird thing to think, but his head is bowed, and his eyes are trained on me, glinting with desire and the reflection of my budget chandelier from Ikea.

'Your room smells like you.'

'Is that a good thing?' A wave of goosebumps washes across my skin, followed by a flash of heat.

'Very.' His fingers trail along the footboard of my bed.

There's another bra hanging from the knob on the left, but Godric either doesn't see it or he ignores it. He comes to a stop when his socked feet are an inch from touching mine. There's a paisley pattern on them. The only splash of color in his otherwise black-on-black outfit.

I tip my head back so I can look at his gorgeous, almost frighteningly intense face. 'Hi,' I whisper.

'Hi.' His grin makes my insides try to flip over. 'Now that you have me in your bedroom, what would you like to do?'

I glance at my bed. The sheets are fresh, but the comforter is rumpled because of all the dresses that were living on it up until a minute ago. 'We could see how squeaky the springs are in my mattress?' I'm going for cheeky-sightly-comedic, apparently. I don't know what to do with my hands, so I clasp them in front of me, but I start wringing them and shift them behind my back instead.

'You seem nervous.' He hasn't made a move to touch me, yet.

'The last time we were alone in a bedroom your brother barged in and you locked yourself in a bathroom.' Both of those things are true, but I don't honestly believe either has anything to do with my current nervous-Nelly state. Maybe it's anticipation masquerading as anxiety.

I figure the best way to handle it is to stop talking and start making out. I wrap his tie around my fist and tip my chin up in invitation. Godric's smile widens and he dips down, lips brushing over mine. I curve my free hand around the back of his neck in case he gets any ideas to pull away.

'I want you to touch me tonight.' I suck his bottom lip between mine and let it slide through my teeth.

He winds his arm around my waist. 'I'm touching you right now.'

He's correct, he is touching me, but there are far too many layers of fabric separating us. I let go of his tie to deal with the zipper on my dress. It's one of those side-zip jobs. Unfortunately, it requires both of my hands to make that happen.

'I think you know what I mean,' I say and then slide my tongue between his lips.

He pushes back against it, the sweetness sending a fresh wave of calm through me, as well as a familiar blanket of want. The anxiety I felt a moment ago dissipates.

I let the hand cupping the back of his neck drift down his chest while we continue to make out. Godric's hands cup my cheeks, giving me the opportunity I need to handle the stupid zipper. I fold one arm behind my back to make it work and get the zipper down without it catching on the way. I tug on the shoulders of the dress and the sleeves slide down my arms. The bodice drops to my waist, I push it over my hips and it falls to the floor.

And now I'm standing in the middle of my bedroom wearing only my bra and underwear while I'm making out with Godric. I wore my very best matching set tonight. Just in case. He breaks the kiss and glances down. His breath leaves him on a low hiss.

He stills, and for several long seconds he seems to be doing an excellent mannequin impression. A sexy one, but he's not moving and I'm standing here with hardly any clothes on, wishing I'd thought this out better.

A low, deep groan rumbles through him and his hands ghost over my shoulders and down my back. They only hesitate for a millisecond before he cups my ass, and then, to my shock and utter surprise, he gives me a rough squeeze and lifts me off the floor. My reaction is immediate. I grab his shoulders and wrap my legs around his waist so he's not bearing all my weight in the palms of his hands.

He spins us around. And then my back meets the comforter, and my head hits the pillows. How he managed to perfectly execute this move so half my body isn't hanging off the bed is a wonder, but I don't have the inclination to ask questions when he's hovering over me with his erection pressed against my stomach. He props himself up on one arm, which makes his biceps bulge enticingly.

Godric follows the arch of my eyebrow with a single finger, skimming along my temple and across the edge of my jaw, down to the hollow of my throat. He continues the descent, trailing a path into the valley of my breasts, until he reaches the scalloped edge of my bra. He follows the lace accents and, as usual, my body responds by breaking out in a wave of goosebumps, followed by a welcome flash of need.

He dips down to kiss me again, the contact is brief, but his lips follow the same path his finger made, traveling along the column of my throat. I turn my head and tip my chin up further to give him better access.

He makes another deep, feral sound. 'So dangerously enticing,' he whispers against my throat, his tongue sweeping out to taste me.

I slide my fingers into the hair at the nape of his neck, anchoring them there. My heart is racing, my body apparently unable to decide whether I'm hot or cold, because I keep alternating between waves of goosebumps and flashes of heat. I'm drowning in glorious sensation. The feel of his lips on my skin, combined with the press of him between my thighs, sends my body into overdrive.

I wish I thought this out better, and at least relieved him of his shirt and tie before I decided to lose the dress.

I'm reluctant to put a pin in things to even our skin exposure, because that would mean diverting his attention, and I would really love to have his talented mouth on my nipple.

As if he can read my mind, his free hand shifts to cover the swell of the breast his mouth isn't close to. His thumb skims the tight peak, and despite the sensation being muted by fabric, I still arch off the bed. At the same time, my legs tighten around his waist, and I moan. The sound is unreasonably loud and exceptionally wanton.

Disappointingly, Godric's mouth leaves my skin, and he lifts his head. His expression sends another bolt of lust rocketing through me. 'Do you like that, then?'

The question is probably both rhetorical and tongue-in-cheek, but I bite my bottom lip and nod anyway. I don't trust myself to speak, because I fear whatever comes out of my mouth will be some garbled, desperate sound. I don't think Godric's ego needs more inflating.

'Shall I do it again?' His lips brush the swell at the same time as his thumb circles my nipple.

I fight not to moan so loud that I wake the neighborhood or send the dog next door into a frenzy. Instead, I fist Godric's hair with one hand and use the other to pull my bra cup aside, exposing the nipple his mouth is two inches away from.

His gaze lifts to mine and my nipple tightens to the point where it becomes a physical ache that spreads through my body and centers between my legs. Still holding my gaze, his lips close over the tight peak and he swirls his tongue.

'Oh my fucking God . . . ric,' I groan, and roll my hips.

Godric makes another noise; this one sends a shiver down my spine that ends between my thighs. I try to run my free hand down his back, but he's still wearing a stupid shirt.

'I need you to be wearing less clothes,' I complain. 'But I don't want you to stop doing what you're doing.'

'It's quite the conundrum.' His tongue continues to circle my nipple, and then, sweet Lord, he applies suction and I feel like I'm being engulfed in flames of desire.

'Oh God, use teeth,' I moan-order.

His gaze flips back up to mine, his eyes wide with something that looks like shock for a second, before the emotion is gone and is quickly replaced with something dark. 'You don't want me to do that, my love.'

His free hand slides under me and a second later my bra snaps free, but it's accompanied by the sound of fabric tearing.

'I'll replace it if I ruined it.' He tugs the strap down my arm, then shifts so he can remove the other one.

I don't get to see the damage because he tosses the bra on the floor and then folds back on his knees, bringing me up with him. He cups both breasts in his hands and gently thumbs my nipples, then covers the right one with his mouth. When he moves to the left, he pinches my nipple with his thumb and finger. I grip his shoulders and grind in his lap, lost in sensation, until I realize this is my opportunity to help undress him.

But when I feel around for the end of his tie, I realize it's already lying beside us on the bed and his shirt is unbuttoned, so all I have to do is push it over his shoulders.

'How the hell did you get your shirt undone?' I moan-ask.

'I'm a very efficient multitasker,' he replies. 'Do you need me to take anything else off while I'm at it?'

'I'd love it if you lost your pants, too.' You can't get what you want if you don't ask for it.

He moves me off his lap. It also means my nipples are no longer getting his undivided attention, but his body is damn well magnificent as he works the buckle free.

And since Godric is kneeling between my thighs, my face is at eye level with his incredible abs. I move his hands out of the way and pull the clasp free, the clink of metal against metal sending another shiver down my spine. Anticipation makes my hands shake as I pull his belt free and let it drop to the floor. I pop the button on his pants and lean in to kiss his stomach as I drag the zipper down.

His hands clench and release at his sides, his expression fierce, his gaze fixed on my lips against his skin, just above his navel and the fine trail of dark hair that dips below the waistband of his boxer shorts. I cup him through the fabric, fingernails scraping across his skin as I tuck them into the elastic. While I've been enjoying all the boob love – I have a feeling he might be a chest man – I find myself completely entranced by the look on his face and the way his nostrils flare. My pointer finger grazes the tip of his erection. His lip curls and the sound he makes induces a full-body shudder on my part.

One second I'm grazing his peen, the next I'm flat on my back, my wrists shackled by his, hands pressed against the pillows on either side of my head, and his face is buried against my neck. His lips part and his tongue strokes my skin as his hips sink into mine. For a second I feel the press of his teeth and anxious energy makes everything clench.

He groans, and then it's just the softness of his lips moving along my throat to my jaw. 'I want your hands on me, but it feels so intense when you touch me . . .' he whispers, slowly releasing my hands.

I raise one, with the intent to run my fingers through his hair, but think better of it. 'It's okay if it's too much for you.'

He makes a lamenting sound. 'Maybe I can focus on making you feel good for now?'

'If that would be better for you.'

'Mm. I think it would.' He shifts and stretches out beside me. 'I love your body.' His fingers drift along my stomach. 'And the way you respond to my touch.' He circles my navel. 'I want to know what you sound like when you come.' He follows the waistband of my panties with a single finger, moving from the right hip to the left. 'Would you let me do that, Hazy? Can I make you come?'

Nothing he says is particularly dirty, but every word and touch makes my body sing with need. 'I would love that.'

'Good.' His smile is halfway to a smirk. 'Me, too.' His fingers slip beneath the waistband of my panties. His touch is feather-light, skimming my sex, finding the place that makes me sigh with pleasure. He's gentle and sure as he explores, eliciting soft groans and pleas for more.

And when he goes lower, fingers sinking into me, and curling in exactly the right way, I fist the sheets and my eyes roll up. 'Oh my sweet Lord, just keep doing that.'

I don't know why, but the fact that I'm still wearing my panties makes this even hotter. As does the way he props his cheek on his fist, eyes on my face the entire time, like I'm the most riveting thing he's ever seen.

The insistent curl and release pushes me closer to the edge. Everything is tightening, spiraling, taking me higher. I'm seconds away from one hell of an orgasm, and based on the way I've started shaking, fisting the sheets like they're the only thing that's keeping me from floating away, I have a feeling that any hope of volume control has gone out the window. Which thankfully is closed.

'I-I-I, oh, God . . . ric.' And those are the last words I'm able to say, before the orgasm drags me down into bliss. I ride it out, because honestly that's all I can do. Just ride the wave.

This isn't one of those orgasms that hits hard and tapers quickly. Not by any stretch of the imagination. Godric knows exactly what he's doing with his magical fingers. For half a second the green monster of jealousy peeks out because the only way he could be this adept is from an exceptional amount of practice. But I can't complain about the fact that he's mind-blowingly competent at providing manual orgasms, so I mentally tell the green demon to shut up and enjoy the experience and the view.

He doesn't stop when the orgasm begins to wane. Like he's aware if he keeps going, it'll fire back up again and keep me swirling around in the tornado of bliss.

Several loud, moan-filled minutes later, I turn into a limp noodle. The orgasm has finally settled into sporadic clenches. My eyes pop open as Godric's hand leaves my panties. He's still watching me as his fingers disappear between his lips.

I make a noise that's hard to define, a combination of lust, surprise and who the hell knows what else.

Godric's lids flutter shut, and he makes a deep sound in

the back of his throat. When they open, they're hooded with lust. 'I want to make you come again, except this time with my mouth.' It's part declaration and part growl.

'I mean . . . Don't you want –' I motion below the waist. 'Shouldn't I return the favor?'

'You can return the favor after, if you'd like. But first, I want more of you.' The furrow in his brow is back and deeper than ever, like it's occurred to him that maybe I've had enough, which is preposterous. 'But only if that's something you want, too.' I'm sure there are some women out there who are good with a single, drawn-out orgasm. I am not one of them.

He blinks at me, and I blink back. Right. He's waiting for me to answer.

'Your face between my thighs is definitely something I want.'

He grins again. 'I was hoping you'd say that.' He rolls on top of me and brushes his lips over mine; at the same time, his erection presses exactly where I need it.

I gasp when he shifts his hips and his tongue slides into my mouth. It's still sweet, as always, but now I can also taste my own orgasm, which is weird. But also oddly hot.

We make out for a while, grinding on each other, with me making little mewling sounds and Godric groaning every so often. And then he begins his descent. It isn't enough for him to kiss a path down my body. He stops at all my most sensitive places and lingers there, whispering naughty, sexy things against my skin.

I moan and grip his hair when he sucks a nipple into his mouth.

'I love that sound.' He kisses his way over my stomach.

'Keep doing what you're doing, and I'll keep making it.'

His gaze lifts to mine when he reaches my navel and hooks his fingers into the waistband of my panties. 'I wonder what it would take to have you screaming my name.'

'I guess we're about to find out, huh?' I swallow thickly as he tugs them down a few inches and kisses a path from hip to hip.

I want to shove my panties down my thighs and guide his mouth to my center, but I have a feeling I wouldn't be all that successful if I tried. Instead, I watch him, completely entranced by his beautiful face and broad shoulders and his deft fingers moving over my skin.

Eventually, my panties are discarded on the floor, leaving me naked and exposed. Godric's nostrils flare as he inhales a long, slow breath and then he drops his head, kissing the inside of my right thigh and then my left. His gaze shifts to mine when he licks up my center.

I bow off the bed. 'Oh my fuuuuuu—'

'Mm. You taste as good as you sound.' His tongue circles my aching clit.

I grip the sheets and try not to writhe uncontrollably.

'I like your hands in my hair.' Soft kiss.

'I might rip it out by the roots.'

'It'll grow back.' He reaches up and his fingers wrap around my wrist, tugging until I release the sheets. He moves my hand to his head, and I thread my fingers through the silken strands, gripping hard.

Godric's talented tongue pushes me over the edge, not once, but twice – and both times I scream his name. He tries for a third, but I'm sweaty and oversensitive, so I use his hair to pull him back up.

And then I push on his chest. 'I want to take care of you now.'

He rolls us over so I'm straddling his thighs.

'You're the reason artists paint women,' he declares, hands on my waist, eyes moving over my naked form.

'You're amazing for my ego.' He makes me feel ridiculously sexy.

'It's the truth. I could touch you for hours. Kiss every inch of you. Covet every moan and sigh and scream when I make you come.' His lips turn up in a naughty grin.

I cup him through his boxers, fingers wrapping around his generous length through the thin, soft fabric. I tease him, then slide my fingers under the waistband, tugging it down to free him from the fabric.

I'm not the least bit surprised that I'm currently stroking a BFD – otherwise known as boyfriend dick. He's the perfect combination of length and girth, with a slight curve. Godric has a pretty peen, just like the rest of him.

I lean down to kiss him as I stroke from base to tip, thumb sweeping over the head, gathering the wetness and dragging it down.

But when I start to kiss my way over his collarbones, Godric takes my face in his palms. 'Stay here, please. Your hand is perfect.'

'You don't want my mouth on you?' I ask.

His smile is wry as his thumb traces the contour of my bottom lip. 'Oh, Hazy. It's not about what I want, it's about how quickly I'll lose control if I do. I'd like to savor this experience, and I won't be able to do that if your pretty mouth is wrapped around my cock.'

Well, then.

I continue to stroke him, slow and lazy, in no rush to make this end. I don't try to take it further, even though the desire is there. It's worth slowing things down with Godric. Especially since I'm already halfway to falling for him.

12

I wake the next morning curled around a very warm, very hard body. *Godric slept over.* I snuggle closer and press my face against his neck. His arm tightens around my waist. Based on my position, there is a distinct possibility that his arm has been trapped underneath me the entire night.

'I know you're awake.' His voice is a low rumble, with a hint of gruffness that wakes up all the lustiest parts of my body.

'How can you be sure?' I mumble, inhaling his sleep-warm scent.

'Because your breathing changed, and you stopped telling me nonsensical stories.'

I lift my head in a rush, then cover my mouth with my hand. 'I do not talk in my sleep.' I take in his expression. 'Do I?'

His amused brow becomes a furrow. 'Why are you doing that thing with your hand?'

'What thing with my hand?' I ask from behind the protective barrier of my palm.

Instead of responding, he tugs gently at my wrist. 'I can't see your beautiful face. Or that gorgeous, smart mouth of yours.'

'It's called morning breath.'

The furrow deepens. 'And that matters why?'

I can't tell if he's being serious. 'Because morning breath is disgusting, and I need to brush my teeth before kissing is even an option.'

'Why do there seem to be so many unwritten rules I don't know about?' he murmurs, almost more to himself than to me.

Before I can respond with something cheeky, Godric rolls over and fits himself between my thighs. I'm entirely naked, and he's wearing boxer shorts. And that is all. We're skin to skin, except for the best parts, but I can feel him, hard and insistent against me.

I scramble to get my palm back in front of my mouth, but Godric gathers both of my wrists in one of his hands and stretches them above my head. He gazes down at me, a wicked smile playing on his lips. 'I quite enjoy having you under me like this.' He drops his head and nuzzles in, with a low hum of appreciation. His lips ghost along the column of my throat until they reach my ear.

'What are you doing?' I'm all breathless and wanton.

'Saying good morning.' He kisses a path along the edge of my jaw.

I turn my head, but he keeps following. I clamp my mouth shut, biting my lips together. When he tries to push past them with his tongue, I make a disgruntled sound.

He pushes up on the arm that isn't currently holding my wrists hostage. His confusion would be adorable if he wasn't two inches from my mouth. As it is, the change in the angle creates delicious friction. Despite wanting to save him from the horrors of morning-breath kisses, I hook one leg over his hip to keep his erection where it is, nestled against my now very awake and excited girl parts. My body and my brain are clearly on two different wavelengths, and I can't get my lower half to follow the directions of my upper half.

'Don't you want to make out with me?' Godric sounds both hurt and mystified. 'Everything about your body tells me that you do, and yet you won't let me in.'

'Well, yeah, I do want to make out, but like I said, I need to brush my teeth first.'

'But you're already under me and I'm hungry for the taste of you on my tongue. I want to swallow down your orgasms like fine wine.' He says all this while wearing an ardent expression.

It's tough to argue with his logic. 'Whatever. Have it your way. Don't say I didn't warn you.'

'Warning acknowledged, but will remain unheeded.' His lips brush over mine again, and at the same time he rolls his hips.

Godric knows what he's doing in the bedroom. My body is already singing with need. The next hip roll causes me to moan, allowing him to slide his tongue into my mouth. He must have had one of those candies he's clearly obsessed with before I woke up. It's a damn miracle he doesn't have a mouth full of fillings with how much sugar he seems to eat. I'm too busy making out with him to point out this issue, though.

Eventually, he pulls back, and I fully expect him to start kissing his way down my body because apparently my vagina is his new favorite place to put his mouth.

Instead, his brow does that furrow thing. 'I have an important question.'

'Yes, you can have my vagina for breakfast.'

He grins. 'That's wonderful to hear, but that wasn't my question.'

'Fire away, then.'

'Am I your boyfriend?'

My eyebrows attempt to disappear into my hairline. 'Uh . . . do you want to be my boyfriend?'

His eyebrows try to touch each other. 'That came out wrong. What I meant to say is that I would like to be able to introduce you as my ma—' He stops. 'As my girl-friend. Which would mean that you could also introduce me as your boyfriend. Would that be something you'd like, as well?'

I bite back a smile and run my fingers through his hair. 'Repeat after me.'

He seems confused.

I continue anyway. '"Hazy, would you be my girlfriend?"'

He blinks at me.

'You're supposed to repeat that,' I instruct him.

He strokes my cheek. 'Hazy, would you be my girlfriend?'

'Yes, Godric, I would love to be your girlfriend.'

He grins. 'I'm your boyfriend now, then?'

'Yes, Godric, you're my boyfriend.'

'Cool beans. I'm going to like being your boyfriend.' He kisses me for half a century. 'And now for breakfast.'

Over the weeks that follow, Godric and I fall into a routine. On Mondays, Wednesdays and Fridays he shows up at my place at eight to walk to campus with me. And that's only if he hasn't stayed over. Most sleepovers take place in my bed, but I have stayed at his place a couple of times.

Ironically, I have yet to formally meet his brother Laz.

I'm not sure if he's actively avoiding me when I come over because he's embarrassed about walking in on us kissing that one time, or if he's so reclusive he doesn't leave his bedroom often. Although, if I'm honest, we usually disappear up to Godric's room and spend a good part of our evening making out. He's also trying to teach me how to play chess, which I suck at, and I've taught him how to play cribbage, which was my grandma's favorite game.

We work on our homework assignments together. I discover that he has an independent study course, and often spends several additional hours in the lab during the week, but he never seems to struggle to keep up with his workload. He's usually done before I am, which means he'll sit and read, intermittently taking a break to stare at me, while I finish my own work.

Despite all the time we spend together, the regular makeout sessions, and the frequent sleepovers, we haven't made it past third base. Actually, Godric has made it to my third base. I'm stuck at his second. But I don't push, because the whole sensory thing is an issue and I sort of love that he's not in a rush to take it to the next level.

A few weeks after establishing our boyfriend-girlfriend status, we head to the campus pub to grab a late lunch once our Friday lab is finished. Next week we're taking blood samples so we can examine DNA structure, which I'm very excited about. Godric seems less than impressed.

Unfortunately, the pub is in the student center, which means passing the student paper office. Until now I've managed to avoid running into Blaine when I'm with Godric. I've also avoided discussing Godric with Blaine, choosing to ignore his questions and ridiculous conspiracy theories about the house and why it's been vacant prior to Godric and his brothers' arrival this fall.

I try to hide behind Godric and speed walk past the office, but we don't go unnoticed. Blaine yells my name loud enough to cause several people to stop and stare.

'Dammit,' I sigh in resignation.

'His voice makes me want to commit heinous criminal acts,' Godric gripes.

'You're not alone.'

'Hazy, baby! We need to talk about your piece on the history of Halloween.' He's still yelling.

I turn around. 'Stop calling me "Hazy, baby". It's Hazy or Hazel, full stop.'

Blaine's eyes drop to where Godric's hand and mine are laced together. His smile also drops. 'Are you two a thing now?' It sounds more like an accusation than anything else.

'Hazy is my girlfriend,' Godric declares. 'And I'm her boyfriend.'

Blaine raises an eyebrow. 'Is that right?'

'It's exactly right.' I swear Godric growls.

'What do you need to discuss regarding my article? Which I handed in on Tuesday, by the way, and it's now Friday.'

'Just some fact checking. I can stop by on Saturday if that works for you,' Blaine says, like he's doing me a favor, not being an annoyance.

'Hazy will be busy Saturday,' Godric snaps.

'I can speak for myself.' I elbow Godric in the side. 'I'm busy on Saturday.' *Probably sitting on Godric's face*. It's a miracle the last part stayed in my head.

Blaine inspects his fingernails. 'Fine, Sunday would work.'

'Just email the stuff you want fact checked.'

'Sure thing, send me a reminder email so I don't forget.' He slides his hands into his pockets and rocks back on his heels, turning his attention to Godric. 'Oh, and we're probably going to host a Halloween party again this year – unless, of course, you and your brothers would like to do the honors. You haven't thrown a party yet, have you?'

I'm about to tell Godric he doesn't have to throw a party, but Hunter appears out of nowhere and slings an arm over both of our shoulders. I startle, but Godric seems unsurprised and unfazed.

'We would love to host a Halloween party. Costumes mandatory,' Hunter says, with a grin that looks more like a threat.

'We would?' Godric arches a questioning eyebrow at his brother.

'Absolutely.' Hunter gives him a hearty pat on the back.

Blaine takes a step back. 'Awesome. I'll get the word out.' He gives them the thumbs up and nearly trips over his own feet as he takes refuge inside the student paper office again.

'Laz isn't going to be happy,' Godric says.

'Laz needs to expand his social circle beyond you and me, and this is the perfect opportunity.' Hunter drops his arms from our shoulders. 'I have class in ten. We can talk more about this tonight.' And with that he disappears into the throng of students.

Despite Hunter's attempts to involve Laz in the party planning meeting, he does not come to the living room to join our discussion later in the evening. Hunter seems particularly intent on getting the ball rolling, since Halloween is little more than a week away.

'Most of the parties around here have a keg and some bowls of chips,' I offer as he agonizes over drink selections.

'Most of the parties around here are thrown by Neanderthal frat boys.' Hunter types away on his laptop. The screen is shared on the massive flat-screen TV, and it showcases several small local breweries. He's trying to narrow down the type of beer he plans to have available.

'Not to be rude, but this place is classified as a frat house, which makes you frat boys.'

Godric scoffs and Hunter hides his smile behind his hand before he schools his expression. 'Good point. But we're the classy kind of frat house. And we need to show Sir Douchecanoe of Dirtbagville what a real party looks like. All I've seen this year are weak attempts at posturing, and a lot of getting drunk and making terrible decisions.' Hunter sips his craft beer, which has been poured into a fluted glass to bring out the hoppiness.

Godric makes a noise of agreement as he sips his Scotch. He's sitting in the wingback chair – apparently, this is his chair – and I'm tucked in beside him, with my legs thrown over his. It's surprisingly comfortable even with the two of us crammed into it.

The position is also intimate, especially since Godric's arm is draped over my shoulder, and he keeps playing with a lock of hair, twirling it around his finger before releasing it. Hunter seems unfazed by our cozy position, his focus on throwing the best damn party this street has ever seen.

And he's already well on his way to making that happen. Between the time he declared they were throwing a party and the time we left my bedroom this afternoon – when he started relentlessly messaging Godric to come home so we could have this impromptu meeting – the front yard has been fully decorated for the impending ghoulish holiday. I assume he enlisted Laz's help, otherwise it would have been nearly impossible to accomplish. Even with help it seems like a small miracle.

Speaking of their third brother . . . 'Is Laz coming down?'

'He's working on an assignment.' Godric noses my hair out of the way to get access to the exposed skin above the wide collar of my shirt.

'You do realize I'm sitting right here and I can hear you heavy breathing all over Hazy, right?' Hunter asks.

'She smells good,' Godric says.

'So do cookies. Go huff those for a while.' Hunter clicks on the cider menu. 'Oh, lavender and honey cider would be a great alternative for the non-beer-drinking crowd.'

I nudge Godric's face away from my neck. 'Satya will thank you for that.'

Hunter decides on four different kinds of beer and two ciders before he moves on to catering.

'You could order pizza from Bobby's Bestest,' I suggest.

'The name of that place irks me endlessly,' Godric gripes.

'But they do have the bestest pizza,' I argue.

'This is accurate,' Hunter agrees. 'Pizza for the heathens, but I'm ordering an appetizer buffet and a dessert bar because this is a Halloween celebration.' Once he's finished emailing three separate companies, he shuts his laptop. 'Now we just need a costume theme.'

'I say we all have to go as a supernatural being from one of our favorite books or movies.' Godric is wearing that secretive smile again.

'Love that idea,' Hunter says with a smirk, then turns to me. 'Hazy, wanna weigh in on this?'

'I'm down.' Thankfully, I have Satya to help me figure out a costume.

13

'How awesome do we look?' Satya props her fist on her hip and Alyssa does a spin.

We're dressed as the witches of Eastwick from one of Satya's favorite movies. Alyssa, who happens to be a complete wizard with a needle and thread, and who has a sewing machine in her bedroom, helped take our Walmart costumes to the next level with some modifications and embellishments and a few YouTube tutorials. We are some seriously sexy witches.

'Has Godric told you what he's dressing up as yet?' Satya asks.

'Nope.' I apply a coat of dark red lipstick. It's not particularly great for making out, but it does complete the look. 'He's determined to make it a surprise.' Every time I've asked him about it all he does is smirk. I've tried playing the guessing game, but he's a fortress when it comes to withholding information. 'I have a feeling it's either ridiculous, or ridiculously hot.'

'He's always ridiculously hot. I'm sure whatever he's decided to be, he'll rock it.' Alyssa adjusts the tulle overlay on her skirt, fluffing it up before she bends to retie the laces on her pointy heeled boots.

I offered our assistance setting up for the party, but Godric assured me that he and his brothers had it covered. I'm hoping tonight I'll finally meet Laz. Up until now he's been the guy I hear about, but never actually see.

At ten to eight we lock up and strut down the street and around the corner to Godric's. They must have a fog machine because the moment we step through the trellis decorated in black rose blossoms and spooky giant spiders, fog swirls around our feet and licks up our legs, all the way to our waists. A ghoulish soundtrack layered with moaning ghosts and eerily haunting music plays quietly as we make our way to the front porch. Cobwebs stretch between the supporting columns, animated spiders scuttling into the corner as we approach; dark shadows loom and recede in the corners, disappearing into the fog. It truly looks like a haunted house tonight.

I spot Hunter in the living room with his laptop open and balanced on his palm. The party doesn't start for a few more minutes, but hordes of people are spilling out of their houses, walking down the street in tight groups toward the house.

'I hope this doesn't get out of hand,' I murmur.

Most of the time the invitation is only extended to the residents on the street. It's sort of an unwritten rule, and we happen to be included because I used to date Blaine and we became honorary street dwellers. In the past there have been a few instances in which word has spread like wildfire, and hundreds of people have shown up to a party. The police rarely get called because everyone around here is a student, but occasionally the non-street partygoers get rowdy. There have been a couple of fist fights.

Alyssa flips her hair over her shoulder. 'I feel like Hunter and Godric will be able to manage things, they're intimidating.'

Satya hums her agreement and taps her lip thoughtfully. 'Especially Hunter, he's always smiling, but there's something dark lurking behind it. Like when he's around people, he's waiting for a reason to put them in their place.'

I've often thought the same thing when it comes to Hunter. I always see him smiling, but no one can be that chipper all the time. Every sun has a moon.

I don't have a chance to knock on the door before it's flung open and Hunter stands there, wearing a pair of ripped shorts, running shoes . . . and nothing else. His cut chest is fully on display, as are his wide shoulders and his massive biceps. He really is a mammoth of a man. 'Welcome to the party. I love the costumes, you're the witches of Eastwick, am I right?'

Satya's eyes light up. 'Yes! How did you know?'

Hunter's grin widens. 'Lucky guess.' He steps back from the door and motions us inside.

Much like the exterior, the interior has been completely transformed. All the living room furniture has been removed, including Godric's beloved wingback chair. In its place are chairs draped in black fabric. The walls are covered in cobwebs with more spiders crawling in the corners. They look eerily real.

The sideboard that typically holds Godric's Scotch has been transformed into a bar complete with beer taps. Instead of red solo cups, they have Halloween-inspired glassware, all of which looks like it could be metal, or plastic that's made to look like metal. There's even non-alcoholic punch with floating ice eyeballs.

The opposite wall boasts a buffet of tiered appetizers,

platters of sandwiches and delicious-looking desserts. As far as parties go, this one is already winning.

'Who are you dressed up as?' Satya asks as she follows Hunter inside, her arm hooked with Alyssa's.

'You'll figure it out soon enough.' Hunter winks.

'Where's Godric?' I ask.

'Right here.' He appears in the doorway between the living room and the kitchen.

'Oh my God.' Satya snort-giggles and slaps a palm over her mouth.

Alyssa slow claps. 'You win for best costume so far.' She motions between the two of us. 'I'm betting a hundred dollars you'll be glittering into next week.'

Godric steps out of the shadows and begins to sparkle. Because his entire face, and any other exposed skin, is covered in glitter. His full lips are stained a slightly darker red and his normally lightly tanned complexion is pale.

As usual, he's holding a glass of Scotch. He somehow manages to look ridiculously sexy while wearing a gray pea coat, a plain navy shirt and dress pants. I'm assuming his hair has an unprecedented amount of product in it considering the way it's been styled into a curated mess.

'Edward Cullen.' I smile and shake my head. Now I know why he wouldn't tell me ahead of time. And why we couldn't go as a couple from a book. Dressing up as Bella would mean wearing a ratty plaid coat, a hairband and looking confused.

He grins into his glass. 'My favorite part is that he sparkles in the sun. Points for creativity. It sure as hell beats the whole death by garlic and holy water.'

'Does that make you Jacob?' Satya asks Hunter.

'I always liked Sam the best, if I'm honest.' Hunter winks again.

Hunter offers us drinks, there's even a wine bar for those who aren't into beer or cider. The glasses aren't plastic at all, they're light metal with an embossed Beta Epsilon Delta engraved into the side. As far as classy Halloween parties go, this one takes the cake.

The doorbell rings the moment the grandfather clock in the hallway strikes eight. Inside half an hour, there are a hundred people crowding the main floor, all dressed in costumes, enjoying the party and the food.

An hour into the party, Blaine and Justin arrive. Justin is wearing actual clothes, which seems like a miracle, and Blaine is dressed as Dracula. Of course. I'm already half in the bag and I don't want him to ruin my buzz. Godric went to drag Laz out of his bedroom ten minutes ago and still hasn't returned, so he can't save me from Blaine. Alyssa is talking to some guy wearing a Batman costume, and Satya and Hunter are deep in conversation with a group of superheroes. I decide a bathroom break is required and that I'll use the one in Godric's room to avoid Blaine.

I make it to the staircase undetected. It's blocked off with a sign that says *No Trespassing. Violators will be executed.* There's a life-sized Grim Reaper standing guard. He's animated and his plastic scythe slices through the air at regular intervals. I skirt past him between swings and jog up the stairs.

It's quiet on the second floor, the hall lit only by the wall sconces. I note that Laz's bedroom door is ajar. The gap is only a couple of inches wide, but it's enough that I get a glimpse of the interior. The bedroom, while decidedly masculine, is also incredibly romantic.

I pause for a moment, but I don't hear voices coming from inside. Maybe Godric managed to get him to come downstairs and we missed each other because I approached the stairs from the hallway, rather than using the front foyer. But I'm already up here and I need to use the bathroom, so I continue down the hall and climb the stairs to Godric's bedroom.

I turn the knob and the door swings open. Standing in the middle of the room are Godric and the Grim Reaper. Which would be fine, since it's Halloween and a costume party. But Godric is holding a bag of dark red liquid. For a couple of seconds my brain struggles to understand what I'm seeing. Godric has expensive taste in alcohol. I know because I looked up the wine I had on our date and it's more than a hundred dollars a bottle. The notion that he would drink bagged wine seems preposterous. As does the fact that he'd be sucking it back like it's a Capri Sun minus the straw.

A trail of red dribbles down his chin as he and the Grim Reaper both turn to look my way. The Reaper's dark hood is pulled up and the only thing I can see is the luminescent red of his eyes and the massive scythe that glints in the chandelier light. Logically I know it must be Laz. But the creepiness, paired with the inexplicable sight of Godric sucking back what looks to be a bag of blood, freaks me right out.

I let out a strangled shriek and step back, but I don't take into consideration that I'm standing at the top of a flight of stairs. I try to grab for the railing, but my reflexes are dulled by the wine I've consumed. I stumble and lose my footing as the Grim Reaper appears in front of me, hand extended.

Godric mutters, 'Oh fuck.'

The Grim Reaper says a bunch of words that don't make sense.

For a moment, time seems to suspend. I should be falling; my feet aren't touching the ground at all. One of my legs is kicked up in the air, my arms are flung out like I'm reaching for an imaginary rope to grab onto. And then a blurred figure slips around the Reaper, causing a gentle breeze to make my hair tickle my cheek. I feel the soft brush of a body as it somehow slides past me. And then time and my body move again. But instead of falling down the flight of stairs, I hit a solid chest and two familiar arms wind around my waist. Between one blink and the next the Grim Reaper disappears.

'Are you okay?' Godric's lips are at my temple.

My entire body is shaking as my feet return to the floor at the top of the landing. Godric keeps his hands on my waist as I brace a palm against the wall and stumble the few steps into his room. He closes the door behind us and guides me to the closest surface to sit down. Which happens to be his bed.

I can't seem to stop shaking. 'What just happened?'

I don't know how to read Godric's expression, but the set of his eyebrows denotes his worry. Which is reasonable, since I think I'm losing my damn mind.

'I was falling down the stairs.' I fling a hand toward the closed door. 'I should have fallen down the stairs. The Grim Reaper was right there.' I point to the middle of the room.

'And then he was there.' I point to the closed door. 'And then he disappeared. What in the world were you drinking? It looked like blood.' Everything that's coming out of my mouth is ludicrous. 'Oh my God. Oh God! Have I been drugged? Did someone spike my drink? Are other people's drinks spiked?' It's the only logical explanation. Although it doesn't make me feel better. In fact, I'm pretty sure I'm on the verge of a panic attack.

If I'm hallucinating, that means I'm in for one hell of a trippy night. And if I'm not . . . well, we have much bigger problems. I stare at Godric, waiting for him to confirm that I am, indeed, tripping balls.

'Aren't you going to say anything? I think you need to take me to the hospital.' I slide off the bed and test out my legs. They're shaky and weak, but I haven't melted into the floor yet, so I'm taking that as a good sign.

I move toward the door, but Godric steps in front of me and settles his hands on my shoulders.

'Hazy, look at me, please.'

I lift my gaze to his pretty, glittering face. There's no dribble of wine-blood on his chin. No indication that what I saw wasn't a figment of my imagination. 'How are you so calm?'

His expression is one of determination, and I don't know what to make of that. I also don't know how he's not freaking out. He's also not answering any of my questions.

'You need to calm down, Hazy.' His hands move from my shoulders up the sides of my neck, and he cups my cheeks. He leans in and presses his lips to mine.

I want to tell him this isn't the time for making out. But for whatever reason, I don't fight him. Maybe because after tonight I'm going to be committed and I might never see him again? I part my lips when he strokes across the seam and his tongue sweeps inside my mouth. I'm hit with the familiar sweetness, and a glorious wave of calm washes over me. There's no wine aftertaste, or the metallic tang I associate with blood. It's the same every time, I'm a little addicted to the feeling. Godric ends the kiss far sooner than I'd like. It's a great distraction from the panic attack I was in the middle of. And maybe that was the point. I'm still freaked out, but no longer freaking out.

'I need to tell you something,' Godric says softly.

'The canapés were full of magic mushrooms? Or the brownies were laced with really strong weed? Or both.'

'No. I would never give you illicit narcotics without your knowledge or consent,' he says.

'What if somebody else spiked the punch?' I grab his wrists since he's still cupping my cheeks. 'It's entirely possible, isn't it?' He's been up here for who knows how long, and Hunter is busy chatting up the guests. There's been plenty of opportunity for someone to throw something in the punch and turn this into a whole different kind of party.

'No one spiked the punch, Hazy.'

'How do you know for sure? And how you do explain what happened with the Grim Reaper. And what the hell were you drinking?'

'The Grim Reaper was Laz.'

'But where did he go? One second he was standing there, and the next he was by the stairs, and then *poof!* He's gone. And how did you get behind me when you were standing in the middle of the room? I feel like I'm losing my mind. And you still haven't told me what you were drinking out of that bag.'

149

'You're not losing your mind. I think you should sit down, though.'

He tries to guide me back to the bed, but I head for the window seat instead. I drop onto the plush cushion, but I'm super restless and feeling a whole lot discombobulated. So I stand up again. And then sit down again.

Godric runs a hand through his hair. And then he starts to pace. 'Okay. I'm just going to spit it out. Tell you the truth. That's the only way forward.' He mutters something I don't catch.

'You're kind of freaking me out.'

'Yeah. I know. I'm sorry about that.' Godric exhales one long breath and turns to face me.

His expression is serious as he drops to one knee in front of me.

'Hazy, I'm a vampire.'

14

Godric

This is possibly the least ideal way to tell Hazy the truth about what I am.

How Laz and I missed her coming up the stairs will forever remain a mystery.

Three centuries is a long time to exist. We've watched humanity nearly eradicate themselves countless times. We've seen how their inability to accept otherness causes needless wars and results in the loss of more good than evil. We've watched Mother Nature do her best to tame the parasite that is the human race. But they're apparently more resilient than cockroaches. And I mean that in the nicest way possible.

After watching humanity evolve and devolve over the centuries, it's easy to understand Laz's sometimes disenchanted view of humans and his reclusiveness. His exceptional disdain for Halloween and the mockery it makes of the evil that lurks in the dark corners of the world is reasonable. As is his obsession with romantic comedies to some extent. They're snapshots of love at its most idealized. We never see what happens fifty years down the road, when one of them gets cancer, or has a heart attack and leaves the other behind. Humans can never truly understand the pain of having found a mate, only to have them ripped away; how it feels to be left alone after having that constant companionship that extends far beyond a human life span.

I even understand why he's angry at me for dating a human girl. Woman. Hazy is definitely all woman. But after nearly half a century of being without a mate, I wanted to feel something beyond passive indifference to my existence. And Hazy, well she's all the things my ceaseless eternity has been missing.

Hazy stares at me. And then she blinks and crosses her arms. Her lips push out in a pout. I've come to recognize it as the expression she makes when she's unimpressed. Most of the time it's directed at Blaine, so I'm not excited that she's now wearing it because of me.

As irritated and upset as she might be, she looks absolutely stunning tonight. Her costume accentuates every luscious curve of her body. It's been a challenge to be an engaging host when all I want to do is get her out of her clothes and into my bed.

I'm concerned that, based on recent events, this may not happen. Ever again. Depending on how she takes this news. Her current lack of reaction is not particularly reassuring.

She pokes at her cheek with her tongue. 'Are you fucking kidding me?' She flings a hand in my direction. 'Why are you making a joke about this?' Her voice rises, along with her heart rate and her breathing, until she's back to a state of panic.

'It's not a joke, Hazy.' If I can kiss her again, it might calm her down enough to make her rational. I step forward, and she puts her hand out.

'Don't you dare try to use your sex appeal on me.' She flicks her hair over her shoulder. 'I need an explanation that makes sense. Because right now I think I'm either high as hell, or I'm losing my damn mind.'

'I can understand how it might feel that way, but I assure you, you are not high, and you are not losing your mind.' I clasp my hands behind my back to keep me from touching her. Obviously she's not in the right headspace for a make-out session. 'Maybe I should take the glitter off?' I have no idea why I suggest this, other than I'm stalling.

'I don't see how glitter removal will help, but if it makes you feel better, have at it.' She motions to the bathroom.

'Come with me?'

'To the bathroom?' Her right eyebrow raises.

'Or you can stay here, but please don't leave.' I swallow compulsively.

I knew I would have to come clean eventually. And that it would have to be sooner rather than later. It seems only logical – since we're getting closer and spending a lot more time together, and my feelings for her are growing exponentially – that I tell her the truth. Hopefully, she can handle it. That was the discussion I'd been having with Laz. He's been on me for weeks. Mostly he's been telling me it's a terrible idea to date Hazy. And while I understand his concerns, apart from that first kiss, for which he's partially to blame, I've managed to keep myself under control.

'I don't plan to leave until you tell me something that makes sense.' At least she's not yelling and pitchy anymore.

I'm relieved when she follows me to the bathroom. She stands on the threshold, watching as I shrug out of the gray pea coat and hang it on one of the hooks by the shower. Getting rid of all this glitter at human speed will take the rest of the night. So I make a choice and hope that once I show her who I really am, she won't run screaming.

I turn on the water and pull my shirt over my head.

Hazy's heart rate picks up immediately, and her breath catches. This always happens when I take my shirt off.

'Getting undressed isn't going to get you out of this conversation,' she says.

'I know. I'm not trying to get out of the conversation. I'm just trying to un-Edward myself before we have it.' I take a face cloth and run it under the steaming water. And then I wipe my face free of the glitter powder, but not at human speed.

Hazy's eyes flare and she blinks a bunch of times, then rubs her eyes. 'I think you need to take me to the hospital. I'm tripping balls.' Her voice is thin and reedy.

She braces a hand against the wall. She's gone white as a sheet, and she looks like she's on the verge of losing it again. Annoyingly, my brother seems to have a point about my plan being half-cocked and full of holes.

I move across the bathroom, faster than a human would, but slower than I'm capable of, and wind my arm around her waist before she sinks to the floor. I move her so she's sitting on the vanity and no longer responsible for holding herself up.

She blinks rapidly several times and glances around. 'I'm so dizzy, did I pass out?' She settles one palm on my bare chest, her expression full of confusion as the shaky fingers of her free hand caress my cheek. 'Seconds ago, you were covered in glitter, and now you're glitter-free. And I was standing there, and now I'm sitting here.' She points to the doorway.

Her breathing grows erratic, and her eyes roll up, only the whites visible. She sags against me, her body limp. This is not at all how I saw this conversation going. Although, to be fair, I hadn't planned past telling her I'm a vampire, which I realize belatedly was not a plan at all.

'That worked well.' Laz is suddenly standing in the doorway, his expression exasperatingly smug.

'Your commentary is unhelpful. As is your presence. The last thing Hazy needs is for you to be standing in here, dressed as the Grim Reaper, when she comes around.'

I lift her into my arms and carry her through the bathroom. Laz moves out of the way so I can take her to my bed.

'Super-speeding all over the place with her is not the best way to explain what the hell is going on,' Laz informs me.

'Yeah, I figured that out.' But in my defense, she was unsteady on her feet and adding a bump on the head to the mix seemed like another bad idea.

'She passed out, huh?' Hunter appears out of nowhere and peers at her still form stretched out on my bed.

'If we're all in here, who's manning the party downstairs?' I adjust the skirt of Hazy's dress since it's riding high on her thighs.

'Everyone's having a great time, except maybe Blaine. Someone gave him a special brownie, now he's passed out on the recliner, and a bunch of people have drawn dicks on his face with a Sharpie. I've also highly encouraged photographs, so I don't think this party is gonna get rave reviews from him. Everyone else is saying this is the best party they've ever been to.' Hunter flings a hand in Hazy's direction. 'Apart from your girlfriend. This probably isn't going to go down as one of her favorite nights either.'

'Can the two of you fuck off? I don't want you in here when she comes around. I don't need an audience, and she doesn't need to be more freaked out than she already is.'

Hunter snorts. 'Whose fault is that?'

'I can tell you exactly how this is going to go,' Laz says, his expression grim.

I would be nervous about that, but his expression is always grim, even when he's watching the funniest of romantic comedies.

'I don't need your crystal ball at the moment, but I'll let you know if that changes.' I wave them off, and the two of them leave as Hazy blinks her way back to consciousness.

15

Hazy

Godric's lovely face slowly comes into focus as the black and white spots in my vision disappear. The way he's positioned turns the teardrop chandelier into a sort of halo crown. Which means I'm lying in his bed. But I have no idea how I got here.

'I don't know what's going on,' I protest, my voice a craggy whisper.

'What exactly do you remember?' Godric's hand hovers in my peripheral vision, as though he wants to touch me, but isn't sure if he should.

His expression is guarded, and he looks nervous. Godric looks a lot of things a lot of the time, but nervous usually isn't one of them. Serious, yes. Determined, absolutely. Deliciously sexy is basically his go-to look. But it is a rare day when I see wariness on his pretty face. And right now, he looks wary as fuck.

'I remember coming upstairs to use the bathroom because Blaine showed up, and I wanted to avoid running into him without you.' Dealing with Blaine is always a pain in the ass, but lately he's been more aggravating than usual. Or maybe my tolerance for him is at an all-time low. He's been relentless with his questions about Godric. I dig around in my head, but the things I'm remembering don't make a whole lot of sense.

'And then what?' Godric asks softly.

'The Grim Reaper was in your bedroom?' It comes out as a question, but I absolutely remember that moment. 'You were drinking a bag of . . . something. And then I asked you if someone spiked the punch. Or drugged me.' I glance around the room as things start to fall into place, and the rest of what happened makes familiar goosebumps flash across my skin. 'And you told me you are a vampire.'

'Do you believe me?' he asks.

I stare at him, and he stares at me. My heart rate jacks up, and my palms start to sweat. I'm suddenly cold and hot at the same time.

'Take a breath, Hazy. Everything is going to be okay.' His words are soft, but they don't match his tremulous smile.

'Vampires are not real,' I say, but it lacks conviction. 'I mean, are they real?'

'I think that would depend on who you ask. Most humans would agree with you.' Godric clasps his hands in his lap, and then unclasps them and runs them down his thighs.

'Most humans.' My gaze moves over his stunning face. 'But you are not one. A human, I mean.'

He shakes his head.

I do some more blinking and staring. 'But . . . How? I mean, what the hell?' I push up on my elbows and when I don't pass out, I sit up fully and scoot back on the bed, putting a little necessary distance between me and my either psychotic or vampire boyfriend. The jury's out on that one for now. 'Prove it. Prove to me that you're a vampire.'

'How would you like me to do that?'

I throw my hands in the air. I'm flustered and nervous.

I've been dating Godric for nearly two months. I hope he's not certifiable. But the other side of that coin is equally off-putting. I don't know what's worse, him believing he's a vampire or him actually *being* a vampire.

'I don't know. Do something vampire-y. Like turn into a bat or something.'

Godric throws his head back and laughs. 'That's a myth. I don't turn into a bat.'

'So none of you turn into bats, or just you?'

'None of us. That's not a real thing. It's one of the many elaborate fabrications used as plot devices in stories and movies.'

'Huh.' I tap my lip, trying to think of other vampire things that I've read about or seen in movies. 'I'm guessing this means you don't have a lair either, and that you don't sleep hanging upside down? Is this what you really look like? Are you taking a human form, but you actually look like something out of a horror movie? Do you even sleep?' I wave a hand around in the air. 'Wait. Don't answer those questions. First, I need to see you do something that proves you are what you say you are.' Unless I have tangible proof, none of his answers will matter.

'Well, to be fair, I have done things that should prove to you that I am what I said I am.' Godric gives me a patient smile. 'So, you'll have to tell me what exactly I can do to prove to you that I'm a vampire.'

'Were you drinking blood out of a bag when I walked in here?'

He's silent for a moment before he nods. He seems almost embarrassed.

I have questions about that, but I still need additional

159

proof first. 'Maybe you should drink mine, then.' As soon as the words are out of my mouth I regret them. In part because of the way Godric's eyes darken and all the hairs on the back of my neck stand on end. 'Wait. No. I take that back.' I hold out a hand, keeping him from coming any closer. 'What about fangs? Don't you have fangs? Show them to me.'

'Fangs are another myth.' Godric runs his tongue along his teeth, and I track the movement.

I try to suppress a full-body shudder, but I'm unsuccessful. Also, for reasons I can't fathom, other parts seem to find this exciting rather than scary.

And then I think about what it's been like with Godric when we make out. How every time he kissed my neck and lingered along the column of my throat, I'd grab his hair and tug hard and ask him to bite me. He would always chuckle, and it was always a dark sound that made me break out in a wave of goosebumps. Then he would drag his teeth gently across my skin and tell me, in that same dark, throaty voice that I did not want him to bite me.

'Oh God.' I skim my throat with my fingers, and then I clasp my hands, because drawing attention to my neck probably isn't a good idea. 'If you're a vampire then doesn't that make me your dinner? Is this you playing with your food before you eat it?' The panic is back. I do a log-roll off the side of the bed and end up in a heap on the floor. I pop to my feet. Godric is still sitting on the edge of the bed.

'You're not a meal, Hazy. And I don't play with my food.' Godric runs his hands up and down his thighs again.

'But you're a vampire. And vampires drink blood. Oh

fuck. You're always telling me I smell delicious! And it's because you want to do more than eat my pussy, isn't it?'

Godric clears his throat, his voice still soft, but that gruffness is there, too. 'Traditionally speaking, vampires usually drink blood to survive.'

Godric follows me with his gaze as I move around the bed. I glance between him and the door. There's a lot of space to cover. I don't know how quickly I can run across the room. I also don't know if super-speed and strength is a real thing, or just part of the Hollywood myth around vampires. I guess I'm about to find out.

I start running, but my feet are apparently useless, because I trip when I reach the halfway point. But I never hit the ground. Because Godric's arms circle my waist, and he sets me back on my feet.

He releases me right away, though, and steps back. But when my legs threaten to give out again, he gathers me in his arms and carries me over to the window seat. He backs off, giving me space and a clear path to the door.

'You said you weren't going to leave.' Now he sounds sad.

'Well, Godric, that was before you told me that you were a vampire. And I'm not sure if you're crazy or if I'm crazy. But this is a lot. I mean logically, if you were a regular person, I guess you would not be able to cross the room in one blink, would you? But then is super-speed an actual thing for vampires? Maybe you're just a superhero. That would make sense.' I honestly still wonder if I'm on drugs. Maybe this is one big hallucination.

'Why would I tell you that I'm a vampire if I'm a super-hero? A superhero at least has redeeming qualities, like being a saver of lives. Vampires are often feared by many, unless it's in those romance books, in which case women fall in love with the idea of them.' He seems annoyed by this.

'Okay, for argument's sake, let's say that you are a vampire.'

'I am a vampire.' He purses his lips.

'This is what you keep telling me.' I raise a hand when he opens his mouth to interrupt. 'And sure, you are definitely fast. Unnaturally so. Up until now, that's the only thing about you that isn't normal. And the whole drinking a bag of blood. But that could be explained by Renfield's Syndrome. Especially since everything else about the package in front of me appears very much human. And you're telling me that all the things I traditionally believe about vampires are inaccurate. That makes it exceedingly hard for you to prove with any kind of definitiveness that you are a vampire. And you said that, traditionally, vampires drink blood, but you also said that I'm not a meal. Those things contradict each other. Because if vampires *do* drink blood then that also makes me a meal. Unless I'm missing something.' I cross my legs, pleased that something logical has come out of my mouth. I'm a science nerd. Logic makes sense. Vampires do not make logical sense.

'You have a point,' Godric concedes. 'Most vampires consume human blood. However, not all vampires consume it directly from the source. Some of us choose more humane methods of obtaining our nutritional requirements.' His gaze moves over me on a hot sweep that would normally make my lady parts zing, but currently that zing is intertwined with real nerves. 'But me telling you this is pointless if you don't believe what I'm saying is true.'

Godric tucks a hand in his pocket and leans against the wall. So casual. 'Before I answer more questions that make me seem unbalanced, we should find a way to prove that I am, in fact, what I say I am, would you agree?'

This is logical. 'And how do you propose to do that?'

He's quiet for a moment. 'I could show you how my teeth work.'

'Not a fucking chance in hell.' I push to a stand. My legs aren't all that steady but I'm not going to turn myself into his next snack.

He holds up a hand. 'I didn't mean on you, Hazy. I meant on myself.'

'Oh.' I sit back down. 'You're going to bite yourself?'

'Seems like a reasonable option, and like it might help get us closer to you believing me.'

He's right to appeal to my logical side. And honestly, I need him to do something other than move at superhuman speed. Although, if I allow myself to process that fact, I should be closer to believing him. But it isn't every day your boyfriend tells you he's a vampire.

'Okay. Go ahead and bite yourself.' I make a *go on* motion. On the outside I think I look pretty calm, but inside I'm still freaking out.

Godric pushes off the wall but doesn't come any closer. 'Is it okay if I sit beside you?'

'I guess.' I scoot until my back hits the wall. The proximity will allow me to better see what's happening.

'Thank you. I know being this close is making you nervous.' Godric looks saddened by this as he drops down on the plush cushion.

And he moves at a pace that is inhumanly fast, proving

yet again that he is not like most humans. He rolls up his sleeve, faster than should be possible.

His gaze lifts to mine as he raises his arms and drops his head. When his lips are an inch from his arm he asks, 'Are you ready?'

'As I'll ever be.' I don't know how true this is, but if he bites himself and nothing happens then I know he's unfortunately a pretty guy with problems. If something does happen . . . well, I have no idea what I'll do then. Other than probably freak out some more.

His lips pull back, almost in a snarl, and his tongue strokes across his forearm. And then I watch as his teeth sink into the skin. The most visceral, discomfiting part is that I can *hear* it breaking. The sudden wave of nausea is unexpected. I've cut open plenty of animal cadavers, but watching my boyfriend's teeth cut through his skin is a serious mindfuck. Yet I can't drag my eyes away from the sight as blood wells around his lips and trickles down his forearm.

'Oh God.' My voice sounds tinny and far away. 'Maybe you should stop that. Oh my God.' My brain is having trouble processing what I'm seeing.

Godric releases his skin from his teeth. It's a macabre sight, his tongue sweeping out to clear away the blood coating his lips. There's a thin trail making its way down his chin.

I don't know why I reach out and try to wipe it away with my thumb, but his nostrils flare and a sound bubbles up from his chest. It's the same noise he makes when his face is between my thighs. 'Don't do that. It's not safe.' He swipes his chin with his sleeve.

My gaze darts back to his arm, where blood continues to well and drip down his forearm. He swipes over the open wound with his tongue, clearing away most of the blood, revealing the outline of his teeth in the broken skin. And then he starts to heal. Rapidly. Right before my eyes, I watch the wound knit itself closed. And within thirty seconds, it becomes a scar. Less than a minute later, the scar disappears, leaving behind nothing but smooth skin.

I pass out again.

16

This time when I rouse, I'm slightly less freaked out. Well, that might be inaccurate, but I'm not high-level panicking anymore. I'm sprawled over the window seat, with Godric leaning over me. His brow is furrowed with concern, which is understandable since this is the second time I've fainted this evening. I take in his stunning face, which is perfect, apart from a streak of blood under his chin. The only remaining evidence that he bit his own forearm.

Human teeth could not pierce the skin that easily. And there is no way a wound could heal in under a minute. 'So . . .' I lick my lips; my mouth is dry. Which happens when I get anxious, and this takes the cake for anxiety-inducing revelations. 'My boyfriend is a vampire.' I try that phrase on for size. It seems to fit.

'You still want me to be your boyfriend?' Godric's eyebrows rise and his expression shifts from worry to hopeful.

'That is a good question.' Do I want a vampire for a boyfriend? I'm not sure. This requires some careful consideration. I pull myself back into a sitting position. 'I could use a drink.' I'm exceptionally parched.

'What do you need? I can get you anything you want. Would you like wine, or water, or maybe something with sugar in it? That's a thing for humans. When your blood pressure is low, you need sugar. Maybe that's why you keep passing out. Because your blood sugar levels are low.'

'My body is freaking out because you're telling me you're a goddamn vampire, and coming to terms with that is a bit of a struggle.'

'Let me get you something to drink. I'll be right back.' Godric is across the room before I can even reach out to stop him.

'Wait!' I call to the empty, open doorway. 'Don't go anywhere. I'm pretty sure you must have some chocolate in here somewhere.' He is a chocolate fanatic, so that would absolutely make sense. I have an emergency stash of gummy worms in my nightstand because they're my favorite.

He appears in the doorway again, wearing an apologetic smile. 'I don't keep human food in my room because it's an indulgence, not necessary for survival.'

'I'll get a glass of water.' I stand but I'm woozy, and my legs aren't up to the task of supporting me, so I sit back down. 'You can get me a glass of water.'

What would normally take an average human at least a minute or two, takes Godric all of three seconds. It's discombobulating to watch him blur around the room. I wonder if this is his normal speed most of the time.

Godric sits at the other end of the window seat and hands me the glass. I take several small sips, and then guzzle the entire thing in three long swallows. It helps a little.

'Do you need more? I can get you more.'

I hold up a hand before he can take the glass from me. 'No. And can you stop with the super-speed stuff, please? Or maybe that's your natural state, and the way you move around humans feels a lot like asking a cheetah to be a snail? But my head is already spinning, so if you could put it in snail mode while I'm in *what is going on?* mode, that would be awesome.'

'I'm sorry. I'm anxious, which makes it harder to maintain my human facade.' His expression is all apology.

I blow out a breath. This is a lot. 'You're a vampire.'

'Yes.' He nods once.

'My boyfriend is a vampire.' If I say it enough out loud, maybe I'll believe it. 'What does that mean, exactly?'

'What does it mean?' Godric echoes.

'Yeah. You look like a human, you act like a human, you blend in with humans when you aren't busy blurring around like a bad acid trip. Why are you trying to blend in with humans? Why are you dating me in the first place? Aren't there vampire ladies out there who would be a more . . . natural fit?'

'My brothers and I are on a . . . sabbatical.'

'Sabbatical?' My echo-y-ness is irksome.

'We take a few years to go back to school to update our education, immerse ourselves in humanity, so we don't lose touch with it.'

'Dating me is an experiment in human relationships?' I cock an eyebrow.

His eyes widen. 'No! You're not an experiment in anything, Hazy. I enjoy you. Everything about you. I find you endlessly fascinating.'

'Why?'

'Why?'

At least I'm not the only one being an echo. 'Yeah. Why do you find me endlessly fascinating?'

'You're not like the other humans.'

'I'm a weirdo, even by human standards?' I cross my arms.

'No. You're not a weirdo. I mean, you're quirky, but everyone can be eccentric in their own way. You're smart, and funny and sexy, and your views on life and relationships are refreshing and you're incredibly fun when you're naked.' His gaze darkens and his eyes dip to my cleavage.

I uncross my arms because their position only draws more attention to my rack. 'Do not give me that look right now.'

He drops his gaze to his lap. 'Sorry.'

'So I'm smart, funny, sexy and you like getting naked with me. That could literally be anyone's dating profile.'

'I have met countless humans over the span of my existence and no one has ever drawn me in the way you do. When I'm not with you, I'm thinking about you. From the moment I laid eyes on you I felt compelled to be near you. To know you. I've never experienced that kind of longing before and the more time I spend with you, the more that feeling grows.'

I nod, processing, absorbing. 'We've been dating for almost two months, why keep me in the dark? Unless there's danger in me knowing the truth.'

He drums on his knee. 'There's no . . . danger, per se.'

'You don't sound all that sure.'

'We don't broadcast what we are. Our plan is to blend in with humanity.'

'This is really fucked up, Godric.'

'Can you elaborate, please, so I can understand where your head is? I want to calm your anxiety however I can.'

'My anxiety?'

He makes a sound, but eventually opens his mouth and words come out. 'Your heart rate is elevated, and you keep wringing your hands, which are clammy, and based on the way you keep swallowing compulsively, your mouth is dry.'

'How do you know my heart rate is elevated?'

'There's a vein in your neck and I can see that the blood is pumping faster than usual. Typically, this only happens when we're . . .' His gaze drops and he turns his head to the side, clearing his throat. 'I'm sure you don't need me to elaborate.' His gaze returns to mine and his voice drops to a barely audible whisper. 'I can also hear it.'

'Excuse me.' I do some more blinking.

'I can hear your heartbeat. It's rather soothing.'

'Like all the time?'

'Not all the time. Just when we're in the same room. Down at the party it's more difficult because of all the noise and the music, but I'm pretty good at picking you out in a crowd. You have a slight murmur. Nothing to worry about, but it changes the rhythm.'

I open my mouth, close it, open it again. I was born with a heart murmur. The kind that requires me to take special medication if I ever have to be put under for surgery. It's sort of like an echo in my heart. 'That's . . . isn't that annoying?' Does that mean when he's in a room full of people he can hear every heartbeat individually? I'd think that would be highly distracting. 'Wait, if you can hear my heart beating does that also mean you can hear my stomach gurgling?'

'I tune out unnecessary noise.'

I leave that alone. Stomach noises are not the most pressing issue. 'Okay, back to the whole you blending in with humanity. Obviously, you knew at some point I would find out what the deal was. I mean, next week we're doing

DNA tests in our lab. That's going to come back all funky, isn't it? If you're a vampire and you live solely on blood, your DNA must differ significantly from mine.'

'I had a plan for that.'

'How long did you plan to keep the fact that I'm your typical Friday night dinner a secret?'

'I don't feed on humans. And I wasn't sure how long we would end up dating, so I hadn't devised a timeline. But I wasn't going to keep you in the dark forever if we dated long term.'

'Long term.' I'm back to echoing again. 'What qualifies as long term to you?'

'My long term and your long term differ significantly.' He goes back to tapping on his knee.

Looks like I'm not the only one who's anxious. 'Care to elaborate?'

'I didn't expect my feelings for you to grow as quickly as they have.'

'That's not an actual answer.' I will my heart not to get all pitter-pattery about that revelation.

'That pleases you, though.' He bites his lip and has the audacity to look boyishly handsome while doing it. 'That my feelings for you have depth.'

'Are you making this deduction based on the things you can see and hear that us normal humans can't?' Of course, it pleases me that my boyfriend is admitting he has feelings for me. And if I'm honest with myself – and I'm not sure I want to be – having a vampire tell me he's hot for me is kind of an ego boost.

'I'm reading your body.' His expression is intense, and his eyes are doing that glinting thing.

It makes my stomach and other parts clench. 'Okay.' I raise my hand so it blocks my view of his face. 'That's super unfair. You basically have a social cue superpower. Does that mean that you knew I was attracted to you before you even started talking to me? Like you read those signs and figured I was a sure thing for a date?'

Godric props his elbows on his knees and leans in, resting his chin on his steepled pointer fingers. 'Being able to sense attraction isn't the same as being able to predict the outcome of asking someone on a date. While I had a certain awareness of your attraction to me, based on the physical signs, there was always a chance that you would have turned me down. Truthfully, the probability that you would say no was significantly higher than you saying yes to spending time with me.'

'Have you been reading *Cosmo* while you've been standing in line at the grocery store?'

A hint of a smile appears in the corner of his mouth. 'No. Those magazines are designed to make women question themselves and their inherent ability to attract a mate. The preening is unnecessary. As are the games. But humans seem to need that kind of entertainment when it comes to finding a partner.' His gaze roams over my face. 'Most humans admire my kind from a distance. They acknowledge that I am physically appealing.'

'Check your ego, Godric,' I mutter.

'There's scientific evidence that we give preference to attractiveness and that humanity equates it with goodness. Look at children's movies prior to the twenty-first century. The villains are always hideous, misshapen creatures meant to be off-putting, but the heroes and heroines are physically appealing. In the real world that's inaccurate. If we measured all of humanity by standards of attractiveness, then only the most beautiful people would have the most power, but this does not hold true. It's true, however, that it's easier for physically attractive humans to get what they want, at least to a certain extent. Although, in the past few decades there's been a shift in how beauty is perceived. A prime example lies with some of the most notorious serial killers. They're wolves hiding in sheep's clothing. Their attractiveness provides a false sense of safety.'

'Are you comparing yourself to the serial killers of this world?' That's highly unnerving, although I can see his point. Would some of these violent, vicious predators have gotten away with the things they did if we as a species weren't conditioned to believe that beauty and goodness were intrinsically connected?

'There's evil in every species. Humans have murderers, serial killers and psychopaths who don't value their own species, let alone others. The vampire world isn't any different. We have good and evil. We have those who believe that because we're at the top of the food chain, everyone and everything else is expendable.'

'But you're not one of those?' I swallow past a lump in my throat.

'No. I don't fall into that category. Part of the reason I'm here at all is so I can retain my humanity. It doesn't matter where we fall on the food chain, every species has value and purpose. I spend time with *you* because you make me feel things I haven't felt in a very long time, if ever.'

I want to ask how long, but I have a feeling the answer might be more than I can handle tonight. I let my eyes roam over his face. He's so damn pretty. And potentially lethal. 'I should be afraid of you.'

'And yet, you're not.' His eyes are soft, and his expression is full of awe. 'Although there are times when your body tries to tell you to be, for whatever reason, our attraction to each other outweighs your basic instinct for self-preservation.'

'Are you saying my danger button is broken?'

This earns me another smile. 'Not broken, it's just triggered by different things. And I tend not to be one of them, for the most part. Not in the traditional human sense anyway.'

I blow out a breath. 'This is a lot to take in.'

He nods. 'I imagine it is.'

'You said you don't feed on humans, but you need blood to survive. How does that work, exactly?' The science nerd in me is all over this.

'My family developed a blood pill. It's not perfect, but it provides the key nutritional components so we're able to survive and thrive adequately.'

'A pill? How does it work? That must have been revolutionary for your species.'

'Mm. It has been.' Godric's eyes light up. Which makes sense, since he's a science nerd like I am. 'Sometimes we need to disappear from society for a while, particularly when humans do things to put their species at risk. And when that happens, food sources become limited. That was what inspired my family to try to find another way to feed, but more than that, my uncle was particularly passionate about the importance of co-existing with humans. As a species we're considered a parasitic host. The relationship between human and vampire is not symbiotic. We take

and give nothing in return, and some of my kind enjoy –'
He purses his lips. 'Anyway, we had hoped to be able to
integrate into human society eventually, without deception.
We knew it would take generations to accomplish, but it's
a utopian concept, and there are those of us who continue
to believe that humans are to us as chickens are to you.'

'A food source,' I finish. 'But they also make good pets.
They're incredibly affectionate.'

He makes a noise and a look crosses his face that I don't
want to read too much into.

I decide to concentrate on the scientific side. Talking
about the logistics of his feeding is preferable to focusing on the fact that the gallon-plus of life source running
through my veins functions as his basic dietary requirement. That he takes a pill instead of feeding on humans
tells me so much about him as a . . . vampire. That he values
humanity. 'How effective are the pills?'

'They make co-existing with humans manageable. The
best comparison would be a gluten-free diet. The option
is usually available, but the gluten-free alternative doesn't
quite live up to its fresh gluten-filled counterpart.'

My hand flutters up to my throat, but I quickly drop it
to my lap. I have so many more questions. And I'm kind of
in awe of Godric's self-control. 'That makes sense.' Over
the years, I've had a few friends who have gone gluten-
free, and while there are some awesome options out there,
including a brownie that's to die for – not literally – at one
of the local cafes, nothing really beats gluten-filled bread,
fresh from the bakery. 'How often do you have to take the
pills? Was my diabetic comparison accurate?'

'How often I need to take a pill depends on how much

contact I have with humans. Prior to coming to Burnham, I hadn't been in direct contact with humans for a long time. Low exposure meant I didn't need the pills as much. At the beginning I wanted to see how long I could go between pills, which is part of the reason I struggled to be around you, and why Laz was . . . acting the way he was.'

'What happens if you're around humans and you don't take your pill?'

'I guess the best comparison I can make is when you're on a diet and someone takes you to a bakery full of your favorite treats. Temptation can be difficult to resist – at first anyway.' Godric runs a hand through his hair, and his eyes drop to my throat, but quickly spring back up to my face. 'When I started spending more time with you, I realized that I needed to manage my situation more carefully. And I need to supplement.'

'Supplement, what does that mean?'

'The blood pills weren't cutting it.'

'Does that mean you needed real, human blood?' My swallow is audible to myself, so I can only imagine how loud it is for Godric with his extra-awesome hearing.

'It does.' He tips his head fractionally.

'And how did you get that human blood?' My stomach churns at the thought of Godric feeding on a human.

'The blood bank,' he says softly.

'Is that what you were doing when I came up here? Supplementing with a blood bag?'

He nods. 'I thought you might stay over, so I was being proactive.'

'Right. Okay. That makes sense.' The green monster inside me calms the hell down.

His lips curve up slightly. 'This is what makes you different from other humans. Instead of being afraid of my need to feed, you're possessive over it.'

'Well, yeah.' I roll my eyes. 'You're my freaking boyfriend. Vampire or not, I don't want you sucking on anyone else's neck. Oh wow. Geez.' I've been putting the puzzle pieces together but it's taken me until this moment to understand the full picture. I wonder what that says – other than finding out that your boyfriend is a supernatural being is a bit of a trip? 'Of course, this is why you won't bite me when we're making out. Holy shit.' Realization is one hell of a smack in the face. 'Here I am always asking you to use teeth and you're always saying no. I can't fathom how hard it must be not to sink your teeth into my skin when I'm basically begging you to use me as a damn feedbag.'

Godric swallows thickly, his smile wry. 'I value your life and your presence in mine more than I need to slake my hunger. And while I can use teeth without hurting you, I'd rather not play with fire, particularly since you were unaware of my vampirism.'

It's all starting to make sense. 'So that first time we kissed, when Laz showed up and beaned you in the head, is that what happened? Were you playing with fire then?'

'I thought I had myself under control. And I did, but Laz . . . he can be hypervigilant, and he is the least comfortable around humans, which is ironic since he is the most human of the three of us.' He shakes his head. 'But I overestimated my control when it came to you. At least in the beginning.'

'What happened exactly when I nicked my lip . . .?' My tongue darts out to touch the spot. There is no physical evidence of that, only the embarrassment that came with him disappearing into the bathroom.

Godric's gaze darts to mine and away again. 'When Laz threw the pill bottle at me it was a distraction I didn't anticipate. I'd been so wrapped up in you and the way it felt to kiss you, how thoroughly enraptured I was, that I didn't clue into my brother's presence until he hit me with the bottle. He hadn't meant to make contact. I should have realized what was happening, but I was too immersed in sensation, and I lost control. It was just a moment, but it was enough.'

'Lost control how?'

'My guard and my humanity slipped. I guess the best comparison I have is that our teeth are similar to cat claws in that they retract when we're not feeding. It's only when we have the intent to feed that they sharpen to the point where they're able to pierce skin.'

'When he hit you with the pill bottle it startled you and that's how I cut my lip?'

'Exactly. But with practice and exposure, my control with you continues to improve.'

'Is that why we're stalled out at third base? Because of your control issues?'

'I've never had a relationship with a human before. Not an intimate one. Everything with you is new, so I've been cautious.'

'Am I in danger when I'm with you?'

'That depends on who you ask.'

'That's a cryptic answer.'

'I'm very careful with you, Hazy, because you're invaluable and because having you in my life makes me happy, and for the first time in a long time, I feel whole.'

178

'How long is a long time?'

'Your measurement of time and mine isn't the same.'

'That's the second time you've said that. You're avoiding giving me a straight answer.'

'I'd like to give you some time to process what I've already told you before we dive deeper into that particular topic.'

'You said you've never been in a relationship with a human before, does that mean you've had a vampire girlfriend?'

'In the past, yes.'

'Was it long term?'

'Yes.'

'If I ask how long term, will you evade the question?'

'Yes.'

'You'll have to tell me eventually, you do realize that, right?'

'I'm aware. But for tonight, I'd like to put that conversation on hold. She's no longer with us, and it was a long time ago. Discussing her isn't easy.'

'I'm sorry.'

'Loss is part of life.' His eyes search mine. 'Being with you fills my heart in a way that no one else ever has. I know this is a complicated situation, but I'm hopeful that since you're still sitting here, that despite me being a vampire, you might still want me as your boyfriend?'

Logically, this is one heck of a complicated relationship, but my heart is in the driver's seat when it comes to Godric. 'It's gonna take a hell of a lot more than finding out you're a vampire to turn me off of you.'

'That's very good news.'

'I have a couple more important questions.'

'Fire away.'

'So far, I know you have super-speed, and you can hear things better than most people. I mean humans. Maybe your hearing is sort of like dog hearing?' I make a face. 'That's probably a bad comparison.'

He gives me a patient smile. 'It's not inaccurate. All my senses are more developed: sight, hearing, smell, touch.' His eyes darken. 'Especially taste.'

'That's uh . . . good to know.' The flush in my cheeks is impossible to control, so I ignore it. 'If all of your senses are more developed, does that also mean that you're stronger?' It seems to be a reasonable conclusion to come to. Most guys would not lift me up with the same ease and proficiency that Godric does. And that's not me being unkind to myself, that's just the law of physics.

'I am, yeah.'

'So could you lift a car over your head and throw it, like the Hulk?'

'That would be dramatic, but possible.'

Godric gets up and retrieves a pencil from his backpack; he moves faster than a human would, but not as fast as he moved when he was getting me water. Within seconds he's seated beside me again, and I don't miss the fact that he's edged closer. He holds the pencil between his index finger and thumb and it snaps in two. He grabs the pieces before they fall to the floor and shows me the broken pencil in his palm before he makes a fist. When he uncurls his fingers the pencil is no more.

'I don't know if the demonstration was necessary, but I get the point. You're exceptionally strong.'

That my boyfriend can turn a pencil into a pile of dust by making a fist should unnerve me. But instead of making me want to run, all I want to do is climb into his lap and make out with him. I cross one leg over the other and clasp my hands around my knee to keep from fidgeting. Or jumping him. I clear my throat.

Godric smiles.

I ignore the heated look on his face. 'Is it hard to moderate? Your strength I mean? Isn't that a challenge?'

'Initially it took some time and skill to learn how much pressure is appropriate. In my early days I destroyed several outfits, because I would put holes in them just by trying to put them on. But I've long since honed that skill.'

'By that same logic, when you touch me, you're basically being the gentlest you can?'

'It's about moderating pressure. You do it all the time. When you pick something up that's fragile, like an egg, you're more careful with it than you are when you pick up something more durable, or heavy, like a rock or something made of metal,' he explains.

'And me? Where do I sit on the fragile scale?' I hope I'm not like an egg, because the idea of cracking like one is highly unappealing.

'You're not fragile, Hazy, you're precious. There's nothing in this world that I want more than you. And when I touch you, all I want is to make you feel as good as touching you makes me feel.'

'Well, you're pretty damn good at touching me.'

He smirks. 'It's nice to hear you say that.'

'But I guess you already know that, don't you? Since you can probably read my body better than I can.'

'It's not so much that I can read you better. It's that I'm in tune with the subtle nuances. Like now, your breathing has changed, it's a tad shallower than usual, which happens when you're nervous, but also when you're turned on. And your heart rate has sped up. There are many reasons for that, but the warmth in your cheeks is another subtle indication that you're thinking about the ways I touch you and how it makes you feel. My ability to read you in ways that human males can't, gives me a distinct advantage. And maybe an unfair one.'

This explains how he always seems to know exactly what to do with his hands and his mouth and his exceptionally talented tongue. Before I can even think to ask for more pressure, he gives it. I never have to tell him what I need. He's always two steps ahead, providing pleasure without exception. While a regular guy would fumble around, and figure out what, and how, and why, Godric just knows.

'There are some serious advantages to having a vampire as a boyfriend,' I admit.

'I'm glad you feel that way. I would be lying if I said that I wasn't worried about how you'd react. I'm sure that you'll have more questions, and I'll do my best to answer them.' He clasps his hands in his lap, then unclasps them, as though he's unsure. He's even sexy when he's nervous.

'Not gonna lie, I'll probably have a list. Now I have one more important question.'

He nods solemnly. 'Go ahead.'

'Have we been stalled out at third base because you're worried about losing control?'

He rubs the back of his neck and gives me a sheepish

grin. 'The short answer to that is yes. The long answer is slightly more complicated.'

'Obviously, I want the long answer.'

'I'm aware that your generation of humans doesn't necessarily experience physical intimacy in the same way as the generations before yours.'

'You mean how people my age are all down to fuck, screw the feelings?'

Godric blushes. And it is freaking adorable. 'That's part of it.'

'And you're a feelings kind of guy. Is this an *all vampires* thing, or a *just you* thing?'

'Most vampires mate for life. But again, there are always anomalies, just like there are in humans. Some of my kind have adopted different schools of thinking, but, uh, I didn't want to take our relationship to the next level, not with this thing between us.'

'Ah, got it. Now that I know you're a vampire and I'm cool with it, we can have sex?'

'Connecting with you in that way will have implications.'

'Are you purposely avoiding the word "sex"?' I ask.

'I'm trying to explain how the vampire connection and the human connection differ.'

'Is there a chance you could pulverize the headboard while we're boning?' Now I'm kind of being a jerk.

'We will not ever *bone*.' He says it like it's the dirtiest of dirty words.

I move in closer and straddle his hips. His expression is deliciously dark.

Dangerously dark, even. It's my new favorite.

'Yes, we absolutely will. We will have sex, we will *bone* and sometimes we will fuck like animals, because that's what we are. Well, that's what I am, and you're a supernatural being. But other times, when you're all up in your feels, we'll make sweet, sweet love, probably to terrible cheesy music circa the nineties, or whatever your favorite decade was.' I run my fingers through his hair. 'And you will love doing all of those things with me, and I will especially enjoy a good fucking, because I'm a woman who is in tune with my sexuality and my boyfriend is a hot-as-fuck vampire.'

17

I lean in to kiss him, but he cups my face between his palms and stops me when I'm within half an inch of his luscious lips. I pucker mine as much as I can but I'm still an eighth of an inch shy. 'Kiss me.'

One corner of his mouth tips up. 'You're a very demanding little human.'

'And you're being a very frustrating vampire. I just want to make out with you. You were telling me all about the ways in which you're a superior lover and now I'm all amped up and you're not helping a girl out.' I pout and shimmy forward on his lap, trying to get my crotch to make contact with his.

Of course, because I now know that he's infinitely stronger and faster than me, he decides to show off. One second I'm wriggling around in his lap, trying to get him to kiss me, and the next I'm laid out on his glorious bed, my wrists shackled by one of his hands and stretched above my head. He hovers over me, his weight braced on his free arm.

His eyes glint with mirth and for a second I get a glimpse of the supernatural being behind the human facade. My heart skips a few beats, then starts to sprint. I try to wrap my legs around his waist, but I quickly realize that only one of his thighs is between mine. The other rests against the outside of my right thigh. He lowers his hips and I feel his erection against my stomach. I bet he could do push-ups for hours and never get tired.

But at least there's friction where I need it. Even if it's just a thigh, I'll take it. I wrap my left leg around the one between mine and start grinding. My whole body is on fire with need.

'What am I going to do with you?' His words hold that same dark lilt as his gaze and his nose skims my cheek.

'You're going to fuck me and we're both going to love it.'

'That's quite a naughty mouth you have.' His lips brush over mine but when I tip my chin up for more he pulls away.

'Maybe you should fill it with your cock,' I suggest sweetly.

The sound that comes out of him sends a wave of goosebumps rushing over my skin and the hairs on my neck and arms stand on end. And it all finally clicks. The way my body reacts to him isn't just lust, but also fear. I should want to run, but all I want is more.

And then his mouth is covering mine, tongue pushing past my lips. He releases my wrists and I immediately shove them into his hair. I don't worry about how hard I'm gripping because he's a damn vampire. I wonder if my hair-pulling is more like a tickle. I'll ask when my mouth isn't full of his tongue.

Like always, he tastes sweet, and that driving need to have more of him, for him to touch me, lick me, fuck me, builds until I'm mindless with want and then the wave of calm follows. The desire is still there, still very present and alive, but I'm no longer in the rush I was a moment ago.

Godric breaks the kiss and gazes down at me, eyes full

of the same lust I'm feeling. 'That's better. Now I can take my time with you.'

'What did you just do to me?' I run my fingers lazily through his hair.

'I didn't *do* anything per se.' He kisses a path along the edge of my jaw.

My breath catches when his lips reach the hollow of my ear, then skim the column of my throat.

'Your scent has changed,' he murmurs against my skin. 'Are you frightened?'

'I'm . . . aware in a way I wasn't before.'

He lifts his head and meets my gaze.

'Is this hard for you?' I ask. 'Being this close to me? Isn't it like putting a piece of your favorite cake in front of you and not being able to take a bite. Literally?'

'I don't see you as a food source, Hazy. You are my ma— my girlfriend. I revere you above all others.'

'That sounds pretty serious.'

'Mmm. Too real for you?' He arches an enquiring eyebrow.

'I can handle it.' I cup his cheek in my palm and bring his lips back to mine. I suck his bottom lip and use teeth the way he won't. 'Why does your mouth always taste like candy?'

'It's the venom.' He strokes along the seam of my lips, but I clamp mine shut.

He pulls back again, this time his gaze is wary.

'Say what now?'

'Venom, Hazy. It's where the sweetness comes from.'

'Why are you using venom on me?'

'It's not intentional. It's what happens when I'm in the

proximity of human blood. I produce venom and it has analgesic, calming and mildly arousing properties.' He drops his head and sweeps his tongue along my throat. 'Say if I were to bite you here.' His lips caress my skin with each word. 'It would cause you discomfort, especially at first. But the venom eases the sting and when it hits your bloodstream it helps to calm.'

'But also to arouse,' I whisper.

Godric's gaze meets mine. 'That's correct. Typically, it takes much longer to absorb when it's not released directly into the bloodstream, but again, all of this is new for me, so I'm learning like you are. But when we kiss . . .' I let him in when he strokes along the seam. His tongue meets mine and that sweetness floods my mouth, stronger and more potent than before. 'I'm very careful to cut off the supply to avoid influencing your desire, but it does seem to heighten it regardless, even with minute amounts of venom.'

'Is that why I turn into an absolute harlot whenever you kiss me.'

'Mm. It's possible, or that our attraction is just that strong. Now that you know what I am, we can test that theory. But first I'd like to make you come on my tongue.'

'And then your cock?' I'm super hopeful we're going to seal the deal tonight.

'If that's what you'd like, then yes, that's what I'll give you.'

My dress comes off with minimal damage and Godric is out of what remains of his costume – which is a normal outfit that any guy would wear, vampire or not – in a matter of seconds. He keeps his boxer shorts on, though, and leaves me in my bra and panties.

And then the slow torment begins. Godric takes his time, kissing every inch of my skin, purposely avoiding my neediest of spots. He doesn't budge a millimeter when I try to strong-arm his face closer to my lady parts.

'This is really unfair,' I whine.

'Mm. How so?' He starts at the right hip and kisses along the waistband of my panties.

'You're using your super-strength to get your way. There's literally nothing I can do to get you to stop torturing me like this, apart from begging.'

His gaze lifts to mine. He's not even halfway to my navel yet. 'Maybe you should try that, then.'

'Is this how it's going to be? You with the teasing, me with the begging?' I'm not sure I'm all that opposed. It might be worth a try if it speeds this up.

'We'll get there one way or another, won't we?' He kisses the space below my navel.

'Yeah, but you've been at this for –' I glance at the clock on the nightstand and guess – 'at least twenty minutes, and my nipples and my vagina have had zero attention. They're feeling very neglected, and the rest of my body is gloating. You can see how unfair that is, can't you?'

Godric chuckles, and it's the same dark sound that makes goosebumps rise along my skin, and my heart stutter in my chest.

'You know what I think?' Godric's thumb slips under the right leg hole of my panties.

'I'm sure you're excited to share your personal musings with me so you can keep dragging this out,' I grumble.

He grins, and man, does it do things to my body. 'I think you quite enjoy all this teasing.'

He's not wrong, but it's frustrating that he's so damn sure about it. 'What if you're reading my body wrong? What if you think this is making me all excited but it's making me frustrated instead?'

'Hmm. I don't want you frustrated.' His thumbs follow the juncture of my thigh until he's an inch from the promised land.

I groan and hope it sounds less breathy and needy and more annoyed.

He keeps kissing a path to my left hip. And his thumb sweeps back and forth, so close, and yet so damn far away.

I give in and beg. 'Please, Godric. I'm aching for you.' I run my fingers through his hair, but don't try to guide his mouth this time. Instead, I keep pushing his hair back off his forehead. I swear the sound that comes out of him is almost a purr.

'I need you to make me feel good,' I whisper-moan. 'Just, please, Godric.'

There's a faint tearing sound and between one breath and the next I'm panty-less.

'I'll replace those,' he promises, and then his mouth is on me.

'Oh, thank God,' I moan, and fist his hair, rolling my hips with every masterful stroke of his tongue. Wave after wave of pleasure washes over me, taking me higher. I come apart when he adds his fingers, and then come again when he uses suction and grazes my clit with his teeth.

He kisses his way back up my body, just as languorously as before he went down on me. This time he devotes some attention to my nipples before he finally settles between my thighs, his erection nudging against me through his boxer shorts.

'I want you,' I whisper when his lips brush over mine. 'I want you to fill me up. I want to be yours.'

His dark eyes move over my face, the hint of a smile pulling at the corners of his mouth. 'You've been mine since the moment I laid eyes on you, you just didn't know it yet.'

A shiver rushes along my spine and I run my hands down his back, sliding them under the waistband of his boxer shorts, digging my nails into his deliciously firm ass as I tip my hips up. 'Then take me.' I push his boxers down, freeing his erection from the fabric.

His weight lifts for the briefest moment and his boxer shorts appear in my peripheral vision before they land on the floor. When he settles between my thighs again, the head of his erection slides along my most sensitive skin and we both make needy noises.

I desperately want to get to the good stuff, but there are a couple of important questions I should've asked before we got to this point. 'Do you have condoms? Do we need them? I get the shot.'

His thumb skims my cheek, and his eyebrows pull together for a moment, as if these are things he hasn't considered until I voiced them.

'Birth control, I mean. I get the birth control shot. Can you get me pregnant? Or give me . . . things?' Yeah, this would have been an awesome conversation to have before his peen was sliding over my happy parts.

He has the audacity to look amused. 'Yes, I could get you pregnant if the timing was right, but you aren't ovulating, and I can't contract or give human diseases, including sexually transmitted ones.'

I blink twice. 'You can tell I'm not ovulating?' I shake my head. 'Let's leave that alone for now, and the STI conversation is something we're coming back to, when we're not about to get our freak on.'

This time he looks unimpressed. 'We are not getting our freak on, I'm going to make love to you.'

'You can call it whatever you want, as long as you're filling me with your cock.'

His cheek tics.

I run my fingers through his hair. 'Sex is supposed to be fun, Godric, you can make love and get dirty with me at the same time.' I pull his mouth to mine and sigh in contentment when that sweetness hits my tongue.

We make out for a minute, me rolling my hips and Godric bracing his weight on his left arm so he can stroke my cheek and feel my pulse racing – at least this is what I'm assuming, with the way his palm rests against my neck – while the bottom half of his body remains immobile.

That familiar need rises, along with the wash of calm. I wonder what the long-term effects of repeated venom exposure are. Could I become addicted? Will my tolerance increase? Will I stop being affected by it after a while? All questions to ask later, when we're not naked and this close to what I've been impatiently waiting weeks for.

'I need you in me,' I whisper against his lips when desire overwhelms me. 'Please, Godric,' I tack on at the end, dragging out the words on purpose. He seems to be a big fan of please.

'You're impossible to deny.' It's almost an accusation,

but he slides low with the shift of my hips and nudges at my entrance.

He disconnects our lips, pulling back to meet my gaze. 'I need you to let me do this at my speed. No rushing me, Hazy.' It's part warning, part plea.

'No rushing you.' I nod my agreement.

He brushes the end of his nose against mine. 'Let me have control, so I don't lose mine.'

'I'm yours to do with what you will.'

His hips sink into mine and he fills me, inch by delicious inch. I don't dare tear my eyes from his face as he joins us in the most intimate way possible. And when his hips meet mine the sound that leaves him can only be described as a purr.

Every roll of his hips takes me higher, every soft kiss, every groan and growl pushes me closer to the edge and keeps me balanced there, suspended above bliss. And when I finally tip over, I'm submerged in sensation, body shaking with release, every nerve ending on fire.

And Godric keeps going, and going, and going. I lose track of the number of orgasms I have. I lose track of time altogether. I'm mindless, boneless, driven only by desire. Eventually, he warns me that he's close and for a second I worry that the things I've seen in movies aren't grandiose fiction: that his orgasm will be a lethal projectile, that he'll destroy the bed with his final thrust and me along with it. But that's not what happens at all.

His humanity is the thing I see most clearly when he finally comes. His eyes flare and roll up, his mouth goes slack, and he groans my name with that final thrust. And then his weight settles on top of me as his chest presses against mine and he turns his face into my neck. I feel his lips part then, his tongue sweeping along the skin. The gentlest, barest scrape of teeth follows, and for a moment I think maybe he's going to bite me. Instead, he presses his lips to my neck, following a path along the edge of my jaw until he reaches my mouth.

He pulls back so I can see his pretty eyes and face. 'How are you feeling, Hazy?'

'Amazing. You?'

'Like I've just discovered my new favorite pastime.' His mouth tips up. 'And all I want is more.'

18

Godric would happily spend the rest of the night in his bed-room providing me with an unlimited supply of orgasms. The thing I learn very quickly is that vampire stamina is practically limitless. Godric can go all night. And not like a round of sex, followed by some pillow talk, and then another round. He requires zero recovery time between one hard-on and the next. Which is awesome, but also on the right side of exhausting.

'How are vampires not complete hornballs all day, every day?' I ask after orgasm number seven thousand and fifty-three. I'd like to say I'm joking, but the count is unreasonably high.

Godric circles a very sensitive nipple with his fingertip. 'Who said most of us aren't?'

I make a strangled sound and grab his hand, lacing my fingers with his. Every part of my body, from the top of my head to the tips of my toes, is hypersensitive. Godric is the picture of sexy sensuality and I'm a dewy, boneless mess. He never even breaks a sweat, while my skin is gritty with salt. The sheets underneath me are damp, and my ability to string a sentence together isn't the best.

Godric has been wearing the same self-satisfied smile for at least twenty minutes. He's ready to go again, but I need to call a timeout. Every time he touches my most sensitive body parts I moan. Loudly. I'm also parched. And hungry.

'You could live in an endless loop of bliss if you wanted to.' I can't decide if an eternity of orgasms would be a good or a bad thing. I'd get literally nothing done as a vampire. At least not with Godric around.

'The newness of this experience inspires the desire to continue having it on repeat. I feel like that isn't much different for humans and vampires. You say you need a break, but your body responds to my touch anyway. And mine continues to respond to yours. The connection we share is strong, and the more we foster it, the more it will grow. And with you –' he lifts my fingers to his lips and kisses the tip of each one – 'already all I want is more.'

'I feel the same.' Am I tired? Yup. Thirsty? Definitely. Hungry? Uh-huh. But I still get lost in his heated gaze. 'I can see how we could end up never leaving this bed. The biggest difference between humans and vampires is our need for food and water and rest, versus yours.'

'That's an unfortunate side effect of your condition.' Godric's finger traces a path along my collarbone.

'My condition?' I huff a laugh. 'You make it sound like my humanity is an inconvenience.'

'Your humanity is delightful, but it does pose a minor challenge when it comes to satisfying my desire for you.' His grin turns salacious. 'I'll have to learn to temper my needs now that you've awakened them.'

He captures my lips with his. I give in for a minute, sinking into the kiss, enjoying the sweet taste of him on my tongue. But eventually, I put my hand on his chest and push.

Now that I know what he really is, I can appreciate the immediacy with which he ends the kiss and pulls back enough that I can see the questions in his eyes. I'm not strong enough to truly push him, but the pressure of my hand is what makes him act and react.

'Does my human need a break?' His voice is dangerously seductive.

'Your human needs about a gallon of water, and probably a snack. Also –' I thumb over my shoulder at the clock on the nightstand. It's an old-school analog alarm clock, with the two bells on the top. It's the most infuriating alarm clock in the history of the universe, and that's saying something considering Alyssa insists on using that grating *beep-beep-beep* factory sound on hers instead of programming her cell phone with a musical wake-up. 'It's going on midnight, and we've been up here for hours. We should probably make an appearance before the party is over.'

I'd be concerned about the state of the house, but with three vampires on the premises, I'm sure Hunter and Laz – if he's decided to leave the security of his bedroom – have it under control.

'I'd argue the merits of remaining in bed, but your stomach is yelling at us. Let's put some food in you, and make sure your friends are okay before I bring you back up here, and fuck you like you've been begging me to.' Godric's smile is full of dirty promises.

I give him the stink eye. 'Of course you dirty-talk to me now. I am one thousand percent holding you to that when we get back up here. No more of this sweet, sweet love-making nonsense.'

I don't care how tired I am, I will absolutely be jumping on the getting-fucked train as soon as I put some food in this body and get rehydrated.

Godric has apparently given up moving at human speed now that I know what he is. One moment he's lying beside me and the next, he's standing at the end of the bed, fully dressed.

I, on the other hand, logroll my way to the edge, then let my left leg slide over the side until my toes hit the floor before I allow my right leg to follow. The area rug is soft beneath my feet. I settle my palms on the mattress and push away, but only manage to lift my top half a few inches. I don't fully trust that my legs will support the rest of me. I've also been on my back for several hours. Tomorrow it's probably going to feel like I ran a marathon. Tylenol is a safe bet. 'We might want to consider using that bathtub at some point tonight.' I doubt he has Epsom Salts.

'A bubble bath with you would be fun.' Godric's voice deepens. 'This view is also incredibly appealing. I think I'll fuck you like this after you've been properly fed.'

I glance over my shoulder to find him standing behind me, his heated gaze locked on my bare butt. 'I thought you were a boob man.'

'When it comes to you, I'm an everything man.' He steps closer, until his toes touch the back of my heels.

If my stomach wasn't growling like a beast had taken up residence in there, I might skip the trip for food and water. I don't make a move to stand, though. Instead, I arch my back and push my ass out towards him. Which, admittedly, isn't the best idea if my intention is to leave this room. But my hormones are all over the place and I'm already excited again. Godric leans in until his thighs press against the back of mine. He palms my ass, gives it a squeeze and then slides his hands up my back. When he reaches my shoulder blades, he skims my ribs and slides his palms under me, cupping my breasts. And then he lifts me, so the back of my naked body is pressed against the front of his clothed one.

Across the room is his dresser and beside that is a full-length mirror giving me an incredible view of naked me and clothed Godric. His eyes lock on mine in the mirror as he releases my right breast and sweeps my hair over my shoulder. His left hand slides up until his palm rests against my throat and his thumb and fingers curl around the edge of my jaw. He tilts my head to the side, exposing my neck.

I moan as his lips ghost the skin until he reaches the hollow behind my ear. 'I need you to get dressed, my love, or we won't make it downstairs before this party ends.'

'We could delay going to the party for, like, half an hour?' I suggest.

'Half an hour won't be enough time to appease my need for you. And I worry, based on the way your body is protesting, that your stomach will soon be growling louder than I do. But I do appreciate how much our desires match.'

Godric kisses my neck and then spins me around. He lifts me, sitting me on the edge of the bed. He zips around the room, and a moment later kneels in front of me, helping me back into my clothes.

Once I'm dressed, minus the panties that no longer exist, I hop off the bed and follow Godric across the room. He's about to turn the doorknob when I put a hand on his arm. I might squeeze because he has nice forearms. 'Wait.'

He glances at my hand and then at me, his smile wry and too cocky for his own good and mine. 'Hazy, my love,

I will happily take care of you as soon as you are fed, but I cannot provide any more orgasms until your blood sugar has returned to normal.'

I roll my eyes. 'I'm hot for you, but I know what my limits are.' Although less than five minutes ago I was ready to forfeit food. My stomach is screaming at me, and I'm light-headed, which I'm sure he's picked up on. Food over fucking for now.

'I'm glad we're on the same page about the importance of you remaining healthy and alive. What are we waiting for, then? Do you have concerns?'

'Not so much concerns, but I do have a couple of important questions.'

He drops his hand from the doorknob and turns to face me. 'I'll do my best to answer them.'

'So the girls are going to know that we boned.' He makes a face and I rush to correct myself, even though I think it's funny that he finds the word 'boning' so offensive. 'I mean, had sex, or as you prefer, made sweet, sweet love.' His eyes narrow and I bite back a smile. 'I have a super shitty poker face. I've never won at cards with either of my roommates because my emotional state is literally written on my face. And when I get my bone on, it's pretty damn obvious.' This time I ignore his irritation even though it makes me all zingy inside. 'Plus, we were gone for hours, so they'll know.'

'There wasn't a question in there, Hazy,' Godric says after I fail to elaborate.

'Right. Okay. Yes. That was me prefacing the questions with some facts about myself and my friends. I guess what I'm saying is that I hope you're okay with them knowing we've done the dirty deed. But my question isn't about that, it's about what I can or can't tell them outside of the stellar sexing. Or is you being a vampire a secret that I'm supposed to keep indefinitely? Also, if you're a vampire I'm assuming that also means your brothers are vampires, or at the very least Laz is one, considering he seems to be able to do the whole moving fast thing, too.' We clearly have a lot to talk about, eventually, after I eat food and hydrate.

'You're right, both of my brothers are also vampires. Laz's situation is different than mine and Hunter's, but for simplicity's sake we'll just call him a vampire.'

Now I have a ton of other questions, but again those will have to wait.

Godric taps his lips. 'With respect to the secrecy issue, as I've said before, we try our best to blend in with humans outside of our home; and usually when there's a threat of being uncovered, we tend to move on.'

'So I shouldn't tell them?' I fight with my hands not to wring themselves.

'This situation is . . . unprecedented, but it would be preferable to keep this between us. The fewer people who know, the better. I'm sorry if that puts you in a difficult position with your roommates.'

'I get it, though, why you want to maintain your privacy and secrecy.' I can't imagine how challenging it must've been for Godric to hide his vampirism behind a human facade all this time, afraid to tell me the truth about who and what he is. I consider what it's probably like for Laz, who hides away in his room. It must make for a lonely existence.

'Thanks for understanding. You're incredibly unique, Hazy, and I'm very lucky to have found you.' He cups my cheek in his palm and kisses me, but doesn't make a move to deepen it, which is good because my stomach is a growl factory.

With my questions out of the way, Godric and I head down to the party. I half expect Laz to pop out of his room, but his door remains closed.

We start down the stairs, rounding the corner at the first landing. Blaine is about halfway up, attempting to remove one of the framed photos from the wall.

'What do you think you're doing?' Godric practically growls.

'Fuck! Shit!' Blaine startles and loses his footing.

Much like I did when Laz scared the crap out of me a few hours ago. Unlike that time, Godric does not make a move to stop him from falling. Blaine does a graceless half-spin and grabs the banister, but misses, bangs his head on the railing and lands on his ass, sliding down a few steps.

Godric steps in front of me and descends the stairs, stopping beside the picture Blaine seemed to be most interested in. It's a black and white one of Godric's uncle and brothers from more than half a century ago. Which I now realize is the current Godric, Laz and Hunter, but taken sometime in the last century. Not going to lie, it's a bit trippy.

Godric crosses his arms.

Blaine hops to his feet and cops a nonchalant lean on the railing. Sharpie peens decorate his forehead and cheeks. He must not have looked in a mirror recently. 'I was checking out your wall of photos.'

'And you thought you'd take one off the wall so you could get a better look?' Godric asks dryly.

'Uh. Well, uh . . . I was, uh . . . that guy could be your doppelgänger.' Blaine waves a hand toward the photos.

'The Hawthorn genes are strong.' Godric takes another step down, placing himself in front of the photo Blaine was trying to pry off the wall, and Blaine mirrors the movement, creating space between them. He's not super steady on his feet, though, so he almost misses the step again.

Blaine's gaze bounces from Godric to the wall of photos behind him, and back again.

'Did you miss the Grim Reaper on the way up?' Godric motions to the hooded cut-out with the steadily swinging scythe.

'I needed the bathroom, but the one on the main floor had a line.' He thumbs over his shoulder.

Godric leans over the banister. 'Looks like it's free now.'

'Right, yeah.' Blaine's gaze shifts to me and he does a full-body scan, pausing for longer than is reasonable at my chest, before his eyes lift. They flare when they reach mine. I'm sure that he knows exactly what we've been up to, because Blaine is familiar with my post-orgasm face. It's the same expression I'm wearing in my contact photo on his phone, because he snapped one basically five seconds after I came, back when we were dating. It's a nice pic, if I'm going to be honest.

He props a fist on his hip like an annoyed mother. 'What have you two been up to?'

I'm not sure why he feels the need to ask a question he already knows the answer to, other than he's stalling and doesn't want to go back downstairs.

'Godric was demonstrating his proficiency at giving multiple orgasms.' Apparently, I've decided blunt honesty is the way to go. Also, while I have a feeling Godric isn't one of those guys who does the whole kiss 'n' tell thing, Blaine is probably the one person he wouldn't mind knowing about his skill set.

Blaine's eyes flare again as Godric glances over his shoulder at me, his expression dark but also amused.

'Right. Nice. That's great for you.' Blaine gives us the thumbs up. This time when he steps back, he does miss the stair again and goes tumbling down the rest of the flight. He smashes into the fake Grim Reaper, knocking it over as he lands on the floor in a heap.

He pops to his feet and yells, 'I'm fine! I got this!' Then sprints in the opposite direction of the bathroom.

'I'm not sure he needed that explanation.' Godric's lip twitches.

'I don't think it hurts for him to know that you're far more capable of pleasing me than he ever was. He needs a slice or five of humble pie anyway. I don't like that he was up here snooping around.' Godric and I descend the stairs and he lifts me over the *No Trespassing* sign like I weigh less than a sack of potatoes.

'He's wasted. He won't remember anything tomorrow.' Godric sets the cardboard cut-out of the Grim Reaper back on the stairs. The scythe is bent, so he straightens it.

'The wall of past memories isn't the best,' I whisper.

Godric seems unconcerned about Blaine's obvious attempt at snooping. 'Which is why the Reaper is standing guard. I'll have Laz manage the situation.' I don't know what that means, but my stomach growls and Godric's brow furrows. 'Come on, let's get you fed.'

I follow him to the living room, which is crammed with

people dressed as movie and book characters. A bunch of the guys are dressed as gladiators, which means there are a lot of abs on display. The naughty version of Disney princesses also seems like a popular option. People congregate in groups and spill into the kitchen and down the hallways. One couple has discovered a darkened alcove to make out in. And the backyard is just as full as the rest of the house.

We cut through the swarms of people, and as I've come to expect, people move out of the way for Godric as he passes. It's weird that I don't have the same desire to give him space as other people naturally tend to. As though my fear-of-dangerous-creatures button is faulty.

A couple of guys I recognize from our street pat him on the back and tell him what an awesome party it is. I leave him to socialize and make a beeline for the buffet table. I'm surprised and grateful it's not empty. I grab a plate and fill it with all my favorite things, most of which fit into the carbs category. I pop a mini quiche into my mouth before adding one to my plate.

Godric appears beside me with a glass of water. I finish chewing and chug it. Then hand him the empty glass.

He has another full one in his free hand, so he passes it to me. 'I'll be right back.' He disappears into the crowd again. I presume to refill the glass, since I'm onto chugging the second one.

'Girl. You've been gone for hours.' Alyssa reaches over my shoulder and steals a mini mushroom quiche from my plate. I grab another one and drop it on the mound of food, then pick a few more things I haven't tried yet before I address her.

'I've been busy.' Finding out my boyfriend is a vampire and then having all the sexy times.

Alyssa moves to stand in front of me. Her right eyebrow lifts and then her left. 'Oh my God.' She grabs my shoulders. 'Oh. My. God. You boned! It's written all over your face.'

'"Boned" is literally my least favorite word in the history of the universe.' Godric appears beside me, yet again, with another glass of water.

He plucks the empty one from my hand and passes me the full one.

'My least favorite word in the universe is "moist". Unless you're referring to cake,' Alyssa announces.

'Preach,' I agree.

She pats Godric on the shoulder. 'Also, good work on making my friend a happy girl. You must've really done her right. The only time I've ever seen her eat like this is when she did one of those charity mud runs, and we went out afterwards and gorged on junk food and beer, she hurled, and then passed out for sixteen hours.'

'Those are two very polar opposite experiences, and this one wins by a long shot.' I pop a sausage roll into my mouth. It could probably use some spicy mustard sauce, but it's still delicious. I turn my attention to my boyfriend, who looks like he's fighting a grin of satisfaction. 'I'm good on the water situation for now. You might want to give me and Alyssa a few minutes to chat, unless you want to be irritated by our overuse of the word "boned".'

'I'm going to find Hunter and Laz, then. Message me when you need me.' He tucks a finger under my chin and tips it up, lips briefly touching mine. His heated gaze moves over my face before he turns around and walks away.

I stare at his butt until he's swallowed by the partygoers. I also remind myself that I'll be back in his bedroom soon enough, so chasing after him is pointless. Also, his ego has had enough stroking in the past five minutes and he doesn't need any more accolades regarding his bedroom abilities.

'Where's Satya?' It's probably best if I wait until we find her before I provide any details, otherwise I'll have to repeat myself.

'Last time I saw her she was outside chatting with Hunter, but that was a while ago.' Alyssa plucks an hors d'oeuvre from the buffet and pops it into her mouth.

'Will finding her interfere with your end-of-night plans? Because me chronicling the details of my night can absolutely wait until tomorrow.' I don't want to stand in the way of either of my roommates' happy endings this evening.

Alyssa waves a hand around in the air. 'Nope. I've had three drinks, and the guy I was talking to started to look and sound like he might be a good idea later. But there's a hundred percent chance if I made the decision to go home with him, I'd end up regretting it in the morning. It would be in my best interests to live vicariously through you and hear all about how awesome your night has been instead.'

'Shall we see if we can find Satya, then?' I pop a mini samosa into my mouth. They taste ridiculously good tonight.

'Seems reasonable, and we can make sure she's not on the path to bad choices either.' Alyssa threads her arm through mine and we weave our way through the crowd of partygoers, heading for the kitchen.

'Crap.' Alyssa comes to an abrupt halt when we're half-way across the room, and then starts dragging me in the opposite direction.

'What?'

'Justin is here. And he's wearing something other than Speedos. He actually looks good.'

I glance over my shoulder, scanning the room as Alyssa drags me away from the sliding door to the backyard. I get a glimpse of a guy in a costume who vaguely resembles Justin. He's dressed as the Joker, circa *Suicide Squad*, who happens to be Alyssa's favorite anti-hero.

'Hold the fuck on. Were you flirting with Justin?' We round the corner and step into the hallway that leads to both the front door and the side door, the latter of which also leads to the backyard.

'Maybe. Don't judge me. Some random was talking at me and every time I tried to exit the conversation he would grab my elbow and keep talking. Then Justin came in dressed as the Joker, and you know I have a weak spot for him. He's just so misunderstood.' She waves a hand in the air. 'Anyway, you know what Justin usually does when he sees me.'

'You mean tells you he's in love with you and asks you on a date?' I supply.

'Yeah. He saw me from across the room and headed directly for me, and I fully expected him to pull the same nonsense, but instead he came up and hugged me and asked if I needed saving.

'And I did, so I said yes. Justin went off on this whole tangent about how sorry he was that he was late and could I ever forgive him. Then he thanked the elbow grabber for keeping me entertained, walked me outside, and made sure I was okay. It was so different from the Speedos and Doritos guy I usually see. And then, I started to realize that he's kind of cute, but I can't tell if that's because of the costume he's wearing, or the booze, or the fact that he saved me from that random elbow grabber, or a combination of the three.' Alyssa makes her duck face; it's the look she wears when she's annoyed with herself.

'It's possible that we lumped him in with Blaine's idiocy,' I muse. 'The douchebagness is strongly associated with that house, and Justin is always in freaking Speedos. It makes sense that we would judge him accordingly.' But he's always been nice, despite the questionable wardrobe and his obsession with eating Doritos and sticking his hand down the front of his pants.

'There's too much to unpack there, especially three drinks in. We can come back to this when there's no alcohol in my bloodstream, and the additional factors impacting my ability to think clearly no longer exist.'

Alyssa and I make our way down the hall and pass a couple who are going at it in the corner. We use the side door and pop outside. The temperature has dropped significantly, but it is the end of October in the middle of upstate New York, so that makes sense. The fresh air helps clear my mind.

'Blaine was trying to sneak upstairs, but we caught him when we were coming down to get me some food,' I inform Alyssa.

Alyssa rolls her eyes. 'Was he trying to find a bedroom to hook up in? Why not take his conquest across the street to his own house?'

'Surprisingly, there was no one attached to his arm. Although that might have something to do with the Sharpie peens drawn all over his face.'

'Ah, yes, he was passed out in a lounger for a while. We all know how dangerous that can be. I'm sure Justin has been biding his time, just waiting to get him back for that party in sophomore year.'

'Oh right. I remember that. Anyway, he's been all up in my grill about Godric and his brothers recently.' Up until tonight I brushed it off as Blaine being Blaine, but now that I know Godric has something to hide, it no longer seems like a harmless infatuation. Me knowing is one thing, but Blaine . . . he'll do anything for a story. Unfortunately, I can't tell Alyssa or Satya that.

'They're shiny and new, that's all.' Alyssa pats me on the shoulder reassuringly. 'There she is.' She points to the brightly burning fire in the middle of the yard. It's surrounded by comfy Adirondack chairs with plush cushions. There are a few couples huddled in chairs. Satya is sitting on her own, but there's a group of guys to her right and another to her left. It's clear she's bored, since her focus is on the phone in her hand.

Alyssa brings her fingers to her lips and whistles shrilly. It's what she does when she wants our attention. It works, despite how loud it is out here. Satya bounces out of her chair and scans the backyard. When she spots us, she rushes over.

The moment she lays eyes on me, she raises her hand in the air. 'You and Godric sealed the deal!'

I slap her hand, and she pulls me in for a hug. The jostling causes me to lose one of my sausage rolls on the lawn.

I mourn the loss for a second, but there are more inside if I need them.

'How can you tell?' I ask when she releases me. 'I haven't even said anything.'

'Godric just came to collect Hunter, and the look on his face matches the one you're wearing. Now I need the details. I hope you haven't already filled Alyssa in, because that means she'll have to listen to it all over again.'

'We came to find you first,' Alyssa assures her.

'Good. Give us all the dirty details.'

19

Godric

'Sounds like you've been treating your girl right,' Hunter says as we move through, away from the various groups of people littering our backyard.

'It's bad enough that Laz is beaning me in the head with pill bottles while I'm making out with Hazy, but now you're listening in, too. It's fucking creepy, you know that, right? Not all of us are exhibitionists,' I snap.

It's only a matter of time before Hazy realizes that our private time isn't all that private when we're in my house. The problem with being a vampire, and living with other vampires, is that everybody can hear everything that's happening in the house, no matter where they are. With time and practice we've gotten good at tuning each other out, but when there are a lot of loud and random noises – i.e. moaning, calling out my name on repeat, and using phrases like 'right fucking there', 'oh God', 'that's it' and 'please don't stop' – it's trickier to close our minds off. Still, calling me out on it is juvenile and unnecessary.

'I was doing my best not to listen.'

'Have you seen Laz?' Changing the subject is the best way to go. There's nothing I can do about my brother's exceptional hearing, or his enjoyment over poking fun at my ability to please my girlfriend.

Of the three of us, Hunter is most likely to engage in casual hook-ups. And until now, he was the only one of us who had had sex with a human. His previous human partners were all casual flings, though, unlike my relationship with Hazy. Having him as a sounding board while I've navigated this path has been helpful. No one wants to crush their girlfriend's pelvis when they're in the middle of an orgasm. It's sort of a mood killer. Among other things.

'He came down for five minutes, an hour ago. And then he disappeared again.'

I'm unsurprised by this. Laz isn't a fan of people on a good day, let alone a house full of them. 'Did he say anything to you?'

'About?'

'Hazy.'

Laz hasn't been on board with our relationship. I get it. Truly. We try our best to keep the fact that we aren't human under wraps wherever we go. My dating Hazy has made that challenging, but we were managing fine until tonight.

He'd insisted we all drink a bag of blood because we had a house full of it. He'd also hassled me about how long I planned to continue to date Hazy. He felt that I should consider breaking it off. I felt like he should mind his own goddamn business.

'He told me what happened in your room.'

'Please tell me he was not doing that creepy thing where he projects himself into my personal space while I was getting it on with my girlfriend.'

Occasionally when Laz wants to talk, but he doesn't feel like moving from his favorite chair, he'll do this thing where he projects an image of himself wherever I am. He basically looks like a two-dimensional ghost when he does that. Texting would be the easier, less invasive route, but he's even less enthusiastic about instant messaging than he is about parties.

Hunter holds a hand up. 'Calm down, dude. I don't mean what happened in your room *after*, I mean what happened to inspire the need to reveal to her that you're a vamp.'

'Oh.' That's far less creepy. 'It still means he was listening in, though.'

Hunter glances around and drops his voice. 'I don't think he was intentionally listening, but Hazy was freaking out and she wasn't particularly quiet about it. And you know how sensitive Laz is about being . . . him. We've had to move for far less.'

'We should take this conversation inside.' Hunter follows me through the throng of partygoers to the side door. 'If he hadn't shoved a bag of blood in my face, our secret might still be safe,' I gripe as I open the door.

Hunter gives me a look. 'It was only a matter of time before you spilled the beans. Don't go blaming it on Laz.'

'It could've gone smoother.'

Things might have gone very differently tonight had either of us been paying better attention to what was going on outside my bedroom door. And I'm sure Laz will happily look into his crystal ball and enlighten me with every different version of the future that might've taken place had Hazy not walked in on me drinking a bag of blood and almost fallen down the stairs. Having a vampire-warlock hybrid as a brother can be fantastic, but it can also be a giant pain in the ass.

'Do you trust her?' Hunter asks as we ignore the *No Trespassing* sign.

'Yes.'

'Completely?' We climb the stairs together.

I nod. While I trust Hazy with my secret, I sure as hell don't trust her ex. Blaine is a problem I'd like to solve by draining him dry and incinerating his remains. However, I'm not sure Hazy would take too kindly to me murdering her ex.

I don't bother knocking before I enter Laz's bedroom.

His decor makes it look like something out of a dark fairy tale. He's seated in his favorite wingback chair, a fire crackling in the hearth. He seems to be nursing a fruity drink. Laz has a weakness for pineapple juice. He's not a big drinker, but when he does imbibe, he tends to go for things like pina coladas or dessert-style martinis.

He sets his glass on the table beside him and slow claps. 'So you had relations with a human and didn't kill her.' He doesn't drag his gaze away from the hearth. 'And you also told her the truth. Well done.'

'She thought she was losing her mind.' Which is reasonable. Today the only vampires around are the ones in romance books, teen dramas and horror movies.

'We'll have to move. We can't stay here.' Laz can be over-dramatic on a good day, so it's unsurprising that this is how he starts the conversation. Hunter and I are used to talking him off ledges.

In previous years when we've gone on sabbaticals, if there was even an inkling of someone knowing what or who we were, he would immediately insist on packing up and leaving. Then we would have to reason with him, citing how disappearing without a trace is more suspect than sticking around and smoothing out a few people's memories.

'You're overreacting.' I sip my Scotch. I should have brought my flask along. This is a more-than-one-drink conversation.

'You're being a hormonal fool,' Laz declares. 'You know there are repercussions for getting involved with a human. Hunter has been the reason more than once for us having to pull up our tent pegs. Did you honestly think it would be different for you? As if it's not bad enough that you're pretending to be one of them, now you've gone and compromised us by revealing who and what we are.'

'Hazy isn't going to tell anyone.'

'How long do you anticipate she'll be able to keep our secret?' Laz's eyes flash and he taps on the arm of his chair. Two sparks jump out of the tip and land on the floor, singeing the pitted hardwood.

We stare each other down.

He breaks first, turning his gaze to the fire in the hearth.

'As long as it's necessary,' I say. 'If you weren't so closed off to the idea of me dating her, maybe we would have been able to talk this through before we got to this point – the same way Hunter and I talked through what I should expect when it comes to being with Hazy.'

Laz grits his teeth. He doesn't love being left out. Unfortunately, his unwillingness to immerse himself in humanity makes it impossible to have these kinds of discussions with him. So does the black-cloud-of-doom attitude he has about basically everything, especially love. He would have preferred to stay in Alaska, but he didn't want to be there alone, so he came with us, albeit grudgingly.

'He has a point, Laz,' Hunter says.

'Of course you're on his side. You've been flirting with the humans incessantly.' Laz huffs and sips his drink.

'What's the point of taking this sabbatical if we can't enjoy the benefits of being college students?' Hunter pushes off the wall. He moves across the room and takes the chair opposite Laz. 'Look, man, I know the last few years have been hard on you. I know there was a lot of isolation, and that you're in a more difficult position than either of us. But I think if you're honest with yourself, some of that has been self-imposed. And locking yourself away in your room, avoiding contact with anyone other than me and God, isn't good for you, and it sure isn't good for either of us.'

His jaw tightens, and Laz keeps his gaze fixed on the fire dancing in the hearth. 'I'm sorry for being such a burden.'

This isn't just about my relationship with Hazy. And it's not just about Hunter having an affinity for human women. Laz is an anomaly. He's one of very few hybrid vampires, and one of even fewer hybrid vampire-warlocks. And it's made all the worse by his unwillingness to use his dark magic to cause chaos. Not only is he not accepted by the warlocks, he's also not accepted by the greater vampire population because of the warlock blood that runs through his veins. It's a shitty situation for sure.

I cross the room and take my place in the last wing-back chair. Laz's room is often where we hang out. Mostly because him leaving it is a rare occurrence. Half the time Hunter attends his classes and records them. Hunter and I had hoped that the sabbatical would give Laz the break he needed from feeling like he's always on the outside.

His edgy vibe should work well with some of the misfit humans, but he seems determined to remain in solitude.

'You're not a burden, Laz. But Hunter isn't wrong, you need to get out more. Socialize. Use this time away to tap into the other aspects of yourself. It's okay to want to indulge in humanity occasionally. It's good for us.'

Old-school vampires don't feel this way, but those of us looking for a peaceful co-existence see the merit in it.

'Doesn't it all feel pointless?' he asks. 'What good can come from forming connections and having relationships with people who are just going to die?'

Our eternal existence is a sore point for Laz.

'Have you thought this through, God?' His gaze moves to me. 'Have you truly considered what this will look like in the future?'

My jaw tics. I have thought about this. Not a lot, because it's all so new, and jumping ahead decades won't do me any good at this stage. 'It's too early to dive down that hole.'

'Is it, though?' Laz arches a dark eyebrow. 'How honest have you been with Hazy? Does she know what it means for *you* to have taken this step with her? Does she even understand the concept of a mate?'

I should've known that this is the first place Laz would go. 'She found out I was a vampire three hours ago. It's not as though I've had a whole lot of time to discuss the finer details with her. And claiming a mate is an archaic practice.'

'Finer details my ass. It might be archaic to humans but it's common practice in the vampire world. And you would have had plenty of opportunity to discuss this with her had you not been busy having a horizontal refreshment for the past several hours. How much of the truth are you going to give her? What details will you conveniently leave out? You've been dating her for all of – what, two months? Humans are fickle creatures, God. They start and end relationships on a dime.'

'Hazy isn't like most humans.'

He rolls his eyes and shakes his head. 'She's fragile like the rest of them. She has a lifespan that's a fraction of ours. All her knowledge about us is based on movies and books that are ten percent accuracy and ninety percent fiction. You have told her nothing of consequence in the hours since you've revealed what you are. Newsflash, God, but your sexual prowess isn't going to carry you through for the next seven decades. You can't keep her under you indefinitely. Unless you've forgotten, she requires sleep and nourishment in the form of something other than your ejaculate.'

The aggravating part about Laz and his cloud of doom is that he's right. Not that I want to face that truth at the moment. Instead, I hit below the belt. 'You would know, since you need the same things.'

Laz gives me a look that could kill. 'Thank you for that reminder. It's so easy to forget that of the three of us, I'm the only one who needs to sleep and consume something other than blood to survive this nightmare of an existence – and yet, I am the only one who seems capable of understanding that I am not human.'

I've definitely hit a nerve. Hunter sighs and leans back in his chair. Before I can apologize, or backtrack, Laz barrels on.

'While I may require sustenance of the non-sanguine variety, and sleep to regenerate, unlike the two of you, I seem to be the only one who can recognize the pitfalls that come from falling in love with someone who will cease to exist within a mere century. How do you plan to manage this relationship?'

I don't bother trying to respond, because Laz is far from done.

'Let's say, for argument's sake, that Hazy decides she wants to spend her *human* life with you. One thing that teen vampire franchise had right, is the fact that she is going to get old and you are going to stay exactly the same. Eventually, you'll look like her son, and then her grandson, and then her great-grandson, which will make her seem like a creepy old lady and you'll be the gold-digging scoundrel.' He holds up a finger. Laz is good at being dramatic. 'Unless your plan is to change her. And that has a whole new host of massive pitfalls. You know, as well as I do, that statistically there is a less than fifty-fifty chance that a human will survive the transition. It's bad enough that we lose close to twenty percent of vampires who naturally transition. Would you have her endure that, only to have a fifty-fifty chance of having her at your side for the rest of eternity? She doesn't even understand the concept of eternity. Look at us.' He motions to his room. 'We are on sabbatical specifically because we're fucking bored. And because the two of you are afraid of losing your goddamn humanity. At least I'm smart enough to realize I don't have any. It's a mask we wear so we can prey on them. Is this what you want for her?'

Underneath his anger is fear. Of what, I can only guess.

'Consider the strides we've made this century,' I urge. 'We've created a blood pill that has changed our entire existence. There are new studies, and new opportunities for change all the time. And I'm not here just because I'm bored. I'm trying to find a way to make the transition easier on vampires. And maybe, while I'm at it, I might find a way to make it possible for the human survival rate to increase, too.'

'And you're willing to use your girlfriend as a guinea pig? She's little more than twenty years old. She's already more than a fifth of the way through her incredibly short life. You are nearly three hundred. There is no comparison. She is an infatuation.'

'She's not a fucking infatuation.'

'You've made yourself one for her.'

'Tell me how you really feel, Laz.' I polish off the rest of my Scotch and wish again for my damn flask. Laz keeps vodka in his room, but that's not my drink of choice.

'You're being obtuse if you think that this isn't going to be problematic.' Laz uncrosses his legs and grips the arms of his chair, leaning forward. 'What happens when she eventually gets bored, or annoyed with your habits? What happens when she realizes you require sustenance that isn't served on a plate? The blood pills take the edge off, but they don't negate the need to replenish straight from the source, as was proven this evening. Or do you plan to use her as your blood bag, too? Will you share your source with us?'

My lip curls and I growl. 'Shut your fucking mouth.'

'Okay.' Hunter raises a hand as he stands and positions himself between us. 'Laz, you're pushing it. You've made your point, and while I'm sure you can magic the house back together after God puts you through a few walls, I don't think you can erase the memories of more than a hundred humans.'

Laz leans back in his chair, wearing a self-satisfied smile.

Hunter crosses his arms. 'Stop being a dick.'

'I'm being pragmatic, not a dick.'

'You're being a pragmatic dick. I get that you're worried about what the future looks like, but maybe give these two a chance to figure their own shit out without being the actual Grim fucking Reaper?' Hunter cocks an eyebrow.

Laz purses his lips. 'This whole thing puts us at risk. And there's the matter of that neanderthal across the street. He seems to have an unhealthy infatuation not only with us but with God's human.'

'Her name is Hazy,' I spit. 'And I'll handle him.'

'And how do you intend to do that? Will you eradicate him?'

And he's back to needling me. 'Murder isn't the only way to deal with a problem.'

'But it would solve it quickly, don't you think?'

Hunter blows out a breath.

'Always with the extremes, Laz,' I observe. 'Would it kill you to at least try to get to know Hazy before you go damning her?'

'Why bother when her ending is imminent?'

'Fuck you, Laz,' I snap.

'As fun as this whole conversation is, we need to put a pin in it,' Hunter says.

I'm about to ask why, when there's a knock on Laz's door.

20

Hazy

I debate knocking on Laz's door for a good thirty seconds or more. It sounds a lot like I'm interrupting a very heated argument. Unfortunately, my options are limited, so I give in, knock, and cross my fingers. The door swings open, but there's no one poised on the other side of it to greet me. Instead, Godric, Hunter and Laz are all standing in front of wingback chairs, arms crossed, lips pursed. When the three of them are together like this I can see the family resemblance. Although Laz has softer features than his brothers, even when he's glaring angrily.

I've only seen a sliver of Laz's room in passing, prior to this moment. It has to be one of the most romantic bedrooms I've ever laid eyes on. There's a fire roaring in the hearth and the color scheme is pale gray with dark gray accents. There are bouquets of blush-colored roses in beautiful vases positioned all over the room, and navy candles line most of the surfaces, dripping wax onto their brass holders.

Based on the stifling silence and the tension that's so thick it rivals mashed potatoes, I interrupted an argument. As much as I'd like to believe it isn't about me, logic implies it probably is. Also, the knowledge that I'm standing mere feet away from not one but three powerful vampires, hits me with a force I'm not entirely prepared for. It's one thing to be in the presence of one hot vampire – who wants to dote on my every need – but it's another thing entirely to walk into a room of irritated vamps.

It's sort of like stepping into a cage full of hungry chee-tahs. I fight with my body not to do something stupid, like scream and run away. My mouth is suddenly dry, my heart is hammering in my chest, which I'm sure they can all hear, and my palms start to sweat. 'Uh, sorry to interrupt, but, uh, there's a fight happening downstairs. And, uh –' I give in to the nerves and wring my hands '– they've already taken out one of the buffet tables. I figured it would be best to come get you before they do more damage.'

Laz is still wearing the Grim Reaper cloak, but the hood is down, which makes him only slightly less terrifying. 'I told you a party was inadvisable.' He stalks in my direction. 'I'll handle this.'

I hastily step out of the way and nearly trip over my own feet as he passes.

'I'll give him a hand. The last thing we need is Laz doing something that requires a whole hell of a lot of memory modifications.' Hunter gives me a sympathetic smile as he passes, leaving me and Godric standing on opposite sides of the room.

'Sorry I interrupted.' I have no less than a million burn-ing questions.

He moves to stand in front of me, his expression tense. 'It's fine. I should go help. Would you like to wait for me in my room?'

'Sure. I can do that. I'd offer to help, but it's a couple of football players and they're fighting over Alyssa, so . . .' I do some more hand-wringing. Satya and I hussled Alyssa out of the living room and into the backyard. I left them with a group of guys from the down the street, then rushed up here for reinforcements.

'I would prefer to handle the unruly football players, rather than sending you in as a lovely distraction,' he says, the tension still visible in his face.

He places a single finger under my chin, tipping it up to press his lips to mine. His tongue strokes along the seam so I let him in. The familiar sweetness hits first, followed by the wave of calm and the warmth of desire.

'Please lock the door behind you for your safety,' he instructs. 'I'll join you as soon as I can.'

My stomach clenches at the gentle command. Everything has gotten startlingly real over the past few hours. 'Okay.'

I do as he says, and lock the door once I'm in his bedroom, then stretch out on his bed to wait. I send a message to my group chat with Alyssa and Satya, to make sure they're okay, and am relieved when they message back right away to let me know they're fine and still hanging out in the backyard.

Godric must have taken much longer than a minute, because the next thing I know, I'm waking up tucked against his side, with my head on his chest, and a thin stream of sunlight is cutting a line across the black comforter.

'I fell asleep.' My morning brain is still half-offline.

'I must've worn you out last night,' he murmurs. I can feel his lips turn up against my skin as he presses a kiss on one temple.

'There was a lot of excitement.' I slept beside a vampire

last night. That's a whole lot of mind blown. 'What happened with the fight last night? I should've come down to help with the clean-up.' When I'd come up to get Godric, Justin had thrown some other guy into the buffet and all the appetizers ended up on the floor. At least the chocolate fountain hadn't gone down at that point. That would have been a colossal mess.

'Human men are very reactive. The fight ended before it even really began. As for cleaning up, we're vampires, remember. We're faster and stronger, and cleaning up was a breeze.'

'There must be some serious perks to being a vamp, huh? I'd love it if I could snap my fingers and everything would be tidy.' I settle my hand over his heart, feeling the steady *thump-thump* under my palm.

'It's certainly handy in some situations. Now, I have an important question for you.' Godric tucks my hair behind my ear.

Under normal circumstances, I would be rushing to the bathroom to manage my morning breath, but since I already know it's not an issue for Godric, I breathe it all over his face when I reply with, 'Fire away.'

'Would you like to start your day with breakfast, or me inside you?'

'Option two, please.'

I forgo brunch with Godric because I promised Alyssa and Satya that we would go to our favorite greasy spoon this morning and I would spill the rest of the beans. Or at least the beans I'm allowed to spill.

As much as I'd love to spend the entire day in Godric's

bed, I recognize that I need time to digest the fact that I'm dating a vampire. Godric has asked me to keep that tidbit between us for the time being. When I asked him about what I walked into in Laz's room, he brushed it off and said everything was fine. I don't believe him for a hot second, but I'm assuming that just like I need to have a chat with my besties, he needs to have one with his brothers. I hope me knowing about his true nature won't be problematic.

Godric walks me to the door, and for whatever reason I expect it to still look like the aftermath of a party in their living room; however, it's been returned to its previous pristine state. 'Wow. I'm coming to you when I need my room cleaned in the future.'

'Laz is the one with the magic touch,' Godric says.

'I don't think he's my biggest fan.'

'He doesn't know you. Give him some time.'

He kisses me goodbye, and I promise to message him later.

I demolish a ridiculous amount of food at brunch and fill Satya and Alyssa in on the parts of the night that I can. I understand that Godric and his brothers need to keep a low profile. Also, I'm not sure I'd believe me if I told yesterday me that Godric is a supernatural being. I also find out that the fight at the party started because some douche was catcalling Alyssa in front of Justin who went all MMA fighter on him.

I dedicate the afternoon to assignments and catching up on reading, and then I fall down an Internet rabbit hole on vampire lore. In the evening I plunk myself down in front of the TV and pull up *The Vampire Diaries*. Satya and Alyssa have been rewatching it lately, so I figure I might as well join in, for research purposes. I make notes on my phone so I can ask Godric questions about what's true and what's not.

On Monday morning I meet Godric at his place so we can walk to class together.

'I missed you last night.' He cups my face between his palms, slants his mouth over mine and lays a kiss on me that makes my knees go weak, my heart stutter and my lady bits flutter.

I groan and push on his chest. 'You can't do that to me.'

He takes a small step back. 'You don't want to kiss me?'

I give him a look. 'Of course I want to kiss you, but whenever I do, my body starts preparing for other things, and we don't have time for *other things*.' I point to my crotch in case it needs more of an explanation. 'Now I'm all worked up and there's nothing we can do about it for hours. You might be able to concentrate like this, but my mind will be hanging out in the gutter and I'll probably take terrible notes.'

'I can take care of your needs now so you're not distracted with thoughts of my hands on your body while we're in class.'

'We don't have time.' I'm pouty.

'I can be exceptionally quick when necessary.'

I narrow my eyes. 'Is this a trick?'

'Absolutely not. I'm happy to prove that I can give you what you need, even under extreme time constraints.'

How can I say no to that?

Five minutes and two orgasms later – both mine – Godric and I leave his house, me on slightly wobbly legs, and him wearing the biggest grin in the history of the universe, and head for the campus.

'I've been doing some research,' I tell him.

He glances at me from the corner of his eye. 'What kind of research?'

'Vamp research.' Our fingers are laced together, hands swinging between us.

'Ah. Online research, or movies and books?'

'All of the above. I'm trying to figure out how accurate some of this stuff is. Or maybe how inaccurate.'

'Most vampire movies are sensationalized nonsense.' His tone implies his irritation.

'Yeah, that's what I thought. I guess I just want to understand how this whole thing works. Like, you don't age, right? You basically look like you're in your twenties forever?'

'We age much slower than humans.'

'How much slower?'

He lifts a shoulder. 'One of your years is probably close to twenty of ours.'

'That's . . . wow.' I bite the inside of my cheek. 'If I ask you how old you are, will you be honest?'

'I'll always try to be honest with you, but in this case, I'd ask whether you feel ready to handle the truth.'

'Throwing the ball back in my court makes me wary of the answer,' I tell him.

'Then maybe we should start with easier questions and come back to that one when you're ready for the answer.'

He has a point. What if he predates the Bible?

At my silence, Godric squeezes my hand gently. 'Why don't you ask me something simpler, such as can I fly?'

'Oooh. That's a good one. Can you fly?'

'Not in the traditional sense of wings. However, my ability to move fast, and my strength, allows me to jump significantly higher than the average human.'

'Like skyscraper high, or more like three-story-building high?' I press.

'Three stories is very doable,' he replies. Like it's totally normal to be able to jump from the ground to the top of the house he lives in.

'You're kind of like superheroes. At least in some ways.'

'Except the vast majority of us aren't all that concerned with the preservation of humanity for anything but our own selfish desires.'

'What about the capes?'

He scoffs. 'That's a ridiculous Hollywood fabrication.'

'So the whole Dracula thing with the hanging upside down or sleeping in coffins is a bunch of bullshit?' I watched *Bram Stoker's Dracula* in bed last night. I'm super glad Godric doesn't turn into a scary demon bat thing.

Godric is quiet for a moment as we pass a group of students. All three of them give him a lingering once-over, their gazes slide to me for a moment and then shift back to him. As a synchronized unit they take two steps to the right, giving us extra space while stealing another glance at him.

He really is that pretty. 'I wonder if it's subconscious when people do that?' I say, more to myself than to him, but he hears me when no one else would.

'Do what?'

'Check you out and give you space at the same time. Sort of the same way you admire a cheetah because it's beautiful, but you don't want to get too close because it's lethal.'

'Ah, yes. I believe it's subconscious.'

'Why don't I react that way to you?' I muse. The fact that he could literally turn me into his next meal should terrify me, yet it does not. If anything, it gets me all hot and bothered, which seems like the very opposite of what it should be.

'I'm unsure, it's possible your fear center is . . . different than other humans.'

'Maybe my wiring is faulty,' I suggest.

'Whatever the reason, I'm grateful for it.' He leans in and kisses my cheek. 'Anyway, back to your question about the authenticity of *Dracula*. Basically, everything is sensationalized to make the movie more appealing to a broader audience. We don't sleep in coffins, although the darkness does help settle the mind, regardless of species. We don't need hours of rest, but brief periods are helpful, particularly when we've exerted ourselves in an extraneous way, and when we need to feed. Our version of rest is more like a state of semi-stasis. Sleeping the way you do could be very dangerous, particularly back when people believed we existed outside of books and movies.'

I'd ask how long ago that was, but it takes us down the same road as how old he is, and it's probably better if we save that for a time when I don't require my attention to be on what my professor is saying. 'How often do you need to feed?'

'That depends on a variety of factors. I believe the best comparison would be how elite athletes eat a lot more than the average human when they're competing. It's the same for us. If I exert myself then I need to feed more often.'

'Does the other night count as exerting yourself?' I ask.

Godric's gaze shifts to me and the look he gives me makes me wish I'd asked this question when we had more in the way of privacy. 'That kind of energy expenditure is a rejuvenator. While you need food and a nap after a night like that, I don't.'

'Would that be different if I was a vampire?'

'The experience isn't the same.'

'You've had a vampire girlfriend before.' I don't want to push him into a difficult conversation, but I'd like to know more about his past relationships.

'I have, the same way you've had a human boyfriend before,' he reminds me.

'Can I ask what happened?' I ask.

His jaw tics. 'Our truth was discovered and she didn't survive.'

I stop and turn to face him. His expression is guarded, but I can see the pain in his eyes. 'I'm so sorry, that must have been awful.'

He swallows thickly, voice clogged with emotion as he whispers, 'Loss is part of living.'

I squeeze his hand. 'Knowing that doesn't make it hurt any less.'

He gives me a small smile. 'You're right, it doesn't. But it was a long time ago.'

I have so many more questions, but all of them can wait. I take his other hand in mine. 'You don't have to hide your pain from me, Godric. If you ever want to talk about it, I'm here, okay?'

'Thank you.' He runs his thumbs across my knuckles. 'It's not something I talk about often.'

'Because it hurts?' I ask softly.

He nods. There's so much anguish in his eyes. I'm about to tell him we don't have to talk about it if it's too hard, but he blurts, 'One of the doctors we were working with found out about her and he killed her to study her. I realized what was happening too late and wasn't there to save her.'

'Oh God.' I cover my mouth with my hand. 'I'm so, so sorry you had to go through that.' I can't even imagine what it would be like to lose the person I love like that.

'Me, too.' He brings my hand to his lips and kisses my knuckle. 'But it inspired us to make changes – and if I hadn't lost her, I wouldn't have found you.' He pulls me closer. 'From pain comes resilience and hope.'

I tip my head up. His expression is earnest, eyes brimming with unspoken feelings. My heart breaks for his loss, but at the same time it swells with new emotion. 'Thank you for trusting me enough to share that with me.'

'Your existence heals my heart in a way time never could.' When he kisses me, my heart swells even more. I'm falling hard and fast, and it seems like maybe he is, too.

Over the course of the week Godric spends three out of the next five nights in my bed with me. I have a queen where he has a king, not that it matters, since I find myself tucked into his side, my head on his chest, when I wake in the morning. I think he would probably spend every night in bed with me if I let him, but we don't do much sleeping and I can't afford to be exhausted every day.

I always wake to him stroking a finger along my spine, or running his fingers through my hair. Morning sex is my

233

new favorite thing. And Godric is an incredible provider of orgasms.

Godric and I are making breakfast on Friday morning. Well, I'm pouring cereal into a bowl and Godric is sipping coffee and eating what's left of our chocolate stash.

'We should start testing your blood for my venom, to see how long it takes for it to leave your system,' Godric says.

'That's a good idea.' I've learned that his venom has healing properties along with being calming, arousing and an analgesic. I've also learned there are trace amounts in his semen, which explains why we can have marathon sex without me feeling it the next day. My thighs ache, but my other parts feel fine.

'We could do a prick test before we leave this morning, and I can take it to the lab later and run some tests,' he suggests.

He has lab access whenever he wants, thanks to his independent study project.

'That sounds good. We should log in the amount of time we spend making out and the number of times you come inside me? That way, we can compare the results over time.' I shovel another spoonful of cereal into my mouth. To anyone else this conversation would sound ridiculous, but there are scientific advantages to documenting these things.

He taps his temple. 'Photographic memory. I can create a spreadsheet later today.' He pops a square of chocolate into his mouth. It doesn't matter what time of day it is, he's always interested in chocolate. And sex.

I shift the subject, otherwise we're liable to end up naked

on the kitchen counter. 'How does your body process human food if you don't need to consume it?'

'It breaks it down and I absorb it.'

I shovel another spoonful of cereal into my mouth and chew thoughtfully, swallowing before I ask. 'Like a plant soaks up water?'

'Basically, yes.'

'So you never have to use the bathroom?'

'Not typically.'

'What does not typically mean?'

'If I ingest copious quantities of food my body won't process all of it.'

'So you need to do a number two on occasion?'

He purses his lips, his gaze dropping to my cereal. 'Doesn't this spoil your appetite?'

I shrug. 'It's basic biology and it fascinates me. It's kind of odd that you have a butthole but it doesn't serve a purpose.'

'Well, prior to transitioning it served the same purpose as yours.'

'What does that mean? Prior to transitioning? Do you mean when you were turned into a vampire?' This is the stuff we haven't talked about much yet, in part because Godric hasn't wanted to overwhelm me.

'There are two ways to become a vampire. Humans are turned, but I was born with the vampire gene.'

'I don't know why I didn't consider that as an option,' I say.

'Maybe because popular movies condition you to believe there is only one way to become like me.' He traces a vein on the back of my hand with his fingertip. 'Transitioning usually happens in the late teens, or early twenties, when our

235

center of reason is slightly more developed. Bloodthirsty toddlers throwing tantrums would make it tough for us to hide our identity from humanity.'

'That would make the terrible twos pretty gruesome. Is transitioning sort of like human puberty?'

'In a very basic way, yes.' He nods. 'But with lower odds of survival.'

'How so?'

'Not all vampires survive the transition. Like humans, some of us are more fragile than others.'

'But you and your brothers survived it.'

'We did.' He sips his coffee. 'Although we weren't entirely sure Laz was going to get through it. Being half-vampire, half-warlock lowered his chances of survival. His transition was rough.'

'That must have been scary.'

He nods somberly. 'They were dark days, but he made it through.'

I feel like there's more to Laz's story. 'He has a different father than you and Hunter?'

'Yes, our mother was seduced with dark magic and ended up pregnant.'

'That sounds . . . not good.'

'It wasn't, but the universe found balance. And Laz managed to survive the transition, so here we are. Of the three of us, he's the only one who requires food the same way humans and pre-transition vampires do.'

'So your intestinal tract is basically dormant for the most part now? Sort of like the appendix for humans.'

'Well . . .' One corner of his mouth tips up. 'I wouldn't say it's entirely without purpose.'

I narrow my eyes, trying to figure out what his expression means.

'Depending on sexual orientation and adventurousness,' he adds.

'Oh. Oh!' My eyes flare. 'Have you? Are you? Have you ever?' I stumble over my words. My body warms and everything below the waist tightens.

'Eternity is endless. Sometimes we try new things to quell the boredom.' Godric reaches across the table and skims my bottom lip with a single finger. I part my lips and touch my tongue to the pad, then wrap my lips around it, sucking softly.

His eyes grow hooded. 'That excites you.' It's not a question.

I glance at the clock on the stove. 'We should go upstairs.'

His smile is full of dirty promises. 'Feeling up for a little adventure then, my love?'

My chair screeches across the kitchen floor and Godric moves at human speed while I take the stairs two at a time. I'm mostly naked by the time he slips into my room. And we're almost late for class. But man, is it ever worth it.

21

I meet up with Godric for lunch before we head to our lab. Now that I know he doesn't need to eat food the same way I do, he no longer orders regular things, like burgers, or a steak sub. Instead, he grabs a giant double-chocolate brownie and a coffee while I hit the salad bar. They have everything, from couscous salad to bean salad, to Brussel sprout salad with a maple Dijon dressing and chopped pecans. I fill my plate, pay for my meal and sit across from my sexy boyfriend.

He uses a fork to cut into his fudgy brownie. He chews thoughtfully for a few seconds before swallowing. 'This isn't the best brownie I've had.'

'It's a college campus cafeteria brownie, your expectations should be pretty low.'

'Apparently, they weren't low enough.'

'I have a brownie recipe from my Great-Grandma Nell that's to die for. I'll make them for you.'

'We could make them together.' He slides his fork into the brownie and frees another small piece.

'Why don't I make my recipe and you make your favorite one and we compare?'

'Like a bake-off?'

'Exactly. How about when we get home, before we get too busy with each other?'

'I like the sound of that.' His gaze heats as it roams over me.

'You probably shouldn't look at me like that in public.' I stab a cherry tomato and pop it in my mouth.

'You like it when I look at you like this. Your heart rate tells me that.'

I roll my eyes. 'Show-off. Save it for when we're not in a room full of people.'

'Did you know that even when you're asleep your body reacts when my eyes are on you?' He continues to poke at his brownie, skimming the icing off the top.

'Do you stare at me all night when I'm sleeping?'

'No.' Godric smiles and licks the tines of his fork. It's hellishly suggestive.

'Do you lie there listening to me breathe all night?'

'Depends on the night. Sometimes I'll lie with you for most of it, other times when temptation is hard to resist, I'll get up and keep myself busy. But when it's clear that you want me beside you, I'll return.'

'What do you mean "when it's clear I want you beside me"? How do you know that?'

'Sometimes you talk in your sleep. Other times you'll become restless, and if I find you hugging my pillow, I'll replace it with myself.'

'That makes me sound needy.'

'You're not needy, and honestly, you would be fine if I didn't pose as your pillow. But I like lying beside you, and I do need rest, even if it's not the same as yours. Besides, your presence calms me.'

'That's good to know.' I spear a slice of cucumber. 'Your presence does a lot of things to me, although you're already aware of that.'

His grin turns sly. 'That I am.'

I finish my salad and Godric eats all the icing off his brownie and then we head to our lab.

Blaine is already at his own station, mostly set up. He frowns at our linked hands, but doesn't acknowledge us otherwise. He's a bit sore after the Halloween party. There were several videos and pictures of him with the Sharpie peens on his face making the round on social media. It doesn't matter that Godric and I had nothing to do with it. It happened in Godric's house, therefore his anger is directed at him.

Godric and I go to our usual table and it isn't until I take a seat that I remember what today is. We're taking blood samples and swabbing our mouths for DNA. I grab Godric's arm and lean in, my lips at his ear as I whisper, 'What are we going to do?'

'Don't worry, I already have it covered,' he assures me.

Professor Barton explains the purpose of the lab and we get to work. First we do the mouth swab. I'm excited to study Godric's DNA. There's so much to learn from him. When we move onto the finger prick, Godric goes preternaturally still for a moment. An image of him going on a rampage, snapping necks and draining bodies of blood, slams into my brain. It should freak me out that my boyfriend could probably wipe out the entire class before they have a chance to process what's happening. And in some ways it does. But the idea of him sinking his teeth into my neck has a whole different effect on my body.

'Please get your head out of the gutter, Hazy. You're making it difficult to focus,' he murmurs, his dark gaze lingering on my throat, as though he knows exactly the turn of my thoughts.

I shake my head. 'Sorry.' I use the device to prick my finger and Godric inhales deeply, his nostrils flaring. I can't help it. I clench below the waist.

He groans.

The pair closest to us looks our way and the girl blushes before returning her gaze to her microscope. Blaine is glaring daggers at us. His partner keeps snapping her fingers, trying to redirect his attention.

I let the drop of blood well before I touch it to my slide. Then do it again with a second one before I bring my finger to my mouth; the metallic, coppery tang hits my tongue and I swear I can hear Godric's teeth grinding together.

'You're killing me softly, Hazy.' Godric uses too much pressure on the pricker device and the plastic cracks. 'Oops-a-daisy.' He shoves the ruined device into his pocket and ambles to the front of the room to grab another one while I stifle a giggle at his phrase.

This time he manages not to crush it in his fingers as he takes a sample of his own blood, puts a drop on two slides and lays the protective shield on top, the blood fanning out. I glance over at Blaine's table, but his partner is micromanaging him and forcing him to take notes while she looks at the slides.

I'm giddy as I slip Godric's slide under the microscope. It's glaringly obvious that I'm not looking at human blood. The cells are frenetic, zipping around like toddlers on red-dye number 40.

'This is so cool,' I whisper. I'm looking at a cellular structure that doesn't break down over the course of a century. Whatever Godric's DNA is comprised of, it allows him to continue to exist for hundreds, if not thousands, of years.

I haven't allowed myself to think too much about that. If his blood got into the wrong hands, or the wrong people learned about his existence, it could mean very bad things for him and his kind. The elixir of eternal life. So much good and evil could come from it.

'I have so many new questions,' I whisper.

'I'm sure you do. And I'll happily answer them when we're alone.'

The point of today's lab is to learn about the history of our genetic make-up. We'll be running it through software that can reveal our genealogy. Before we submit our slides, Godric switches ours for samples from his backpack because my blood has trace amounts of venom floating around in it.

I wait until we're on our way home before I ask any questions. 'Whose blood did you swap ours out with?'

'Donors.'

'You have donors?' That green monster rears her head.

'Laz made a visit to the blood bank. My sample is from a male human in his twenties with O negative blood type, yours is from a woman with AB negative.'

'Ooooh. That's a lot different than where my head went.'

'Your heart rate tells me you don't like the idea of me accepting donor blood.'

'Your smirk tells me you like that I don't like the idea of donor blood.'

'As I've said before, I like you in green.'

'Do you always get your donations from the blood bank?'

'It's been a very long time since I've tapped from the source.'

I wonder what a long time for him is. I haven't been brave enough yet to ask how old he is.

I understand the basics of vampirism, that most are born, but that humans can be turned. When I asked more about that, Godric distracted me with a make-out session that turned into several orgasms. I didn't realize until after, that it was likely intentional.

I change the subject, before he can get in more digs about my jealous side showing. 'We should stop at the grocery store for brownie supplies.'

'Good plan. Once I get you into bed, I won't be inclined to let you leave it.'

'My green side is that appealing?'

'It makes me feel like the playing field we're on is close to level.' He threads his fingers through mine and gives my hand a gentle squeeze.

We make a right instead of a left so we can go to the bigger, better grocery store. The November chill is in the air, my breath puffing out in clouds that hang in the air for a moment before they disappear.

'Do you get cold?'

'Not the same way you do. Cold is uncomfortable, but I'm not at risk of losing limbs or digits in sub-zero temperatures like you.'

'Huh. That's cool.'

We pick up all the things we need from the grocery store and Godric pays for everything before I find my wallet, which was hiding at the very bottom of my backpack.

'Should we go back to your place to make these?' I haven't had an opportunity to enjoy Godric's kitchen, and now would be an awesome time to make that happen.

Godric hums and runs his fingers through his hair. 'Your place is closer.'

'Your kitchen is bigger.'

'Laz is probably home.'

'Is that going to be an issue? Is that why we've been having sleepovers at my place instead of yours this week?'

He gives me a curious look. 'Is that a serious question?'

'We haven't spent any time at your place since the party. And I get the feeling Laz isn't my biggest fan.'

'It isn't personal.'

'Is it because I'm human?'

'Your being human isn't the reason I've been sleeping over at your place.'

'Then what is the reason?'

'I live with two other vampires, Hazy.'

'Is my feedbag status a problem?' That might make sense. And it could explain Laz's standoffishness. Maybe being around me is a reminder of the fact that he's taking blood pills instead of consuming human blood to survive. It may also explain why he avoids in-person classes as much as possible.

'Both of my brothers have a good handle on those particular impulses.'

'If my fresh blood isn't a problem, what is it?'

'I can hear your heart beating right now.'

'Can you stop trying to change the subject.'

'I'm not trying to change the subject. I'm making a point. You can be in a different room in the house entirely, or a room full of people, and I can still pick out the sound of your heart from everyone else's.'

'I still don't – oh. *Oh.*' I stop walking and turn to face

244

him, my voice dropping to a whisper as it finally clicks. 'Which means they can hear everything that's happening in your bedroom, even when you have music on and they're on the main floor. Even during the party?'

'They're good about blocking things out, but I don't want you to feel compelled to be quiet, or self-conscious, and your roommates don't get home for a couple of hours. I was hoping I might be able to entice you up to your bedroom while the brownies are baking. I miss the sound of my name on your lips when you're in the middle of an orgasm.'

'You gave me one this morning.'

'You were being quiet because we were standing in your foyer – and I intend to make you scream.'

'My house it is, then.'

But en route home, I get a message in our group chat that my roommates skipped their last class after hitting the bar for a liquid lunch. Their plan is to watch *Super Troopers* again, for the seven-hundredth time, and Alyssa's snort-laugh doesn't make a very romantic soundtrack, so I convince Godric that we're better off at his place, and he concedes, albeit reluctantly.

I glance over at Blaine's house while Godric rummages around in his messenger bag for a key. It's a distinctly human thing to do. I swear I catch movement in the window on the second floor. I wave, on the not-so-off chance that Blaine is being a Creeping Creeper, before I follow Godric inside.

He announces our arrival, but it appears no one is home. We unpack our brownie baking supplies and I set the oven to preheat. I've made these so many times I know the recipe by heart, so it's just a matter of Godric helping me find the measuring cups and spoons, and we're good to go.

He zips around the kitchen, pulling things from cupboards and setting them on the counter before he's off again. He reminds me of the Tasmanian Devil from old Bugs Bunny cartoons.

Once everything is lined up in front of us, he takes his place beside me and props his fists on his hips. 'Do we have everything we need?'

'All that's missing is a double boiler.'

'Ah. Let me get that for you.' He zips across the room and returns a second later.

In the time it takes me to set up the cutting board and unwrap the boxes of baking chocolate, Godric manages to assemble all his dry ingredients and he's on to creaming the butter and sugar for his recipe. By hand.

I stop what I'm doing to watch him for a few minutes, which is how long it takes him to prepare the entire recipe. Without the help of a Kitchen Aid mixer.

The water has just come to a low boil. I've added the butter to the pot along with the chocolate. His brownies are ready for the oven, which is still heating.

Godric props his hip against the counter while licking the batter off a spatula. 'Want some help?'

'Show-off.' I give him the side eye. 'You can keep me company while I make human magic happen.' I finish measuring the dry ingredients into a bowl.

He pulls up a stool and takes a seat across from me. 'Did your grandmother teach you how to bake?'

I nod and move to the stove, adding the chocolate to the melted butter, using a whisk to stir it in. 'She lived down the street when I was growing up and she loved baking so much. When I was a kid, I'd go there in the afternoons once school was finished and we would bake cookies together. She made the most amazing chewy triple-chocolate fudge cookies. She was a wizard with flour and butter. What about you? Who taught you how to bake?'

'My mother taught me the basics pre-transformation. And when I lived in France for a few years, I discovered I had a real passion for it.'

'You lived in France? Where else have you lived?' It makes sense that he's moved around a lot. Ten years would be about the longest he could stay in one place without people realizing he's not aging.

'All over the world, really. Once commercial planes were invented it became a lot easier to move from one country to another, but I spent a lot of time in Europe post-transition. My mother is there right now. There's a large community of vampires in Italy and Spain, and many of them share the same goals as my family.'

'Have you lived in Spain and Italy, too?' I add more chocolate, stirring it until it's smooth.

'I have. Portugal is lovely, and they have great wine and amazing food.'

'I would love to go there one day. A trip to Europe is on my bucket list.' I imagine that, with a long lifespan, traveling the world would help quell boredom and give someone a much broader understanding of how the individual societies work, as well as a much deeper appreciation of cultural differences.

'I'll take you anywhere you want to go. We could travel the world together.'

'It sounds like you've already done that.' I crack the eggs into a measuring cup, one at a time, then beat them with a fork.

'But going with you would be like seeing it all again through fresh eyes.' Godric props his chin on his fist. 'I've seen almost all of Europe, and we spent some time in Australia, and I've visited China and most of Asia.'

'What brought you to North America?' I turn off the burner and remove the chocolate and butter mixture from the heat so I can add the eggs and vanilla.

'We came to Canada first and worked our way across the country. The east coast is beautiful, but the people are exceedingly friendly, which is great if you're looking for a community and not so great if you're trying to keep things hidden.' Godric passes me the bowl with the dry ingredients. 'Are you sure you don't want my help?'

'Nope, you can just keep me company.' I whisk in the flour mixture one spoonful at a time. 'I'm taking it you didn't stick around the east coast very long.'

'No, we kept moving. Quebec has great food, and Ontario has amazing lakes, the west coast is stunning and lush, but the Northwest Territories are pretty barren. The polar bears don't particularly enjoy our company and the population is sparse. Once the blood pill was developed, that wasn't as much of an issue. But prior to that, we had to live in bigger cities where we could access blood banks without being noticed.'

It's on the tip of my tongue to ask when the blood pills were developed, but then we're back down the rabbit hole of how old he is.

'Do you have a favorite place? One that you love more than all the others?'

'Right here. With you.' He smiles down at me.

'What's your second-favorite place?'

'My bed. With you.'

I laugh and try to wriggle away when he nuzzles into my neck. 'I need to pay attention to what I'm doing!'

'It'd be easier if you let me help. I'm very good at multi-tasking.' He lets me go, though.

I finish mixing in the dry ingredients. I pour the mixture into a pan lined with parchment paper, then put both trays in the oven and set the timer on my phone for fifty minutes. 'Feel like working up an appetite while these are in the oven?'

'Absolutely.' Godric grabs me by the waist and hoists me up.

I wrap my arms and legs around him koala-style. And then we're zipping up the stairs. It feels like being on a roller coaster, but without the loop-de-loops and twists and turns.

Godric doesn't waste any time getting us both naked and laying me out on the bed.

'So much for the striptease I had planned,' I chuckle as his lips move across my neck.

He freezes for a moment, then lifts his head. How his eyes manage to light up and darken at the same time is a wonder. 'Striptease?'

I arch an eyebrow.

'I can re-dress you, if you want.'

'I was kidding.' I've never given a striptease. I'm not exactly the most coordinated dancer in the history of the universe, although I have watched *Magic Mike* an unreasonable number of times. Still, watching a movie about stripping and actually stripping are two very different things. 'Maybe another time,' I offer when he doesn't make a move to put his lips back on my skin right away.

'I would very much like that.' His lips return to my jaw and his hips settle into the cradle of mine.

I hook my feet at the small of his back and run my fingers through his hair, tipping my chin up and turning my head, giving him better access to my throat. He peppers my neck with kisses, breathing in deeply. He groans and parts his lips, his tongue sweeping over my skin.

'I'm sorry, my love, I need to hit pause. I should've taken a pill earlier and you're far too tempting.' The warmth and weight of him leaves for a few seconds. I barely register his absence before he's back, thumb caressing the spot where his lips just were, hips nestled in the cradle of mine again.

Our lips meet, but before he can deepen the kiss and scramble my brain I say, 'Today must have been a lot for you.'

'Nothing I can't handle.'

'Still, it was a lot of exposure.'

'I prepared for it, although I didn't fully consider the impact of you and probably should have.'

'How do you mean?' I skim the contour of his bottom lip with my fingertip.

'You're more alluring than most, so despite taking the necessary precautions my body still responded in inconvenient ways.'

'What were the necessary precautions?'

'The donor wasn't only for the samples.' He kisses the tips of my fingers. 'But it was still a challenge to control myself in a room full of people. Not in that I was concerned about my ability to keep you safe, but my base instincts kicked in.' He drags the tip of his nose along my cheek. 'I covet your life force.'

'So you want to drink my blood?' I ask.

'Maybe we should talk about this later, after I've made you come.'

'I'd rather talk about this now.' I suck his bottom lip between my teeth. 'You want to feed from me.'

'Of course I do.' He rolls his hips and his erection slides over my already slick skin. 'You're my girlfriend. I want every part of you.'

'Do vampires feed from each other?'

'Yes.'

'Is it the same as feeding from human blood?'

'Not quite. It regenerates us, but for shorter periods of time. It's not a replacement for the real thing – or, in my case, blood pills and the occasional bag of blood.'

'Then why do it?'

Godric gazes down at me, his expression unreadable. 'Sex and feeding often go hand in hand for vampires. It's less about the actual feeding and more about connecting, and . . . claiming your . . . partner in the most base and primal way possible.'

'Would you want to feed from me during sex?' I'm all breathless and my muscles below the waist clench deliciously, despite the lack of friction and physical stimulation.

'The idea excites you.' His erection kicks between us.

'It seems to have the same effect on you,' I whisper.

He clears his throat. 'It wouldn't be a good idea for me to feed from you while I'm inside you.'

I can't hide my disappointment. 'Why not?'

'I'd need to be in control, and that would be a challenge. When I'm feeding I'll be able to feel all the things you feel. Like an echo of your emotions. It can be overwhelming, and it wouldn't be safe for you.'

'But you could feed from me while we're not having sex?'

'Yes.'

'And you'd like to do that?'

'Yes.' His voice is guttural and thick.

'Then you should.'

'Right now?' His eyes flare.

'Please.' My voice is barely a whisper. 'I want to give this to you. I want to give myself to you in this way.' There are so many other questions I still need answers to, but I know without a doubt that I want this. 'I can give you this, I can take care of you like you take care of me.' *Plus, it's hot as fuck.*

I tip my chin up and expose my throat. 'Bite me.'

22

Godric

It takes an ungodly amount of restraint not to give in to Hazy's request immediately. My mouth is so full of venom I need to swallow several times. It's futile. My body's already preparing to feed. Hazy's pulse hammers in her throat and when I drop my head to press a gentle kiss to her pulse point, she sucks in a gasping breath and slides her fingers into my hair. They curl around the strands and she arches, exposing more of her deliciously appealing throat.

But I don't sink my teeth into the skin. The throat is a fabulous place to feed from if it's vampire to vampire, or if the intent is to take as much as quickly as possible, and potentially drain the victim in the shortest span of time. It's also close to the heart, allowing the venom to hit the bloodstream much quicker, subduing the feedee. But it's risky for a human and a first-time feed. Especially since I haven't had fresh blood from the source in over a century. My connection to Hazy figures in as well, and I don't want to put her in that kind of danger. But I don't share all of this with her.

Maybe I should, but I don't want to scare her unnecessarily. 'The throat, while effective, is conspicuous.' I kiss my way along her jaw, back to her lips. 'And while the venom will heal the wound quickly, there may still be a very obvious bite mark that could last for days before it disappears completely.' I take one of her hands in mine and bring her wrist to my lips. 'Here would be better, and easier to hide the marks.'

Hazy bites her bottom lip, the disappointment in her eyes clear. 'What about my inner thigh? You're the only one who sees that part of my body.'

I stare down at her, considering. The femoral artery is there, but I can certainly avoid it. That would be like opening a fire hydrant. It could get messy and disastrous. Besides, she's right; it's very hidden. 'The inside of your thigh it is.'

I kiss my way down her body, taking my time, forcing myself to relax and steadying my mind and body. I need to be in complete control for this. I have no idea how I'm going to react to her blood in my system – but hell if I don't want to know what she tastes like on my tongue.

When I reach the apex of her thighs I nuzzle in, burying my face between her legs, licking her until she comes. It's while she's riding out the orgasm that I turn my head, part my lips and swipe my tongue over the inside of her thigh.

'No sudden movements, my love,' I warn.

She moans in response.

I take a deep breath, excitement making my cock kick and the venom flow. And I sink my teeth into her skin. It gives way like soft butter. Hazy gasps and I feel the sharp pain echo through me. I settle a palm over her abdomen, gently keeping her hips pinned to the bed. Venom floods the wound and travels through her bloodstream in a rush, the initial shock of pain ebbing and in its place a wash of calm.

Lust and desire, strong and violent, flood my senses as

her blood pools in my mouth. The flavor coats my tongue. It's the finest wine, the most decadent, luscious dessert, the richest chocolate, threaded through with the headiness of an orgasm.

I suck, drawing out more blood, swallow, letting it coat my throat as I take her inside me. It only takes a moment for her blood to enter my own system and for the initial shock and fear that came with the bite to shift. The orgasm I interrupted surges, overwhelming my senses with pure, unadulterated bliss.

Hazy moans, loud and long. When I'm no longer worried about sudden movements, I adjust the position of my hand so I can circle her clit with my thumb as I feed.

It's a fabulously stupid idea. Fabulous because it sends Hazy careening back over the cliff of bliss. Stupid because I experience her orgasm right along with her.

I make the mistake of lifting my gaze, in part to ensure she's enjoying this as much as I am, but also because watching Hazy come apart is one of my favorite things in the entire universe. I'm not disappointed by the view. Hazy grips her right breast in her hand, finger and thumb pinching the nipple. Her teeth are pressed into her bottom lip but her head isn't thrown back. She's staring down at me, dark desire making her eyes glint.

I growl and suck again, and her eyes roll up.

Suddenly, a spiral of smoke appears above her head, forming itself into letters that spell out *TOO MUCH*. They hover in the air for a few seconds before they disappear.

Laz must be home.

I resist the urge to continue sucking, instead retracting my teeth and lapping over the wound, licking at her skin

255

until I feel it start to close against my tongue. I pull back and swipe over it again, cleaning away the last of the blood as her skin knits back together.

It isn't until I'm lying beside her that I realize I've taken a heck of a lot more than the cup or so I'd allotted myself. I've probably taken more than half a liter. Which is a lot of blood.

Her alarm on her phone pings, signaling the brownies are done. I silence it.

Hazy blinks up at me, her gaze the same as her name.

'Holy shit,' she whispers, so quietly it's almost soundless.

Her pulse is slower than usual, blood pressure lower than it should be. In hindsight, I probably should not have fed from her for the first time while she was in the middle of coming, because her blood literally tasted like a bottled orgasm. 'I need to feed you.'

She slow blinks at me.

I quickly dress her and lift her in my arms.

'S'going on?' she mumbles, her forehead resting against my neck.

'Getting you a sugary snack,' I tell her.

She makes a little noise, but she's a limp ragdoll in my arms. It's alarming and jarring. I open the door and find Laz standing there with a plate of brownies, fresh from the oven, and a mug of hot chocolate piled high with marshmallows and topped with whipped cream and chocolate shavings.

We stare at each other for a second and he raises an eyebrow, like he's daring me to get mad at him for creeping on us, but if he hadn't interrupted, I may not have stopped the way I should have. It's sobering. And a whole fucking lot unnerving.

256

He sets the tray by the window seat and disappears down the stairs, not giving Hazy a glance. Hazy is half passed out, but I rouse her and feed her brownies and hot chocolate. Her color returns slowly, but it's clear in the lethargic way she moves and how languid she is in my arms, I've taken more than I should have. At least her blood pressure has returned to almost normal after three brownies and the mug of hot chocolate.

'I could use a nap,' she murmurs.

'I'll take you back to bed.' I carry her across the room and lie with her until she falls asleep, which takes all of thirty seconds.

I'm assuming she'll be out for a while, considering, so I make sure she's tucked in with plenty of blankets and head down to my brother's room. The door opens before I can knock.

'I wasn't being a creeper.' He steps back and allows me to enter.

There's a fire going in the hearth, which is typical no matter the time of year.

'I know. Thanks for the warning.' I cross over to the wingback chairs and take a seat. A glass floats across the room from Laz's minibar, along with a bottle of Scotch. The bottle tips, pouring three fingers, before settling on the table beside me. I down it in two swallows and refill the glass myself.

Laz drops into his chair and picks up a martini glass. From the look of it, there's chocolate liqueur in it. There's a plate with a single brownie beside it.

'Thanks for taking those out of the oven.'

'No problem. The ones Hazy made are incredible.'

'How do you know they're the ones she made?'

'Because I've had yours a thousand times. They're good, but Hazy's are fudgy and decadent. I've never had a better brownie.'

'You should tell her that, when she's awake.'

'Mm. I should.' He gives me a half-smile, then looks away. 'If I'd realized what was going on I would have stayed out longer – although, brownies aside, it seems my arrival was appropriately timed.'

'I misjudged our connection.'

He nods once. 'It's stronger than you anticipated. I also think that a century of blood bags and pills isn't quite the same as drinking from the source.' He sips his martini, his gaze shifting from the fire to me. I see the envy in his eyes. The curiosity. 'It seemed like it was quite the experience for both of you.'

'Like all my favorite things rolled into one,' I admit. 'Also like the best cheat day ever, after years on a diet.' Part of me worries now that I've had a taste, I'll struggle with returning to blood pills and the occasional bag of donor blood.

'Do you think she'll allow you to do it again?'

I shrug. 'I don't know if I want to put her at risk like that.'

'It's been a lot of years since you've fed from a partner, and never with a human. It was a ballsy location choice, and I would suggest a less . . . carnal moment next time, if you're planning to make a regular thing of it, at least until you have a better command of your own emotional state.'

'It seemed like a good idea at the time,' I mutter.

'And may have been had this not been the first time you've fed from a human in over a century.' He's unnervingly calm about this whole thing.

'I expected you to be pissed at me for this.'

Laz taps his lips. 'I, too, underestimated your connection to her and hers to you. I could feel it the moment I walked into the house. Your emotions were leaching into every corner of the place. You love her, and she loves you. Providing you with sustenance is the ultimate show of commitment, although I'm not entirely sure she recognizes that on a conscious level.'

I stare at the fire, watching the flames dance and flicker. 'I can't imagine the future without her.'

'That will be inevitable, unless your plan is to change her eventually.' He's matter-of-fact about it, but there's something lurking under his words, a nervousness I haven't heard from him before.

'I don't love the odds on that,' I admit.

'They aren't particularly favorable for either of you,' he agrees.

'My hope is I'll be able to find a way to make it easier while we're on this sabbatical.' It's part of the reason I'm back in medical school. It gives me access to labs and supplies we would otherwise have to purchase illegally. And plenty of humans. I hadn't expected to fall in love with one, however. Or to feel so connected to her that the thought of losing her would most definitely create a hole in my chest. Bigger than the first one.

'My hope is that you're successful.'

The heaviness of potential failure hangs in the air. Because if I'm not successful . . . well that's something I don't want to think too much on. Not now. We have time on our side. Hazy is young, and my family has made such huge strides over the past century. Maybe with her help, we'll be able to make more of those.

I head back upstairs when I sense Hazy waking. I stretch out alongside her and she curls into me. Her eyes flutter open slowly. She's still lethargic, but based on her heart rate and her blood pressure, she's regenerating the way she should. By morning she'll feel like herself again.

'Hi.'

'Hi.' I run my fingers through her hair and skim her cheek with my thumb.

'I had a nap.' Her voice is raspy with sleep.

'That you did.'

'You fed from me.' Her hand appears in my peripheral vision and her fingers drift down my cheek.

'I did.' I nod once and swallow down the venom that instantly starts pooling in my mouth at the mere mention.

'Was it good for you? I'm assuming my blood is better for you than a synthetic pill, but did you enjoy it? I didn't even get to ask you any questions. I just gobbled down brownies like I hadn't eaten in a week.' Her brows pull together, as if she's trying to reconcile the events that took place earlier. She cranes to look over my shoulder at the clock on the nightstand. 'How long have I been out?'

'A few hours.'

Her eyes flare. 'A few hours?'

'I'm sorry.' I stroke her cheek. 'I took a little more than I should have,' I admit. 'Hence your need for sugar and a nap.'

'Oh.' She bites her lips together. 'What's "a little more than you should have" mean?'

I swallow past the lump in my throat. 'I believe I took somewhere in the vicinity of twenty ounces.'

'Huh. Well, that explains me being all loopy and passing

out. Am I particularly delicious, then?' Her eyebrows dance on her forehead.

I chuckle. 'You are a delight to the senses, and an utter treat in all ways, Hazy. One of the things I didn't account for was how strongly your emotions would come through when I fed from you.'

'What do you mean?'

'Biting you while you were in the middle of an orgasm seemed like a smart plan because you were at the height of bliss, which acts as a natural analgesic. The sting of the bite would be lessened, but I didn't anticipate how potent your emotions would be when they hit me, or the way it affected the flavor of your blood.'

Hazy props her cheek on her fist, her eyes alight with curiosity and excitement. 'Explain that, please. This is so fascinating. I want to know all about your experience with me and how it's different from other experiences you've had before.'

I lace my fingers with her free hand. 'Your blissful state was hardly interrupted by the bite, which was my intention. Fear has a taste, often it's bitter, or tangy, like wine that's sat for too long. But your moment of fear and pain had a smokier flavor, like burning cedar. Coupled with the taste of your orgasm, it was . . .' I swallow down more venom. 'Overwhelmingly intoxicating. But more than that, I felt what you felt, the pang of fear, the wash of calm, then the waves of desire that grew stronger with my feeding. It discombobulated me and made me forget myself for a few seconds. Hence my taking more blood than I should've.'

'So biting me during an orgasm makes my blood taste better?' she asks.

'It does. Although I'm imagining it tastes incredible no matter what, the flavors are enhanced when your emotional state is heightened.' I stroke the edge of her jaw, my palm resting against the side of her neck, the steady thump of her pulse a balm and a reminder that I need to be more careful in the future. If she'll ever allow my teeth near her again. 'How was the experience for you?'

'Unreal, to be honest. It felt like my orgasm was echoing, which makes sense if you were feeling it right along with me, and there was this . . . sense of euphoria that came with it. Like I never wanted it to end.'

'Interesting.' The word comes out mostly a croak.

'Why is that interesting?'

'Usually that bond is reserved for vampire-to-vampire connections, but then, most vampire-to-human interactions aren't like ours.'

'Would you feed from me again?'

'Would you like me to?'

'Yes. Definitely.'

'The pain doesn't bother you?'

'It's brief, and the pay-off is so worth it. That was the best orgasm I've ever had.' She hooks one leg over mine.

I allow her to pull me closer and our lips connect in a soft kiss. 'I think it would be better to avoid feeding from you in that state until I have things under control, and that may increase the initial discomfort for you.'

She bites her bottom lip. 'But eventually you'll feed from me again during sexy times?'

'If that's what you want, then yes. But I'd like to ensure my control and your safety moving forward. There's also the matter of my venom running through your veins. The more I feed from you, the more venom you'll have in your bloodstream. I'm not sure what the effects of that will be in the long term.'

'Hmm. Okay. We should take blood samples after feedings to determine how long it takes the venom to cycle through me. As soon after as possible, most likely. And we can monitor me for any changes as a result. And the next time you feed from me, we should pick a more neutral location, and I can be stimulated but not in the middle of an orgasm.'

'I absolutely agree.'

'Should we take a sample now?'

I always have lab supplies here now, since we've been routinely checking Hazy's blood post-sex to see how long the venom stays in her system. I expect this will be different, with the way it's going directly into her bloodstream. I gather what I need and take a quick sample – putting it in the fridge to look at later – before I return to the bed. It all takes less than a minute.

'I have an important question.' Hazy bites her lip.

'Sure.'

'Can we make out? This whole conversation has me excited all over again.'

I adjust our position so I'm nestled in the cradle of her hips. 'Looks like we match, then.' I drop my head and cover her mouth with mine, swallowing her giggle-moan.

23

Hazy

'Check this out.' Blaine slaps a piece of paper on my desk.

I've been trying to avoid the office in the weeks since the Halloween party by copyediting the pieces for the paper at home instead, on my laptop. Blaine is being extra annoying these days, constantly asking me questions about Godric and his brothers every time I see him. Which would be fine if my boyfriend wasn't a vampire.

Blaine's most recent strategy to get me into the office has been to have me copyedit hard copies of the formatted pages because 'the reading experience is different on paper than it is on the screen'. Eye roll.

He's not wrong, but if he sent me the proof pages as a PDF I could at least print them at home. Instead, he's been holding the copies hostage in the office and ignoring my emails when I press him for printable files. I've about had it with his shit. But at the same time, keeping tabs on what he does and doesn't know is probably a good idea.

Especially since he's taken to conveniently being around in the mornings when Godric and I are leaving for class. He's always hanging around on the front porch, pretending to look at his phone. I'm grateful he doesn't walk to campus, otherwise we might have to deal with his nonsense more than we already do.

Blaine props his fists on his hips and awaits my re-action. There's a photocopy of an old article sitting directly on top of the proof pages I'm supposed to edit, so I have no choice but to look. The photocopy is from the school paper dated almost fifty years ago. A group of students in the science department are posing for a photo, apparently having won a competition.

'Go science nerds.' I push the paper aside and focus on what needs my attention.

'You're not looking.' Blaine stabs the center of the photo. 'Look at this. It's your boyfriend.'

I glance at the grainy image. While the hairstyles have changed some, and the outfits are dated, I can very clearly see that it's Godric standing in the midst of the group. He's wearing that infamous smirk that makes my panties want to climb into his pocket for safe keeping.

'And look here.' He stabs the names with his finger. GODRIC HAWTHORN is typed in the caption below.

'It's a family tradition to come here. That's his great-uncle, who he was named after.'

'Why is he named after his great-uncle? Why isn't he named after his own damn father?'

'Why do you even care? You're perseverating again, Blaine. Last year you were sure our advanced microbiology professor was sleeping with one of his students and it turned out that she was his niece. And the year before that, you were determined to prove the Delta Iota Kappa were running a secret meth lab in their basement, but they were growing hydroponic lettuce. What is proving that Godric looks like his great-uncle going to do for you? Or is this because you're upset that I'm dating him and we're happy in a way that you and I never were?'

He ignores my points about the microbio professor and DIK. 'You were always happy in my bed.'

I purse my lips. 'You're treading the harassment line again.'

'I'm stating facts. I made you come every time we were in bed together.'

'And then you ruined the afterglow buzz by timing them, like a weirdo. Take a cue from Taylor Swift. We are never ever getting back together. Ever. Get over it.'

'There's something going on at that house and I'm going to figure it out. I've never seen that third brother. Not once.'

'Because he's basically agoraphobic and takes his classes online.'

Laz seems to be warming up to me. Over the past few weeks, I've run into him in the kitchen or the hall a few times and he always says hello. I also discovered that he has an affinity for cooking almost anything. And while Godric is usually the baker, Laz makes chewy oatmeal chocolate chip cookies I'm in love with. I ball up the photocopy and toss it in the garbage. 'If you're done playing Sherlock Holmes, I have articles to edit.' I motion to my desk.

'I think you're hiding something.'

'I think you need to find something new to fixate on. You're butthurt that I'm over you, and your poor fragile male ego can't take it. I have twenty minutes to finish these, thanks to you, so if you could kindly screw off and let me get them done, that would be awesome.'

Blaine huffs and stomps off.

As soon as he's gone, I nab the crumpled piece of paper

from the trash can and shove it in my backpack. Godric needs to see this. Also, that one question I've avoided asking again keeps popping up like a whack-a-mole. I should probably get over myself and get the answer so I can start processing the fact that my boyfriend is well over a century old. Maybe several centuries. On the upside, at least I'm getting used to the whole mindfuck-i-ness of dating a vampire.

I show Godric the newspaper article from fifty years ago when we get back to his house that evening.

'What did you say about this?' Godric's eyebrows are pulled together and his mouth tips down in a frown.

It's a sexy look for him, but then, all his looks are sexy.

'I told him it was your great-uncle.'

'That's good. It looks like I need to pay a visit to the school paper archives.'

'I have access. I could do a search for you.'

'That would be helpful.'

'I have a question.'

Godric looks up from the wrinkled piece of paper, his expression wary. 'Okay.'

'How old are you really?'

He blinks at me.

I blink back. 'We can't avoid this topic forever, Godric. You're a vampire. You've been around the block a few times. Keeping my head in the sand about it doesn't make a lot of sense.'

He sighs. 'Knowing I'm a vampire and the reality of my lifespan is not the same. You should sit down for this.'

I don't argue. If he wants me to sit, I'll sit. I drop down

onto the window seat and clasp my hands in my lap. 'I'm ready.'

He runs a hand through his hair. Not at human speed. I'm used to that now, though. 'I'm two hundred and seventy-three.'

I don't know what I expected him to say, but that wasn't it. 'Did you say two hundred?'

'And seventy-three, yes.'

'Wow.'

He takes a seat beside me and puts his hand on the cushion between us, palm facing up. It's a request for contact. I press my palm to his and let that truth sink in. It's a number I can't even begin to comprehend. My great-great-grandmother lived to be a hundred and three. At the end she was a tiny, wrinkly little lady, but she was still full of fire. She was the kind of woman you see in memes, making clay peen sculptures in the retirement home.

'The things you've seen,' I whisper. Plagues, world wars, famine, droughts, natural disasters, the theory of evolution, the development of technology and AI. He's been here through it all. And my twenty-two years seem utterly insignificant. My meager existence is infantile in comparison. Literally. 'How can you be in a relationship with me, when I'm so . . . inexperienced in life?'

His expression softens. 'I've never met anyone like you, Hazy, vampire or human. You have a fresh perspective, you're incredibly intelligent, curious, and the most beautiful creature I've ever had the pleasure of laying eyes on. I've been here a long time, and there's a staggering loneliness that comes with existing in an infinite loop. You breathe new life into me. I feel like I have a purpose, like there is meaning in my existence again. You invigorate me.' He squeezes my hand. 'It's okay if this information freaks you out, though.'

'It probably should,' I agree.

'But?'

'But I kind of expected it to be a significant number. Nearly three centuries is a bit more than I bargained for, but you're damn hot for someone who was born in the previous millennium.'

He laughs and I climb into his lap. Sometimes the best way to deal with another mindfuck is to drown it out with love.

I'm in the middle of frying an egg for breakfast. Godric is toasting the English muffin for my egg, cheese and ham sandwich while he nurses a coffee.

'I'd like to start infusing venom doses into donor blood samples to compare them against yours,' Godric says.

'We should use multiple donor samples. Maybe pull from various blood types, both male and female, so we can create our own testing variables.' I break the yolk so it's not overly runny.

'And we should test three different donors with the same blood type as you, and see how their variables differ from yours,' Godric agrees.

'This would make the most amazing master's thesis, don't you think?' I flip the egg. My reaction time lately seems to have improved, so I no longer need a spatula to make this happen. 'Too bad there aren't vampire colleges.'

'There are vampire research facilities, mostly in Europe, but the human component has been lacking.'

269

I smile up at him. 'Maybe we can change that.'

'You two are giving me a toothache with all the sappy-nerdy love vibes.' Hunter appears out of nowhere and zooms around the room collecting things. He pauses to steal a piece of bacon from the plate next to the stove.

'We're talking about creating a control group to compare the effects of venom on different blood types.'

'Yeah, like I said, sappy-nerdy *science* love vibes.' Hunter grabs a second piece of bacon.

'You're up early,' I observe.

'Group project for my Deviant Behavior class and one of the members is a serious hottie. We're meeting at her place and I'm in charge of bringing coffee. How you humans consume that shit is beyond me. Makes me jittery and tastes like the inside of a shoe.'

I thumb over at Godric. 'He likes coffee.'

'He also likes Scotch, which tastes like peat moss.' He nabs another piece of bacon, folds it into his mouth accordion-style and speaks while chewing. 'You two have a good morning. Laz will probably be down in the next fifteen, so you might want to plan your kitchen antics accordingly.'

'I'm making breakfast.'

'Yeah, but this guy is looking at you like *you're* breakfast and it's only a matter of time before he makes a move.' And with that he zooms off toward the front door. It slams a moment later, and we hear the muffled sound of his voice carrying across the street. 'Blaine, my man, it's a little chilly for morning spy sessions, don't you think?'

Godric rolls his eyes. 'I wish he'd find something else to focus on.'

'Same. Typically, he would have moved on to something else by now.' It makes me nervous, but Godric and his brothers seem more exasperated by Blaine's attention than worried that he'll uncover their secret.

I did manage to pull a bunch of old papers and microfiche files with more of Godric's 'relatives'. There are a couple with Laz and Hunter as well, all involved in various clubs in the school. But never athletics. That would be far too obvious.

'Back to Hunter's comment about me being breakfast.' I glance over my shoulder.

'Your butt looks good in those jeans. Biteable, really.'

'That's a thought, maybe you should have a nibble.'

'Tempting, but Laz is moving around upstairs and none of us need that awkwardness. And I'd like to wait until you test almost clear for traces of venom before I take another bite out of you.' His arm snakes around my middle and his lips ghost along my throat. The presence of venom in my blood drops daily, but it was a lot higher post-feeding compared to the trace amounts that were present when I was just swallowing his venom through kissing.

The toaster pops and Godric sighs. His arm drops from around my waist, and he pulls the slices free and adds the cheese slice and ham while I finish frying my egg. He's not a fan of egg in sandwiches, so I'm preparing food for one.

'The holidays are coming up.' I check the egg for doneness and deem it ready.

'Mm. Yes, they are.' Godric sets the plate next to the stove.

I slide my egg onto the melty cheese side. 'Do you and your brothers celebrate?'

271

'Sometimes. After three centuries, it can be tough to come up with unique gift ideas. Is it a big deal with your family?'

'Yeah, we all gather at my parents' place. My brothers come in from out of town and bring their significant others. It's chaotic and loud and overwhelming, but it's also a lot of fun.' I carry my sandwich over to the island and slide onto one of the stools.

Godric stands on the other side, coffee in hand, eyes roving over my face, head tipped fractionally to the side. 'How long do you visit them for?'

'Usually at least a week.' I take a bite of my sandwich and chew. Slowly. I'm gathering the courage to ask the next question. I swallow down the mouthful and my nerves, and blurt, 'Maybe you'd like to come visit for Christmas?'

Godric goes still in that way I've become accustomed to. It usually happens when he's trying to stay in control of his actions and reactions. I don't take this as a good sign.

'Or maybe we're not at the meet-the-family stage. Just forget I asked.' I take a huge bite of my sandwich. My mouth is suddenly dry, though, and my eyes are doing that stupid prickly thing, like my feelings are going to leak out of them.

He sets his coffee down. 'I would love to meet your family.'

I put a hand in front of my mouth. 'You would?'

'Of course. I love you, you love them. Meeting them would be an honor.'

My sandwich slips from my fingers and plops onto the plate.

'Hazy?' Godric looks concerned now.

272

I swallow my half-chewed mouthful. 'You love me?'

His brow furrows. 'I tell you this all the time, Hazy. Why do you look so surprised?'

'I think I would remember you dropping the ILY bomb.'

'I always call you *my love*,' he argues.

'That's not the same at all. *My love* is a pet name, like darling, or sweetheart, or babe, or baby, or baby doll or sweet cheeks.'

He makes a face. 'I will never call you sweet cheeks, or baby doll, or babe.'

'Not the point, Godric. You just dropped the ILY bomb. This is like . . . a moment.' I push my stool back. It screeches obnoxiously, but my feet hit the floor and I round the island to stand in front of him. 'I love you, too, in case you didn't already know.'

His grin lights up my entire world. 'I'm happy to hear that, my love. And because I believe it bears repeating, I love you with every fiber of my supernatural being and I would also love to spend Christmas with you and your family, in part because I want to know them, but also because the thought of being away from you for an entire week is utterly absurd.'

24

Godric

'Let the record show that I do not think this is a good idea. At all.' Laz stands in the middle of my room with his arms crossed, wearing a grim expression.

'You don't think anything is a good idea, so I'll take that with a pound of salt.' I fold two pairs of boxer shorts and set them in my duffle. I bought a new travel bag because the suitcase I prefer is a century old and looks more like an heirloom than something I should use.

'It'll be fine, Laz. He's meeting the rents, not asking for her hand in marriage.' Hunter is lounging on my bed, his arms folded behind his head. 'My biggest concern is what the sleeping arrangements will look like. How in the world are you going to keep your hands off Hazy for forty-eight hours?'

'As if putting us in separate rooms will stop me from sneaking into hers,' I scoff.

'She's not particularly quiet,' Laz grumbles.

'Which is a good thing.' Hunter gives me the thumbs up. 'You're clearly taking care of her needs.'

'Of course I'm taking care of her needs. It's my damn responsibility to know what makes her feel good and how to bring her pleasure.'

'Good for you.' Laz slow claps. 'My concern isn't you getting caught in your girlfriend's room, it's her potentially letting the cat out of the bag. Or you slipping up somehow and accidentally revealing who and what we are. Didn't you say she has four brothers? It's human custom to give new boyfriends the third degree, and brothers tend to be protective of their sisters, regardless of whether they're older or younger. It's bad enough that Hazy knows what we are, we can't have her entire family knowing as well.'

'Hazy isn't going to tell them, and I'll handle the third degree just fine. You need to relax. I'll only be gone overnight.' I add a dress shirt, a pair of dress pants, a pair of jeans, a T-shirt and a sweater to my bag.

'We'll have our Christmas dinner tomorrow evening, when you get back,' Hunter says.

Laz makes a noise but doesn't comment otherwise. Laz is big on decorating for holidays. He goes all out for Christmas, even though the entire premise conflicts with our existence. It's a human holiday, one that isn't typically celebrated by our kind. But Laz watches every Christmas movie out there, drinks spiked hot chocolate and makes a gingerbread house that he keeps in his room so we don't start breaking pieces off before Christmas Day. I have a feeling his ire over my trip has less to do with my meeting Hazy's family and rather more to do with the disruption to our Laz-inspired family traditions.

Every few years we take a trip to Europe to see our mother, and mine and Hunter's father. They tend to move around a lot but currently live in Sweden. Those trips are a challenge for Laz because of how he came to exist. His adopting of human traditions, despite his continued belief that he lacks humanity, is a rebellion against himself, because he feels he fits nowhere.

'Why don't we exchange one gift now, and then we can open the rest when I'm back?' I don't wait for a response but rush over to my nightstand and pull two small gifts from my top drawer, passing one to Hunter and one to Laz.

'I suppose that would be okay,' Laz grumbles.

He and Hunter disappear for a moment and return with gifts. I drop down on the window seat and bite back a smile over the memory of what happened the last time I sat here. Hazy suggested we read the chapter for our class together. Except she had me read it aloud. We didn't make it through more than two pages before she was straddling my thighs and asking me to whisper dirty things in her ear.

'Stop thinking about sex!' Hunter lobs wrapping paper at my head.

I don't bother to defend myself. Instead, I peel back the paper and carefully open the gift from Hunter. It's a new shirt that says '*Never Forget*' with a floppy disk, VHS tape and a cassette tape holding hands.

Hunter whoops when he opens the six-pack of craft IPAs.

Laz's brow furrows in concentration as he opens the gift from me. His frown deepens as he takes in the holiday-themed illustrated cover. 'It's a holiday romcom in book form. I know you love movies, but these are portable, and you can enjoy them anywhere.'

He flips the book over and scans the back. 'Hmm. This sounds like something I might like. It ends happily?'

'Yup. Satya says that's basically a requirement for romance books. Unless it's the first of two volumes of a trilogy – those apparently can end with cliffhangers – but this is self-contained, so you get the fulfillment of the happily ever after, like the movies you're fond of.'

'Thanks.' A faint smile pulls up the corners of his mouth.

'No problem. Just trying to keep things fresh.'

I open my gift from Laz, which happens to be one of those pill case things that the elderly use to keep track of their medication. I snort and roll my eyes.

'I'll be fine for a couple of days, but thanks.'

'It seems like feeding from Hazy might be turning into a regular thing. It would be a good idea to bring blood pills with you, since engaging in such activities while you're at her parents' would be unadvisable.'

'I fed yesterday.'

This time from her wrist, while she was straddling my lap. The sex came after.

'We're aware,' Laz says dryly.

I finish packing and throw in things like the toothpaste Hazy leaves in my bathroom, and the toothbrush that sits on my counter but only requires use after I've eaten human food. I also toss in deodorant, which I don't need because I don't sweat, but it's all in the name of playing the part of the human boyfriend.

My brothers help me load everything into the trunk of my car.

'I made a cheese ball for you to take with you.' Laz opens the small cooler to reveal the pecan-crusted ball. It's one of his favorite recipes and he's been making it every year for Christmas since he discovered their existence in the seventies.

'Thanks, that was really nice of you.'

He shrugs. 'I was already making one for us, it wasn't hard to make a second one.' Laz's gaze shifts to the house across the street and his half-smile drops.

A flash of light comes from a window upstairs.

'For his own safety, I sincerely hope Blaine is going away for the holidays,' Laz says darkly. 'Or maybe it would be more fun for me if he stuck around.'

'Don't torment Hazy's ex while I'm gone,' I order.

Laz sighs. 'Just suck the joy out of the holidays for me, why don't you?'

'He'll be too busy partaking in a Christmas movie marathon with me to torment anyone,' Hunter assures me.

I pick Hazy up just before eleven. Hunter and I drove her car out to Niagara yesterday so she and I could make the trip to her parents mostly together, and so I'm able to drive myself home after we celebrate, meaning she can spend more time with her family and I can do the same. Her family celebrate on Christmas Eve, followed by Christmas brunch and gift opening on Christmas morning, and Laz always cooks a turkey dinner on Christmas Day, so I'll be able to participate in all of the best parts of the holiday with all my favorite people. It's a two-and-a-half-hour drive adhering to the speed limit, and having to follow her in a separate vehicle seemed like a torment neither of us needed.

I help Hazy get her bags into the car; she has three, plus all the gifts for her family members to go alongside the ones I wrapped earlier today. She settles into the passenger seat, and I take my place behind the wheel.

She runs her hands up and down her thighs. 'Thanks for driving. And for taking my car all the way home yesterday. I feel bad that you wasted all that time.'

'I wouldn't consider it a waste of time. Not when I get to spend several hours marinating in your luxurious scent and having your undivided attention.' It also only took Hunter and I three hours to make the trip. Two and a bit of those hours were spent in Hazy's car, because it can't get past a hundred and ten miles an hour without the engine protesting. It only took us forty-five minutes to run home.

'You make me sound like a bath bomb.' She shifts in her seat so she's semi-facing me.

'You're more like my favorite brownie. Laz is a fan of bath bombs, though.'

'Why does this not surprise me even a little? Did you leave my gift for him under the tree?'

'I did. I'm sure he'll be delighted on Christmas Day.' I pull onto the freeway and merge into holiday traffic.

'I hope so. Thanks for agreeing to meet my parents. I know it's a lot to ask.'

'Why do you say that?'

'Because I have four brothers and they're going to grill you like a steak.'

'Ah, yes, well that's to be expected. You're the youngest of five and the only female. Protective instincts kick in, and all of that.' I tap on the steering wheel. 'Who do you think I'll have to work hardest to impress?'

Hazy taps her enticing lips and I remind myself that I'm driving and that my eyes need to stay mostly on the road. 'Maybe the twins? Curtis is almost ten years older than me, and he was married and out of the house by the time I hit my mid-teens. The twins were just starting college, so they were still partly around. Francis and I are the closest in age, and he can take a while to warm up to new people.'

'He's the one with a sensory processing disorder?' I

smile at the memory of Hazy's original assumption that I struggled with the same issue before she learned the truth.

'Yeah. That's right. And he's the quiet one. At least when the whole family is around. But when it's just the two of us, he's super chatty.' Hazy plays with the charm hanging around her neck. 'Curtis's wife's name is Olive and she's super preggers and due to have the baby in the new year, so he'll be preoccupied with her. Dawson's partner's name is Greg. They've been together since college, and they got married two years ago. Devon broke up with his long-time girlfriend last year and I don't think he's dated anyone since. It was a rough break-up for him. She decided to move to the West Coast and he didn't want to be that far from family.'

'And your parents have been married for thirty-seven years, your mom is a neurosurgeon and your dad is a biochemical engineer, correct?' I fact check the information Hazy has shared with me since we've started dating.

'That's right.' Hazy smiles. 'Your mind must be like a library.'

'In a lot of ways it is, but meeting the parents like this is a brand-new experience for me. While I've gone to college many times before and immersed myself in your world, I've never gotten this close to a human before, or been able to take part in family celebrations this intimately.'

'Not even with your vampire girlfriend?' Hazy asks. 'I don't even know her name.'

'Elsbeth. And no, her coven didn't agree with our philosophy and shunned her when we . . . got involved. My family became her family.'

'Because of the blood pills?'

'Basically, yes. The vampire world is polarized when it comes to their belief systems. Some stick very closely to tradition, and while that worked a couple of hundred years ago, a lot has changed and we need to change with it. It was during a particularly bad epidemic that my family discovered how to clone human blood and concentrate it into capsule form. We performed some trials and realized it was nearly as effective as drinking the real thing, which at the time was exactly what we needed. Humans were succumbing to illness and we needed an alternative. What at first was a cause to celebrate became the source of a lot of controversy, once humans started to rebound and repopulate.'

'Because some vampires didn't see the need to continue with the blood pills?'

'Exactly, they thought we should go back to feeding from humans and abandon the pills.'

'The side of change is always the hardest one to be on.'

'It can be. We're natural-born predators, and at the top of the food chain. There was understandable resistance to change. Some vampires believed we were trying too hard to humanize ourselves. Others thought we were forsaking our true nature. But during the times when humanity was already at risk, we couldn't threaten to render our nutrition source extinct. The blood pills prevented that from happening, and many covens started to use them as a supplement.'

'What about now?'

'The vast majority use blood pills at least some of the time. There's still controversy around them, but we continue to make headway with those who are resistant. And there are benefits to being on the side of progress. Like getting to meet your family.' While I appreciate Hazy's curiosity, not everything surrounding our discovery was beneficial to our family, so I redirect the conversation.

Hazy must sense that because she doesn't press me. 'Are you excited to meet them?'

'Excited. Nervous. I want your family to like me. I'm aware that it's important for you to have their approval, particularly since you're close to them, which I realize is not the case with all families.'

She nods thoughtfully. 'We are close, and I feel lucky to have such great relationships with them.'

'Has it been hard for you, hiding what I am from them?' I ask.

She's quiet for a moment. 'I think of it more like selective information dissemination. You have to protect yourself and your brothers. I get it, in a way I couldn't before we started running samples of my blood. I see the difference in my own samples and the potential for new discoveries, and how in the wrong hands, it could be a very bad thing.'

'It's the same with any new discovery. There are always two sides to a coin. If we can manage it, I'd like to take another sample tomorrow before I leave,' I tell her.

'And I'll take samples every day while I'm at my parents so we can analyze them when I get back.'

'Thanks for doing that. I know it's not the most convenient.'

'It's important, though. And we're learning so much.'

We've been taking daily samples to document how long the venom stays in her system and the effect it has on her cells. It seems the more often I feed, the longer the venom lingers in her system. In addition to collecting data, we also record her physical, emotional and psychological state to see if there are correlated, compounding changes.

We stop to pick up Hazy's car from the hardware store parking lot in the next town over from where her parents live. Before she hops out of my car and into hers, I pull Hazy in for a long, lingering kiss.

She sighs into my mouth. 'Kissing you is one of my favorite things to do.'

'Good. I feel the same.'

She pulls back, catching her bottom lip with her teeth as she reaches for the door handle, but she leans back in to kiss me one last time before she switches cars.

For better or worse, it's time to meet the family.

25

Hazy

The nerves kick in on the final leg of the drive. Possibly because Godric's presence calms me, and my body seems to be aware of his absence in my car. It's been like that more and more lately. Feeling connected to him beyond a physical or emotional level. It's almost as though my cells recognize his nearness and seek him out.

I don't know if that's a venom thing or a love thing. What I do know for sure is that I'm head over heels for Godric.

I pull into the driveway of my parents' home. It's a nice place on the outskirts of town, in one of those subdivisions with bigger lots. The house is surrounded by lush green lawns and manicured gardens. My mom is the best neurosurgeon in the state, and my dad is the vice-president of a biochemical engineering company, but they never lived an extravagant lifestyle. My parents are serious overachievers. It seems to be an inherited family trait. Curtis is also an engineer, and Dawson went into family medicine. Devon took a slightly different path and is a math professor at a local college. Francis is the deviant of us all and I love him for it. He's pursuing a doctorate in musical therapy.

Cars line the driveway, all of them black or gray, all of them expensive. That I'm still driving the same car I've had since high school is a running joke in our family. As is the fact that it's red and in desperate need of a paint job. My parents have offered several times to upgrade my car, and to help me out financially, but I'm on a scholarship and my summer job pays for groceries and rent throughout the school year. Driving around in a fancy car is asking for attention I've never sought, and there's merit in living like a regular college student. Plus, my place is so close to campus I hardly need to use the car, apart from big grocery trips and coming home for a visit.

Godric parks behind me and we climb out of our respective vehicles. My palms are damp, and my mouth is dry.

He meets me at the trunk and tips his head. 'You're anxious. I'm sorry I can't help you manage that now, but I promise that later, regardless of sleeping arrangements, we'll find a way to expend all that nervous energy.'

'I love that even when you're talking about giving me orgasms you sound like the science nerd you are.' I grab the front of his coat and tug.

He concedes and drops his head, lips meeting mine. He cups my face in his palm, thumb finding my pulse point. 'Keeping my hands to myself until we're alone will be a feat, Hazy. But I'm up for the challenge.'

'I'm not sure if I am.' I sigh, swallowing down the sweetness of his venom. 'Shall we do this? I'm about ten thousand percent sure that my family is standing at the windows watching us.'

'You're right. They're trying to hide behind the curtains. Also, your mother thinks I'm handsome and one of your brothers has already referred to me as a pretty boy and hopes that I'm not like that douche, Blaine the Pain,' he tells me.

'I don't know if your super-hearing is going to be a good thing.'

'I guess we'll find out soon enough.' He presses the trunk button on the keys dangling from my finger and it pops open.

Godric gathers all our bags in one arm, and I give him a look. 'We should probably make more than one trip, don't you think?'

He glances at his loaded-down arm. 'Good point.'

I reclaim one of my bags and I also grab a plastic tote full of gifts. He does the same, leaving behind my laundry basket of clothes I didn't have time to wash before we left, my toiletries bag, the cheese ball Laz so kindly made for us, and the final bag of gifts, for our second trip.

The front door swings open as we reach the porch.

'Baby sis, it's good to have you home!' Francis steps out to meet us, his gaze shifting to Godric before returning to me with an arched eyebrow. 'Let me help you with this stuff, then we can do the whole intro thing.' Francis takes the tote full of presents from me and staggers back a step. 'What the hell do you have in here? Bricks? Have you been working out, or something?' He passes the bin to Dawson, who has come out to greet us, before going to get what is left in the trunk.

Dawson adjusts his grip on the bin. 'Wow, you must be hitting the gym.'

I smile and shrug. 'Godric is a good influence, I guess.'

I make a mental note to add this to our lab reports. Maybe his venom has an impact on my strength that we haven't noticed until now. Regardless, it's worth studying.

As soon as my hands are free of bags and gifts, I'm

enveloped in a round of hugs. The whole family converges on me. And then it's time for introductions.

My heart is thudding in my chest, my palms are damp with sweat, and I can feel my face turning red.

Godric's fingers skim the back of my arm, a silent assurance that everything will be fine. I hope he's right. I want my family to like him. It's one thing to introduce my boyfriend, it's another thing to introduce my *vampire* boyfriend.

He shakes hands with my dad and my brothers, but my mom and Curtis's wife, Olive, both hug him. Dawson's partner, Greg, calls him a snack.

'Why don't you two get settled and then we'll get you a drink,' Mom suggests. 'I've made up the bed in your old room.'

'You can keep your stuff in Hazel's room, Godric, and we'll pull the couch out for you down here when everyone's ready for bed.' Curtis grins and gives Godric a hearty clap on the shoulder.

Olive rolls her eyes and pokes Curtis in the side. 'Don't listen to him, if anyone's ending up on the couch tonight it's him because he always snores when he drinks too many beers.'

'The day bed in Mom's sewing room is all ready for you, Godric,' Dawson says.

Mom's gaze darts to mine, full of apology. I'm sure my brothers are responsible for the sleeping arrangements.

'Whatever makes everyone the most comfortable,' Godric says amicably.

'Come on.' I grab his sleeve and tug him toward the stairs. 'Let me show you my childhood bedroom.' I'm grateful we have a minute, and that he won't have to sleep in the living room like Blaine did when I brought him home for Easter in my freshman year.

I lead Godric down the hall, past my brothers' bedrooms. As the youngest of five, and the only girl, I was fortunate to end up with the biggest bedroom when Curtis left for college. Although I realized later part of the reason had to do with it being at the end of the hall, past all the other bedrooms. If I ever decided to sneak out, I'd have to overcome the obstacle of tiptoeing across creaky floorboards without waking any of them. It was genius really, even if it was unnecessary.

I push open the door to my room. It hasn't changed much since I left for college. There are still a couple of band posters on the walls. The comforter is navy with an atom pattern on it.

'This is it.' I motion him ahead of me.

'It smells like you.' Godric steps inside and sets the bags on the floor by the dresser. 'And feels like you, too.'

I peek around the door and check the hall, making sure none of my brothers followed us up here. 'Sorry about Curtis.'

'It's fine. He's your brother. He's allowed to give me a hard time.'

'I'm also sorry the bed in my mom's sewing room is a single.'

'I don't mind that either, especially since I'll be sneaking up here when everyone is asleep to cuddle with you in your double.' He drops his head, and his lips ghost the column of my throat. He inhales deeply and I tip my head, smiling when his tongue sweeps out, followed by the gentlest scrape of teeth and a soft press of his lips.

Which reminds me . . . I turn to face him and run my hands over his chest, because I can and because his pecs are fantastic. I drop my voice to a whisper only he can hear. 'Have you noticed a change in my strength post-feeding?'

'I was careful to only take a liter last time.' He still gets upset with himself over taking more than that, the first time. And when he fed before we came here, we agreed that my wrist was the safest location. With time I'm sure we'll graduate to less PG locations, but one step at a time.

'I know, but that's not what I meant. Both of my brothers commented on how I must be lifting weights.'

'We are getting an extraordinary amount of exercise in the bedroom lately.' Godric's grin is salacious.

I roll my eyes. 'Head out of the gutter for a minute, please. What I mean is, should we be checking for an increase in my physical strength after I've had a chance to recover from a feeding?'

'Oh.' He blinks. 'Yes. Now that you mention it, I'm not sure how I didn't notice it before.'

'Probably because you're already ridiculously strong and because we're both distracted afterwards.'

'Hmm. Probably. One of the twins is on his way upstairs under the guise of getting something from his room,' Godric warns.

I roll my eyes. It's a trait I've apparently inherited from my mother. 'Seriously. Like we can't wait until after everyone has gone to sleep before we get freaky. Come on, let's go down and get the third degree over with so we can relax and enjoy ourselves.'

He smiles and kisses me. 'I am rather looking forward to seeing how quiet you can be later.'

'That makes two of us.' I head for the door, aware one of my brothers is on the way up to be a nuisance.

We run into Dawson in the hall. 'You two all settled, then?' He does the arched eyebrow thing, and his gaze moves over my boyfriend, clearly assessing.

'Yup. I'm taking Godric down to get the inquisition over with. I'm sure you won't want to miss that.'

Dawson grins but moves so he's standing closer to me. 'Wouldn't miss it for the world. Better get him a stiff drink.'

I shake my head and pull Godric down the hall. 'I'm sorry. They're all going to give you the gears. Blaine was the last guy I brought home and he wasn't a fan favorite.'

'Was he his normal foot-in-mouth self?'

'Yes. Very much. I honestly thought Devon was going to challenge him to a fight in the backyard. It wasn't the best,' I admit.

'I'll do what I can to outcharm him.'

'I don't think you'll have a problem with that,' I say.

The first twenty-four hours were fine, until the charming facade dropped and the douche appeared. Then it was all downhill.

When we reach the living room Curtis offers Godric the seat beside him and my mom drags me into the kitchen to help pour drinks and set up the charcuterie board.

Olive has already made the cheese ball the central focus of the board. She's currently rubbing her rounded belly with one hand and popping a grape into her mouth with the other. Her eyes light up when she sees me. 'I can't remember the last time I had a cheese ball.'

'Godric's younger brother made it for us.'

Mom's arm is laced through mine. She glances over her shoulder, presumably to make sure we're alone, and drops her voice to a whisper. Which would be adequate if I wasn't dating a vampire with exceptional hearing. 'He's so handsome. He looks like he stepped out of the pages of a magazine. And he's so polite.'

Olive raises her fist. 'Nice work, Hazy, he's a hottie.'

I return the bump. 'Yeah. He is.'

'And way nicer than whatever that guy's name was you brought home your freshman year,' Olive adds.

She's been around since I started high school, so she's seen her fair share of boyfriends come and go.

'How did you two meet again?' Mom asks as she pours me a glass of spiked egg-nog. 'And what does Godric drink? Do you think he'd like the egg-nog? I know it's an acquired taste.'

'He's a fan of Scotch or red wine. We have a class together this semester and he lives down the street and around the corner.'

'Even his taste in drinks is sophisticated,' Olive muses. 'He's got my vote.'

'Hmm. The Scotch is probably in the liquor cabinet,' Mom says.

'I can get it,' I say.

I rush to the dining room and scour the cabinet for my dad's Scotch. I find a Glen something or other in a fancy box that's never been opened and bring it back to the kitchen. Mom gives me one of the lowball glasses and I pour a hefty amount.

'I'll deliver this and make sure they're not going at him like vultures.'

'I'm sure it's fine.' Mom pats my hand but doesn't try to stop me.

'My parents are in Sweden for a few months on business, but me and my brothers always celebrate regardless,' Godric is saying.

Curtis has taken on his favorite Godfather-type seated position. My dad is reclined in his favorite chair, looking relaxed and amused. Dawson and Greg are cuddled up on the couch, Devon is stuck in the middle beside Curtis, and Francis is wearing his pursed-lips expression, as if he's waiting his turn to lob a question at Godric.

I cross over to Godric and hand him the glass. 'I hope they're not turning this into the Spanish Inquisition.'

He gives me a warm smile as I lean in and kiss his cheek.

'It should be me serving you, not the other way around, my love, but thank you,' he murmurs.

'Later,' I whisper so only he can hear.

His grin widens and I catch Devon giving us the raised eyebrow.

'I'll be right back.' I give my brothers and my dad a warning look and return to the kitchen.

I don't know what I think is going to happen. It's not like Godric is at risk of blurting out the fact that he's a vampire to my family on a whim. That's more likely something I would do.

When we're finished prepping the food, I bring in the bowl of assorted crackers and my mom follows with the charcuterie board, while Olive brings in the fruit tray. Apparently, all she wants to eat lately is pineapple and berries.

Godric shifts in the oversized chair, making room

for me. It's one of those barrel chairs designed to seat two people. I join him on the chair, and he extends his arm across the back, his fingers grazing my shoulder as I snuggle in.

All my brothers' eyes are on us. Their attention isn't unexpected, but it is annoying.

'Hazel tells me you have a class together and that you're also pre-med,' Mom says conversationally.

'That's right. We're lucky enough to have the same lab section in our biochem class, and it gave me the perfect excuse to talk to Hazy.' Godric smiles down at me. 'We had a one in seven chance of having that lab together and luck was on my side, it seems.'

I give him a wry grin.

'That is so cute. Isn't that so cute?' Olive rests her head on Curtis's arm.

'Yeah. So cute,' Curtis mumbles.

'Hazy told me you have two brothers and you're all going to Burnham. You must be close.'

'We are.' Godric nods.

'But you're spending Christmas with us,' Devon interjects.

'My brothers were happy to tweak our celebration so I could meet all the people who are most important to Hazy, and my parents travel a lot, so we're used to celebrating after the fact.'

The conversation shifts, my mom mentioning that she's always wanted to travel to Europe, but that flying makes her nervous. That leads to a discussion about how travel has changed over the course of history, and Curtis – who is a self-proclaimed history buff – starts talking about 9/11.

'I remember when that happened. It caused an incredible shift in travel on a global scale,' Godric says.

Curtis's brow furrows. 'How would you remember that? You would have been all of what, two years old, when that happened?'

My hand is currently resting on Godric's arm and my fingernails bite into his skin, while I try to keep my expression neutral.

'I mean I remember my parents talking about it when I was a child. My mother's family is from England and for a while they couldn't make the trip to see my grandparents,' Godric explains. 'And then of course we talked about it in school, particularly when we were discussing world events and geography.'

'Right. Yeah. That makes sense,' Curtis says.

26

Godric

I can imagine Laz's reaction if he'd witnessed my accidental slip. Hazy's brother Curtis, while being the one to ask the most questions, isn't nearly as leery of me as her youngest brother, Francis. He's the quiet observer. I find his eyes on me often, and I remind myself that I'm not alone with Hazy.

I realize I've grown accustomed to just being me when I'm with her. I don't slow my movements or attempt to do most things at human speed when we're on our own or in my house. Sure, I temper myself when we're in class, but my comfort level with Hazy is high, which means I need to play the part of the regular human boyfriend in the presence of her family unless I want to blow this whole thing apart.

It's a reality check I don't like all that much.

Hazy's family clearly adores her, and her brothers are inclined to take on the protector role, while Hazy, being Hazy, shoots them down at every pass.

Christmas Eve dinner is an elaborate affair even Laz would approve of. I do my best to keep up my human charade, accepting offers for seconds on turkey and stuffing and dessert.

Later in the evening, once dinner dishes have been

tackled and leftovers put away, we end up playing Trivial Pursuit and I flub a few questions, otherwise I'd end up winning by a landslide.

Olive is the first to go to bed, followed by Hazy's parents. We're sitting around the living room, chatting with her brothers. I excuse myself to go to the bathroom for a moment, not because I need to use it, but because I can hear her parents whispering to each other from their bedroom on the main floor and curiosity has gotten the better of me. It's also a human thing to do, and I need to keep up the ruse.

The water is running and it's clear someone is brushing their teeth.

'He seems like a nice young man. He's got his head on his shoulders and he's clearly ambitious if he's pre-med like Hazy. I like him a lot more than the one she brought home freshman year,' her dad says.

Her mom spits out a mouthful of toothpaste. 'Blaine. He was . . . not her best choice.' There's some rustling. 'Godric seems nice and he says all the right things.'

'But?' her dad prompts.

She's silent for a moment before she sighs. 'I don't know. There's something about him. I can't put my finger on it. I worry she'll get her heart broken. They're so wrapped up in each other, it's almost like the rest of the world doesn't exist outside of their bubble. Maybe I'm being an overprotective momma bear. It's been a long time since she's brought someone to meet the family.'

I head back to the living room, feeling bad that I've been eavesdropping on her parents' conversation. As I'm walking down the hall, I pick up on the conversation between Hazy and her brothers.

'I don't know, he seems pretty nice to me,' Dawson says.

'He's pretty, that's why you think that,' Greg fires back. His tone is teasing, though.

'There's just something. I don't know,' Francis, who has said all of twenty words this evening, mutters.

'Yes! Exactly. He's almost . . . too good to be true,' Curtis says.

I'm unsurprised; he's been the most vocally wary of me since I arrived. Some people have a better danger radar than others, and Curtis fits into that category.

'Can you guys stop, please?' Hazy snaps. 'He's my boyfriend. Feel however you want, but the interrogations stop now. Don't ruin this for me the same way you did when I brought Blaine home.'

'He was a dick,' Francis says.

'I'm aware. But you and Curtis made it super uncomfortable for me by being giant d-bags the whole time he was here. And while I realize he and I weren't destined to walk down the aisle together, you certainly helped expedite the end of our relationship. I would appreciate it if you didn't do the same thing to Godric. He's important to me and I want him to feel welcome and not like he's under a damn spotlight.'

'Woah, woah, walk down the aisle? You two have been dating how long? A few months? And you're already planning your wedding?' Francis sounds aghast at the possibility, which I don't appreciate.

'That's not what I meant!' Hazy sounds flustered and her heart rate is elevated. 'I just mean I know Blaine was not destined to be long term, and I have no idea what the future holds for me and Godric, but I would like it if you

297

didn't chase him off by being judgemental jerks or pulling the whole big-brother-protector garbage because you still feel you have to treat me like I'm a teenager, not a grown-ass woman capable of making good boyfriend choices.'

'Calm down, Haze, we're giving you the gears because you get all riled up about it,' Devon says.

'Speak for yourself,' Francis says. 'There's something about him. I don't know what it is, but he makes me nervous.'

'Can you guys please stop talking shit? How awful would you feel if your significant other's siblings were bad-mouthing you, and you overheard.'

'He's in the bathroom, he can't hear us,' Curtis scoffs.

I take that as my cue to make some noise. Their voices drop to a whisper, and when I round the corner the room goes silent.

Hazy fakes a yawn and pushes to a stand. 'Well, I think I'm going to call it a night. Dad always gets up early and bangs around in the kitchen, so sleeping in is impossible. Want to come up and say goodnight?' She turns to me and holds out a hand.

'Yeah. Sure.' I thread my fingers through hers. 'Night, all. Sleep well, see you in the morning.' I wave to her brothers.

They all say goodnight, Devon and Dawson both wearing chagrined expressions. Curtis and Francis share looks, but I follow Hazy out of the room and up the stairs.

She waits until we're in her bedroom and the door is closed before she turns to me, her lips pursed. 'How much did you hear?'

'All of it.' Lying is pointless and isn't going to help either of us.

'I'm sorry they're being jerks.'

I cup her face in my hands and press my lips to hers. 'They're being brothers, it's okay.' Do I love their wariness? No. Do I understand it? Absolutely. 'I'm literally a predator, Hazy. I would be more concerned if none of them had reservations.'

'I just want them to like you. You're important to me,' she admits.

'And you're important to me. Give them time to get used to me and get to know me. And I'm sorry about my slip-up. I was out to lunch.'

'You covered it well.'

'I'm used to being around you. My guard is down, and I need to remember where I am and who I'm with.' I kiss her again. 'I should go to my room. Your youngest brother is currently devising a plan to check on you for stupid reasons. I'll come back when everyone else is asleep.'

'That we're sleeping in separate rooms is ridiculous. I've been living away from home for four freaking years.'

'I think it's sweet of you to take your parents' feelings into consideration and next week we can make up for all the missed sleepovers.' I leave her room and slip back into mine seconds before Francis knocks on Hazy's door.

I put in my earpods and crank the music so I'm not listening in on their conversation. It takes nearly two hours before her brothers finally decide to call it a night. I try not to tune in while they're talking, but it's tough when I keep picking up my name. Curtis is not a fan. Francis continues to have a feeling about me, Dawson thinks I'm too pretty, and Devon is neutral. He doesn't want what happened with the last guy to happen with me.

Hazy is fast asleep when I slip into her room. I don't wake her. Instead, I slide into bed beside her and enjoy the comfort of her presence. She rolls over and tucks her body against mine.

All night I lie there, rubbing an errant curl between my fingers, listening to the soothing beat of her heart and her regular breathing. At times I'm almost lulled into a state of semi-consciousness. But my mind keeps going back to her mother's worry about me breaking her heart.

I'm in love with Hazy, and not in the sometimes fickle way of humans. She's the beginning and the end for me, and all of Laz's original worries niggle at me. Because he's right, we have about a decade before it starts to become obvious that she's getting older and I'm not – not at the same rate as humans do anyway. But maybe there's something in this whole venom transfer situation. She's stronger than usual, and it's only been a couple of days since I last fed from her. We need to run more tests, gather more data.

A decade is a blip in eternity, but it's significant for Hazy. It could be enough time for me to find a way to keep her human and slow down the aging process. Ten years is nothing for me, but the twenties are an exciting time in a human life, there's so much personal growth. Those are experiences I would never want to take from her. But I do have to consider the very real possibility that there will be a time limit on our relationship. Even if she did want to transition from human to vampire, the odds aren't in our favor, and I would rather walk away than take that risk. And that's a terrifying thought, because losing her would make my existence feel like a death sentence with no end.

*

I sneak out of Hazy's room when I hear movement in the kitchen. She's still dead to the world, but I kiss her cheek and extract myself from her arms. She woke up at four and did a little groping, but she was too out of it to do more than pat my junk and nuzzle into me.

I'm not quick enough in my exit and I run into Francis on the way back to the sewing room.

He's standing in the middle of the hall with his arms crossed. 'Can't spend one night apart from her?'

'To be fair, I'll be spending the better part of a week separated from her, and her presence is calming in a way no one else is.'

He pokes at his cheek with his tongue. 'She seems to have a bad habit of falling for pretty boys.'

It's my turn to cross my arms. 'If you're referring to Blaine, I think it's safe to say his pretty boy status declines fairly quickly after he opens his mouth and speaks.'

'You've met him?'

'I have. I happen to live across the street from him.'

His lip curls. 'So you're a frat boy.'

'My brothers and I aren't from the cast of *Neighbours*, if that's where your concern lies. I'm quite serious about my academic standing. I have a four-point-oh GPA and so does my youngest brother. We're all serious about our degrees.'

'You're not really Hazy's type.'

'And why is that?'

'Shouldn't you be dating some . . . sorority girl or something?'

'Why do you believe a sorority girl would be more my type than Hazy?'

He gives me a look. 'Come on, man.'

'Hazy is incredibly intelligent, she has an amazing sense of humor, she's fun to be around, she makes the best goddamn brownies in the history of the universe, and she's the most beautiful woman I've ever had the privilege of laying eyes on. In my eyes she is absolutely the perfect woman and I feel blessed beyond measure to have the opportunity to be with her. I'm grateful for every smile, every laugh, and every moment I get to spend in her presence. She is a joy and a delight. I don't think there's another woman out there who will ever hold a candle to her, regardless of who they are and what their hobbies consist of.'

He blinks at me a few times. 'Don't break her goddamn heart.'

'If anyone is at risk of having their heart broken, Francis, it's me. Now if you'll excuse me, I'd like to get changed so I can join your father downstairs and have coffee with him, because it seems as though I'm facing quite the battle for acceptance here, and my plan is to do everything in my power to prove that I am, without a doubt, wholly dedicated to Hazy and her happiness.'

My speech seems to have the desired effect, as Hazy's brothers back off, and some of the hostility from Francis seems to dissipate. Curtis is too busy fawning over his pregnant wife – she'll be going into labor before the new year, based on her body's signals – to pay much attention to me this morning.

Hazy comes downstairs half an hour after me, her hair tousled, sleep lines still on her face, eyes alight with excitement and nerves. I stand as soon as she enters the room, and she heads straight for me.

I don't think about the fact that her entire family is observing our interaction as I cup her face in my palms and she tips her head back, puckering her lips as I brush mine over hers. 'Merry Christmas, my love. I hope you slept well.'

'Sorry I passed out before we could celebrate,' she whispers, so quietly only I am able to catch the words.

'No apologies necessary.' I keep my lips closed when she strokes along the seam with her tongue.

Her father is sitting fifteen feet away from us, and Hazy's body and mind are not online together.

One of her brothers clears his throat and Hazy backs off, her cheeks flushing as she realizes that she tried to make out with me in front of her entire family.

Once we all have coffees in hand, the gift opening begins. I must admit, despite the challenge of winning over her family, celebrating with them is a new experience I would happily repeat, inquisition and all, if it means I can see the joy on Hazy's face as they exchange gifts and smile and laugh and hug.

And it makes me question what the future will hold for us, and whether it would be kinder to walk away from her before I do exactly what her family worries about. It doesn't matter how much she thinks she loves me. If by some miracle we manage to increase the odds enough that transitioning becomes possible, and she survives, she will have to watch her family grow old and pass away from afar. She'll lose her parents, her brothers, their partners, her nieces and nephews, their children. The cycle will go on and on, and she'll be on the periphery of it all. That isn't a heartache I want to be responsible for.

After Christmas brunch I pack up my bag so I can head home and join my brothers for dinner and Hazy can have time with her family, without me there to make them edgy.

'I'm sorry we didn't get any alone time.' Hazy wraps her arms around me and settles her cheek against my chest.

I press my lips to her crown, enjoying the closeness, aware that once I leave, I'm opening the door for her brothers to plant seeds of doubt about us. I can sense it's coming, and I don't love it, but it's inevitable. 'We'll have plenty of opportunities for alone time next week.'

'I'll try to head back early if I can.'

I pull back and take her face in my hands, shaking my head. 'Don't do that. Spend time with them. Enjoy them. I'm not going anywhere.'

'You feel far away already,' she whispers.

'Just a couple of hours' drive, my love. I'll see you in a few days and we can spend an entire day naked in bed together, how does that sound?'

'Divine, to be honest.'

This time when she kisses me, I don't stop her from deepening it. Selfishly, I want the memory of my kiss to stay with her when she goes back into that house.

The moment I pull into the driveway, Laz throws open the front door. He's wearing a black sweater with a white Christmas tree on it. His arms are crossed, and his expression is grim, which is typical. I grab my bag from the truck and my gifts from her family and meet him in the foyer.

'Merry Christmas. I think we need to terminate Hazy's ex.'

'Merry Christmas, we would have to move if we did that.'

'Yesterday he came over three times. Once to ask for

a cup of sugar and then he brought us some weed-laced cookies and tried to invite himself in.'

'Did you answer the door?' I think Laz has avoided any face-to-face interactions with Blaine.

'Of course not.' He sneers with disdain. 'Hunter answered and I listened from the other room. He had all kinds of questions about where you were and when you were expected back. The third time he stopped by was under the guise of polling the street about what house should host the New Year's bash. I'm sure you would be unsurprised to hear that we're winning by a landslide.'

'I figured we'd have a low-key New Year's, particularly after what happened on Halloween. Has he been by today?'

'No, he left this morning to visit his parents, so we have a few days before he returns to bother us. Memory modification would go a long way in making him less of a problem.'

'He's harmless, and that's a last resort.'

Laz makes a sound of disagreement. 'He's exceptionally interested in us and I don't like it. He also seems to think majority rules apply under these circumstances. It might be advisable for you to pay him and his Speedo-wearing roommate a visit and let them know that we are not interested in hosting another party. As I'm sure you're aware, Hunter always believes a party is a good idea.'

'I'll deal with Blaine,' I say, wishing I'd stayed with Hazy's family and dealt with her brothers rather than my own.

27

Hazy

'There's something about him. I can't put my finger on it.' Francis is wearing his pensive expression as he shuffles the cards. We're playing a game of cribbage in the living room, just the two of us.

This conversation is zero percent surprising. Francis has always been exceptionally perceptive and a quiet observer on the best of days, so the fact that he's picked up on something isn't unexpected. It is challenging to talk around, though.

'He's not like Blaine if that's what you're worried about.'

He lays down a nine and I lay a six, making fifteen. I move my back peg forward two points. 'He's a hell of a lot prettier than Blaine was, that's for sure.'

'Blaine's personality made him ugly.'

'That's accurate.' He lays down a face card. 'Godric ticks all the right boxes. And it's clear he's completely head over heels for you. I mean, the way he looks at you.' Francis rolls his eyes. 'It's borderline inappropriate.'

I'm in the middle of a sip of my tea and I almost choke on it. As it is, I cough a couple of times when the sweet liquid tries to enter my lungs.

Francis arches an eyebrow. 'Please be smart with this one, Hazy. You have a lot of years of education left to go if you're planning on being a doctor.'

'Can you please not with the lectures? I have a dad, I don't need you trying to be a second one.' I lay a four, bringing the total to twenty-nine.

He holds up a hand. 'Noted. I just don't want your future derailed because of some cute guy who turns you into a walking hormone.' Francis puts down an ace and reaches for his pegs, but I hold up a hand.

I drop my own ace, making it thirty-one, giving me two points, plus two more for the pair.

'Dammit, you're kicking my ass,' Fran gripes.

'That's what you get for being a pain in mine.'

'I just want what's best for you.'

'I appreciate that, I get that the last time I brought a guy home you all wanted to pummel him, but the only thing he and Godric have in common is that they're both pre-med. Give me the benefit of the doubt that I can make better boyfriend choices than I did in my freshman year.'

But that conversation with my brother, and the one I had with my mom – who shares the same 'there's something' concern – hang over my head. Especially when the messages I'm getting from Godric are . . . not his typical flirty, fun, I can't wait to get you back into bed ones.

Hazy: *having fun with your brothers?*

Godric: *Absolutely. Almost as much fun as I had with yours.*

I frown, because there are no jk or laughing emojis that follow.

Hazy: *I'm sorry if it was a stressful trip*

Godric: *It wasn't stressful, it just gave me a lot to think about.*

Hazy: *such as . . .*

Godric: *Your family only wants what's best for you, and I want the same.*

Hazy: *which is you*

Godric: *I don't know that they would agree, especially if they knew the truth.*

Everything feels off – and I don't like it. I make a quick decision.

Hazy: *I'm calling you on video chat.*

I hit the video button and wait for him to answer.

As soon as he does, I blurt, 'What's going on?'

'Nothing. I'm sitting here, drinking Scotch, watching bad TV, awaiting your return.'

Godric is lounging in his wingback chair in the living room. It's dark, with only the faint glow of what I assume is the TV lighting up the right side of his face in short bursts.

I give him a look. 'What's with the whole "I don't know that they would agree, especially if they knew the truth"? Did something happen that you're not telling me about?'

'You can't tell me they would still be okay with us dating, if they knew what I really was.'

Until we started dating, I didn't realize vampires existed outside of movies and books, so his statement isn't all that fair. 'They don't know you the way I do.'

His gaze shifts away, focused somewhere beyond his phone. 'And they never will, because I'm making you lie to them about me.'

I don't love the churning in my gut, or the set of his jaw. 'You're not making me do anything, Godric. I understand why that needs to remain a secret.'

'The secrecy is only one small piece of it, though.'

'Can you look at me, please? What's happening right now? I feel like you're not telling me something.'

His gaze shifts back to me, his eyes roving over my face, but I can't read his expression. 'I'm sorry. It's not intentional. Maybe Laz's melancholy is rubbing off on me. I miss you.'

'I miss you, too, but I'll be back before you know it. Talk to me. Tell me what's going on. Are you upset about my brothers? They just need time, Godric. That's all.' I feel like I'm talking in a circle, getting nowhere.

Godric smiles, but it's strained. 'I would prefer to have you with me if we're going to discuss how your family feels about me. It's unsurprising that they have reservations.'

'Does that mean you're having reservations about us?' I swallow down the lump forming in my throat.

'I have no reservations about you and me, my love.'

'It sounds like there's a "but" attached to that statement.'

'I wish I could reach through this infernal device and put you at ease. You're the best thing in my life, Hazy.'

I blow out a frustrated breath, certain there's more to that statement, but he's holding back. 'Okay. I'll probably head back the day after tomorrow.'

'Enjoy your time with your family.'

'You, too.'

'I'll do my best.'

I end the call feeling worse instead of better.

Weather reports show a storm rolling in later the following afternoon. As much as I love my parents, I don't want to end up snowed in for several more days. I get up early the following morning, load my car with my gifts and clean

309

laundry, and text Satya and Alyssa to let them know I'm on my way back. They both went home to visit their parents for the holidays, but we all planned to be back for New Year's.

I also text Godric, who responds with *drive safe* and *I can't wait to see your beautiful face*. My stomach does its usual somersault over his message, but there's a knot forming with every mile that passes. I don't like the physical or the emotional distance between us.

I'm half an hour into the drive when the snow starts, and an hour from Niagara the visibility begins to degrade. Swirling snow makes it tough to see more than a few yards in front of me. I squint when I notice a black spot up ahead. The last thing I need is to hit a moose or a deer. But as I get closer, I realize it's not an animal, it's a person.

I don't want to leave someone out in the middle of a snowstorm, but I also don't want to end up the victim of a kidnapping. It's a real conundrum. At least until my phone starts to ring from its spot in the holder on the dash, and Godric's name flashes across the screen.

I hit the answer button and his voice filters through, the reception not the best. 'It's me you're about to pass. I'd love to keep you company on the ride home.'

'Huh?' I pass the figure with a phone in his hand, who happens to be male and my boyfriend. 'Oh shit.' I brake and the back tires skid out for a few terrifying seconds before they find traction again.

'Be careful, please,' Godric's voice is laced with concern.

'Pulling over,' I tell him as I signal, tapping the brakes again, carefully this time. I ease onto the shoulder and Godric appears at the passenger-side door.

'Why don't you let me take over driving from here,' he says before he ends the call.

I check my mirrors before I exit the vehicle. He's right there, though, guiding me around the hood and helping me in the passenger side. We don't kiss or hug; the snow is pelting my face and my eyeballs feel like they're at risk of freezing in the few seconds it takes to get from the driver's to the passenger seat.

Godric slips behind the wheel. His lashes and eyebrows are coated with snow, along with every other part of him.

'How the hell did you get here?'

'I ran.'

'Aren't you frozen?'

'I was moving fairly quickly, so I'm fine.'

I grab him by the lapels of his jacket and fuse my mouth to his. His lips are cold but soft, and his tongue is warm, mouth sweet.

Eventually, he pulls back. 'As much as I love making out with you, we're losing visibility by the minute. Why didn't you wait out the storm at your parents' house?'

'I wanted to get home so we could talk. I've been a bag of anxiety since you left, and that video chat we had yesterday ramped it right up to intolerable levels,' I tell him.

He strokes my cheek with cold fingers. 'I'm sorry. That wasn't my intent. I felt this conversation would be better when we're in the same room, not miles apart.'

Swallowing feels like it's basically impossible with how big the lump in my throat is.

'Let me get us off this road and somewhere safe.' He shifts the car into gear and signals us back onto the road.

The visibility is garbage. I don't know that I would have

been able to get us much further with the white-outs we're currently facing. I search for a place to stay on my map and half an hour later we stop in a small town with a tiny run-down motel. It's not that Godric can't navigate the road, it's that there are pile-ups all over the place and getting around them is proving impossible. Also, while he can survive a car crash, I'm not immortal, and putting me at risk like that is not something he wants to do.

I unload my bags from the car and follow Godric into the seedy accommodation. His lip curls as he takes in the small space. 'It would be lovely to have Laz's powers,' he sighs.

'Are you going to break up with me?' If the answer is yes, tonight is going to be long.

Godric turns to face me, his expression full of emotions that make my heart sink. 'Your brothers and your mother are worried I'm going to break your heart.'

'Is that your plan?' I wring my hands. My mouth is dry, my palms sweaty.

'Of course not. But their concerns aren't unfounded. Although, if anyone's heart is at risk of being broken, it's mine.'

'I'm not going anywhere.'

'My life is endless, Hazy. I'm here until the world implodes or someone removes my heart from my chest, chops my head off for good measure and incinerates me before I have a chance to regenerate.'

'That's exceptionally graphic and a horrible way to die.'

'It's also the truth. And so is the fact that our relationship is complicated, and those complications will be compounded the longer we're together. Meeting your family has shown me this with a clarity I had previously been unwilling to entertain. It's fine for now, because you're in your early twenties and I appear to be in mine. But what happens a decade from now, when you're in your thirties and I continue to defy the aging process? There will be questions we can't answer without your family finding out I'm not human, and that will put everyone at risk. And more than that, I don't think it's fair to make you choose between me and the people you love.'

'Okay, but I'm only twenty-two and we've been dating for less than six months. I feel like you're drinking the Laz Kool-Aid and you've veered into fatalist mode. We don't have to make the future today's problem. We have time to figure things out. It doesn't have to be all or nothing, and we don't have to plan forever right now, do we?'

He lifts his hand, fingers drifting down my cheek. 'No, we don't have to plan forever right now.'

There's something in his tone. 'What aren't you telling me?'

He's silent for a long while before he finally whispers, 'Comparatively, your decade is a couple of months for me.'

I drop down on the edge of the bed. It creaks loudly and I bounce a couple of times. 'That hurts my brain.'

He sits down beside me, knee touching mine. 'I know. I'm trying not to overwhelm you, Hazy, but these are the things I think about while you're sleeping. In the same way that I'm stronger and faster than humans, I also tend to experience emotions in extremes, and my feelings for you are deep and layered and complex. Being with your family, seeing the love you have for each other, makes me question a lot of things.' He plays with my fingers, his eyes on our hands.

'Can you explain what and why, exactly?' I bite the inside of my cheek.

'When humans think about the future, they plan in terms of months, and years and what their five-year plan looks like. Maybe it's about graduating, then going on to graduate school. Or getting engaged after that, starting a career, getting married, having a family. It's a chronological order of events. Most human lives follow a similar path. There are ups and downs, roadblocks and challenges, high points and low points. It's a cycle with a beginning, a middle and an end.'

'But your life isn't like that,' I whisper.

Godric shakes his head. 'No, because the cycle is broken. There is life with no certainty of death.'

I let that sink in. Really sink in for the first time.

Godric runs his thumbs across my knuckles. 'Time moves differently when there is no end to it. My brothers and I have been planning this sabbatical for the past forty-six years. For Hunter it's been a countdown to party time. I've been planning to access labs and use the resources at my disposal to further my research on blood pills and figure out what we can do better. But then you came into my life and that goal changed. *I've* changed, Hazy. Everything I want out of this existence has shifted and it all aligns with you. So I can sit here and say that we don't have to plan forever tonight, and while it's true, in my head, I'm already skipping decades.'

'While I'm over here thinking about New Year's, you're thinking ahead to the end of my life cycle?' I ask softly.

Godric bites his bottom lip and nods once. 'I don't want to overwhelm you or scare you with my honesty, but there are few ways forward and all of them cause some-one pain.'

'And you already know what it's like to lose someone you love,' I muse. 'How long were you and Elsbeth together?'

Godric stares at me for a few long seconds, not moving, not breathing. His voice is barely a whisper. 'Seventy-two years.'

'A human life span.' I absorb that information. Let it sink in. 'How long has she been gone?'

'Forty-three years.'

'Is that enough time for your heart to heal? Or does it ever recover from a loss like that?'

'Some vampires are together for hundreds of years. It's a fraction of an existence. And the meaning of time isn't the same for me. But what I felt for her is nothing com-pared to how I feel about you. Imagining what that pain would feel like is . . . untenable. I already know how much it hurts to lose someone whose heart is close to mine, and I don't want that pain for you.'

'What about you, what do you want for yourself?' I'm trying to see outside of my narrow scope, but I don't know that I can. Not in these shoes, this body, this life with an imminent ending, no matter how far into the future it is.

His gaze lifts. 'Say we're together for the next ten years. Eventually, a choice will have to be made, and no matter what it is, it will hurt you. Me being with you, loving you, it's entirely selfish. If we went our separate ways it would hurt us both, but in some ways that pain is far easier to tolerate than the alternative. Because if you wanted to transition, even if we ignore the low odds of survival, it would also hurt you because it would mean taking you away from your family. And worse, you would lose them, one at a time, from a distance. I don't ever want to do that to your heart. What if you resented me for it? What if you hated me? What if, after everything, I locked you into forever and you didn't want it with me anymore?'

I cup his cheek in my hand. 'You went to some dark places these past few days, didn't you?'

He raises his eyes to the ceiling and he nods. 'Maybe a little.'

I blow out a breath. 'I'm not going to lie. This is a lot to process.'

I consider what it would be like to spend the next ten years with him, loving him, growing with him, only to have something happen that would take him away from me, or me away from him. I try to multiply that feeling by ten, by a hundred, but it makes my heart ache too much. 'There are so many conversations to have about this. It's not the kind of thing to talk about once and then leave it alone. Whatever the future looks like for us, whatever the choices we make, together and separately, we will talk them through, one fear, one worry, one step at a time. We'll poke around in the places that make us uncomfortable. We'll disagree, we'll get angry, we'll be scared and hopeful and every emotion in between. But we'll figure it out together.' I take both of his hands in mine. 'I love you, you love me, and for now, tonight, it can be enough, because we have the gift of time. We have time to learn, time to talk things through, to make a list of pros and cons and decide it's crap and write a new one. Don't decide what to do tomorrow based on what you're afraid of ten years from now.'

'You are the most incredible gift,' Godric whispers. 'I don't know what I did to deserve you.'

He drops his head and slants his mouth over mine, and I get lost in him, in the need for connection, in a love that might be bigger than either of us knows what to do with. But hell if I'm going to let fear of what hasn't happened yet get in the way of right now.

28

New Year's is low-key. Despite Blaine stopping by half a dozen times to remind us about his party, we skip it. Instead, me and Godric and his brothers, plus Satya and Alyssa, make dinner together and hang out and play games while drinking Laz's fancy cocktails. It's the perfect ending to the holidays.

And then second semester begins. Blaine is in two of my classes. I guess I should be grateful that he was only in one last semester. I'm also grateful that Godric happens to be in our shared genetics course. While I avoid sitting near Blaine in our first shared class, Godric's height makes it tough for us to hide in the genetics class.

Blaine spots us the second we walk through the door and starts waving his hands around like he's doing an impression of the inflatable balloon guy. 'Hazy, God, got seats saved for you!' He pats the chairs on either side of him.

'Can we ignore him?' Godric asks.

'Not if we want to avoid unnecessary embarrassment.' I squeeze his hand.

'Maybe Laz is right about taking care of him,' Godric grumbles.

'We can't terminate our classmates, even if they are infuriating. Besides, I think this is one of those cases where you keep your friends close and your enemies closer.'

'You're right, which is unfortunate,' Godric agrees as we head for the front of the class.

'Let's make a Blaine sandwich!' My annoying ex motions energetically to the seats on either side of him.

'We should leave the left-handed desk for someone who needs it,' Godric announces.

He ushers me down the aisle, past Blaine, and takes the seat directly beside him, acting as my vampire shield.

'How great is it that we're in another class together this semester?' Blaine says.

'So great,' I mutter.

Godric makes a sound that's more like a growl than anything else.

Blaine seems to be oblivious to Godric's annoyance. He motions between the two of them. 'You and me have a lot in common, huh?'

'You mean because we're both breathing and have Y chromosomes.'

Blaine laughs. Loudly. 'And we're both pre-med. And we've both dated Hazy. If you need any pointers I'm here to help.' He nudges Godric's elbow.

I lean forward. 'This is one of those occasions when your helpfulness and honesty make you look and sound like a complete douche, Blaine.'

'I'm trying to be a good friend,' Blaine says.

The pencil Godric is flipping between his fingers snaps in half. 'I take my pointers from Hazy, since she's very capable of telling me what she needs.'

'Right. Cool. She's vocal, I'll give her that.' He gives Godric the double thumbs up.

I lean in and drop my voice to a whisper only Godric can hear. 'You can't murder him in a room full of people.'

Thankfully, the professor enters the room and Blaine

319

can't say anything else that's horrifyingly inappropriate.

I'm also grateful that the class we all have together is twice a week instead of three times. Because every single class, Blaine saves us seats. We learn to arrive only a minute or two before class begins so Blaine only ever has a chance to ask Godric one or two questions, usually about his family and more specifically about his great-uncle and the house they live in. Blaine has been doing an awful lot of research around that house, and subsequently, Godric's family.

Unfortunately, luck is not on our side and Blaine is not only in our genetics class, but he's also in the same lab section. He manages to partner up with the curly-haired girl from last semester's biochem class. Her name is Ursula but she goes by Sula. She seems nice, which means I feel bad that she's stuck with Blaine. I also feel bad for me and Godric, since they're at the table to the right of ours so Blaine is forever leaning over, asking about our findings and blah, blah, blah. He's about as subtle as a flashing neon sign.

My hope was that by sitting beside him twice a week in our genetics class, Blaine's obsession with Godric and his brothers would wane, but the opposite seems to have happened. If it isn't bad enough that I have to constantly remind Godric not to murder him in our genetics class, Blaine almost always manages to get a seat next to me in our other shared class and that one *is* three days a week. So I'm a captive audience for Blaine and his nonsense five times a week.

It's a Monday, and unfortunately, I have articles that need copyediting for the paper. After the class I have with

Blaine, I head to the office. Blaine, being the infernal micro-manager that he is, decides to tag along. On a positive note, he's stopped giving me paper copies only. In part because two weeks ago I failed to proof more than ten articles for him, and the paper was full of blank spots as a result.

He couldn't blame it on me, because the office had been locked and I couldn't get in to proof them. While that problem has been solved, he's started sending them to a folder I can only access on the computer in the office, with a password that changes on a weekly basis. He is literally the most bothersome person in the history of the universe.

Blaine leans in close and drops his voice to a whisper, even though no one is paying attention to us as we trudge across the salted pathway. 'I have something I need to show you when we get to the office.'

Most of my face is covered by my scarf. It's freezing today and the wind is bitingly cold. My eyes are watering and my eyelashes feel like they're trying to weld themselves together with every blink. 'My excitement is boundless.'

'Did you hear me? It's important. I found something out about your boyfriend. He's hiding things from you.' This time he doesn't whisper.

I turn my head enough so I can blink at him, then focus on putting one foot in front of the other.

Blaine doesn't try to say anything else on the subject, mostly because his tongue is probably at risk of freezing off if he talks too much. The paper office is empty when we get there, but at least it's warm and my eyeballs don't feel like they're icing over anymore. I don't even have my jacket off before Blaine slaps a small stack of handwritten articles on my desk.

I frown at the papers. 'Who the hell writes articles by hand these days?'

'These aren't articles, they're essays. I've been doing some digging and there are some strange coincidences concerning this boyfriend of yours and the previous Godric Hawthorn who attended college here fifty years ago.'

I exhale through my nose in frustration. 'We've already been through this, Blaine. Godric's named after his great-uncle.'

'Yeah, you told me. But look at these.' He jabs a finger at the stack of photocopied essays.

'I'm looking. They're essays written by Godric Hawthorn. So what?'

'There's an archive in the school library documenting all students who graduated with honors.'

I shrug, trying to appear nonchalant, but already I'm connecting the dots. 'So Godric's great-uncle was a good student, too. That's not a crime, Blaine.' Godric gets mostly nineties in his classes. He purposely sits below the top one percent of students to avoid drawing too much attention to himself, but intentionally making mistakes irritates him.

'Check this out . . . ' He flips open the manila folder, revealing a photo of an open spiral notebook. 'The handwriting is *exactly* the same. Look at the loops in the l's and the p's.' He stabs at the piece of paper.

I stare down at the samples. I recognize the handwriting as Godric's. And the spiral notebook is definitely his. There's a heart in the top corner of the page with my name in it and an arrow through it. He's cheesy like that.

'You took pictures of Godric's notebook?'

'To prove a point,' he says defensively.

How I manage to keep my voice even is a wonder, although I suppose I'm used to brushing off people's concerns when it comes to my vampire boyfriend. 'So you're saying what, Blaine? That he's traveled here from the past? That he's from another time? Or that there's a portal to a parallel dimension and he's managed to make his way from –' I glance at the date on the newspaper article – 'the nineteen seventies to the twenty-first century?'

'No. That's not . . . I'm not saying that.'

'What are you saying, then? Because if he's from the seventies, he's aged incredibly well.' I choke back a slightly hysterical laugh.

Blaine mashes his lips together. 'How do you explain two people having the exact same handwriting? What if he stole the original essays and replaced them with these?'

'Why would someone steal a fifty-year-old essay? You need a new hobby, Blaine. Your obsession with Godric is getting out of hand. You're veering into stalker territory.'

'I'm uncovering the truth!'

'Like you did with that poor microbio professor last year, or that guy from DIK, two years ago? This is what you do, Blaine. You fixate. You've been doing it with me for four years. And now you're doing it with Godric and his brothers. Is this transference or what?'

He gaze drops to the V in my V-neck. 'You're hiding something. Your chest is going blotchy. That only happens when you lie.'

'It also happens when I'm annoyed.' And when I'm about to have an orgasm. But he's right about the lying part, and I'm clearly trying to throw him off the trail. 'And you're getting on my last damn nerve, Blaine.'

'What if they aren't who they say they are? What if they've stolen their identities? What if they're fugitives?'

'Are you listening to yourself? Fugitives who have decided to jump to the twenty-first century, go to college and live on Frat Row? If I was a fugitive, I don't think I'd be pre-med. I also don't think fugitives get into relationships with their fellow college students. I've been dating Godric for six months. I think I'd know if he was on the lam.'

'Maybe you're keeping your head in the sand, have you considered that?'

I roll my eyes. 'Keep it up and you'll be proofing the articles on your own.'

Blaine drops it, and gathers his handwriting samples, huffing about my inability to see what's right in front of me. He stuffs the papers into his desk and locks it, slipping the key back into his pocket.

I take a seat at my desk, hands shaking with the anxiety of it all. I need to talk to Godric about this. Laz has already mentioned more than once that Blaine's continued interest in them is problematic. He's also suggested that they cut their sabbatical short. If Godric moves back to Alaska – or worse, decides to leave the country – I have no idea what will happen to us. Relationships are hard work, long-distance ones are even more of a challenge.

I go directly to Godric's at the end of the day. As soon as I reach the front door it swings open and Godric wraps his arms around me and zips me up the stairs.

But before he can get to work removing my clothes, I yell, 'Wait! I have something I need to tell you!'

One hand is already under my shirt, the other is about to pop the button on my jeans. Most of the time whatever I need to talk about can wait until after sexy times. But not this.

He stills and tips his head slightly. 'You've never told me to wait before. What's wrong?'

'Blaine took photos of your handwriting during class and found old essays written by your "great-uncle"' – I do the air quotes – 'in the archives. The handwriting matches. On the upside, he probably thinks you're traveling through time; on the downside, Blaine is still digging around and it looks like maybe the sabbatical tradition has some holes in it unless we can find a way to get the essays back and remove them from the archive.'

His hand slides out from under my shirt and falls to his side. 'He's more persistent than a cockroach, isn't he?'

'And just as gross, yes. How are we going to fix this?'

Before Godric has a chance to answer, there's a knock at his door. It swings open half a second later and Laz enters dramatically, Hunter on his heels.

'What the hell is going on with that little gnat across the street, now?' Laz demands.

'Thanks for the privacy,' Godric gripes.

'Normally I tune you out, but Blaine continues to be a problem.' Laz turns to me. 'No need to start at the beginning, just fill us in on what that fool has been up to.'

I explain what Blaine showed me earlier today, and how he's been taking pictures of Godric's handwriting and comparing it with a sample from fifty years ago.

'I told you!' Laz levels Godric with an accusatory glare.

'You should get comfortable with using a tablet to take notes.'

'Cursive is a dying art.' Godric flips a pen between his fingers.

'Cursive may be the reason we'll have to cut this sabbatical short.'

'What can he prove with a sample of cursive writing?' Hunter asks from his spot on the window seat. He's nursing a beer, not nearly as wound up as Laz and Godric.

'He could have it analyzed and find out that the samples are indeed penned by the same hand,' Laz says.

'But they'd determine it would be impossible, or that you had your great-uncle write your notes from the grave. Or that one of the samples must have been planted. It's a circle he'll never be able to close,' I argue.

'My primary concern isn't what he has, it's how closely he's looking at us. We need him to stop digging.' Laz crosses his arms.

'We can solve that problem pretty easily, no?' Hunter tosses a stress ball in the air and catches it. Where he got it from, I have no idea.

Laz's gaze shifts his way. 'We can.'

'What am I missing?' I glance between the two of them.

'Whatever you two are thinking, you can stop now.' Godric eyes his brothers with irritation. 'Hazy, you know where these samples are, yes?'

'They're in his drawer in the paper office, but he locks it, and he keeps his keys on him all the time.'

'That won't be a problem for me. I can get in and manage the situation,' Laz says.

'But if the papers go missing he'll know it's me,' I argue.

'They won't go missing. I can adjust them so the connections he made no longer apply,' Laz explains.

At my confused expression, Godric adds, 'He'll use magic to doctor my handwriting.'

'If you'd have let me, I could have tweaked his memories earlier in the year,' Laz says.

'But you can't do it now?' I ask.

'I can, but there are risks, and I can't be sure I'd get everything. Not without making a mess anyway – which I'm not opposed to. However, Godric seems to think it's a bad idea.'

'What kind of risks?' I ask.

'Too much memory modification can lead to . . . bigger issues,' Godric says.

'The human brain is astonishingly fragile.' Laz inspects his black-and-white painted fingernails.

'Also, memories tend to bleed through, so it's not the best strategy. Doctoring the samples is the better, less risky way to achieve the same ends,' Godric adds.

'I'll manage the situation. You're welcome in advance.' Laz whirls around, and strides across the room, using magic to open and close the door.

Hunter hops to his feet. 'He's all drama. It'll be fine.' He pats me on the shoulder as he passes.

I wait until he leaves before I turn to Godric. 'Should I be worried?'

'It's fine. Laz is just being dramatic. We'll get it taken care of.'

'I wish Blaine would let this go.'

'He will. He just might need help.'

I hope he's right, because Blaine seems determined to

uncover the truth, no matter the cost. And while I might not be his biggest fan, exterminating him seems like a harsh punishment, and one I'm not sure I want to live with for the rest of my life. However long that ends up being.

29

'Add another plate,' Hunter says.

'She's already benching a hundred and ten pounds. I'm not adding another plate.' Godric's expression is a mixture of pride, lust and annoyance. The annoyance is directed at his brother, the rest is directed at me.

'I was benching one hundred a week post-feeding last time, wasn't I?' I tap the bar.

Godric nods. 'One-ten at day five, one hundred at day seven.'

'So, a five pound a day decrease, but now I'm at one-ten at day seven. That's a significant increase in strength retention.' I cock an eyebrow. 'You should add another ten pounds. We want the most accurate measurement of my physiological changes.'

'I'd like to do a comparative analysis of all of our findings after this.'

'And then we can make some predictions as to what we think the results will be next time!' My voice rises with my excitement.

'Exactly.' Godric makes a low sound that I've come to recognize as his horny purr.

'Okay. This is starting to sound a lot like foreplay.' Hunter makes a gagging sound and heads for the door. 'Looks like I'm going for a walk. Text when the fun times are over, and we can review the newest stats.' He raises his fingers, but Laz appears before they touch his lips.

'There's a matinee of *How to Lose a Guy in 10 Days* playing at the theater downtown. I'll pay for your popcorn with extra butter.' Laz shrugs into his trench coat. He's been slightly more social lately.

'Deal,' says Hunter. 'See you two in a few hours.'

And with that they're out the door.

Godric's gaze moves over me on a slow, hot sweep as he adds five-pound plates and positions his palms under the bar, in case I'm unable to handle the extra weight. So far it hasn't been an issue. I lift it up over the bar and slowly lower it to my chest. Pausing for a moment to take a deep breath in before I push up on the exhale. I follow with two more reps before I allow him to help me rack the bar.

As soon as I release it, Godric picks me up and carries me to his bedroom. In a matter of seconds we're both naked, him stretched out on top of me, our mouths fused in a searing kiss, his erection sliding over my sensitive skin.

'I need you in me.' I shift my hips until the head of his erection nudges my entrance.

'I needed to be in you half an hour ago.' His lips brush over mine, his grin salacious. 'So it's your turn to wait.'

He kisses along my throat and I tip my head, my breath catching as I wait for the sting of his bite, but I should know better by now. He teases me for what feels like forever, but eventually, Godric's desire wins out over his need to torment me.

When he's finally filling me, I cup his cheek in my palm and urge his gaze to meet mine. 'I want to feel what you feel this time.'

He catches his bottom lip with his teeth. 'You can't

ask me for things like this when I'm inside you, Hazy. It's unfair.'

'Please. Just a few drops.'

His throat bobs with a nervous swallow, but the lust in his gaze tells me I've already won. This isn't the first time we've done this, but never when he's been inside me.

He braces himself on one arm, hips still making slow circles, hitting that place deep inside that pushes me closer to the edge of bliss. Godric's eyes stay on mine as he runs his index finger over his teeth. Blood wells even as the cut begins to knit itself closed and he wipes it along my bottom lip. I drag my tongue across it, the metallic, slightly sweet taste hitting my tongue.

It only takes a few seconds before the effect hits me and my pleasure doubles as I feel not only my own, but Godric's, too.

'Your turn.' I bring my finger to his lips.

'Hazy.' It's a warning mixed with need.

'You can stay in control.' And I'm strong enough to handle it if he loses it a little.

He allows me to slip my finger between his lips. I run it over his teeth, the sting almost too brief to register, and then my pleasure doubles again, his and mine echoing through me. I come in waves that never seem to end, body weighted down with desire and floating on clouds of bliss at the same time.

Between one wave and the next I find myself on top of Godric instead of under him. I roll my hips, chasing the orgasm that radiates through both of us. It isn't until we've both found our release and our bodies are no longer connected in the most intimate way that he feeds. He's no longer concerned about leaving marks because I heal quicker than I used to. Within an hour, the scar has disappeared and the bite is only a memory.

We lie there for a while, just being. The echo of him lingers in my system, and it will remain for several hours. At first it was discombobulating to experience his emotions along with my own, but over time I've gotten used to it, and I miss it when it's gone.

'Should we shower and record our findings before your brothers get back?' I ask eventually.

'I suppose it would be a good idea,' he says on a sigh.

We leave the comfort of his bed and head to the bathroom.

'So I can bench one-twenty, a week after you've fed. That's an eleven-percent increase from the last feeding,' I say as I step under the spray, letting the warmth soak in.

'And you're healing in under an hour, where it took more than forty-eight hours after the first time. It's astonishing, how exponential the change has been.' His fingers drift along the column of my throat, where he bit me earlier. The bump of scar tissue has already smoothed out, the skin returned to its pre-bite state.

It wasn't until after the Christmas holidays that Godric explained the way feeding works, and why, traditionally, vampires chose not to feed from the same host more than once, unless it's their mate. While, typically, blood bonds form between mated vampires, apparently we're experiencing something similar. Because human-to-vampire mating research is limited, it's difficult to determine if I'm unique.

We've learned that Godric's bond to me is strongest post-feeding and it dissipates slowly over the days that follow. It takes nearly a month for my blood to cycle through his system completely. The twenty-seven-day stretch in which he did not feed from me in order to find this out felt exceptionally long. And Godric needed to increase his blood pill intake more than twenty-five percent over that time. But when he feeds from me regularly, in half-liter doses, he only requires the pills during labs where we're taking blood samples, and near the end of the week.

I also learned that the connection we share post-feeding is how Godric was able to pinpoint my location when I was driving home in that storm. My blood in his system functions like a tracking app. He can sense me wherever I am, even with hundreds of miles between us.

'I imagine my ingesting your blood impacts the percentage gains,' I muse as I soap up a loofah and run it over his chest.

'I believe so. Originally, I thought the amount was negligible and wouldn't linger or have lasting effects, but your recent gains suggest otherwise. So much of transitioning is steeped in ritual, and that may be part of the reason so many human-to-vampire transitions have failed over the years.'

'Because you'd basically have to drain most of my blood and replenish it with your own. Maybe it's too much of a shock to the system, just like if you flooded me with venom, it probably wouldn't go well. But consistent feeding at regular intervals, and introducing your blood to my system in small doses, allows me to build up a tolerance.' At this point, we've agreed that the fifty-fifty chance of successfully transitioning from human to vampire isn't a risk either of us want to take with my life. But we have years to gather data, to find new solutions and to come up with a plan that works for us.

'I think there's merit in it. And we have the luxury of time, so we can take this as slowly as we want. Seeing how my blood impacts you physiologically will help us inform our decisions moving forward.' He smiles down at me. 'I see so many changes in you already, Hazy. Little things that no one else will catch.'

'You mean beyond my ability to become a female weight-lifter as a side hustle?'

He grins. 'Humans age rapidly. Your century of life is a fragment of what mine can be. There are vampires whose existence spans millennia. You grow rapidly, and there's a period in which things slow, but it's brief, and then you begin to degrade. Currently you're in what I would call a state of stasis. And if I'm correct in my hypothesis, and we continue our current course, we might see a reversion.'

'You mean your venom and blood combo will start to reverse the aging process?'

'Or at least prevent it from progressing.'

'Which could buy us more time.' And that's the one thing we can't manufacture.

'It could. We'll have to see over the long term what the effects are, positive and negative, and weigh our options, but it could give us a few extra years. We could have time on our side instead of against us.'

'Time is good.' I'll take as much of it as I can get, especially when it includes Godric.

The next day, I'm on my way to meet up with Satya and Alyssa so we can walk home together, when I hear my name being shouted. I know that voice. Outrunning Blaine isn't an option. Actually, it's totally an option. I can probably run a marathon now, where six months ago I couldn't jog down the block without being winded.

Last week Godric took me for a run in the forest. I fully expected to sprain an ankle, but along with an increase in strength, and being able to run a six-minute mile, my reflexes have improved. I'm a big-ass fan of the side effects of venom and trace amounts of Godric's blood these days.

Except all these perks are currently useless because I don't want to draw attention to the new changes in my body by outrunning Blaine. Still, I'm not going to make it easy for him.

When he finally catches up to me, he's huffing and puffing. It's April, so it's still cool enough to need a jacket. The back of my neck is dewy with perspiration, but that's about it.

'Didn't you hear me calling your name? I've been chasing you across campus!' He's angry. And winded.

I pop out an earbud. 'Huh? Sorry, what was that?' The music was on, but I could still hear him. That's another thing I've noticed, my hearing has improved.

'We need to talk.'

'I got all the pieces to you on time this week, so what could we possibly need to discuss?' I'm aiming for cavalier.

'Can you slow down? What are you training for, the speed walking Olympics?'

I realize he's basically jogging in order to keep up with me, and throw it into sloth mode.

He glances around and leans in, lowering his voice. 'I know you broke into my desk. Lying about it is pointless.'

Thankfully, I'm not the one who did the breaking in, so I don't have to fabricate a lie. 'Why would I break into your desk, Blaine?'

'To protect your boyfriend.' He grabs my wrist, which is a stupid thing for him to do.

I twist out of his grip, and two seconds later I have him in a chokehold. Damn, my reflexes are amazing these days.

I quickly release Blaine, who stumbles back a couple of steps. 'The fuck is wrong with you?'

'You grabbed me.'

'So you put me in a sleeper hold?' His voice is shrill, and he rubs the back of his neck.

'It was a reflex. I've been taking self-defense.'

Again, I'm not lying. I've been learning how to do a lot of things with Godric and Hunter lately. Like parkour. And fencing. And archery. And self-defense. Apparently I'm good at all of them.

'You're the only person I showed those essays to and they've been switched out.'

It's good to know he hasn't been passing those around. 'Switched out?'

'Yes! They changed.'

'Changed?' I figure repeating things back to him doesn't count as a lie.

'Yesterday the handwriting samples matched and when I checked them again this morning they don't! Everything pointed to a theory and now they don't match up at all!' He throws his hands in the air and then props them on his hips. 'Someone got into my drawer and messed with them – and since you're the only person who knows about them, it had to be you.'

I give him my best sympathy face. 'Have you considered that they never matched up in the first place and you were so determined to turn Godric and his brothers into villains that you fabricated this nonsense to begin with?'

He gets in close, dropping his voice. 'Yesterday they matched. I know they did. And you swapped them out because you're protecting them.'

'How would I even do that when I don't have a key to the office, let alone your desk?' I raise a hand, intending to put it on his shoulder in a comforting gesture, but he takes a nervous step away from me. 'Are you sure you're okay, Blaine? I know the stress of exams can be a lot for you, and they're just around the corner.'

'This has nothing to do with exams and everything to do with whatever is going on with those Hawthorn brothers.' He's raising his voice now, drawing attention.

'Are you sure you aren't projecting, Blaine?' For a moment I feel bad. I know what it felt like when I first found out Godric was a vampire. I thought I was losing it for real. But Blaine has been on a mission all year and it needs to stop.

'I'm going to figure out what's going on.' He turns around and stalks off, still rubbing the back of his neck.

I sigh. So much for throwing him off the trail. There are only a handful of weeks left in the semester, and Blaine seems more determined than ever to get to the bottom of this mystery. And I can't let that happen.

30

Two days later, we walk into our genetics lab and Professor Easton announces that we're swapping partners for this one. I exchange a look with Godric. We both carry around a small, insulated pack with extra blood samples these days. Just in case. At least we're supposed to. He's diligent about it. Me, not so much. We're only a handful of weeks away from the end of the semester. We've *always* had the same lab partners.

Except I remember Blaine staying after class last week. That fucker.

Godric gives me a questioning look and I round my eyes at him in panic. We've been looking at my blood samples for months. There are distinct, marked differences between my blood and that of a human who isn't feeding a vampire. The kind of differences that are hard to ignore. Although it's been four weeks since I've ingested any of his blood, even the minute amounts linger in my system three times as long as the venom does. And these days there are always trace amounts of that hanging around in my blood.

This is not an ideal situation. At all.

Godric leans down until his lips are brushing my ear. 'Do you have your spare samples?'

I purse my lips and shake my head.

I don't dare look at him.

And it gets even worse when Godric is paired with Blaine and I end up with Sula.

I don't know what to do. I cross my fingers that Godric can pull through for both of us.

Sula seems oblivious to the tension as we set up our station. 'How are you feeling about exams coming up?' she asks, making polite conversation.

'Pretty good. Godric is a great study partner.'

She smiles. 'I can only imagine. He's like an encyclopedia with the way he retains facts.'

Godric steals a glance at us.

'That's an accurate description.' My hands are shaking as I do the prick test. Blood wells and I touch my finger to the slide.

Sula passes me a tissue and a small red dot spreads across the white flimsy paper when it touches the tip. I ball it up and shove it in my pocket before I lay a cover on my slide, moving it to the side of the table closest to Godric. If Godric can't find a way to switch it out, Sula will see first-hand the changes my body is going through. Ones that can't be explained with modern medicine.

Thankfully, Godric is closest to me. His hand shoots out, swapping the slides. Months ago I wouldn't have been able to detect the movement, or see Godric exchange the blood samples, but now I'm able to catch things other humans cannot. I have to guess that it's a result of the combination of venom and Godric's blood in my system. Regardless, my relief is palpable. We've managed to avoid disaster.

'Let's have a look at you under the microscope first.' Blaine's tone is all smarmy asshole as he picks up Godric's slide.

Sula puts the slide that Godric swapped with mine under the microscope and puts her eye to the lens, adjusting it. 'Want to take a look at your blood?'

'Sure.' My focus is completely divided, half of me with Sula, the other half trying to listen in on Blaine and Godric's conversation. My head feels like it's full of cotton. I'm not sure if I'm on the verge of a panic attack or what.

I glance in their direction as Blaine puts his eye to the scope, his mouth turning down in a frown. My brain inconveniently cycles through every gory vampire movie scene where the vamp goes on a murder spree and unalives an entire room full of people, but always leaves one person to tell the tale. And that person will be me. I don't know if I can handle my own conscience if Godric slaughters our class in a bid to keep his blood safe from Blaine's eyeballs.

'That's not what I expected,' Blaine grumbles.

I try to make eye contact with Godric, but he's busy staring at Blaine. 'Really? What exactly did you expect?'

'Thanos DNA,' Blaine says under his breath.

It's everything I can do not to let loose a hysterical laugh because I'd originally assumed Godric was a superhero, rather than a supervillain. But more concerning is Blaine having any expectations whatsoever.

I bring my eye to the microscope for Sula's sample and I swear the blood I'm looking at isn't entirely human. But between one blink and the next the minor anomalies I thought I picked up are gone. The stress of this lab is making me see things.

For the next half an hour, we put the samples through several tests, and the entire time I feel like I'm going to pee my pants. In the last ten minutes we take fresh samples that we mix with legionella to examine during our next lab. There's no way Godric can switch out the sample without someone noticing.

We label them and place them in individual Petri dishes with our names on them. I'm on the verge of hyperventilating. I try to take my time leaving class, hoping for a chance to get my slide back, or give Godric an opportunity to deal with it, but it's proving impossible.

And fucking Blaine is right there.

Godric leans down and whispers, 'I can't get to the samples now.' His expression is tense, and he looks like he's going to freak the hell out.

So I do the only thing I can think of to distract Blaine. 'I can't do this anymore!'

Godric's brow furrows. 'Can't do what?'

'This! You and me. I can't do it anymore. Look, Godric. I really like you, you're a great guy, and an awesome lab partner, but this, this . . . possessiveness is too much! I can't deal with it.'

He stares at me like I have two heads.

People gawk and whisper, some rush to leave, trying to escape the embarrassment of it all, others find a reason to stall and watch the train derail.

'I don't understand.' Godric's voice is low and soft, and his expression reflects his confusion.

'She's breaking up with you, dumbass,' Blaine says from ten feet away. His tone is gleeful.

I want to punch his smirk right off his face, but I'd probably break a few bones if I did that. His, not mine.

'Can we talk about this somewhere less public?' Godric's voice is laced with anguish.

And suddenly I'm flooded with emotions. On top of my own panic and worry comes a debilitating wave of devastation. I will him to understand that I'm not seriously breaking up with him, but the onslaught of emotions feels like a sucker punch to the gut, and tears leak out of my eyes. It gets worse when I try to stifle a sob and it bubbles out in a horrifyingly loud cry.

Godric takes a step forward and I hold out a hand. 'Please don't. I can't.' I have no idea what the hell I'm doing, but I'm committed to making this distraction work. 'I need . . . I need a break. I need . . . I have to go.' I whirl around, my vision blurry with tears, and stumble into Blaine.

'I got you. It's okay.' He slings an arm over my shoulder.

I want to elbow him in the ribs and tell him to fuck off, but getting him out of the lab to allow Godric to take care of things, is paramount. So I don't elbow Blaine in the ribs or shake off his arm.

'Let's get out of here,' Blaine says as he ushers me down the hall.

I'm bawling uncontrollably.

We're only on the second floor, so he opts for the emergency stairs instead of the elevator. He glances over his shoulder a couple of times on the way down.

'Do you have a tissue?' I sniffle. Loudly.

Not that one is going to do much against the relentless flood of tears.

'Here.' He pulls one from his breast pocket, but frowns when he notices the reddish-brown spot on it. 'Wait. Not that one.' He stuffs it back in his pocket and pulls out another, this one unused as far as I can tell.

I wipe my eyes, then blow my nose. The spontaneous

bawling fit has decreased in severity, which is good, because it feels like I can catch my breath again. I hiccup every few seconds, though. The whole thing looks pretty authentic as far as break-ups go.

I sniffle again. 'Do you have another tissue?' I'm worried that the other one might have blood on it, and that it might be my vampire boyfriend's.

He tries his breast pocket again. 'Sorry, I'm fresh out. Do you want me to walk you home?'

The last thing I want is to hang out with Blaine.

'I think I need to be alone, but thanks.' I tap my temple. 'I need to process. Thanks for getting me out of there, though.' I take a step backward and thumb over my shoulder, toward the women's bathroom. 'I'm going to get this under control.'

'I can wait for you if you want.'

'It's okay. Thanks, though.'

I disappear into the women's bathroom. My phone is buzzing with messages.

I lock myself in a stall and pull out the device. Godric is freaking out. Obviously, I did a good job with the fake break-up. I compose a message, but before I can press send, my freaking phone dies. And of course, because the universe is having a laugh at my expense, I don't have a charger. I'm crossing my fingers the break-up ruse gave Godric the time he needed to switch out my sample, or that whole embarrassing scene was for nothing.

31

I stay in the bathroom for twenty minutes. In part because I want to make sure Blaine has left, and also because the torrent of emotions keeps ebbing and flowing, and every time I think I have my eyeballs under control they start leaking all over again.

Finally the tears stop, and I'm able to leave the bathroom. Godric is gone, and I can't text to find out his whereabouts, so I head to his place, hoping he'll be there.

I spot him on the front porch when I'm halfway down the block. He stops with the pacing and turns in my direction.

His face is a mask of pain. And my eyes start leaking all over again.

Maybe the idea of breaking up with him is so overwhelming that I can't deal with it. Which tells me a lot about my feelings for this man.

'What the hell is going on, Hazy? I messaged you more than half an hour ago and you never replied. Why are you breaking up with me?' His voice is craggy with emotion.

'My phone died and I didn't have a charger with me.' I skirt around him to the front door.

I don't want to say anything else until we're in the privacy of his house, in case Blaine is lurking around close by. I wouldn't put it past him, and Godric seems too distressed to be able to think clearly. Godric follows me inside and I pull the door closed. When I turn to face him, his eyes are red-rimmed.

'I was trying to throw Blaine off the trail,' I say.

His furrowed brow furrows further. 'What?'

'Blaine. I was trying to throw him off the trail. It's obvious he suspects something, and I wanted to give you a chance to switch out the samples before you left the lab. He's committed to whatever conspiracy theory he has going on in his head. Staging a break-up was the only thing I could think of that might work as a distraction.'

'So you're not breaking up with me?'

'No. Of course not.'

'Thank fucking God.' His hunched shoulders relax.

He steps in and wraps his arms around me, hugging me so tightly it feels like my bones are bending.

'God, ease up,' I groan.

He releases me and steps back. The furrowed expression is back. 'Please don't do that again, Hazy. My emotions aren't like yours. Blaine is fortunate I didn't separate his head from his body.'

That visual should not make my lady parts zing, but it does.

Godric arches an eyebrow. 'I still could.'

I shake my head, trying to erase the image. 'Murder probably isn't the solution here.'

'In my world, when we fight over a mate, it's to the death.'

'Well we're living in my world, and I'm still a human, and murder is still a punishable offense, so let's shelve that option.'

'I would prefer it if you didn't use breaking up with me as a ruse ever again,' Godric repeats.

'You believed me.' I'm a much better actress than I realized.

'Your body indicated strong distress.'

'Yeah, because I had to leave a blood sample behind that's going to show anomalies that aren't easily explained, and Blaine's obsession with you has reached serial killer levels.' I grip the back of my neck. 'Were you able to swap out the samples before you left the lab?'

'Dammit. No. I was too busy being devastated by your very public break-up that came out of nowhere.' Godric is back to pacing.

'Not to add more stress to this already stressful situation, but Blaine had a tissue with blood on it in his pocket.' A bad feeling makes my gut swirl. 'I'm hoping it's his?'

Godric's eyes flare and he stuffs his hands in his pants pockets, but when he pulls them free they're empty. 'Fuck. He passed me a tissue after I did the prick test. I must've been distracted because I was trying to make sure your sample was swapped out, and he pocketed it before I could.' He scrubs a hand over his face.

'This is all my fault for not being prepared today,' I gripe.

If I'd brought my decoy samples we'd be fine. And now Blaine potentially has a sample of Godric's blood in his hands.

Laz appears on the stairs, Hunter behind him. I don't know what it says that I've already gotten used to the fact that conversations in this house are rarely private. Maybe that's why I was able to pull off the public break-up.

'I vote we erase his memory. It's the quickest way to solve the problem,' Laz says.

'I'd be happy to beat him into submission,' Hunter suggests.

'I thought you said if you erase his memory, it'll basically be like a full lobotomy.' I prop my fists on my hips.

Laz inspects his black-and-pink painted nails. 'He's not a particularly useful human.'

'We're not lobotomizing Blaine,' I protest. 'Or beating him up, even if he deserves it. All we need to do is get the tissue back before he can run tests on it, swap out my blood sample in the lab, and make sure Blaine doesn't have any other dirt on you in the form of handwritten essays from fifty years ago or archived documents.'

If I was dealing with normal humans, this would seem like an impossible task, but I have two vampires and a vampire-warlock hybrid on my side, so I'm pretty sure we can pull this off.

'We're not pretending that we're broken up for the rest of the semester,' Godric states emphatically.

'Can we worry about that part later?'

'Easy for you to say. You're not the one who had your heart ripped out and stomped on in front of your entire class,' he grumbles.

I put my anxiety and worries on hold for a moment and cup his lovely, angular jaw in my palms. 'Look at me.'

His gaze moves over my face in a caress I feel like a squeeze to my heart.

'My tears were real, Godric. The thought of being without you is more than I can bear.' My breath hitches. 'If anything, that fake break-up proved beyond a shadow of a doubt that you're my person, my vampire, my mate.'

'You do realize that half of the emotions you're currently

processing are Godric's because you have traces of his blood floating around in your system, right?' Hunter says.

'Shut up and let them have their moment,' Laz snaps.

Godric ignores them. 'I thought you were serious for more than half an hour. The last three centuries felt like a snap of my fingers in comparison to the mere handful of minutes that lasted an eternity.'

'I'm so sorry. I didn't mean to do that to you. I honestly thought you'd realize it was all a ruse.'

He covers my hand with his and turns his head, so his lips brush my palm. 'Please don't break my heart again.'

'I won't. I promise.'

Hunter starts slow clapping and I shoot a glare his way, catching Laz dabbing at the corner of his eye with the sleeve of his hoodie.

'Okay you two, time to put a pin in all your feels until we can get this situation with Blaine the Pain sorted out. The sooner the better, too, since apparently, he may have access to God's blood and we need to fix that, stat.'

'Shall we convene in the living room and make a plan?' Laz suggests.

I plug in my phone and Godric pulls me into his lap, wrapping his arms around my waist. I have a feeling he's going to be extra needy for a while. Which is understandable, all things considered.

'I've already managed the archives and scrubbed the local library of all traces of us, so we should be fine there,' Laz informs me.

'But what about the stuff that Blaine has gotten his hands on? What if he's made copies we don't know about?'

It's definitely a Blaine thing to do. He always saves things in multiple folders.

My phone turns back on and starts buzzing. Godric's name flashes across the screen. Apparently, I missed seven calls from him and thirty text messages. I also have new ones from Blaine that were sent less than fifteen minutes ago.

'I wish you weren't opposed to murder,' Godric gripes.

'He's such a dick,' Hunter grumbles.

'Should I check his messages?' I ask.

Laz drums on the arm of his chair. 'I'm sure he's planning to move in on you, which we could use to our advantage.'

I click on the messages, and am unsurprised by the texts asking how I'm doing and an invitation to meet up later.

'You should say yes.' The corner of Laz's mouth turns up when Godric growls.

'So I can distract him while you do what needs to be done?' I check.

I respond to Blaine and ask if I can meet him at his place when he's done with class.

'Exactly,' Laz confirms. 'Although, I think Hunter will be able to manage the tissue situation in –' he glances at his watch – 'half an hour or so. Blaine usually goes to the gym after his Protein Structure class.'

'How do you know that?' I ask.

'Blaine isn't the only one who's been snooping. I've been watching him just as much as he's been watching us. Probably more. I'm sure it would give him nightmares if he knew.' Laz's smile grows sinister. 'In fact, I'm inclined to send a few bad dreams his way for being such an infernal pain in the ass. Although, on the flip side, he has made this year slightly less monotonous. It's a real conundrum.'

'Anyway,' Hunter clears his throat. 'I think it would be best if we divide and conquer. Hazy can distract Blaine while we see if we can get our hands on that tissue. Godric, you have lab access, so it'll be up to you to swap out the samples. And Laz, it might be advisable to do a deep dive into Blaine's files not only in the paper office, but probably on his personal devices, too.'

Godric crosses his arms. 'I don't want Hazy alone with that jerk.'

'She won't be alone with him. I'll be in the house with her,' Hunter assures him.

'I think it would be better if we tackle this one thing at a time, together. What if we find something in Blaine's house that requires Laz's magic to deal with it?' Godric argues.

'I have to agree with Godric on this. I think it would be advisable for me to erase any possible trails that lead back to us through Blaine.' Laz taps on the arm of his chair.

'Okay. Say we do all of this and it doesn't solve the problem? He's frustratingly persistent when he wants to be. What if he keeps digging?' I ask.

It's a very real possibility. See his mounting obsession with my boyfriend and his brothers for details.

Godric and Hunter both look to Laz.

He sighs, and that ominous grin of his makes another appearance. 'There is an alternative to lobotomizing him.'

'Which would be,' I prompt.

'I could opt to use the power of suggestion to dissuade him.'

'Can you explain that?'

'The human concept I can liken it to would be hypno-therapy. Whenever he has the notion to go snooping where we're concerned, I can create a trigger than will . . . encourage him to shift his focus elsewhere.'

'What kind of trigger?'

'It can be anything really. He just needs a shiny new object to obsess over, and since we already know his personality is prone to such behaviors, in theory, it should be a highly effective means to manage him.'

I narrow my eyes. 'Why haven't you suggested this before?'

'It hadn't seemed like the most logical course of action, in part because it's too kind a way to manage him when he's been such a pest. But for you, Hazy, I'm willing to make a concession.'

'Thanks?' I'm not entirely sure how good I feel about this option, but it seems to be the only one that doesn't result in Blaine's brain being liquefied, so I guess it's the best chance we've got.

Since Blaine isn't supposed to be home until later, we decide to tackle the blood samples first. The four of us hop into Hunter's old pickup and drive to campus. I'm sweaty and nervous as we make our way back to the lab.

Laz is wearing a baseball cap, brim low, and a hoodie with the hood pulled up. The back of it reads *President of the Anti-Social Committee*. His brothers flank him, like imposing bookends.

When we pass other students on their way to class they shift aside without even looking our way. The door to the lab is locked, but Godric has a keycard. He holds it to the sensor and ushers me and Laz into the lab while Hunter stands guard outside the door.

Once we're sure the lab is empty apart from the three of us, Godric and Laz move through the room at their usual speed, heading for the area where our samples should be.

By the time I reach them, they've already swapped out my sample with a generic one from a human female.

Laz looks grim, which is normal, but Godric is frowning instead of looking relieved.

I make a circle motion around my face. 'I don't like this look on you.'

'My sample was tampered with.'

The heat comes on, making the vents rattle, and I almost jump out of my skin.

'Relax. There's a repelling spell on the door. Besides, anyone who came in here would think we're nerding out over bacteria,' Laz says.

'Repelling spell. Right.' Laz's powers mystify me. I turn back to Godric. 'Tampered with how?'

'Someone took a scraping from it –'

'Not someone. Blaine. His scent is all over everything. Someone should inform him that cologne does not cover up the smell of neanderthal, no matter how much one wears.' Laz's voice drips with disdain.

'Amen to that.' Godric nods his agreement.

'Are we not worried about the scraping?' My stomach is trying to tie itself into a knot.

'I'd already swapped mine out with regular human DNA before class ended. Yours appeared untouched, so we're safe there, but it would be good if we could have access to his files to make sure we scrub those as well,' Godric says.

'Should I text Blaine to see where he is under the guise of wanting to meet up with him sooner?'

'That's unnecessary. He's currently at the gym.' Laz checks his wristwatch. It's old-school, probably from early last century if I had to guess. 'And will be there for another hour. Then he'll make a stop at the science lounge where he'll meet up with one of the TA's for a quick hook-up in an old storage closet.'

'Uh, is this you reading the future?'

'No. It's Blaine's schedule. He's quite predictable. I wondered if he was sleeping with his TA to increase his GPA, but now I believe it's more likely that he's been using her for lab access outside of regular hours, which would explain how he managed to get the scraping,' Laz informs us.

'Well shit. Next stop is the student commons, then?'

'First the gym to retrieve the tissue, then the student commons,' Laz says.

We leave the lab and hop back into Hunter's truck since the gym is a ten-minute walk from the science building at human speed. The student commons is close by and will be our next stop.

Godric and I wait in the truck while Hunter and Laz visit the locker room to retrieve the used tissue. It takes all of three minutes for Laz to magic his way into the locker, and then we're off to the student commons.

I assume accessing the paper office will be a heck of a lot more challenging since there are always people around, but Laz mutters an incantation to unlock the door and puts up a repelling shield when we're in the office.

Once again, Hunter stands guard outside the door, while me, Godric and Laz head for Blaine's desk. I'm seriously sweaty now, recon missions are clearly not my jam.

Unlocking Blaine's desk drawer is as simple as another murmured spell from Laz.

'Oh, you've got to be kidding me.' Laz frees a Post-it from the perimeter of Blaine's monitor. 'What an idiot.'

He shows us the Post-it with Blaine's login and password on it. Laz takes a seat at his desk while Godric and I comb through his filing cabinet. It takes less then fifteen minutes for Laz to pull every single file related to Godric from the computer and scrub any images. 'Now all I need to access are his laptop and his phone so I can take care of whatever he might have on his personal devices.' He steeples his fingers. 'I can manage both without too much trouble. What time are you supposed to meet up with him?'

'Five-thirty at his place.' I check my phone when I see I have a new message from him. 'Wait, now he wants to meet at my place. That's weird. He's totally the kind of guy who would want to rub it in that he's spending time with me.'

'He truly is that much of a jerk, isn't he?' Laz's lip curls in a malevolent sneer.

'Blaine has a desktop, it's a Mac, and he has an iPad, but from what I remember everything was synced up. I know where they keep their spare key. It's just a matter of whether Justin is home or not.'

'He has class tonight until five-thirty, and he often goes to the pub after with his football friends,' Laz announces.

'How do you know all this?' I ask.

'I don't leave the house much, and Justin is rather entertaining. Did you know he plays guitar and laments his love of Alyssa in rather well-written songs?'

For a second I think Laz is joking, but then I remember

that Laz doesn't make jokes. 'I had no idea. Shall we engage in a little breaking and entering?'

'It's only breaking and entering if the police are called.'

We pile back into the truck and head for home.

There's zero attempt at sneakery when we walk across the street. Although I do knock on Blaine's door on the off chance Laz is wrong about them being out. When no one answers, I move the smiling Buddha, which proves unnecessary since Laz unlocks the door with a spell.

'You could literally creep on every person in the neighborhood if you wanted,' I muse.

'I could, but I already know more than I'd like about most people. Sometimes it's nice to allow people their secrets.' He opens the door and we're hit with a wave of stench.

'What is the repugnant odor?' Laz does that retching thing that reminds me of cats puking up hairballs.

'I call it Eau de Dudebro.'

'These humans are repulsive.'

The four of us make our way through the cluttered living room to the kitchen, which looks like it hasn't been cleaned since New Year's. The stairs are covered in dust bunnies. Justin's door is only open a crack, but that narrow glimpse tells me Blaine is the slob of the two, which I already knew. Justin's room is spotless and organized.

When we reach Blaine's room, I start to take a deep breath, but the smell outside his door is worse than downstairs so instead I steel myself and turn the knob.

I'm hit with another terrible odor, dirty clothes, unchanged sheets and smelly shoes being at the forefront. I gag and pinch my nostrils, then realize I'll have to breathe through my mouth and that's probably worse.

The stench has nothing on the creepy contents of Blaine's room.

'The fuck? Stalker much?' Hunter says.

There is a magnetic whiteboard full of pictures of me and Godric walking into Godric's house over the course of the year, and old newspaper articles about the Hawthorn house, along with Blaine's barely legible scrawl. The wall beside his bed has more photos. The most disturbing one is a cut-out of my face on the body of a swimsuit model.

There's also a microscope set up on his desk and a bar fridge on the floor beside it.

'I will rip his head off and pull his spine out through his throat,' Godric growls.

'Whoa. Wow.' I put a hand on his chest. 'I understand your murderous rage, but that's exceptionally violent.'

His gaze drops to mine. 'Your words contradict your body, Hazy, my love.'

'Can the foreplay, you two.' Hunter takes a step inside the room and whistles. 'This is next level obsessed.'

'I guess now we know why Blaine wanted to go to your place. This looks like something from a crime scene, minus Hazy's body strapped to the bed where he clearly plans to keep you like a pet,' Laz observes.

Godric moves toward the microscope, but Laz steps in front of him. 'Under the current circumstances I feel it might be best for you to be the sentinel. I fear that your rage will make it a challenge for you to moderate your strength and you will crush anything you touch.' Laz turns to me. 'Hazy, if you would be so kind, physical contact will go a long way in keeping Godric from obliterating the entire house.'

'Makes sense.' I step in front of Godric and put my hands on his chest. 'I love you, but murder is still illegal, even if Blaine is apparently a fully-fledged stalker.'

Hunter pulls his phone from his pocket and starts snapping photos. 'Not gonna be hard to blackmail the hell out of this guy.'

Laz crosses to the microscope and puts his eye to the lens. 'Just human DNA, nothing to worry about.' Hunter opens the fridge door. 'Oh, now this is hella weird. Does this say toenails?' He holds up a Petri dish.

The bar fridge is full of them. Some of them are labeled with Blaine's name and Justin's, but several belong to Godric, and there are a number labeled 'miscellaneous' that date back to the Halloween party.

'This does not look good.'

'Blackmail-wise it's great.' Hunter keeps snapping photos.

Godric is standing still as stone, nostrils flared, murder in his eyes. He's unreasonably hot when he's angry.

Laz takes all of thirty seconds to hack into Blaine's computer. Although it's made that much easier since Blaine keeps his password on a Post-it note stuck to his monitor. When he runs across an album of photos with my name, he double-clicks and an ocean of photos appear. A significant chunk seem to have been taken while I was sleeping, back when Blaine and I were dating.

'Murder is looking more and more appealing at the moment,' Godric says gruffly.

Laz spins around in his computer chair, taking in Godric's expression and me with my hands on his chest. 'Hazy, why don't you message Blaine and let him know you didn't see his message, and that you're waiting for him at his house. And that you think you need to have a talk.'

'Hazy will not be speaking with Blaine,' Godric growls.

Laz smiles patiently. 'I agree that it would be in our best interests for Hazy to avoid direct contact with Blaine, but attaching a picture of this room to accompany the text message will inspire him to panic, and I imagine he'll return home quickly. I will be here waiting to manage the situation.'

'By manage you don't mean disposing of his body in a shallow grave?' I ask. I might have extreme dislike for Blaine, and find his behavior exceptionally creepy, but death is pretty damn final.

'Unfortunately, no.' Laz sighs dramatically. 'I shall keep him alive.'

Hunter gathers the Petri dishes with Godric's name on them, and the ones from the Halloween party, while I send the text message with a pic of Blaine's room attached to it. He messages back telling me it's not what it looks like.

Part of me would like to see how this all shakes down, but I don't think Godric will be able to keep himself from literally ripping Blaine's head off. So Hunter and I usher him across the street.

Hunter lays all the Petri dishes on the kitchen table. There are a concerning number.

I have a bunch of messages from Blaine, but I haven't checked them. I don't want to incite my angry boyfriend, and not responding will make Blaine sweat.

Five minutes later, Blaine's old-school BMW from the early 2000s pulls into his drive. We watch from the window as he stumbles out and rushes up the front steps into the house. Godric leaves finger indents in his flask, which he's filled twice since we walked through the door. He might as well drink straight from the bottle.

I nudge him in the side and he passes me the flask. I take a sip and gag. Yeah, Scotch isn't my thing.

Hunter kindly gets me a goblet of wine and cracks a beer.

'How long do you think this will take?' I ask.

'Depends on how much Laz wants to drag out the torture. It's been a while since he flexed his magic like this,' Hunter replies.

'Hopefully, he doesn't go too easy on him,' Godric says darkly.

Since standing by the window won't do much good, the three of us take our seats in the living room and wait.

Less than half an hour later, Laz walks through the front door. 'Blaine has been dealt with!' His grin is downright evil.

'Please tell me he's still alive.'

'Killing him would have been too easy and much too kind.' The bottles on the bar begin pouring into a shaker, along with ice from the bar fridge. It swirls around in midair for a few seconds before tipping into a martini glass. Laz holds out his hand and it floats over to him.

'So what happened?' I realize I'm gripping one of Godric's arms, my nails digging into his skin.

Laz takes a seat in his chair and sips his cocktail, sighing with contentment before he begins. 'I downloaded all his albums and erased anything that could lead him down a path we would prefer he avoid. I also downloaded all the photos he's taken of you over the years, Hazy, and followed that up by threatening to go to the police. Obviously, that's not something I intend to follow through on, but no one wants to hire a doctor with stalker charges, so he seemed to realize it was in his best interests to cease and desist.'

'That's it?' I sort of expected more – and some magic.

Laz's grin widens and he taps his temple. 'I also installed a couple of triggers, so any time he starts to fixate on myself or my brothers he'll learn that it's best to avoid thinking of us at all.'

'Do I want to know what the trigger is?' Even if I don't, my curiosity is too big to contain.

He waves a hand in the air. 'It's a harmless thing.'

Godric chuckles.

I narrow my eyes. 'How harmless?'

'His body will respond in a way that will make him slightly uncomfortable.'

'Uncomfortable how?' I press.

'He'll become aroused.' Laz's expression is downright malevolent. It's the first time I've ever seen him look like the warlock he is.

I wrinkle my nose. 'You mean he'll get a hard-on when he thinks about you guys?'

'Yes! Exactly. Harmless, right?' He seems pleased with himself.

'I guess. How long will it last?'

'A few hours.'

'A few *hours*?'

Laz cocks his head. 'Yes. You have those medications that assist with that issue in humans. There are commercials about them all the time, and if the problem persists more than four hours one should seek medical attention, hence I chose three hours, long enough to cause discomfort, but not so long he should seek medical attention.'

'Uh, I realize a three-hour hard-on probably isn't a big deal for vampires, but it kind of is for humans.'

'Which is the point. I can reassess after a couple of weeks. The desirable outcome is that his fixation with us, and frankly you, ceases.'

'Hold on a second. You said triggers. What's the other trigger, and what activates it?'

Laz looks slightly bothered that I'm smart enough to deduce that there's more here. 'The second trigger is activated when Blaine thinks about you.'

I make a *go on* motion.

'He'll experience a ripe stench of old cheese, cooked cabbage and roadkill.'

I make a face. 'That's horrible.'

'Precisely.'

'I have one more question.'

'Go on.'

'Why didn't you do this months ago?'

'Because existing for three centuries becomes monotonous and though he was annoying, he was also a source of ongoing entertainment. However, his fixation with you and my family has become inconvenient, and I would like to be able to finish my degree in peace.'

'What if he comes back in the fall?'

'He won't. He's leaving for London next month and a college will be offering him admission to their master's program, which means we'll be able to enjoy the next few years without his interference.'

'His grades are good enough to get into a program in England?'

'Not really, but I helped make it possible in a bid to get him out of our hair. And hopefully, this will allow Justin to find a few new, less creepy friends.'

'Huh. So the problem is solved.' Justin does deserve to have better friends than Blaine.

Laz frowns. 'You seem disappointed.'

'It's just a little anticlimactic, is all.'

Suddenly shouting erupts from outside. I'd know that voice anywhere. I unwrap Godric's arms from around my waist and head for the window. The blinds are drawn, so I peek through the narrow gap.

Blaine is standing on the front lawn, one hand covering his junk, the other one pinching his nose. 'Why does it smell so bad? What is wrong with me? Oh God, it's awful!'

Hunter gives Laz a look. 'Might want to dial down the effects – unless you want him to lose his mind.'

'I don't know that he has much of a mind to lose,' Godric muses.

'Just let me have five minutes to enjoy the fruits of my labor.'

Blaine runs around his front yard like a chicken with his head cut off. A few of the neighbors come out and start filming it.

Laz huffs when Hunter points out that this isn't the most inconspicuous use of his magic.

'Fine. I'll scale it back. Party-poopers.'

Blaine's screaming stops a few seconds later.

Laz snaps his fingers and the TV turns on, the movie *50 First Dates* starts playing.

'Oh! I love this one!' I hop back into Godric's lap.

'I'll make popcorn.' Hunter disappears into the kitchen.

'Make the sweet and salty kind!' Laz calls after him.

And we settle in to watch a romantic comedy. Laz with a box of tissues at his side, and the rest of us with smiles on our faces.

Epilogue

One month later

'I can't believe you'll both be gone all summer.' Alyssa flops down on my bed, her pout in full effect.

'I know. I'm sorry. But I couldn't say no to an internship at the New York Library,' Satya protests.

She flops down beside Alyssa and rests her head on Alyssa's shoulder. The two of them have found the one spot on my bed that isn't covered with clothes and my open suitcase.

'I'm just jealous. Especially since this one is spending the summer galivanting around Europe with her deliciously enamored boyfriend.' Alyssa tosses a pair of shorts at me.

I catch them and add them to my already overflowing suitcase. 'It's a once-in-a-lifetime opportunity and I could not pass it up.'

'I need a once-in-a-lifetime opportunity,' Alyssa grumbles.

'Justin will be hanging around this summer, you could always let hell freeze over and give him a chance to take you on a date,' I suggest.

'Ugh. Stop. I don't want to like him.' Alyssa grabs one

of my pillows, pulls it over her head and says something we can't make out.

'What was that?' Satya steals the pillow away.

'He looks so good in a suit.'

'He really does,' Satya agrees.

Justin and Alyssa ended up beside each other at the commencement ceremony because their last names are similar. He graduated with honors and is coming back for his master's next year. Alyssa is too, and now they're both sticking around for the summer. Who knows what could happen?

Blaine already graduated, and took off for London at the end of the semester. The first few times I ran into him on campus after his chat with Laz, he would start gagging the second he tried to talk to me, and then he'd run off to the bathroom. Laz adjusted his triggers, but the conditioned response already existed. I'd feel bad, but after the stalker bedroom scene, he needed to be dealt with and I needed him not to be my problem anymore.

I finish packing my bag, making sure my passport is in my purse, and I have everything I need for my summer abroad. Once I'm done double-checking my essential items, I put away the clothes that aren't coming with me, and Alyssa and Satya help me carry my stuff downstairs.

We exchange hugs and there are a few tears as Godric loads my bags into his car. Laz and Hunter come out to say goodbye as well, although they're planning to join us for a few weeks later in the summer.

'Send lots of pictures!' Alyssa hugs me for the third time.

'Have the best time!' Satya comes in for another hug. 'And bring back chocolate.'

And then we're in the car, heading for the airport.

We've barely made it out of the driveway and my phone buzzes. I smile when I see who's calling and I put it on speaker phone.

'Hi, Mom! We're on our way to the airport.'

'We wanted to wish you safe travels,' she says.

'You remembered your passport, right?' Dad calls out.

'Yes, I remembered my passport.' My dad once forgot his on the counter before a trip and they almost missed their flight.

'You'll text as soon as you land?' Mom asks.

'We absolutely will. And I'll send tons of pictures to the digital frame so you can see what we're up to.'

Godric picked up one of those frames where you can email new photos directly, so we can share our adventures with my family.

'I'm excited for you. For both of you –' Mom's voice cracks.

'You take care of each other over there,' Dad says.

'We absolutely will,' Godric promises and squeezes my hand.

'And as soon as you're back you'll have to come for a weekend visit,' Mom sniffles.

'That sounds perfect.'

We say our goodbyes and I end the call, dabbing at the corners of my eyes with a tissue.

'You okay?' Godric asks, his smile soft and a little worried.

I wave a hand in the air. 'I'm fine. Just a lot of feelings is all.' I've been living away from home for years, but there's so much more to this trip than a summer away. But we'll have phone and video calls to keep us connected while we're across the ocean.

'Feelings are definitely allowed. And you know, if you want to fly them out at any point, we can certainly make it happen.'

'Maybe. One day at a time, right?'

'One day at a time,' he agrees.

When my nephew, baby Braden, was born, we went to visit and meet the baby. We fully expected him to scream his tiny little lungs out when Olive insisted that Godric hold him, but all he did was make a face and pass gas. As a result, Francis is slowly warming up to Godric, one visit at a time. With the arrival of my first nephew, we made sure to visit regularly during the second semester, not wanting to miss out on the cuteness of those first special months.

We spent last weekend with my parents and my brothers. This time I got to show Godric the town where I grew up. We visited my old high school, and went to my favorite restaurants and cafes. We took a walk in the park where I used to hang out after school with friends.

My mom even brought out the old family albums, and she and Godric sat on the couch for hours, him asking questions and her telling him stories about what I was like growing up. I couldn't find it in me to be embarrassed.

We've decided that exposure therapy is the only way to get them comfortable around my vampire boyfriend. Once we return from our summer abroad, we plan to visit my family as often as possible.

I shift in my seat so I can look at his pretty profile. 'I'm excited to meet your parents. Nervous, but excited.'

Godric squeezes my hand. 'You have nothing to

be nervous about, my love, they'll adore you the same way I do.'

I've talked to Godric's mother on video chat a couple of times, but meeting her in person is different. She's stunning, which I expected, and I can see pieces of Godric in her. They look more like siblings because of how slowly they age, but it's clear in their interactions that they're mother and son.

We'll be spending part of the summer on an internship at a prestigious college in Amsterdam, but the most exciting part of this trip comes later. We'll be traveling to a small island off the coast of Ireland to meet with a coven of vampires who have adopted the use of blood pills, and there are several human-vampire couples living there. From what Godric's mother has learned, one couple has been together for more than fifty years without transitioning, in part because they've adopted a similar practice to ours.

We're hoping to share our findings and learn from them, and possibly, with time and persistence, we'll find a way to increase the success rate of human-to-vampire transitions.

While time is on our side for now, I've learned to cherish every single day of this human life I've been given. I talk to my parents and tell them that I love them every chance I get. I text my brothers random daily nonsense just to keep in touch. I hug my roommates and make sure they know they're important and loved.

Godric has taught me so much about life, about who he is, about who I am. But most of all, he's taught me not to take love for granted. My heart has no limit to how much love it can hold or give, but it's up to me to make sure the people who occupy the most space in there are told often how much they mean to me.

'I love you,' I tell him.

'And I love you, always and forever.'

'Always and forever.'

Godric is my person, my mate, my other half.

My vampire boyfriend.

Acknowledgements

As always, thank you to my family and my incredible husband and amazing daughter. None of this would be possible without you. I'm so grateful for your inspiration, love and support.

Mom, Dad and Miss Mel, thank you for always being my cheerleaders. I love you so much.

Kimberly, thank you for bringing me this opportunity, and to Rebecca and my team at Penguin Random House UK for giving me a chance to do something new and different, and giving it the perfect home.

Deb, we've been at this for a long time. I adore you and our friendship. Thank you for coming on every ride with me, especially this one.

Sarah and the Hustlers, you're my safe space and my warm hug. Thank you for always being behind me, even when I veer off the path to try something new.

My SS Crew, you're magicians and I appreciate all the things you do behind the scenes to help me make these stories shine.

Beavers, I've been at this for a while now and I love your enthusiasm for words and new things. Thank you for being amazing readers, and for giving me a space to be excited about what's next.

Deb, Tijan, Sarah, Melissa, Tricia, Catherine and Xio, I'm so fortunate to have amazing women like you in my life. Thank you for being incredible peers.

Kat, Mandy, Krystin and Marnie, thank you for years of friendship, for checking in when I fall down the edits rabbit hole, and for being such badass women. I'm lucky to have friends like you.

To the bloggers, bookstagrammers and booktokkers and readers, thank you for loving love stories and sharing that passion with me and each other. You're the heartbeat of this community and I'm so lucky to have you in my corner.

He just wanted a decent book to read ...

Not too much to ask, is it? It was in 1935 when Allen Lane, Managing Director of Bodley Head Publishers, stood on a platform at Exeter railway station looking for something good to read on his journey back to London. His choice was limited to popular magazines and poor-quality paperbacks – the same choice faced every day by the vast majority of readers, few of whom could afford hardbacks. Lane's disappointment and subsequent anger at the range of books generally available led him to found a company – and change the world.

'We believed in the existence in this country of a vast reading public for intelligent books at a low price, and staked everything on it'
Sir Allen Lane, 1902–1970, founder of Penguin Books

The quality paperback had arrived – and not just in bookshops. Lane was adamant that his Penguins should appear in chain stores and tobacconists, and should cost no more than a packet of cigarettes.

Reading habits (and cigarette prices) have changed since 1935, but Penguin still believes in publishing the best books for everybody to enjoy. We still believe that good design costs no more than bad design, and we still believe that quality books published passionately and responsibly make the world a better place.

So wherever you see the little bird – whether it's on a piece of prize-winning literary fiction or a celebrity autobiography, political tour de force or historical masterpiece, a serial-killer thriller, reference book, world classic or a piece of pure escapism – you can bet that it represents the very best that the genre has to offer.

Whatever you like to read – trust Penguin.